TIMETIPPING

Books by Jack Dann

WANDERING STARS (editor) (1974)
FASTER THAN LIGHT (editor with George Zebrowski) (1976)
FUTURE POWER (editor with Gardner Dozois) (1976)
STARHIKER (1977)
IMMORTAL (editor) (1978)
JUNCTION (1980)
ALIENS! (editor with Gardner Dozois) (1980)
THE MAN WHO MELTED (forthcoming)
DISTANCES (forthcoming)

TIMETIPPING

JACK DANN

DOUBLEDAY & COMPANY, INC.
GARDEN CITY, NEW YORK
1980

ISBN: 0-385-14338-9
Library of Congress Catalog Card Number 78-20067
Copyright © 1980 by Jack Dann
Introduction, copyright © 1980 by Roger Zelazny
All rights reserved
Printed in the United States of America
First Edition

ACKNOWLEDGMENTS

Lines from "Howl," by Allen Ginsberg, from *Howl and Other Poems*, by Allen Ginsberg, copyright © 1956, 1959, by Allen Ginsberg. Reprinted by permission of City Lights Books.

I'm with you in Rockland, copyright © 1972 by Random House, Inc. Originally appeared in STRANGE BEDFELLOWS, edited by Thomas N. Scortia. Copyright reassigned to the author.

Rags, copyright © 1973 by Ultimate Publishing Co., Inc. Originally appeared in *Fantastic*, April 1973. Copyright reassigned to the author.

Timetipping, copyright © 1975 by Robert Silverberg and Roger Elwood. Originally appeared in EPOCH, Berkley Books. Copyright reassigned to the author.

Windows, copyright © 1971 by Jack M. Dann. Originally appeared in NEW WORLDS QUARTERLY 3, Sphere Books, Ltd. Berkley Books edition copyright © 1972 by Michael Moorcock. Copyright reassigned to the author.

A Quiet Revolution for Death, copyright © 1978 by Robert Silverberg. Originally appeared in NEW DIMENSIONS 8, Harper & Row. Copyright reassigned to the author.

The Drum Lollipop, copyright © 1972 by Damon Knight. Originally appeared in ORBIT 11, Putnam. Copyright reassigned to the author.

Days of Stone, copyright © 1979 by Ultimate Publishing Co., Inc. Originally appeared in *Fantastic*, January 1979. Copyright reassigned to the author.

Night Visions, copyright © 1979 by Charles L. Grant. Originally appeared in SHADOWS 2, Doubleday & Co., Inc. Copyright reassigned to the author.

Fragmentary Blue, copyright © 1975 by Ultimate Publishing Co., Inc. Appeared in *Fantastic*, April 1975. Copyright reassigned to the author. Originally appeared under the title *There are no Bannisters*, in NEW WORLDS 5, Sphere Books, Ltd., edited by Michael Moorcock. Sphere Books edition copyright © 1973 by Jack M. Dann.

The Dybbuk Dolls, copyright © 1975 by Robert Silverberg. Originally appeared in NEW DIMENSIONS 5, Harper & Row. Copyright reassigned to the author.

Camps, copyright © 1979 by Mercury Press, Inc. Originally appeared in *The Magazine of Fantasy & Science Fiction*, May 1979. Copyright reassigned to the author.

for the
Guilford Gafia:

J.C.H. II
J.W.H.
G.R.D.
G.A.E.
T.M.
T.W.
W.N.
R.T.

CONTENTS

INTRODUCTION

I have known Jack Dann since my Baltimore days, when he used to come to town for the peculiar rites of the Guilford Gafia. Meeting in Haldeman Manor, a place reminiscent of a crowded Gormenghast with cats, the G.G. was a writing group that seemed to exist just at the periphery of Chaos or perhaps even a little nearer. Though I was not a member, I lived nearby and was occasionally bewildered by the strange lights and sounds, puzzled at the function served by the shark's brain in formaldehyde with a room all to itself, and enjoyably attracted by late-night invitations to artichoke cookouts. The most impressive thing about that group is that everyone involved has become a well-known writer. It would be pleasant to be able to find in this the wherewithal for intellectual smugness, to be able to point to something in Jack's writing and say, "Aha! A clear example of Jules Romains's theory of unanimism! It is the Guilford influence. They do that sort of thing." But, alas, everyone in the group turned out to write quite differently from everyone else in the group, and there is absolutely no interchangeable literary scenery visible. I can only point to the time and the place and recall that it was then and there that I became somewhat better acquainted with Jack Dann and his work.

That Jack is a personable and intelligent man with a keen sense of humor and a sharp eye tells you nothing about the way that he writes, I suppose, but I knew him before I knew his writing, and I'd like to give you this much of the same advantage, albeit secondhand. Jack is a person with whom I enjoyed talking, and I naturally found myself wondering what sorts of stories he wrote. I have to confess that I was wrong when I tried guessing. This is not a unique experience with me, however. I can seldom guess how a person I know will appear in print. For that matter, I can seldom tell from a piece of writing what its author might be like in person. If writing is a mirror of the soul, I am pleased by its reinforcement of my belief in the complexity of this entity's nature. I like to be surprised, although literature should, I suppose, ideally serve as an inoculation against surprise.

Jack Dann's writing surprised me then and continues to do so. It is not only among his circle of literary acquaintances that I fail to find similarities. There may be something of Kafka and Borges in his background, but I have never asked him, and the comparison is not really fair to any of the parties concerned. Every writer has his literary antecedents, whether or not he is conscious of them. I doubt the value of digging for them beyond a certain point when one is not a scholar or a critic but simply a reader, and would much rather leave the act of excavation to those who would mirror their own souls in this fashion. With Jack's writing, I believe that I could use adjectives such as surreal, dreamlike, and expressionistic, and be striking some part of the truth with each of them. Andy Warhol said somewhere that whenever people start talking to him about subjective and objective he gets confused. I sometimes feel the same way. Jack's stories are often good examples of a universe in which any such dividing line has been erased. People and things possess a peculiar immanence, every act persists for eternity, every perception is somehow universal, and the whole place is haunted. There is a hallucinatory quality to these stories, and much of the artistry lies in Jack's ability to induce a kind of hypnosis. It is not until the experience is finished that you really begin to wonder about it. While it is occurring, you simply follow where he leads you, across a constantly shifting landscape. And after each story, I find myself wondering what he could possibly do next. Then he shows me—and I still wonder.

Jack is a reality magician. Like Castaneda, like Lewis Carroll, like Philip K. Dick, he is a master of a nothing-is-what-it-seems-and-everything-may-or-may-not-be-seeming viewpoint. This is a difficult sort of writer to try pigeonholing when it comes to meanings, because the relativistic viewpoint is a part of the meaning, and much of the rest is a matter of tone, of feeling, of character. Jack's visions are generally complex, are sometimes baffling, are never boring. I do not doubt that I will occasionally stumble upon a piece of personal symbolism. But this is the privilege of a gifted lyricist. He does not have to hang labels on everything. There should be enough beyond such points to more than adequately repay the reader for any stubbed toes along the travel route. I enjoy the pictures he draws as I do the imagery in a piece of poetry. I enjoy the moods he creates and the presence of the people who move through these pieces. And I am amazed that each story can be as different as it is from each of the others.

Looking back now, I wonder whether I have been making Jack sound too obscure and somber. If so, I hasten to say that there is clarity of expression here and humor, along with the mystery and dark. shading. Ultimately, as with any writer, you must of course judge his accomplishments for yourself. I find that his stories have a way of working themselves into the mind and producing echoes and correspondences. For this reason, I think that you will remember them for a long while. And just when you feel that he has inoculated you against surprise, he will surprise you again. He's that good. Whatever he plans to do next, I look forward to it. Turn a few pages and see for yourself.

Roger Zelazny
Santa Fe, New Mexico

TIMETIPPING

I'M WITH YOU IN ROCKLAND

I'm with you in Rockland
  where we wake up electrified out of the coma by
  our own souls' airplanes
I'm with you in Rockland
  in my dreams you walk dripping from the sea-
  journey on the highway across America in tears
  to the door of my cottage in the Western night
    —ALLEN GINSBERG, "Howl"

Flaccus decreased the pressure on the accelerator pedal and the speedometer needle drifted back to 100 m.p.h. That's better, he thought. The evening rain was making the road slippery. He glanced at the hitchhiker sitting beside him and pressed his back into the cushioned seat, his arm resting on his leg, the steering stick held loosely between his thumb and forefinger. His eyes were half shut. He could feel the cement being sucked under the car, inches below his feet. He could almost feel his feet melting into the floor as he tried to merge himself with the car.

Like this, he could drive his best. He didn't need to look to the side to judge distance; he could feel it. He was walking with a new body and it was better and stronger than his own. But it was not enough. The car could not satisfy Flaccus; it could only remind him of a stronger, better body.

Flaccus had worked up a good sweat piling up steel beams for the past two hours. He was wearing an exoskeletal harness, a light metal framework equipped with sensors that picked up his every movement and transmitted them to artificial muscles. With the harness, Flaccus could support 2,500 pounds in each hand.

Flaccus moved smoothly through his work, dipping and pushing, lifting and pulling, his motions smooth and easy. He imagined that his muscles rippled as he swayed back and forth. He stretched out his arms. The harness felt good. It was all around him, thin, light strips of body armor, giving him all the power and security he needed. He was soft tissue surrounded by a steel and plastic carapace. Fifty feet away from him stood the new construction project, a jagged framework of plastic and steel.

"Of course I love you," Flaccus said as he stared out the window at the New York skyline. The recent temperature inversion had put an invisible lid on the city. The air, saturated with pollutants, would be difficult to breathe. And the media would play up the increase in deaths by asphyxiation and emphysema. The extreme humidity put Flaccus's nerves on edge.

"Well, you certainly don't show it," Clara replied, pulling her synthetic silk nightgown together.

Flaccus continued staring out the window. He could see her reflection: she was wearing another frilly nightgown. He hated lacy, flowery nightgowns. And Clara had grown to be just the type of woman to wear them. He looked through the reflection of her face at a string of lights near the river. The heavy smog softened the city, merged the sharp interplay of shadow and light into a gray sea. Only the brightest lights were in sharp focus.

"I just can't. I can't love you that way; that's the way I am. I don't mind if you get a lover. I realize you have needs, but I cannot satisfy them."

"But I don't want a lover; I want you." She put her arms around Flaccus's waist. Flaccus ignored her, pretended that he couldn't feel her hands massaging his stomach. He felt the city all around him. He could feel himself blending into the gray smog, drifting down to the cement below. The apartment was a prison, keeping him from the outside, forcing him to play games with this trapped stranger.

"Could you put some heat on? I'm really freezing."

Flaccus turned off the Headway Control and passed two cars ahead of him. The luminescent road divider slithered back and forth, and Flaccus tightened his grip on the stick. The thin metal bands on his hand reflected the road lights. Flaccus increased the air flow and turned the heat up a bit.

Shouldn't have picked up a hitchhiker, he told himself. But what the hell; he was celebrating. He glanced at her: brown hair to her shoulders, tanned face, hook to her nose. Her blouse rippled as she allowed her body to find a more natural position. Knee touching dashboard, hand resting on her lap.

Force yourself. Try to talk to her, you need to talk. You've got to talk. But he had forgotten her name, or maybe he had never asked. Well, you could ask her, he thought. You could say, "What's your name again?" Then you could add, "I never can remember names," and take it from there. Instead, he ignored her.

Try a tree, he thought. That might be easier. If you could feel comfortable around a tree, that would be a start. He chuckled. The girl raised her eyebrows—obviously a studied habit—and huddled against the door.

The trees formed a wall on each side of the highway. They appeared preternaturally green in the artificial light. Although he could see city exits every mile, Flaccus still felt he was in the wilds. He did not like being outside New York.

Who the fuck cares, he thought. You don't need New York. You need a vacation. A guideway exit sign blinked on and off above the highway. He took the next exit. Flaccus could not concentrate on his driving; he was too aware of the girl.

He stopped at the check-in station, inserted his credit card in the roadside meter, and then followed the car ahead onto the access ramp. He stopped the car, cut the engine, and pushed a dashboard button to activate the guide arm.

"Better on the guideway," the girl said. "I mean I don't care which way you take, just as long as we're in the general direction."

Answer her. He thought of moving his hand to her lap, but lit a cigarette instead. She was too young; no, that's not it, he thought. He thought of her breasts pushing into his face. Masturbation would be better.

He watched the car ahead. A small retractable arm emerged from its side and clamped onto one of the guideway's two side rails. Then the car accelerated and merged into the traffic on the main guideway.

Flaccus remembered he was wearing the harness. He could feel it coiled tightly around his body, waiting for a signal to transmit to its own muscles. But for the last twenty minutes Flaccus had forgotten about it. It was his own strength that pushed and balanced the steel beams; it was his own firm, gentle touch that directed everything to its proper place—girders, huge plates of glass, heavy machinery. He did not need anything but himself. But he felt a claustrophobic fear of being swallowed when he thought of the harness wrapped around him. He shrugged off the thought and tried to get back into the rhythm of his work. For Flaccus, the harness had to be his freedom.

"Come on," Clara said, "just sleep with me tonight. We don't have to do anything, just be close together." She pulled him away from the window and helped him into her bed. He was still thinking about the outside. The cool, recirculated air was giving him a headache. He wanted to sweat; he would much rather be at work.

Clara pushed herself against him, resting her leg on his thigh. Her body had become flabby, soft where it was once hard. He let her touch him; it was better than listening to her cry for half the night. Flaccus tried to get an erection. Clara knew how to touch him, but he couldn't respond. He tried thinking about other women. He imagined himself in a car with a brown-haired girl. She was begging him to stop, throwing her head back and moaning. But he was so strong, so hard. He often fancied himself in a car making love.

Clara was beneath him; he supported his weight with his elbows. Was she pretending too? he asked himself. He had to do it now. He could do it. She positioned herself under him. If I can get in, he thought, I'll be all right. He became soft. She said, "Come on, please. . . ."

Think about the harness, think about working on the buildings. You're strong, powerful. You've got to do it. Think of the girl in the car, her breasts pushing against you. You're enclosed in steel, crushing out her life.

"God, it's cold," the hitchhiker said. She had just awakened after sleeping fitfully for an hour. "Christ, you can see your own breath." She raised the temperature without asking for permission.

Flaccus turned the dashboard lights up and looked at the girl shivering beside him, her arms pulled close to her chest for warmth.

"How can you stand it so cold?" she asked.

It would be easier in the car, Flaccus told himself. Especially now. It would be much more erotic if he could just touch her, squeeze her breasts, without talking and playing seduction games.

He reached over and touched her breast. She examined the thin metal bands on his hands, but didn't stop him.

"Did you hurt your arm in an accident?" she asked. Flaccus did not answer. She rested her head on the window and closed her eyes. "Why don't you put the seats down?" she asked. She made no move to be near him when he reached over to fondle her other breast.

Flaccus didn't want her to move closer. He just wanted her to be still while he touched her. And he would not ask her name. She was just there; that's how he wanted it.

And she obliged. She waited a proper amount of time before she removed her blouse and began conversation. "You didn't tell me why you put the temperature down so low. I think I've got pneumonia now." She removed her pants.

Flaccus cleared the windows and watched the shadows draw patterns on her face and chest. With his finger he followed the shafts of light that intermittently cut her into pieces. She touched herself, but did not try to touch him.

It was almost quitting time. In five minutes some two thousand workers would be going home for dinner, but Flaccus would not be one of them. He waited around while the other harness workers discharged their equipment in the construction hut.

Flaccus stayed out of sight long enough to make Tusser, the keeper, properly impatient. When Flaccus finally entered the hut, Tusser was swearing and pacing back and forth. Flaccus told him that he would lock up. He knew the alarm system and had once served some time as a keeper. When Tusser was hungry he did not mind bending rules for his friends.

As soon as Tusser left, Flaccus turned off the alarm system. He took off his harness, lowered it over the support hooks, where it hung from the wall like a skeleton in a dungeon. He did not remove its power package. Flaccus then took off his workclothes and slipped back into the harness. He felt strong and real again, and also clean, as if he had just washed and rested. He put on his street clothes. There were a few bulges, but they were not very obvious. The harness was now a part of his muscle and bone; it was as familiar as his skin. Flaccus would remember to keep his hands in his pockets when he left the hut.

It was the weekend. Flaccus would have three days' grace. The only people on the premises would be the night watchmen, and they would not notice that anything was wrong.

Clara was asleep. Flaccus touched her, grew bolder, kissed her. She moaned and started to awaken. Flaccus got up and walked to the window to watch the city. The smog covered everything with a gray gel. Flaccus imagined his building was a steel stick wound round and round with gray cotton candy.

"Are you going to put the seats down or do you want to do it like this?" The hitchhiker leaned toward Flaccus. "Either way, I don't care, but let's just do it." She turned on soft music, but blanked the screen.

The windshield fogged a bit, then cleared. Flaccus watched the dividing lines in the road. Straight for the city, he thought. He felt a surge of power. Straight for the city. He repeated it to himself. There were cars all around him, all moving at the same speed. But he could not see very far: everything was covered with smog or fog. Smog meant the city.

"Come on," she said, reaching for his crotch, touching the fleshy part of his leg. She found a metal band and traced her finger along its edge. Flaccus pushed her hand away.

"And that's all of it," Clara said, lighting a new cigarette with an old one. "I've been seeing him for about six months, and I just didn't know how to tell you before. So I'm going to stay with some friends for a while until I decide what to do. Is that all right with you?"

She had chosen to talk to him in the living room, rather than the bedroom. Her hair was piled high on her head and her makeup was rather heavy. Flaccus suddenly found her desirable.

"I think this is for the best. It's what you wanted all along, isn't it?" She paused, her breathing was heavy. "Doesn't what I'm telling you upset you?"

Flaccus could find no reason to set her mind at ease.

Flaccus could take her now. He was strong enough. The harness was no longer an extension of Flaccus: it was Flaccus. Gently, he touched the hitchhiker's shoulder, then squeezed, crushing it between his fingers. The girl screamed and fainted. Flaccus shook his head wildly, looking for a way out. He jerked at the door latch, but it broke apart in his hand. He smashed the window and looked down at Clara.

She was breathing heavily and making stupid little noises. "Put it in," Clara said, her teeth clenched. She reminded him of the Cheshire cat, smiling and leering up at him. He could feel himself disappearing until there was nothing left but his penis, and that getting smaller and smaller until it, too, disappeared.

RAGS

Joanna huddled against the side of a stairway leading into an apartment house and studied the brownstone buildings across the street. In the cinereal light of late afternoon, they lost their formal structure. Gray buildings blended their lines with sky and concrete, leaving gaps in the smile of brownstones. She counted the stairways, just to see if they would make an even number: they didn't.

She thought about painting all the buildings yellow. That would clean up the street. Joanna wanted to paint everything yellow. Then everything would be all right and she could always remember nice things. She had yellow hair—proof that everything would be all right—but it was dirty and stringy. It would just take her a little longer to be lucky.

She stood up, waited the proper time, and then stepped into the street. Although the street was crowded, she didn't see anyone about; but, then, she never did. Joanna could not see other people. Joanna's streets were empty, except for garbage cans that occasionally rattled—she had decided that the wind made them jump—and parked cars. The cars were all dented, rusted, and discolored. Like everything else she could see.

She had taught herself a new way to walk; it wasn't that the old way didn't work—that worked sometimes, but not on the streets. She could not walk in a straight line without bumping into invisible beings. So she would stop and skip, sidestep, take a step backward, perhaps run, or fall down and crawl into a cellar or alleyway. That was the new way she had taught herself to walk, and it worked very well. Joanna often had urges to simply walk a straight line, but she fought them down. She had to live by rules. Joanna made up many rules for herself. She didn't always know why, but that didn't matter—making up the rules was enough.

This time, Joanna took three steps, sidestepped toward the curb, then edged back toward the buildings on her left. But Joanna was too slow.

Something bumped into her. She tried to move faster, but was short of breath. You have to eat more, she told herself. That was a new rule. Joanna could see an old neighborhood bar at the end of the street, its large window broken and opened cans and boxes scattered around the doorway. She knew the names of the street and the bar: the large street was First Avenue (she was walking on Tenth Street), and the bar was called The Purple Cat. There was no usable refuse here, no signs of life; the street was dead. Or almost dead.

A bottle crashed in front of Joanna, spraying the street with sparkles of glass. She looked up, saw nothing but window overhangs that looked as if they were stacked on top of each other. Something knocked her against the building. She slipped and fell. Can't stay here, she thought as she tried to stand up. She was nauseous and her ribs hurt. She had to hurry before something pushed her again.

Joanna walked as fast as she could. She stumbled and had to stop for a few minutes. She leaned against the only standing wall of a collapsed building. Joanna could not catch her breath; she was shivering and her face was flushed. You can't get sick, she told herself. That's an old rule. She tried to visualize herself running down the street, sidestepping back and forth, ducking in and out of alleyways, jumping off the curb and landing on her toes. Her face would be flushed and her hair long and clean and yellow.

But her face *was* flushed. That would make it easier to pretend. She pretended that she was not sick and hurried down the street, dreaming of pretty clothes and music. Joanna remembered that she had been sick before. She had the chicken pox and the flu, a cold every year, and the plague. No, she thought, I don't have that. Neither did her mother; she had already died. Remember Uncle Milton and Aunt Kate? Joanna always wanted to have big breasts like her Aunt's. She touched her chest, felt her small lumps.

Joanna was breaking the rules; she stopped remembering and concentrated on the street. This was First Avenue; she was safer on small streets. She could turn down Eleventh Street and hope it was better than Tenth. But Joanna felt sick; she could not pretend anymore. She had to stop, sit down, get food, get well, and get off the avenue; all at the same time, all equally important. Joanna forgot her rules. She touched her stomach, which was slightly distended, and giggled; then put her palm against her mouth to stifle her noises. She wasn't hungry.

Pretending she was in a safe cellar or alleyway, she sat in the street.

She could not stay here. The thought was so obvious that disobeying it made her feel better. She was doing the impossible. She couldn't stay here, but here she was. And she was alive and not even hungry. The street looked different to her, clear in spots, yet obscured in others. Joanna could almost see moving shapes on the street; they dissolved before she could link them to memory. She focused on the cars and ash cans and paper birds that would soar a few feet in the air and then return to the ground to be newspaper animals, rolling around. This empty street was dangerous, meant scars and sores and death. But the street was already dead, except for the papers, and they would die when it rained.

She giggled: it had begun to drizzle. She was proud of herself—she could sit here in the street and face death. She heard a buzzing sound beside her. Joanna looked around, saw nothing out of the ordinary—the droning continued. It relaxed her, began to put her to sleep, although there was a small part of her that wanted to run. And that part screamed and shouted while she fell asleep. But she had fitted it into a soundproof part of her head, somewhere just forward of her right ear.

When she awakened—she wasn't quite sure she had really fallen asleep—she saw a purple cat pacing back and forth in front of her. It stood six feet tall, had large almond eyes—they were blue, but sometimes turned green—and black markings on its face. Two lines, which turned out to be deep furrows, ran from its nose to the corners of its mouth, cutting its face into thirds, creating an appearance of age and wisdom. And it was definitely a male.

The droning took the form of voice, and Joanna accepted it as she accepted the cat. There would be no more rules. She knew that, because she wasn't afraid of the cat or the voice or the street. It didn't matter that she felt sick; she was just weak, not nauseous.

"So you *can* see it too," the voice said. "I made him out of the bar down the street. Take a look, the bar isn't there anymore. I used it all up. There wasn't anything in it, anyway. Why don't you answer me?"

Joanna noticed that the cat could easily look into first-story windows.

"He looks in windows a lot," the voice said. "And he jumps on top of cars"—Joanna watched him leap atop an old Chevrolet convertible, pushing his foot through the soft top—"and sometimes crushes. . . ."

She could not hear the end of the sentence. Some sentences just dangled, unfinished, merging into other ones just beginning, changing their accents and rhythms. It had begun to rain again, plastering the papers to the street, forming rivulets and pools that made gushing noises when they found their way to the gutter and finally the sewer.

"Come on," the voice said. "We can't sit here in the rain. That's dumb. I'm already soaked, and I'm scared sitting here for so long, even with Rags. That's his name." (Joanna stared at the cat, pronouncing his name over and over.) "Just sitting here with . . . you'd better say something. Do you want me to leave you here? Are you just stupid? I've got a place and everything and cans of food, and good locks on the door. It's raining too hard. Look at . . . are you coming?"

Joanna would allow the voice, but that was all. She could not answer it yet. The rain stung her cheek; it began to hail dirty crystals that bounced on the sidewalk. The sky turned dark, creating the illusion of twilight.

"I know you can see Rags. He's coming with us, look what he's doing to that. . . ."

Rags walked slowly toward St. Mark's Place, once a colorful boulevard that sported theaters and crazily painted shops. A black cube, balanced precariously on its corner, had stood in the middle of the street. That was still there, farther west, but not standing on its corner. Rags stopped at St. Mark's Place and waited.

The cat could walk a straight line, she thought, but she did not dare try it herself. She could only guess when to skip and sidestep. Joanna tripped and fell a few times; she was dizzy and weak and couldn't concentrate on her rules. But once she was behind Rags, he zigzagged back and forth, sometimes stepping off the curb, sometimes pausing. Joanna followed without tripping. She watched his tail—it pointed out directions. When it pointed up, Rags would take a giant leap and Joanna would follow with a smaller one.

The buildings were drab, but Joanna didn't want to paint them. They contrasted nicely with Rags's deep, rich fur, made him look more solid and real. She splashed through oil-streaked puddles. Although everything seemed to be occurring at a normal pace, Joanna dimly recognized that she was moving very slowly, lifting her feet with difficulty, and neither skipping nor kicking at the soggy paper birds.

"Hurry up, let me help you. We can't go so slow. It's that building down there, number 260.

"His name is Rags, did I tell you that? I named him that—watch out, there—because I have a doll named Rags. It was a toss-up between the bar or the doll, and I wanted to keep the doll. So I used the bar. But I still felt badly about the doll so I named the cat Rags. That way the doll doesn't feel bad." A few more sentences passed, but Joanna couldn't hear them.

"Rags," the voice said. "Can you say 'Rags'? R-a-g-s."

Joanna tried to blot out the voice. Of course she could say "Rags." But once she said it, she would have to accept more things than she cared to. The streets might change their form and substance, and the voice might grow a body. And other things might take form, things that would be better left unsubstantial. The voice claimed it had created Rags, although it was probably the other way around, Joanna thought. The voice was too thin and tinny to create such a great, full-bodied animal. Rags was probably making the voice squeak just for fun.

"I'll have to shrink Rags before we go into the building. Once, he was impatient to get inside and got stuck in the doorway. I shrank him down to the size of a cockroach, just to teach him a lesson. And then I couldn't find him. I didn't have enough time to look because . . . still in the halls . . . there he was on the bed, jumping up and down on the pillow and smelling like flowers. That's the last time I ever fooled around like that."

And Rags began to shrink. Joanna patted his tail as it grew smaller. Don't listen to the voice, Rags, she thought. Joanna closed her eyes and tried to make him larger. But he was still shrinking. She thought that the voice was laughing at her, was afraid Rags might grow fangs. She followed him up the stone steps. He stood three feet tall under the doorway.

"It's on the sixth floor." A shadow was developing around the voice. Joanna would have to reckon with this voice, for it would soon grow a body. But that shouldn't happen, she thought—she had not said anything yet. She ran her hand along the worn wooden handrail and listened to her shoes tapping on the steps. Spider webs glistened in a small window overlooking a yard that was strewn with garbage and overgrown with weeds. A faint musty odor hung in the air, reminding Joanna of her grandmother's room. But she quickly forgot about that and sat down on the stairs. Joanna felt faint; her mouth was filling with acrid-tasting saliva.

"Come on, we can't stay here." The voice, made visible by its shadow, moved toward Joanna. She would turn her face away and ignore it. Rags, resting on the step above her, touched her neck with his paw, then snuggled up against her. Joanna looked up at him, into his green eyes, and followed the lines and furrows that gave his face character. He seemed a little larger. I did that, she thought—he likes me a little bit. He smelled like flowers, bouquets of yellow flowers, just picked and piled in wicker baskets.

"Do you want me to carry you?"

Joanna shook her head, then caught herself. I must not answer, she thought—that would spoil everything. She tried to stand up but was too weak: her knees buckled.

"See," the voice said as it extended a shadow arm and put it around her waist. Joanna watched its fingers curl around her belt.

"You'd better let me help you. Do you want me to leave you here?" With that, the shadow grew fuzzy and the voice faint; but Joanna let herself be supported.

The voice lulled her, spoke soothingly; its shadow gradually transmuted itself into flesh. Once inside the apartment, Joanna found herself leaning against a young girl with long hair like her own. She wore faded dungarees, a tight orange blouse that showed off two bumps for breasts, and blue shoes. She didn't have a face yet, just a blank pink oval.

Joanna touched the girl's hair, smoothed it between her fingers, wanted to wash her face in it. And she fainted. But in the instant before her swoon, her eyes automatically scanned the room, turning objects into afterimages: a worn oriental rug, two cushioned chairs, a mattress pushed against the wall, comic books in the corner, a writing desk with a hinged cover. She took these with her, rearranging them to fit her dreams, splicing and cutting, adding Rags and subtracting the girl.

She woke up to a blank face, eyebrows just beginning to sketch themselves in. "Are you hungry? I've got lots of food and medicines. Maybe you have the plague?" The eyebrows disappeared. "Don't worry, I can't catch it." But her hair was long and fell on Joanna's face. Long, thick, beautiful hair that curled at the ends, that felt cool and smelled like soap, that was yellow. And that meant luck and food and sleep.

"Say my name and I'll get you some food. Sandra. S-a-n-d-r-a. Say it."

Joanna simply nodded; she was not ready to talk yet. Sandra brought in an armload of cans, a can opener, and two spoons. She dropped them on the floor. "Well, what do you want? Soup? It tastes like scum; it's made out of turtles. This is caviar—the red stuff is better than that beluga. Those are artichokes; I never tried them. And liver pate, and lobster, and kidney parts—that's dog food, but the tuna isn't bad."

While she was eating, Joanna thought about Rags. Come here, Rags,

she repeated to herself. Finally, he walked over to her, giving Sandra a
wide berth. Joanna played with him, patted his ears, fluffed his fur; but
Sandra did not seem to notice. Sandra pulled a chair to the window.
Rags followed her. Joanna called him, but he would not turn around.

"Look . . . built a fire in the street. It's a big one. Come over and
look. Come on."

Unable to hear all of Sandra's sentences, Joanna was growing impatient with herself. She wanted to hear everything, know what was
going on around her. She moved to the window to be near Rags and
watched the fire, feeding on itself, growing larger in the empty street.
It spat flames at the dark faces of the brownstone buildings, set the
windows aglow.

"Look what. . . ." Sandra's hands crawled about on her lap. She
stood up, imposing herself in front of the window, breathing two cir-
clets of steam onto the glass. Joanna could not determine whether
Sandra was upset or having a good time (or both).

But the street really isn't different, Joanna thought, crouching in
front of Sandra so she could see. The fire was getting larger, but it
would be out by morning; she had seen other fires before—this was not
unusual. She moved away from the window and called Rags, but he
would not leave Sandra.

The apartment was a bit cool now. It was autumn, although the city
couldn't reflect the colorful palette of this season. The city was either
cement sweating in the heat, or snow, dotted with soot, soon transformed into slush. But always gray, except for the nights, which traded
one monochromatic monotony for another.

Shivering, Joanna curled into a ball. The mattress smelled. She
watched Sandra moving about excitedly in front of the window. The
glow from the street backlighted her into shadows. Joanna fancied she
saw a bird, a dog, a pistol in Sandra's fluttering hands. All shadow
forms. Rags jumped around playfully. He leaped on Sandra's head, balancing himself with one paw—his weight discarded—without distracting
her from the fire.

Joanna called Rags, but he ignored her. Only when Joanna grew
tired and closed her eyes, did he leave Sandra and settle down beside
her. Joanna fell asleep, later awakened by a finger touching her hair,
then a pale arm around her waist. Hair brushed across her face, and
she dreamed that everything was yellow and long and flowing. She
yawned and turned over, feeling fingers and palms, touching, pushing,

circling, putting her into soft coma. She bathed in yellow hair, dreamed of Rags, and snored.

Later, Joanna woke up and saw Sandra standing before the window, squeezing her small breasts and looking toward the ceiling, then out the window. She was mumbling, "Rise tomorrow." Rags got up, stretched, and walked to the window. Joanna told him to come back, asked him, and then pretended to shout at him. He spat, bristled his fur, and returned to Joanna. When Sandra turned from the window, her formulary completed, Joanna feigned sleep.

Sandra was beautiful in the morning, Joanna thought. Her face, no longer a blank pink oval, was delicately molded; deep-set eyes were accentuated by thin eyebrows—noticeably darker than her hair—that indicated the root of her long, sharp nose, her most prominent feature. But she was older, had had more time to be beautiful.

Joanna had begun to talk. But, after an hour, suffering from dizziness and a headache, she cut the conversation short by falling asleep. When she awoke, her headache relieved, it was still sunny; yellow bands streamed in through the dirty window while Sandra sprayed the walls and floor with an aerosol. Rags was sneezing and jumping about. As a test, Joanna told him to stop. He lay down in the corner, his front paws curled under his chest. Joanna felt stronger.

"What's that?" Joanna asked.

"Bug spray. I don't allow any bugs in this room. I don't care if they're in the other rooms; I only live in this one. You want to see the bugs?"

"No," Joanna said. "Tell me what you were doing in front of the window last night. You were holding your tits and saying things."

"That's supposed to be a secret, but I might as well tell you—it won't make any difference, anyway. I make the sun come up by doing that. I do it every night. I invented all those motions, but they all mean something. Whoever was doing it before me is probably dead now. If . . . get him, then the plague probably did."

I want to hear everything, Joanna told herself.

"If the crowds didn't get him, then the plague probably did. But I'm doing it now. Anyway, I'm immune to the plague—it has to be me."

"I don't believe that. The sun comes up by itself."

"Well, it's true. You believe in Rags—nobody else can see him except you and me."

"That's different."

"And he's getting mad at you," Sandra said. "See, he's glaring at you. He wants to kill you because you don't believe me."

Rags snarled at Joanna. Teeth bared, claws extended, he circled around her. Stop it, she thought. Sit in the corner. Joanna started to cry. She closed her eyes very tightly.

"I'm sorry," Sandra said. "Rags isn't mad anymore. See?"

"He's sitting in the corner," Joanna said, her eyes still closed.

"That's right. Stop crying and I'll show you the other room and the bugs. But I do make the sun come up. That's a secret; no matter what happens, you can't tell anybody."

She's too strong, Joanna thought. And she did make Rags. Maybe she could make the sun come up. But I made Rags sit in the corner. And I have yellow hair. Maybe if I wash it. . . .

"I just make the sun come up. Somebody else makes it rain, somebody makes it snow. That's what keeps everything going. And when someone dies, or say, gets crippled or something, then someone else takes over. And so on. It's not as if I was making *everything* work."

Joanna nodded. She felt sick again. So she huddled into a ball, arms against her chest, knees touching chin: that felt better. I won't vomit, she told herself. It's only fever, not plague. Plague doesn't come and go like this. But everything would be all right. Sandra had yellow hair and made the sun come up; Joanna had yellow hair and would get well.

Joanna pretended she was asleep, so that Sandra would not disturb her. By squinting her eyes, she could see Rags and still appear to be sleeping. She ordered him to skip around the room, to lie down, sit up, beg. Soon Joanna was strong enough to make him snarl at Sandra. But that wasn't enough; she still wasn't sure of herself. So she made him urinate on Sandra's hair. But Sandra did not notice; she was too busy eating. Cans peppered the floor, luring the bugs from other rooms.

"Do you want to see the bugs now?" Sandra asked. Her hair was damp and clung to the back of her neck.

Joanna shook her head—she hated bugs.

"Well, you're going to."

"No," Joanna said. She was tired and comfortable, and getting well.

Sandra, the stronger of the two, pulled Joanna to the door. Joanna called Rags, but he would not respond—Sandra was too powerful now. "You've got to see the bugs," Sandra said.

"Why?"

"Because I know you're afraid of them."

"How do you know that?" Joanna asked.

"Because I am too. Everybody's afraid of bugs. That's why you've got to look at them and keep them around. They make you strong." Rags snarled and pawed at the door.

"I don't want to go in," Joanna said, but she did not resist. It would make her stronger. Sandra opened the door and Rags leaped into the room, squashing brown bugs, running after more, his mouth open and tongue lolling.

Garbage littered the floor and provided holes and folds to hide the cockroaches. There was no furniture. A calendar hung on the wall opposite the door, partly covered by a large flap of plaster that hung from the ceiling.

Joanna tried to make the insects disappear. She kicked a bottle, thinking it was alive. A huge, glass bug. There are no bugs, she told herself, only garbage. But the bugs remained and multiplied. They'll give me strength, Joanna told herself. She ordered Rags to wait by the door.

"There's water bugs in here too. I imported them. Rags loves those best."

"No he doesn't."

Sandra looked surprised. "Yes he *does*. Look, see how he sniffs them out, then squashes them? He's squashing one right now, under the calendar. See that?"

"He's sitting by the door." Joanna felt stronger.

"Can't you see him?" Sandra asked. "He's tearing up bugs. That's it, you can't see him anymore. And you're afraid of the bugs."

Joanna felt something crawling up her leg, moving quickly past her knee. She slapped at it.

"See, you're afraid."

Rags snarled and exposed his claws, but Sandra didn't notice. "He's snarling at you," Joanna said, not quite sure who Rags was snarling at. "He hates you."

Joanna could feel insects crawling up her legs. She bolted for the door, but Sandra was blocking the way. Hoping Rags would not attack her, Joanna picked up a bottle and started swinging it in front of her. There were several cockroaches trapped inside it. She could feel insects crawling all over her.

Sandra backed away, but Joanna followed her. She struck Sandra across the jaw. The bottle shattered into sparkles of glass. Only the jagged neck of the bottle remained in Joanna's hand. Sandra covered her face with her hands as Joanna pushed the remains of the bottle into her throat. And twisted, as if she were neatly cutting out a piece of dough.

"You can't get out now," Joanna said. "And your hair's all red." Joanna looked for Rags. He was sitting in the center of the room, his head cocked to one side like a dog, watching. Joanna stepped to the door, opened it, and ordered Rags out of the room. He bounded out of the room, a piece of roach still hanging from his gum. Joanna followed and closed the door behind her. She coulde hear Sandra's screams inside her head; they made her eyes water. She sat down in the chair by the window and watched the street.

Joanna had washed her hair and combed it dry with her fingers. She had sprayed the room and opened up a can of tuna. Everything was clear and real—but I must keep Rags, she thought. She could still hear screams inside her head, but they were turning to whispers. Joanna watched a few people hurrying down the street, handkerchiefs to their faces.

It was late—Joanna could stand up and squeeze her breasts now. She touched the tiny lumps and giggled. But she would not stand up; she would not do anything. Rags stood beside her and sniffed at the can of fish still in her hand.

And Joanna watched a few boys build a fire across the street for the dead.

TIMETIPPING

Since timetipping, everything moved differently. Nothing was for certain, anything could change (depending on your point of view), and almost anything could happen, especially to forgetful old men who often found themselves in the wrong century rather than on the wrong street.

Take Moishe Hodel, who was too old and fat to be climbing ladders; yet he insisted on climbing to the roof of his suburban house so that he could sit on the top of a stone-tuff church in Goreme six hundred years in the past. Instead of praying, he would sit and watch monks. He claimed that since time and space were *meshuggeh* (what's crazy in any other language?), he would search for a quick and godly way to travel to synagogue. Let the goyim take the trains.

Of course, Paley Litwak, who was old enough to know something, knew from nothing when the world changed and everything went blip. His wife disappeared, and a new one returned in her place. A new Golde, one with fewer lines and dimples, one with starchy white hair and missing teeth.

Upon arrival, all she said was, "This is almost right. You're almost the same, Paley. Still, you always go to shul?"

"Shul?" Litwak asked, resolving not to jump and scream and ask God for help. With all the changing, Litwak would stand straight and wait for God. "What's a shul?"

"You mean you don't know from shul, and yet you wear such a yarmulke on your head?" She pulled her babushka through her fingers. "A shul. A synagogue, a temple. Do you pray?"

Litwak was not a holy man, but he could hold up his head and not be afraid to wink at God. Certainly he prayed. And in the following weeks Litwak found himself in shul more often than not—so she had an effect on him; after all, she was his wife. Where else was there to be? With God he had a one-way conversation—from Litwak's mouth to God's ears—but at home it was turned around. There, Litwak had no mouth, only ears. How can you talk with a woman who thinks fornicating with other men is holy?

But Litwak was a survivor; with the rest of the world turned over and doing flip-flops, he remained the same. Not once did he trip into a different time, not even an hour did he lose or gain; and the only places he went were those he could walk to. He was the exception to the rule. The rest of the world was adrift; everyone was swimming by, blipping out of the past or future and into the present here or who-knows-where.

It was a new world. Every street was filled with commerce, every night was carnival. Days were built out of strange faces, and nights went by so fast that Litwak remained in the synagogue just to smooth out time. But there was no time for Litwak, just services and prayers and holy smells.

Yet the world went on. Business almost as usual. There were still rabbis and chasids and grocers and cabalists; fat Hoffa, a congregant with a beard that would make a Baal Shem jealous, even claimed that he knew a cabalist that had invented a new gematria for foretelling everything concerning money.

"So who needs gematria?" Litwak asked. "Go trip tomorrow and find out what's doing."

"Wrong," said Hoffa as he draped his prayer shawl over his arm, waiting for a lull in the conversation to say the holy words before putting on the tallis. "It does no good to go there if you can't get back. And when you come back, everything is changed, anyway. Who do you know that's really returned? Look at you, you didn't have gray hair and earlocks yesterday."

"Then, that wasn't *me* you saw. Anyway, if everybody but me is tripping and tipping back and forth, in and out of the devil's mouth, so to speak, then what time do you have to use this new gematria?"

Hoffa paused and said, "So the world must go on. You think it stops because heaven shakes it. . . ."

"You're so sure it's heaven?"

". . . but *you* can go see the cabalist; you're stuck in the present, you sit on one line. Go talk to him; he speaks a passable Yiddish, and his wife walks around with a bare behind."

"So how do you know he's there now?" asked Litwak. "They come and go. Perhaps a Neanderthal or a *klezmer* from the future will take his place."

"So? If he isn't there, what matter? At least you know he's somewhere else. No? Everything goes on. Nothing gets lost. Everything fits, somehow. That's what's important."

It took Litwak quite some time to learn the new logic of the times, but once learned, it became an advantage—especially when his pension checks didn't arrive. Litwak became a fair second-story man, but he robbed only according to society's logic and his own ethical system: one half for the shul and the rest for Litwak.

Litwak found himself spending more time on the streets than in the synagogue, but by standing still on one line he could not help but learn. He was putting the world together, seeing where it was, would be, might be, might not be. When he became confused, he used logic.

And the days passed faster, even with praying and sleeping nights in the shul for more time. Everything whirled around him. The city was a moving kaleidoscope of colors from every period of history, all melting into different costumes as the thieves and diplomats and princes and merchants strolled down the cobbled streets of Brooklyn.

With prisms for eyes, Litwak would make his way home through the crowds of slaves and serfs and commuters. Staking out fiefdoms in Brooklyn was difficult, so the slaves momentarily ran free, only to trip somewhere else, where they would be again grabbed and raped and worked until they could trip again, and again and again until old logic fell apart. King's Highway was a bad part of town. The Boys' Club had been turned into a slave market and gallows room.

Litwak's tiny apartment was the familiar knot at the end of the rope. Golde had changed again, but it was only a slight change. Golde kept changing as her different time lines met in Litwak's kitchen, and bedroom. A few Goldes he liked, but change was gradual, and Goldes tended to run down. So for every sizzling Golde with blond-dyed hair, he suffered fifty or a thousand Goldes with missing teeth and croaking voices.

The latest Golde had somehow managed to buy a parakeet, which turned into a bluejay, a parrot with red feathers, and an ostrich, which provided supper. Litwak had discovered that smaller animals usually timetipped at a faster rate than men and larger animals; perhaps, he thought, it was a question of metabolism. Golde killed the ostrich before something else could take its place. Using logic and compassion, Litwak blessed it to make it kosher—the rabbi was not to be found, and he was a new chasid (imagine) who didn't know Talmud from soap opera; worse yet, he read Hebrew with a Brooklyn twang, not unheard of with such new rabbis. Better that Litwak bless his own meat; let the rabbi bless goyish food.

Another meal with another Golde, this one dark-skinned and pimply, overweight and sagging, but her eyes were the color of the ocean seen from an airplane on a sunny day. Litwak could not concentrate on food. There was a pitched battle going on two streets away, and he was worried about getting to shul.

"More soup?" Golde asked.

She had pretty hands, too, Litwak thought. "No, thank you," he said before she disappeared.

In her place stood a squat peasant woman, hands and ragged dress still stained with rich, black soil. She didn't scream or dash around or attack Litwak; she just wrung her hands and scratched her crotch. She spoke the same language, in the same low tones, that Litwak had listened to for several nights in shul. An Egyptian named Rhampsinitus had found his way into the synagogue, thinking it was a barbarian temple for Baiti, the clown god.

"Baiti?" she asked, her voice rising. "Baiti," she answered, convinced.

So here it ends, thought Litwak, just beginning to recognize the rancid odor in the room as sweat.

Litwak ran out of the apartment before she turned into something more terrible. Changes, he had expected. Things change and shift—that's logic. But not so fast. He had slowed down natural processes in the past (he thought), but now he was slipping, sinking like the rest of them. A bald Samson adrift on a raft.

Time isn't a river, Litwak thought as he pushed his way through larger crowds, all adrift, shouting, laughing, blipping in and out, as old men were replaced by ancient monsters and fears; but dinosaurs occupied too much space, always slipped, and could enter the present world only in torn pieces—a great ornithischian wing, a stegosaurian tail with two pairs of bony spikes, or, perhaps, a four-foot-long tyrannosaurus' head.

Time is a hole, Litwak thought. He could feel its pull.

Whenever Litwak touched a stranger—someone who had come too many miles and minutes to recognize where he was—there was a pop and a skip, and the person disappeared. Litwak had disposed of three gilded ladies, an archdeacon, a birdman, a knight with Norman casque, and several Sumerian serfs, in this manner. He almost tripped over a young boy who was doggedly trying to extract a tooth from the neatly severed head of a tyrannosaurus.

The boy grabbed Litwak's leg, racing a few steps on his knees to do so, and bit him. Screaming in pain, Litwak pulled his leg away, felt an unfamiliar pop, and found the synagogue closer than he had remembered. But this wasn't his shul; it was a cathedral, a caricature of his beloved synagogue.

"Catch him," shouted the boy with an accent so thick that Litwak could barely make out what he said. "He's the thief who steals from the shul."

"*Gevalt*, this is the wrong place," Litwak said, running toward the cathedral.

A few hands reached for him, but then he was inside. There, in God's salon, everything was, would be, and had to be the same: large clerestory windows; double aisles for Thursday processions; radiating chapels modeled after Amiens 1247; and nave, choir, and towers, all styled to fit the stringent requirements of halakic law.

Over the altar, just above the holy ark, hung a bronze plate representing the egg of Khumu, who created the substance of the world on a potter's wheel. And standing on the plush pulpit, his square face buried in a prayer book, was Rabbi Rhampsinitus.

"Holy, holy, holy," he intoned. Twenty-five old men sang and wailed and prayed on cue. They all had beards and earlocks and wore conical caps and prayer garments.

"That's him," shouted the boy.

Litwak ran to the pulpit and kissed the holy book.

"Thief, robber, purloiner, depredator."

"Enough," Rhampsinitus said. "The service is concluded. God has not winked his eye. Make it good," he told the boy.

"Well, look who it is."

Rhampsinitus recognized Litwak at once. "So it is the thief. Stealer from God's coffers, you have been excommunicated as a second-story man."

"But I haven't stolen from the shul. This is not even my time or place."

"He speaks a barbarian tongue," said Rhampsinitus. "What's shul?"

"This Paley Litwak is twice, or thrice, removed," interrupted Moishe Hodel, who could timetip at will to any synagogue God chose to place around him. "He's new. Look and listen. *This* Paley Litwak probably does not steal from the synagogue. Can you blame him for what someone else does?"

"Moishe Hodel?" asked Litwak. "Are you the same one I knew from Beth David on King's Highway?"

"Who knows?" said Hodel. "I know a Beth David, but not on King's Highway, and I know a Paley Litwak who was stuck in time and had a wife named Golde who raised hamsters."

"That's close, but—"

"So don't worry. I'll speak for you. It takes a few hours to pick up the slang, but it's like Yinglish, only drawled out and spiced with too many Egyptisms."

"Stop blaspheming," said Rhampsinitus. "Philosophy and logic are very fine indeed," he said to Hodel. "But this is a society of law, not philosophers, and law demands reparations."

"But I have money," said Litwak.

"There's your logic," said Rhampsinitus. "Money, especially such barbarian tender as yours, cannot replace the deed. Private immorality and public indecency are one and the same."

"He's right," said Hodel with a slight drawl.

"Jail the tergiversator," said the boy.

"Done," answered Rhampsinitus. He made a holy sign and gave Litwak a quick blessing. Then the boy's sheriffs dragged him away.

"Don't worry, Paley," shouted Moishe Hodel. "Things change."

Litwak tried to escape from the sheriffs, but he could not change times. It's only a question of will, he told himself. With God's help, he could initiate a change and walk, or slip, into another century, a friendlier time.

But not yet. Nothing shifted; they walked a straight line to the jail, a large pyramid still showing traces of its original limestone casing.

"Here we are," said one of the sheriffs. "This is a humble town. We don't need ragabrash and riffraff—it's enough we have foreigners. So timetip or slip or flit somewhere else. There's no other way out of this depository."

They deposited him in a narrow passageway and dropped the entrance stone behind him.

It was hard to breathe, and the damp air stank. It was completely dark. Litwak could not see his hands before his eyes.

Gotenyu, he thought as he huddled on the cold stone floor. For a penny they plan to incarcerate me. He recited the Shma Yisroel and kept repeating it to himself, ticking off the long seconds with each syllable.

For two days he prayed; at least it seemed like two days. Perhaps it was four hours. When he was tired of praying, he cursed Moishe Hodel, wishing him hell and broken fingers. Litwak sneezed, developed a nervous cough, and his eyes became rheumy. "It's God's will," he said aloud.

Almost in reply, a thin faraway voice sang, "Oh, my goddess, oh, my goddess, oh, my goddess, Clem-en-tine!"

It was a familiar folk tune, sung in an odd Spanish dialect. But Litwak could understand it, for his mother's side of the family spoke in Ladino, the vernacular of Spanioli Jews.

So there, he thought. He felt the change. Once he had gained God's patience, he could slip, tip, and stumble away.

Litwak followed the voice. The floor began to slope upward as he walked through torchlit corridors and courtyards and rooms. In some places, not yet hewn into living quarters, stalactite and stalagmite remained. Some of the rooms were decorated with wall paintings of clouds, lightning, the sun, and masked dancers. In one room was a frieze of a great plumed serpent; in another were life-size mountain lions carved from lava. But none of the rooms were occupied.

He soon found the mouth of the cave. The bright sunlight blinded him for an instant.

"I've been waiting for you," said Castillo Moldanado in a variation of Castilian Spanish. "You're the third. A girl arrived yesterday, but she likes to keep to herself."

"Who are you?" asked Litwak.

"A visitor, like you." Moldanado picked at a black mole under his eye and smoothed his dark, thinning hair.

Litwak's eyes became accustomed to the sunlight. Before him was desert. Hills of cedar and piñon were mirages in the sunshine. In the far distance, mesa and butte overlooked red creeks and dry washes. This was a thirsty land of dust and sand and dirt and sun, broken only by a few brown fields, a ranch, or an occasional trading post and mission. But to his right and left, and hidden behind him, pueblos thrived on the faces of sheer cliffs. Cliff dwellings and cities made of smooth-hewn stone commanded valley and desert.

"It looks dead," Moldanado said. "But all around you is life. The Indians are all over the cliffs and desert. Their home is the rock itself. Behind you is Cliff Palace, which contains one hundred and fifty rooms. And they have rock cities in Cañon del Muerto and, farther south, in Walnut Canyon."

"I see no one here but us," Litwak said.

"They're hiding," said Moldanado. "They see the change and think we're gods. They're afraid of another black kachina, an evil spirit."

"Ah," Litwak said. "A dybbuk."

"You'll see natives soon enough. Ayoyewe will be here shortly to rekindle the torches, and for the occasion, he'll dress in his finest furs and turkey feathers. They call this cave Keet Seel, mouth of the gods. It was given to me. And I give it to you.

"Soon there will be more natives about, and more visitors. We'll change the face of their rocks and force them out. With greed."

"And logic," said Litwak.

Moldanado was right. More visitors came every day and settled in the desert and caves and pueblos. Romans, Serbs, Egyptians, Americans, Skymen, Mormons, Baalists, and Trackers brought culture and religion and weapons. They built better buildings, farmed, bartered, stole, prayed, invented, and fought until they were finally visited by governors and diplomats. But that changed too, when everyone else began to timetip.

Jews also came to the pueblos and caves. They came from various places and times, bringing their conventions, babel, tragedies, and hopes. Litwak hoped for a Maimonides, a Moses ben Nachman, a Luria, even a Schwartz, but there were no great sages to be found, only Jews. And Litwak was the first. He directed, instigated, ordered, soothed, and founded a minyan for prayer. When they grew into a full-time congregation, built a shul and elected a rabbi, they gave Litwak the honor of sitting on the pulpit in a plush-velvet chair.

Litwak was happy. He had prayer, friends, and authority.

Nighttime was no longer dark. It was a circus of laughter and trade. Everything sparkled with electric light and prayer. The Indians joined the others, merged, blended, were wiped out. Even a few Jews disappeared. It became faddish to wear Indian clothes and feathers.

Moldanado was always about now, teaching and leading, for he knew the land and native customs. He was a natural politico; when Litwak's shul was finished, he even attended a maariv service. It was then that he told Litwak about "Forty-nine" and Clementine.

"What about that song?" Litwak had asked.

"You know the tune."

"But not the words."

"Clementine was the goddess of Los Alamos," Moldanado said. "She was the first nuclear reactor in the world to utilize fissionable material. It blew up, of course. 'Forty-nine' was the code name for the project that exploded the first atom bomb. But I haven't felt right about incorporating 'Forty-nine' into the song."

"I don't think this is a proper subject to discuss in God's house," Litwak said. "This is a place of prayer, not bombs."

"But this is also Los Alamos."

"Then we must pray harder," Litwak said.

"Have you ever heard of the atom bomb?" asked Moldanado.

"No," said Litwak, turning the pages in his prayer book.

Moldanado found time to introduce Litwak to Baptista Founce, the second visitor to arrive in Los Alamos. She was dark and fragile and reminded Litwak of his first Golde. But she was also a shikse who wore a gold cross around her neck. She teased, chased, and taunted Litwak until he had her behind the shul in daylight.

Thereafter, he did nothing but pray. He starved himself, beat his chest, tore his clothes, and waited on God's patience. The shul was being rebuilt, so Litwak took to praying in the desert. When he returned to town for food and rest, he could not even find the shul. Everything was changing.

Litwak spent most of his time in the desert, praying. He prayed for a sign and tripped over a trachodon's head that was stuck in the sand.

So it changes, he thought as he stared at the rockscape before him. He found himself atop a ridge, looking down on an endless field of rocks, a stone tableau of waves in a gray sea. To his right was a field of cones. Each cone cast a flat black shadow. But behind him, cliffs of soft tuff rose out of the stone sea. A closer look at the rock revealed hermitages and monasteries cut into the living stone.

Litwak sighed as he watched a group of monks waiting their turn to climb a rope ladder into a monastic compound. They spoke in a strange tongue and crossed themselves before they took to the ladder.

There'll be no shul here, he said to himself. This is my punishment. A dry, goyish place. But there was no thick, rich patina of sophisticated culture here. This was a simple place, a rough, real hinterland, not yet invaded by dybbuks and kachinas.

Litwak made peace with the monks and spent his time sitting on the top of a stone-tuff church in Goreme six hundred years in the past. He prayed, and sat, and watched the monks. Slowly he regained his will, and the scenery changed.

There was a monk that looked like Rhampsinitus.

Another looked like Moldanado.

At least, Litwak thought, there could be no Baptista Founce here.

With that (and by an act of unconscious will), he found himself in his shul on King's Highway.

"Welcome back, Moishe," said Hoffa. "You should visit this synagogue more often."

"Moishe?" asked Litwak.

"Well, aren't you Moishe Hodel, who timetips to synagogue?"

"I'm Paley Litwak. No one else." Litwak looked at his hands. They were his own.

But he was in another synagogue. "Holy, holy, holy," Rabbi Rhampsinitus intoned. Twenty-five old men sang and wailed and prayed on cue. They all had beards and earlocks and wore conical caps and prayer garments.

"So, Moishe," said Rhampsinitus, "you still return. You really have mastered God's chariot."

Litwak stood still, decided, and then nodded his head and smiled. He thought of the shul he had built and found himself sitting in his plush chair. But Baptista Founce was sitting in the first row, praying.

Before she could say, "Paley," he was sitting on a stone-tuff church six hundred years in the past.

Perhaps tomorrow he'd go to shul. Today he'd sit and watch monks.

WINDOWS

Sequestration, he thought. Books, bound in heavy leather, filled with parched yellowed paper; tapestries on the walls, depicting Boshian revelries, Bokian monstrosities, woven by a Gypsy wife who lived in a cellar on Thirteenth Street; American oriental rugs, one piled on top of another to give the impression of luxury, to hide the gouged hardwood floor and broken linoleum underneath, all combined to suffocate him with their air-sodden weight.

John paced the room; if he stopped, he would sink into the multicolored carpet of translucent mud, or heated plastic—greens, golds, ochers flecked with blue thread, puddles of vermilion rippling against a sand border of copper, drenched, glistening with his sweat. At eye level, his prints, overlaid with gummed plastic, steamed inside their penny frames.

Pausing at the open window, John gazed at the silhouette skyline of gray buildings. The room bulged with new mass seeping in from the outside. John turned from the window and walked to the opposite wall; a thousand faces jelled out of the dampness and then blanched, leaving only a few lines of pink ooze in their wake. As he paced faster, tracking footprints in the carpet, thoughts whirled in his mind. Throw some offal over your shoulder. It's only a paper moon. He kicked at the carpet. The room dimmed for a few seconds. A film clouded his eyes, softening everything in the room. He allowed his eyes to unfocus, enlarging the ceiling lamps, chairs, bookcases, and other props into rarefied blurs.

The room grew steadily warmer. John wove paths between the ballooned fuzz forms that took up most of the space; soon they would finish off the last of the free air and fester into a solid block.

Remembering a paperback he had promised himself, John paused before a large wall bookcase. The musty smell of the books reminded him of a party downstairs and a blond giantess who called herself Miss Urania.

"Don't touch me while I'm talking." She pushed herself firmly against him.

Pacing back to the window, he tried to remember what she had said. "I said the *Yellow Book*. No, not the Beardsley thing." Her long hair completely hid her arms. "Crumpled an era. . . ." Her mouth formed a perfect O, drawn with a compass. "The Decadents' last word." She shook her head; strands of hair clung to the dampness of her face. "You should really read it."

John remembered his thoughts as she bounced against him, defining poetry. The book probably mirrored the present—that would not be unusual. Chunks and pieces of one era might be similar to another period, but for all the wrong reasons. Events might repeat themselves in form only. But none of this mattered; he only wanted to see if the book reflected any of his own attitudes. His pleasure would be in personal comparison.

The colors of the carpets were bleeding into each other, each layer of colored mud sinking into the next, until they filled the cracks and separations in the wood beneath, pouring through the floor, bathing the little old lady downstairs in a drunken holiday of color.

John could not breathe. The outside was rushing in and breaking through the walls, only to be sucked into the carpet, which was quickly growing out of its two-dimensional state. Phantasms of strange faces hovered beside him, blinking out of existence when he turned to face them. They swooped behind him, gurgled, became the hiss of the icebox, the shudder of the windows. The cat hanging by its claws from his trousers was a blob of gray cotton with two holes plucked out of the middle, reflecting the glare of the carpet.

John stood up suddenly, shook the cat from his leg, and reached for the door, the only solid object in the room. Frustrating afterimages fed his anxiety as he tried to suppress a vague homosexual urge. Walk down the street, he thought, imagining his anxiety to be bad posture. Stand up straight. It should be cooler outside now—whistle at the people, swill a beer, buy some books. That's it. Buy that book. That is the reason for going outside. You're not running. You're not escaping from a cage. You are going out to buy a book. A soft musky odor brought Miss Urania back to mind: maybe he would pick up a prostitute.

It was damp outside, but much cooler than in his hotel apartment. A few girls were on the street, leaning against a metal railing that fronted the building; others were standing in the rouge-lit doorway of the hotel bar. They all have dark hair, he thought, remembering Miss Urania's blondness. And they were too skinny. He did not answer any of the familiar catcalls.

He passed the subway station. It was too hot to go under the steaming cement. Broadway was choked with summer Saturday-night crowds. The ice-cream bars with their bright canopies over the street were doing weekend business, taking care of the children and hustlers, the pimps and grandmothers. The gays were out in full force, seeming to appear on Saturday rather than Sunday, wearing yellow pantaloons and green shirts, orange jackets and pink turtleneck sweaters, skrunching the ground with leather shoes and white and gold spats, all carrying leashes, leading German shepherds through the crowds. The upper-Broadway smash show was just over, and small groups formed, boulders in the stream of the street, to discuss the aesthetics of body movement and method acting; bright students jabbered at their dates about nudity as a state of mind or the hero as nonhero, while silently mechanizing their next move.

Pushing at the crowd, John walked faster. Broadway was too hot; there were too many perspiring bodies sliding against each other. Crossing the street, he walked to Riverside Drive, almost smelling the water, reminding him of Halloween cider and soggy cigarette butts dried with a match. Once in Riverside Park, with its luminescent trees, he could finally breathe. The Boat Basin, a silent, lurid battlefield after dark, was his favorite haunt. It exuded calmness and solitude; its denizens, strolling about, were only cardboard cutouts. But John felt reasonably safe on the cobbled avenues lit by yellow streetlights.

A man walking a large mastiff approached him, his squared face marred by a double chin. Nodding as he passed, he said, "Hello, Richard."

A mistake; someone else. The face was vaguely familiar, yet John could not place him. The face again, a sardonic face, mouth curled up at the ends, hiding a slight smile. The face was loaded: a normal blanched face. Blanched. The word stood out in his mind and then passed, forgotten. John descended a red stone perron that overlooked a large wading pool where Riverside girls showed off their elegant dogs on Sundays. Maybe it was the horn-rimmed glasses he wore. Probably lived in the building.

Reaching the quays, John fell into step with the strollers. Not many at this time of night, he thought as he stopped for a few seconds to watch the lights of a moored yacht play on the water. Too late for the timid, too early for trade. A girl wearing an orange bikini giggled and sat down on a deck chair to scowl at him. Pushed by the few paraders that walked his way, he moved on, listening for laughter behind.

A young woman with long hair piled elegantly on top of her head walked toward him. Somehow, she reminded him of the man walking the mastiff. He smiled at her. She did not respond. Whom did she look like? Passing by. Peripherally, John noticed her mouth move, silently verbalizing around a wad of chewing gum. A whisper. *Richard Richard, 'round the cahner, twitch, twitch, twitch, she's a gahner.*

Something hung behind him—if he turned around it would only disappear. There were not enough people on the esplanade, just cutouts, manikins that all looked the same. A girl passed, followed by an old man and a very young girl. Look-alikes. John whistled back at them as they mouthed, "Hello, Richard." They needed mastiffs. A little girl, blank, sodden, wearing a gingham dress walked past him and winked. *Richard.*

Look-alikes. Analogues. They'll smile. Cautiously he walked away from the esplanade; behind him, they were watching. Move gracefully. A jerky movement is a giveaway. The leaves are yellow-green, artistically accentuated into monstrous shapes by tiny spotlights. He crawled through the foliage. Feeling a sudden need to be reabsorbed into a crowd, John listened for the hiss of Broadway—it held enough people for every taste and smell. Broadway was efficient.

Detecting a movement about twenty yards away, John stopped, crunching a dried branch. Two figures leaped out of the high bushes, heading upground over a grassy hillock toward the highway above.

Taking advantage of a surge of courage, he ran to investigate, aware that the runners were out of view. A bleached form was lying in a dim pool of light, deep shadows accentuating her essential features.

Staring at her, John noticed that her red taffeta dress, skin-colored in the artificial light, had been ripped away. A black brassiere lay beside a coiled belt, half hidden in the leaves. He circled around her, horrified, yet intrigued by the subtle, sophisticated play of light on her body.

Groaning, she turned toward him, her eyes closed. Got to get help, he thought. Attract attention. Her hair was almost green in the light. Dark brown. Autumn. Get help. She shivered and her head snapped to the side to reveal three irregular gouges that reached from her throat, across the bump of her chin, to her fragile cheekbone. She convulsed and then her body relaxed. And like tumblers dropping after the right combination has been executed, her eyes fell open. Soft blue eyes, diminished, hazy, staring at him. Microscopically, figures appeared inside her pupils, tiny swatches of yellow, growing larger, effacing her irises, acting on two screens.

John could almost make out their forms, even before they came into focus: a tall blond youth, dancing in place, balancing a gravity knife on his index finger, and a sallow boy with long black hair cut short across his forehead, his hands in his pockets. He bent over her for a clearer view, smelling the acrid odor of her skin. Another figure—the girl, only dressed. And screaming. Her throat was contorted into a screw, slowly turning, pushing out her screams. The tall blond boy began dancing around her, affecting an Indian war dance, followed by his friend. She held her face. The boys stopped dancing; the blond boy quickly circled around the girl and pressed his palm against her mouth, effectively cutting off her screams. Her eyes were closed.

John watched the movements with fascination: it was a ballet without music.

The blond boy closed his knife and stuffed it into his jacket pocket. As his companion released her, he grabbed her arm and covered her mouth to block her fresh screams. His fingernails cut into her face, drawing broken lines of blood. Pulling her to the grass, he supplanted his palm with his mouth, undid her belt, and pulled off her dress.

Don't look. Close your eyes. They were transfixed. The film whirred toward its conclusion, quickening its pace with each movement. The ballet sucked him into her eyes, filling him with revulsion. Wiping his nose after they finished, John pulled his face from her cool rubber skin. But he still watched.

They combed their hair. Satisfied that they were presentable, the boys shifted scene, each taking a full eyeball, leaving the empty expanse of skin in between to hide the girl's specter. Standing very straight and proper, they both waved in unison. "Hello, Richard." Laughter, then a few giggles before their eyes lost their pupils and filled with a gray film.

Pressing his nose against hers, he tried to get a better view of the boys' draining orbits, clouded opals that stared dumbly ahead. Tears, he thought. Her perfume, rank with sweat, reminded him of something warm. A pinpoint of yellow appeared in the gray of the boys' eye sockets; a microscopic movement, a miniature man walking a subminiature mastiff waved at him. The little man's face was flushed, as if he had been running.

The dark-haired boy did a pirouette and turned his back to John, thereby ending the stereo effect. Closing his left eye, John looked into her right eye. The blond boy's eyes were glowing. John could see two figures entwined, writhing against each other. One was his neighbor, the man with the mastiff; he could not see the other.

The dark-haired boy turned around with a wink and screamed for John's attention. John opened his left eye. It was a different angle of the same scene. John was the other figure, hiding behind his neighbor, clutching him tenderly with modest delight. "Richard, Richard, take a look—it's you." John closed his eyes.

"Look, we've got more," the blond boy said. "Look, look. The woman with the bun, want some? It's your Mom. The old man and the young girl, take a look. Watch," and with a wink he produced, "babies making babies, dropping off metal settees into the streets. More, we have more."

Enough. He followed the boys up the hillock, mentally erasing his footprints, carefully stepping into the boys' hastily hollowed spaces. Behind him, the girl's body was still whispering *Richard*. It was someone else.

John wanted to see people, scores of them. The gray buildings ahead reassured him. Forgetting his claustrophobia, he ran across Riverside Drive against the light, dodging the cars, up Seventy-ninth Street, back to Broadway. The lights shimmered in the heat rising from the cement, a collage of colors melting, swirling, clashing against each other. The smells of the street, unabsorbed by the cement surrounding him in a stunning cocoon, were too much for him; he fell against the crowd, his balance momentarily lost. The crowd buoyed him up.

Gasping for air, John pushed himself toward crumbling buildings, away from the smog and fumes of the road, away from the people rushing down the street.

Standing in a doorway, John watched them pass. They ignored him, passed him without a wink. He remembered the oppressiveness of the heat and shrank against the cool stucco.

They multiplied. They mirrored each other, their eyes reflecting other people that reflected other people: mirrors of mirrors. Shutting his eyes, John turned from the crowd. The man with the mastiff passed behind him.

Turn around again. They had multiplied. He ran into the crowd. It passed around him unbroken. No one noticed him.

They purposely ignored him. John pushed, kicked, screamed, sang, railed at people, and, defeated, sank into the doorway. The same doorway.

"I'm over here. In the doorway. It's Richard. I don't care; I'm Richard. Over here." A few people turned toward him and smiled, but their faces were continuously reflecting reflections of reflected faces. He could not breathe.

Lost in the people around him, lost in their eyes that had long ago lost his reflection, he walked through a glass tunnel. Outside, faces pressed against the curved pane, flattened noses, steaming the Lucite.

Richard, Richard, over here. He smiled at his neighbor walking the dog. The dog growled at him. Forget it; it's not worth it.

Noticing a policeman bending over the curb, John stopped to watch. The policeman was pulling a drunk out of the road.

Turn your head. *Turn your head.* "Turn your head." John found himself screaming in the policeman's ear. The policeman, his arms wrapped around the chest of the drunk, shook his head and turned with a start.

He was different. Don't make him different. His eyes were blue; inside, a warm fire was going out. The family was sitting in front of it making out shapes in the diminishing flames. "Look, a giraffe, a monster. See that piece of wood? It looks like an antler. What made you think of that?" The mother interposes herself and, smiling, swats the youngest gently on his rear. Her hair is auburn and she had gained another five pounds.

"What the hell is wrong with you, mister?"

A country house, isolated from reality by a blinding snowstorm. No school for the kids. A smile, a cup of coffee in a dirty cup spilled on the rug. An oriental rug. One piled on top of another to give the impression of luxury, to hide the gouged hardwood floor and broken linoleum underneath.

It doesn't exist; it's beautiful. He shook off an icicle.

"I'm very busy, mister. Go about your business. And stop staring at me."

Inspiration. John lunged for the policeman's holster, one hand unbuckled it, the other grabbed the gun. As his fingers closed over the plastic grips, it became part of his arm. He waved it to embrace the people scattering away from him, to tell them he was Richard, that he didn't care. He was anything.

A well-aimed shot into the policeman's belly, clasped together with shiny gold buttons. For the father in the country house. The policeman crumbled, his cap somersaulting twice into the gutter. It landed beside the drunk, who in a moment of consciousness tried to put it on.

A young girl backed away, her eyes wide, reflecting reflections. John cradled the gun, caressed the trigger, and opened the space between her eyes. For the young girl watching the fire. But how could he stop?

A heavy, middle-aged woman bowed, her spine shattered. For the mother swatting her child.

He squinted at the little child clasped in the arms of her mother. There was quite a large space. That was for the child dreaming of giraffes in the fire.

Tears drew heavy lines across his cheeks, acrostics of love and adoration.

He could not stay; it was for other people to puzzle out. Jumping into the crowd, John was, once again, in the glass tunnel, pushing toward the subway station. Hands of fate, he thought. Seventy-second Street.

Remember your token. They must be behind me. They have to get me. Not yet. Down the stairs, past the teller. He dropped the token in the machine, passed through the turnstile, and ran down the stairs.

There was no commotion in the station. He had no need to convince them that he was Richard. A train. Waiting there for him. A few people in the car. Pick an empty one. Doors closing, John slipped between them.

And he was shot into the tunnel, protected for a second, or a minute, or an hour. Settling into his plastic seat, John noticed that the girl across from him seemed to be screaming. No wonder, he thought; he was still holding the pistol. He aimed carefully and fired. Only a click. The girl ran out of the car, steam rushing from her mouth.

Only a little time, he thought. The car suddenly came to a halt, throwing him from his seat. Pain numbed his head; he could not move. He was covered with fuzz.

Move your arm. John could not find it. His head lolled and he turned upside down. Have to get up. His other arm moved back and forth; it was not enough.

He looked into the window. A smeared thumbprint near the latch. Little time. His reflection passed over him. He looked again. The window grew fuzzy, melted, fused into the metal of the car. And locked him in.

A QUIET REVOLUTION
FOR DEATH

No other epoch has laid so much stress as the expiring Middle Ages on the thought of death.

—J. Huizinga

It is a lovely day for a drive and a picnic. There is not a hint of rain in the cerulean sky, and the superhighway snakes out ahead like a cement canal. The cars are moving in slow motion like gondolas skiffing through God's magical city.

"What a day," says Roger as he leans back in his cushioned seat. Although the car is on automatic, he holds the steering stick lightly between his thumb and forefinger. His green Chevrolet shifts lanes and accelerates to a hundred and thirty miles an hour. "This is what God intended when he made Sunday," Roger says as he lets go of the steering stick to wave his arms in a stylized way. He dreams that he is an angel of God guiding the eyeless through His realms.

The children are in the back seat, where they can fight and squeal and spill their makeup until Sandra becomes frustrated enough to give them some *Easy-Sleep* to make the trip go faster. But the monotony of the beautiful countryside and the hiss of air pushing past rubber and glass must have lulled Sandra to sleep. She is sitting beside Roger. Her head lolls, beautiful blond hair hiding her beautiful face.

"I'm practicing to be an angel," shouts Bennie, Roger's eldest, and favorite son. The other children giggle and make muffled shushing noises.

Roger turns around and sees that his son has painted his face and smeared it with ashes. He's done a fair job, Roger thinks. Blue and gray rings of makeup circle Bennie's wide brown eyes. "That's very good indeed," Roger says. "Your face is even more impressive than your costume."

"*I* could do better if I wanted to," says Rose Marie, who is seven and dressed in a mock crinoline gown with great cloth roses sewn across the bodice.

But Bennie is unimpressed. He beams at his father and says: "You said that everyone, even kids, must have their own special vision of death. Well, my vision is just like yours." Bennie is twelve. He's the little man of the family, and next year with God's help he will be Bar Mitzvah, since Sandra is half Jewish and believes that children need even more ceremony than adults.

Rose Marie primps herself and says, "Ha," over and over. Samson and Lilly, ages five and six respectively, are quietly playing "feelie" together. But Samson—who will be the spitting image of his father, same cleft in his chin, same nose—is naked and shivering. Roger raises the car's temperature to seventy-nine degrees and then turns back to Bennie.

"How do you know what my vision is?" Roger asks, trying to find a comfortable position. His cheek touches the headrest and his knee touches Sandra's bristly leg. Sandra moves closer to the door.

"You're nuts over Guyot Marchant and Holbein," says Bennie. "I've read your library fiche. Don't you think I'm acquainted intellectually with the painted dances of death? Well, ha, I know the poetry of Jean Le Fèvre, and I've seen the holos of the mural paintings in the church of La Chaise-Dieu. I've read Gédéon Huet in fiche and I've even looked at your books—I'm reading *Totentanz*, and I'm almost finished."

"You must ask permission," says Roger, but he is proud of his son. He certainly is the little man of the family, Roger tells himself. The other children only want to nag and cry and eat and play "feelie."

Sandra wakes up, pulls her hair away from her face, and asks: "How much longer?" Her neck and face are glossy with perspiration. She lowers the temperature, makes a choking noise, and insists that this trip is too long and she's hungry.

"I'm hungry too," says Rose Marie. "And it's hot in here and everything's sticky."

"We'll be there soon," Roger says to his family as he gazes out the large windshield at the steaming highway ahead. The air seems to shimmer from the exhaust of other cars, and God has created little mirages of blue water.

"See the mirages on the highway," Roger says to his family. What a day to be alive! What a day to be with your family. He watches a red convertible zoom right through a blue mirage and come out unscathed. "What a day," he shouts. He grins and squeezes Sandra's knee.

But Sandra swats his hand as if it were a gnat.

Still, it *is* a beautiful day.

"Well, here we are," says an excited Roger as the dashboard lights flash green, indicating that everyone can now get out of the car.

What a view! The car is parked on the sixteenth tier of a grand parking lot that overlooks the grandest cemetery in the East. From this vantage ground (it is certainly worth the forty-dollar parking fee) Roger can view beautiful Chastellain Cemetery and its environs. There, to the north, are rolling hills and a green swath that must be pine forest. To the west are great mountains that have been worn down by God's hand. The world is a pastel palette: it is the first blush of autumn.

The cemetery is a festival of living movement. Roger imagines that he has slipped back in time to fifteenth-century Paris. He is the noble Bouciquaut and the duke of Berry combined. He looks down at the common folk strolling under the cloisters. The peasants are lounging amid the burials and exhumations and sniffing the stink of death.

"I'm hungry," whines Rose Marie, "and it's windy up here."

"We came up here for the view," Roger says. "So enjoy it."

"Let's go eat and put this day behind us," Sandra says.

"Mommy lives in her left brain, huh, Dad?" says Bennie. "She suffers from the conditioning and brainwashing of the olden days."

"You shouldn't talk about your mother that way," Roger says as he opens the trunk of the car and hands everyone a picnic basket.

"But Mother is old-fashioned," Bennie says as they walk toward the elevators. "She thinks everyone must conform to society to tame the world. But she is only committed to appearances, she cares nothing for substance."

"You think your father's so modern?" Sandra says to Bennie, who is walking behind her like a good son.

"You're an antique," Bennie says. "You don't understand right-brain living. You can't accept death as an ally."

"Then, what am I doing here?"

"You came because of Dad. You hate cemeteries."

"I certainly do not."

But the argument dies as the silvery elevator doors slide open to take them all away from left-brain thinking.

"Let's take a stroll around the cemetery," Roger says as they pass under a portiere that is the cemetery's flag and insignia. Roger pays the gateman, who wears the cemetery's "colors" on the sleeves and epaulets of his somber blue uniform.

"That's fifty-*three* dollars, sir," says the gateman. He points at Bennie and says, "I must count him as an adult, it's the rules."

Roger cheerfully pays and leads his noisy family through the open wrought-iron gates. Before him is Chastellain Cemetery, the "real thing," he tells himself—there it is, full of movement and life, neighbor beside neighbor, everyone eating, drinking, loving, selling, buying, and a few are even dying. It is a world cut off from the world.

"This is the famous Avenue d'Auvergne," Roger says, for he has carefully studied Hodel's *Guidebook to Old and Modern Cemeteries*. "Here are some of the finest restaurants to be found in any cemetery," he says as they pass under brightly colored restaurant awnings.

"I want to go in here," Rose Marie says as she takes a menu card from a doorman and holds it to her nose. "I can smell Aubergine Fritters and Pig's Fry and Paupiette de Veau and I'm sick of Mommy's cooking. I want to go in here."

The doorman grins (probably thinking of his commission) and hands Roger a menu card.

"We have a fine picnic lunch of our own," Roger says, and he reminds himself that he's sick of French food anyway.

As they stroll north on the beautiful Avenue d'Auvergne, which is shaded by old wych elms, restaurants give way to tiny shops. Farther north, the Avenue becomes a dirty cobblestone street filled with beggars and hawkers pushing wooden handcarts.

"I don't like it here," says Rose Marie as she stares at the Jettatura charms and lodestone ashtrays arrayed behind a dirty shopwindow.

"You can find all manner of occult items in these little shops," Roger says. "This cemetery is a sanctuary for necromancy. Some of the finest astrologers and mediums work right here." Roger pauses before a shop that specializes in candles and oils and incense made of odoriferous woods and herbs. "What a wonderful place," Roger says as he takes Sandra's hand in his own. "Perhaps we should buy a little something for the children."

A hunchbacked beggar pulls at Roger's sleeve and says, "Alms for the poor," but Roger ignores his entreaties.

"The children are getting restless," Sandra says, her hand resting limply in Roger's. "Let's find a nice spot where they can play and we can have our picnic."

"This is a nice spot," Bennie says as he winks at a little girl standing in an alleyway.

"Hello, big boy," says the girl, who cannot be more than twelve or thirteen. "Fifty dollars will plant you some life in this body." She wiggles stylishly, leans against a shopwindow, and wrinkles her nose. "Well?" She turns to Roger and asks, "Does Daddy want to buy his son some life?" Then she smiles like an angel.

Roger smiles at Bennie, who resembles one of the death dancers painted on the walls of the Church of the Children.

"C'mon, Dad, please," Bennie whines.

"Don't even consider it," Sandra says to Roger. "We brought the children here to acquaint them with death, not sex."

"That smacks of left-brain thinking," says the little girl as she wags her finger at Sandra. "Death is an orgasm, not a social artifact."

"She's right about that," Roger says to Sandra. Only youth can live without pretense, he thinks. Imagining death as a simple return to nature's flow, he hands Bennie a crisp fifty-dollar bill.

"Thanks, Dad," and Bennie is off, hand in hand with his five-minute friend. They disappear into a dark alley that separates two long, tumbledown buildings.

"He shouldn't be alone," Sandra says. "Who knows what kind of people might be skulking about in that alley."

"Shall we go and watch him, then?" Roger asks.

"It's love and death," Rose Marie says as she primps her dress, folding the thin material into pleats.

"I want to go *there*," says Samson, pointing at a great Ferris wheel turning in the distance.

Roger sighs as he looks out at the lovely gravestone gardens of the cemetery. "Yes," he whispers, dreaming of God and angels. "It's love and death."

Sandra prepares the picnic fixings atop a secluded knoll that overlooks spacious lawns, charnel houses, cloisters adorned with ivory gables, and even rows of soap-white monuments. Processions of mourners wind their way about like snakes crawling through a modern Eden. Priests walk about, offering consolation to the bereaved, tasting tidbits from the mourners' tables, kissing babies, touching the cold foreheads of the dead, and telling wry jokes to the visitors just out for a Sunday picnic and a stroll.

"All right," Sandra says as she tears a foil cover from a food cylinder and waits for the steam to rise. "Soup's on. Let's eat everything while it's hot." She opens container after container. There is a rush for plates and plasticware and the children argue and fill their dishes with the sundry goodies. Then, except for the smacking of lips, a few moments of silence: a burial is taking place nearby and everyone is caught up in profound emotion.

"It's a small casket," Roger says after a proper length of time has passed. He watches two young men clad in red lay the casket down on the grass beside the burial trench. "It must be a child," Roger says. A middle-aged man and woman stand over the tiny casket; the man rocks back and forth and rends his garments while the woman sobs.

"You see," Bennie says after he has cleaned his plate. "That kind of crying and tearing clothes is for the old, left-brain thinkers. *I* wouldn't mind dying right now. Death is wasted on the old. Look at Mommy, she's haunted by silly dreams of immortality. Old people are too perverse to joyously give themselves back to nature." Bennie stands up, looking ghoulish and filthy in his death costume.

"And where are you going?" Sandra asks.

"To dance on the fresh grave."

"Let him go," Roger says. "It is only proper to continue great traditions."

The sun is working its way toward three o'clock. There is not a cloud in the sky, only the gauzy cross-hatching of jet trails. A few birds wing overhead like little blue angels. Roger sits beside his lovely Sandra, and they watch Bennie as he dances stylishly with the two young mourners clad in red. Roger is proud and his eyes are moist. Bennie has stolen the show. He has even attracted a small crowd of passersby.

This is a sight that would have made Jean Le Fèvre turn his head! Roger says to himself as he watches Bennie work his way through a perfect *danse macabre*. The mourners are already clapping. Bennie has their hearts. He has presented a perfect vision of death to his spectators.

"Wave to Benjamin," Roger says to his family. "See, he's waving at us." Roger imagines that he can hear the sounds of distant machinery. He dreams that God has sent angels to man the machinery of His cemetery.

And with the passing of each heavenly moment, the noise of God's machinery becomes louder.

But God's machines turn out to be only children, hundreds of noisy boys and girls come to join in the Sunday processions. They're here to burn or bury innocents and bums and prostitutes, to learn right thinking and body-knowing, and share in the pleasures and exquisite agonies of death's community. The children seem to be everywhere. They're turning the cemetery into a playground.

As Roger watches children playing bury-me-not and hide-and-seek between the tombstone teeth of the cemetery, he thinks that surely his son Bennie must be in their midst. Bennie might be anywhere: taking a tour through the ossuarium, lighting fires on the lawns, screwing little girls, or dancing for another dinner.

"We should not have permitted Bennie to leave in the first place," Sandra says to Roger. "He's probably in some kind of trouble." She pauses, then says, "Well, *I'm* going to go and look for him." Another pause. "What are you going to do?"

"Someone has to remain with the children," Roger says. "I'm sure Bennie is fine. He'll probably be back."

Sandra, of course, rushes off in a huff. But that's to be expected, Roger tells himself. Bennie was right: she is perverse. After a few deep breaths, Roger forgets her. He stretches out on the cool grass, looks up at the old maple trees that appear to touch the robin's-egg sky, and he feels the touch of God's thoughts. He yawns. This bounty of food, fresh air, and inspiration has worn him out. He listens to the children, and dreams of tractors.

A fusillade echoes through the cemetery.

"Daddy, what's that noise?" asks Rose Marie.

"The children are probably shooting guns," Roger says. He opens his eyes, then closes them.

"Why are they shooting guns?"

"To show everyone that death must be joyous," Roger says. But he can't quite climb out of his well of sleep. He falls through thermoclines of sleep, and dreams of tractors rolling over tombstones and children and trees.

"When is Mommy coming back?" asks Rose Marie.

"When she finds Bennie," Roger says, and he buttons the collar of his shirt. There is a slight chill to the air.

"When will that be?"

"I don't know," Roger says. "Soon, I hope." He watches the rosy sunset. The western mountains are purple, and Roger imagines that rainbows are leaking into the liquid blue sky.

Another fusillade echoes through the cemetery.

"Maybe Mommy was shot," Rose Marie says in a hushed tone.

"Maybe," Roger replies.

"Maybe she's dead," says Rose Marie, smoothing out her dress, then making cabbage folds.

"Is that so bad?" Roger asks. "You must learn to accept death as an ally. If Mommy doesn't come back, it will teach you a lesson."

"I want to ride on the Ferris wheel," Samson says. "You promised."

"If Mommy doesn't return soon, we'll go for a ride," Roger says, admiring the cemetery. Even at dusk, in this shadow time, Chastellain Cemetery is still beautiful, he tells himself. It is a proud old virgin, but soon it will become a midnight whore. It will become a carnival. It will be Ferris wheels and rides and lights and candlelight processions.

Lying back in the grass, Roger searches for the first evening stars. There, he sees two straight above him. They blink like Sandra's eyes. He makes a wish and imagines that Sandra is staring at him with those cold, lovely eyes.

In the evening haze below, the candlelight processions begin.

THE DRUM LOLLIPOP

The argument had been going on for an hour. It ebbed, rushed forward, then ebbed again—a steady, calculated rhythm. The flow began for the last time; it carried an echo, as if it were being mouthed in a whisper somewhere else.

Frank Harris remained a little ball while the rest of him screamed at his wife. "I can't love you like that. I just don't have it. It isn't there. You want something I just can't give you. And I won't." A wand lifted him from his seat and pushed him toward the door, into the hall, past the sunken dining room, and through the pantry.

His wife rushed after him, calling, crying, pleading. She overtook him as he fumbled with the screen-door latch. Slipping her arms around his stomach, she dropped to her knees, her fingers wrapped around his belt for support. It would be useless for him to pull himself out the door; she would hang on, crying, and he might hurt her, trying to wrench free. It was an old ploy; it had worked before. The argument was over. Whimpering, she would follow him into the den and tell him that she loved him more than anything in the world.

Upstairs, Maureen put her pick-up sticks away in her toy chest, deep inside, past the toys she did not care about, but she could not find space for the drum. The wands were safe, but the drum, she thought, the drum. Hide it in the closet, in the hamper, under the bed.

"Maureen," her mother called from the foot of the stairs. "Dinner will be ready soon. Clean up your room and come down. Everything's all right now, baby. So come downstairs."

It's broken. A rivulet bubbled under the skin, cracking the taut drumhead. Leave it on the bed. It's broken. She centered it on the pillow, controlled her tears, and calmly went downstairs to eat.

They ate quietly. Maureen played with her food, drawing circles in the corn, and thought about her drum. It would be better to leave it there and make something else. She would never touch it again; she would curl around it when she slept and protect it.

She looked at her father, who was ponderously eating a muffin. She never protected him. She wasn't supposed to. He was supposed to protect her. *I want you to love me the way I love you.* "What's that mean, Mommy?" The wands sang in the toy chest.

"What's what mean, honey?" she asked as she stacked the plates. "Give me your plate."

She's cold. She's like that dead lizard. The drum on the bed. The drum is on the bed. "Nothing. Can I go back to my room and play?"

"No, dear. You've been in your room too long today. You should go out for a little while, at least. It won't be dark for another two hours yet."

Her father left the table.

"Okay." Maureen left everything as it was before. The drum was heavy on the bed. The pick-up sticks hovered in their nook. The dolls were faceless, carelessly thrown about the room. They would be all right. But the drum was cracked. The air pushed inside it. She could leave the house, but this time she would not build a bridge as she left. She reconsidered: a very small one without spokes, or beams, or spongy girders.

She could feel the tension grow behind her. She sat down under a tall oak in the back yard and stared at the white stucco house. Dumbly, it stared back at her through its second-story windows.

But I love you. In my own way. I have always thought of our relationship as something beautiful, something sacred. But I can't love you that way. You're like a daughter to me.

Start with a fence, a white picket fence. Draw a fence around the house. No, that isn't any good. Okay. Eight dogs in the driveway with pointed teeth to protect the house. She laughed: she could not visualize a dog. They looked like horned doughnuts. Pointed teeth, not square teeth.

Closing her eyes, she let her thoughts form around the drum, puffing air each time she slapped it. She shuddered. It was not the drum. It was not a wand. She had drawn something she had never seen. It escaped from her. It settled in the living room, hiding behind transparent walls. The fence collapsed and she stood up. She could not see it; she did not want to see it. She took a step toward the house. And then another: it was fun to be scared.

It was not in the pantry. She passed the washing machine and opened the door into the kitchen. The kitchen was empty. The hall, to the right, down three stairs, there it was. A half image of its substance was concentrated in a tiny puddle. It oozed and grew and contracted. It tossed stimuli of coagulation, vomit, and infection at her as it settled into a scarred asterisk. It was brown, then ocher flecked with black. It grew tentacles and digested itself.

Maureen turned away from it. It pulled her back, enticing her, flooding her. She hated it; it grew fangs.

She could not hear anyone in the house. They were probably upstairs. But why didn't she know? The puddle turned her around and began to disappear, leaving only an aura of warmth. It expanded, engulfing Maureen in a thousand pinpoints of heat. She was free; it did not hold her. But she did not want to go. There was no need. She could stay. She was in love. It had changed; it smelled pretty.

She felt warm and concealed. The aura was a fire to protect her and color the room. It followed her, tracing patterns in the air, up to her room. There, it spun a web from the walls and cradled the bed, careful not to touch the drum.

She heard a creak from the next room. It was the bed. She visualized her parents clutching each other and jarring the springs. She had never heard that before. They had not done it since she was born.

She listened and fell asleep. The web thickened, then turned into a cocoon.

She was up early the next morning. Her room smelled musty, as if the warmth pouring through the open window had not yet evaporated the dampness. The toy chest was closed. She counted three dolls on the floor. The fourth was hidden under the bed, its stuffed sunflower head ripped off and lying upside down beside the torso.

Holding her breath, she tiptoed down the stairs and jumped three steps into the living room. She could not make out the image of movement that had held her last night. She concentrated on the wavering lines; they became more distinct. She closed her eyes, allowing it to sketch its form on her dark retinal field.

It was a drum. Opening her eyes, she glimpsed the dank puddle decaying in the rug. It changed shape, became a bubbling star. It vibrated and emitted a thin glint of warmth. It was a drum pounding. She reached out and caught it with her finger, pressed it into her palm, and imbibed it slowly. She was happy. But it passed quickly.

She waited. Ordering it into being was futile; begging, coaxing, singing did not work either. She took a few steps toward it; it dimmed into an outline. She imagined it had grown another tentacle. It had.

The drum, get the drum and cover the pick-up sticks. The drum was on her bed, but she could not touch it. She had promised. It is not a drum anymore. She ran out of the living room and up the stairs. Secure in her room, she picked up the drum and examined the torn head. It could not be fixed. She slapped it angrily. A flood of revulsion cascaded up the stairs and into her room. She threw the drum on the bed and held her palms tightly against her eyes. The smell dissipated.

Tapping the drum carefully, she listened for a pop of air. It was not an old drum. It should not have ripped. A glimmer sneaked into the room, a very tiny ray of warmth. She could not see it, but she knew it was close to her. Tapping her drum, she watched the door; she concentrated; she giggled; she tried not to urinate in her pajamas. She had not made the drum and she could not fix it. Another drum would not be the same; she could never make another one like it.

Another glint. But softer, a bit wider. She shuddered as it passed through her.

They were awake. She sensed her parents' blurred awareness. The sensation dissolved. She put the drum on top of her toy chest and stared out the window as they quietly got dressed. The sunlight splashed on the floor, then escaped into the suspended stiffness of the house. She breathed mass around the dust motes that floated in the yellow liquid. Invisibly, they dropped into the cracks in the floor.

Her mother was downstairs first. The smell of margarine, a whiff of ozone, then eggs, toast, the clatter of the icebox door, the gurgle of water in the pipes. Maureen could not see any of this, but she was happy.

It was dead. Her drum was on the chest. The puddle in the living room couldn't work without the drum. The drum couldn't work without her. It couldn't work without her. She heard her father swear in the bathroom and a slight odor of nausea swept the room. If you cry it will get worse; it will turn black and gore into the rug. She combed her hair back into a ponytail and admired herself in the mirror. The odor thickened. She leaned out the window to feel the warm air, to see the bright morning. Don't think about the drum. Leave it on the chest. Torn. Leave it alone. It's not there.

She could not smell the cooking odors—they were lost in the heavy waves of nausea rolling into the room. Thicker. Pulling her into the room, stabbing into her mouth and nose, plucking her insides until they strained to vomit. But she could not vomit. She could not take her eyes from the drum, now wavering in sympathy. She could rake the drum, pull its head off, tear the wood into splinters, crack the plastic shoulder strap into red squares.

She lunged toward the toy chest, but found she was still by the window. She was crying, then laughing, then clenching her teeth, dreaming of fangs, and hating everything in the room, especially the drum. She felt her mother forced into her. She could not close her pores; they were gaping holes. She was naked. Her mother. A swill of anger and screaming, a flattened mask of tenderness. A doll yellowed with years, cracking, pulling taut. She screamed at everything that had been taken away. Inside, her mother swelled, tantalizing with promises of depth, promises of emotions yet unfelt, thoughts to tingle her spine, sensations greater than herself. But they were only surface reflections.

Forcing her mother out, she reached for her father. She shrank back and he did not embrace her. He was heavy; he would have smothered her. She snatched at his face, clawing off a piece of withered skin. She gouged at him, concentrating her hatred into her fingers. Stop it. Go away. She looked at the clawed image of her father and began to cry. Go away. She concentrated on the drum; it reflected the puddle downstairs. Change into something else. She visualized animals, trees, designs on bedspreads, dolls' faces, colored pictures. The clot of substance in the living room remained unaffected. You can't change it; you didn't make it. The clot wavered and distorted the wall behind it. I did, she thought. I made it, I made it. She grabbed the drum and ran out of the room. I didn't make the drum; I don't care about it.

She stood on the stairs, her drum nestled in her arm. She could not make the puddle disappear. Concentrating on its imagined shape, she destroyed it in her mind. It remained unaffected. Have to make it go away. She wanted to scream, cry, run to her mother basking in the smells of the kitchen.

She looked at the drum. She was calm, suddenly very old. It bubbled; she snatched at it and it popped. She was very warm and sad. She sat down on the stairs, her legs extended. A golden thread crawled up the stairs and she caught it between her fingers and imbibed it with a pop.

Thoughts of crying and shouting became remote. It was a game. It was fun to be scared. She was flooded with warmth. Loving threads crawled up the stairs, flashing, protecting her, laughing with her, suddenly sad, but pleasantly sad.

"Call your father; breakfast is ready." Her mother stood in the hall below. She looked relaxed; a slight smile twitched at the corners of her lips and then dissolved. "When did you break your drum? It's almost brand-new, and you've already broken it. Were you banging it with a stick? It's made to be hit only with your fingers, not with a stick. Well, it's not any good now. Take it downstairs and throw it away."

"Okay. But do I have to do it now?"

"Now. This minute. Throw it in the wastebasket in the kitchen."

She could not throw it away yet. It would start all over again: the vomit, the smell, teeth, claws, kicking, pulling, hitting, crying, punching, hating. No, I won't throw it away.

She threw it away, her mother before her, her father behind her. And in a rush.

Nothing happened. She ate breakfast and went out to play under a tree, ate her lunch, studied the puddle in the living room—now a tan stain in the rug—played under the tree for a few more hours, tried to draw things in her mind, thought about the drum and the protean stain. The stain was still there, bubbling unnoticed, but the drum—that was hidden in the garbage.

Maureen waited for something to happen. She spent each day under the tree and watched the house. The stain remained in the living room, unobserved by the rest of the family, including Uncle Milton, who dropped over at least once a week. She did not think about the drum anymore; she had not made it.

She forgot about being scared. It was a game, like the others, and she had used it up. But she could not make anything, not even a bridge or a fence. The smear in the living room had taken everything from her. Now she could only work with tangibles. It muffled everything around her; she could not sense words or people.

Slowly things began to change. There were no more marital clashes; her mother and father were falling in love. They held hands, whispered in the bedroom, bounced on the springs, and went out on Saturday night. Even Uncle Milton began dropping in more often; he claimed it was the only place where he could relax.

The laundryman came twice that week, he said he had forgotten that he already collected the laundry.

And the telephone man repaired the wires twice.

And the stain assumed an honest shape. Maureen had been outside when it became active. She had learned to use her hands, but it was not the same. The drum was lost: she had relinquished all control. She was making mud pies in the rain. This would be her last mud batter: she was getting too old for mud pies.

Shouting, "Mother, come and see," she ran into the house, her hands and lacquered boots covered with mud. Through the pantry, kitchen, dead-end in the den, up three stairs into the hall, and there they were in the living room. Why hadn't she looked there first? Because it's there now. It's working. She shrugged off a familiar sensation; everything seemed clearer.

The room was red—she had not noticed that for a long time. A fake stone fireplace was propped against the far wall for decoration. A large mirror hung directly above it, reflecting a fat velvet sofa and an oil painting of the family. A glass table, chairs, a few pieces of crystal, maroon curtains, and a red plush carpet completed the scene.

The tentacled asterisk was visible. It palpitated in front of the fireplace. It had grown four more tentacles, and its black speckles had turned to crusted sores oozing goo into the air. It was radiating long thin yellow spokes of love all over the room. It threw a few wisps at Maureen, but she stepped aside, only to see her mother and father sitting sleepily on the companion rocking chairs near the entrance to the dining room. Bathing in love, they held hands across the doorway.

A wisp of yellow settled on Maureen's braid, hung loose, dropped to her shoulder, and disappeared into her crinoline dress. She felt a burst of security, a cushion of warmth. As she stepped into the living room, the doorbell rang.

"Darling," her mother said, "would you get the door?"

Maureen opened the door for Uncle Milton. He marched into the house, beads of sweat gleaming on his bald pate. Skimming a line of perspiration from his barely visible mustache, he said, "How's my Maureen? Jesus, what the hell happened to you? Fall into a hole? You've ruined that pretty dress. Better go tell your mother. Wait a minute. You're getting tall, almost as tall as me." He puffed his stomach out. "Where's Mom and Dad? In the den?"

She shook her head and pointed toward the living room. She stood in the hall; she did not want to go into the room just yet. And the mud was sticky.

"Maureen," her mother said, "go upstairs and take a bath. And leave that dress in the bathroom. You can put your pajamas on when you're done. Then you can come down and join us."

Yes, Mommy, I'm covered with fuzz, closed in the room, I don't care. Into the bath, peel off the mudskin, no bra yet, red dress in the hamper. A few threads wiggled under the door to keep her company and burst in her hair.

She washed quickly, jumped into her pajamas, and tiptoed into the living room. No one noticed her entrance. The room had turned gray, but it was gradually building up strength. She breathed strength into it. She could feel, taste, hear.

"You know," Uncle Milton said, "I don't know what it is, but I feel so comfortable here lately."

"Sure you do," her mother said, her smile drawing back her thin lips.

"Well, there were a few times when I thought I would have to let you sign those separation papers."

Everyone laughed. It did not have to be funny: it felt good. Maureen sat on the rug, her blond hair untied, enjoying the feel of everything and everyone.

Outside, the noises trickled in. Maureen heard them first. *Leggo, oh, here, eat it then. Too warm tonight, doesn't matter—feels good. I don't know why, just felt like coming over. Relax. Get dark in a while. Put that dirty handkerchief away.*

"Mommy, hear the people outside the house? They're on our lawn. Sounds funny. Hey, Johnny Eaton's mother's out there. Johnny's coming too."

"I don't hear anything," Uncle Milton said, staring at the new tentacles growing out of the asterisk. It readied itself for another burst of energy, its suckers grasping for support. It emitted a gurgling noise, but no one seemed to notice. Contracting, it threw off a puddle of phlegm and radiated full force. The yellow bars passed through the soft walls and wallowed in the grass and people outside. Uncle Milton poured himself another drink, spilling a jigger as a strong wisp passed into his throat.

"Four more people, Mommy. Mr. Richardson and his kid Wally and Mr. and Mrs. Allen from Snow Street. Remember them? They gave us all those vegetables last summer."

It grew, then fell back on itself, preparing for another surge through friendly streets and houses.

Maureen closed her eyes and drew pictures. She could see the lines clearly, only a little fuzz where she could not remember a color. *Johnny, look in your pocket, fingers around it, matches there too, don't worry how, let it go, under the tree, there.* The colors were darker than she imagined. It's getting late.

"That sounded like a firecracker, didn't it?" her father said. "Sounded like a pretty big one, too."

"Could have been a backfire," Uncle Milton said. He leaned back into the couch, hands folded, eyes closed. He inhaled a flood of love, soft clouds perspired by the asterisk. He giggled with contentment.

"No," her mother said, standing inside the curtains and peering out the jalousied window into the front yard. "Why, it's that Johnny Whatshisname. He's playing with firecrackers. And no one's even paying any attention to it."

"Johnny Eaton," Maureen said.

"Yes, Maureen's right; there are over twenty people on our lawn. Look, Mr. Logos is waving at me. It's a regular picnic. They've even got blankets and radios."

Maureen watched the slick tentacles growing out of the asterisk. Better not wait, do it now. Be too late soon. Where's the drum?

The room turned yellow with love, thick strong rays that rolled over the carpet, too heavy to float. And out through the walls. Uncle Milton was asleep. He turned over, burying his face in the soft velvet of the sofa.

"Strange we're in the living room," her father said. "Usually I prefer the den."

Sandra Harris sat down on the floor beside her husband's chair, rested her head on his knee and said, "I guess it doesn't matter if they stay on the lawn. I'm too lazy to bother. Frank, I'm glad everything's settled. Better than before. Frank. Do you see something on the rug? There, in the middle of the room, in front of the fireplace. Jesus, it's ugly. Frank. Frank. I think I can smell it. Can you smell it?"

Maureen faced the wall and stared through minute cracks into other cracks that led outside. Don't look or it'll happen. Can't happen behind me, isn't there. Can't see it.

It equalized the pressure in the room and bathed Sandra Harris. She rested her head on her husband's lap and said, "I love you."

He didn't flinch. Stroking her face, he said, "I know you do. And I love you, too." He yawned and fell asleep. It was dark outside. A few torches flickered in the yard and the street light glowed dimly.

Uncle Milton stayed the night. He slept on the sofa, clutching a pillow. He said he felt so good he would stay another day. And another night. Until it turned into a week. And the front yard population grew until it covered the back yard. They brought pup tents, Coleman stoves, guitars, a green water hose, and more relatives and friends. They packed themselves into the yard until everyone was in some sort of physical contact with the others. No one minded. It was good. It was pure. It was in friendship and love.

Maureen's mother and father tacitly agreed not to talk about the neighbors that had suddenly moved in. The neighbors pressed their faces against the windows and smiled. Uncle Milton periodically yelled at them in good humor.

Maureen did not like it. She knew the ending, only she did not realize it.

Until the next day. It was early in the morning; breakfast was bubbling in a greased frying pan, sunlight was streaming in the kitchen windows, and Maureen was catnapping in the living room. Uncle Milton had been ordered to sleep in her room, cutting off access to the pick-up sticks and drum, almost grown.

Her mother stepped into the living room as she untied her red apron. The asterisk became active; it stretched its tentacles across the carpet. "Come on, honey. Help Mommy get the food on."

"Do I have to do it now?" she asked. Don't let her look at it. It wants her to see it. Protect her. But she moves, she walks, she says things. Something's burned out or burned in. Not real enough.

"Is that a stain on the rug over there? What is it?"

Maureen was locked into the room. The asterisk bubbled, smiled at her by raising its tentacles, passed a beam into her, a shaft of glass connecting her to it. She loved her mother now, very clearly. All the fond remembrances became real; they flowed through the beam. A reassuring drum thumped upstairs. Her mother was beautiful. All her age lines were lifted; her hair faded into gray.

"It's ugly." Her mother watched it, spellbound. "I seem to remember seeing it last night. Like a dream. Fell asleep with your father. I can't think." She stepped backward and screamed. It drew itself into a ball, squelched half its substance to the side, stank, decayed a bit, and shot a beam of love right into her heart. It thickened and held her by the liver and collarbone.

"Mother, don't touch it. Leave it alone." She changed the picture. Nothing happened. She could not move. Mother is beautiful, she thought. Long beautiful hair. "Mother, you are beautiful. I have long hair just like yours. Yours is prettier. Daddy loves your hair. I know he loves your hair."

Her mother's hand sank into the porous putrescent mass, into the heart of it. She looked at her daughter, her face a landscape of disgust and fear. She smiled her special loving smile and retched as it took her arm with its tentacles.

"Mother, I love you," Maureen cried. She felt too content to move.

Her mother smiled at her again, overcome with love and revulsion. She was halfway into it: half mother, half blob. She became a distorted Greek legend squirming with love. Her face snapped in rictus, a mask of fright and love. Maureen could only watch. She loved her mother. "You are beautiful, Mother."

It belched and flattened itself on the rug. She could not smell it.

She finished the picture. Father came downstairs and tripped over a tentacle, waving bye-bye. She drew it quickly. It was easier that way. She could construct the memory later. She wanted the full bloom of love now.

Uncle Milton departed with a loving frown. She did not say good-bye. He had never really been.

The asterisk was perfect, fully grown, carefully tended by its retinue of self. It spurted pus into the air. It was a cereal-box sun radiating cereal-box love.

The drum was upstairs. She ran into her room, found the drum on her toy chest, and carried it downstairs. Before she could reach the living room, it disappeared.

It was late. She had to get on with it. Now. For Mother. And Father. And maybe Uncle Milton.

Outstretching her palms, she walked toward the trembling star, measuring her steps with its palpitations. Sliding her hands under it, she lifted it into the air. It hung between her fingers.

She took it inside her; she ate it, she osmosed it; she transformed it. She felt it in her eyes, a heaviness, a largeness that could span anything, envision everything—with love.

Dream the dream, paint the picture. It's all in the cereal box, ready to eat. Can't be changed now. The drum's disappeared again. You had the chance.

She opened the door carefully, squinting her oval eyes at the morning sun.

And everyone was there. Standing. Smiling. Laughing.

DAYS OF STONE

It was dusk, and Mrs. Fishbine was still lolling about in bed, changing channels with her teevee selector, thumbing through fashion magazines, and occasionally staring at the window across the room. Evening threatened to be long and deadly cold; but she would turn up the heat, smoke her menthol cigarettes, and watch the frost-fingers etch midnight scenes on the glass. She would wait for the phone to ring. She would wait for her sons to surprise her with a visit.

I won't eat, she thought, until they call me.

She went back to her magazines.

Mrs. Fishbine could lie in bed, almost without moving, for hours. She would stare at the whorls in the ceiling and dream of a young man who would quietly give her all her dreams in return for a kiss and a smile. But gradually her memories would poison her daydreams and turn them into stark, cold things. She would remember that she was sixty-two and her hair was thinning. Makeup caked on her face now— she had to use too much of it to cover the wrinkles. Then, after she felt old and ugly and fragile, she would remember that Damon had left her, after thirty years. After she had given up everything for him.

So now she was old and dead—she repeated the words to herself: *deadead and old.* But he was a man, and a man could do anything. A man could find a younger woman to take care of him. There were always plenty hanging around. *Younger woman,* she said to herself. Damon's new plaything was forty; she'll wrinkle soon. *Let her face fall off.*

Usually when she thought of Damon, she would awaken from her trance. This time, however, she would not open her eyes. She would die, even as she breathed. Her thoughts roiled like cigarette smoke in the infinities of red behind her closed eyelids. She devised ordinary, but bloody, deaths for Damon and Lorna. She ran through the usual stock list of car accidents and muggings and settled for a prosaic rape:

Damon would be tied up and forced to watch young men with slick hair torture and kill Lorna.

Dreams uncoiled as she sank into lower thermoclines of sleep.

I love you I'm sorry I love you I'm sorry, he whispered to her in a dream bright as klieg lights. But he still had his face. He was still young. He would have his mistress, and they would both stay young until Mrs. Fishbine's skin cracked away. For an instant, a delicious second, she could see herself: She was beautiful and dressed in a stiff skirt and lacy blouse. Her hair was black and piled high on her head; ringlets hung loose over her ears, and her skin was soft and smooth.

But her face became gray and fell off and she woke up. The television was blaring. A talk show. She looked out the window. How much time had passed—an hour? fifteen minutes?

She waited and read. She had that feeling—it was just about time for a visit. David and Carl, her sons, had been spending too much time with their father. Granted, he was sick, but they owed her an hour. *I'm still their mother.*

She heard footsteps downstairs about ten o'clock. She waited while one of her sons, probably David, she thought, fixed himself a snack. *He can at least yell, "Hello."*

Let him come up here. I'm not going down to him.

It was David. She had always thought he was the better of the two boys: Carl didn't give a damn about anyone, except his father.

"Did I wake you, Mom?" he asked as he entered the room. He sat down on his father's bed, opposite hers. David looked like his father— same high forehead, deep-set brown eyes, shock of hair, and rugged, lined face. Mrs. Fishbine hated him for that and sometimes forgot that she was talking to her son instead of her husband.

David did not wait for small talk and chat, but told her right away that Damon was sick, that he had cancer, that he was going to New York City for an operation. She tried to look bored, tried not to let her facial muscles give her away, but they did: she grimaced. It was a nervous smile, no more. It was a sigh of relief, an affirmation that justice still had a balance. Her hatred and pain stiffened her, gave her strength and wore her down.

She listened to David and watched him change. First his eyes—they were watery and shallow, tiny birdbaths scooped out of his plastic face; and his face was soft and lineless. He looked like anybody else, but not her son. He was a featureless worm, a pale thing that was slowly melting.

"If he dies," David went on, "then you'll have nothing. Do you know that? So you'd better hope that he lives."

But it didn't mean anything. Cancer. Memorial Hospital. Lorna. She lit a cigarette. Of course it was a triumph, but now she didn't care. It was already done. She had only to finish the conversation, hold on to her son so she could watch his metamorphosis. She wasn't afraid. It was as if she had expected the world to dissolve, lose its lines and faces. But her room still had its cloying presence. It was hard and sharp, full of angles and ornaments.

"Well," she said, "that's what he wanted. He caught it from her. She had it, right in her filthy crotch."

David talked on. He was angry, but that was alright: it seemed to quicken his change. His face was a smooth oval. His hands were too long; they seemed to melt like candle wax on his knees.

She let him talk until he started to smell, a putrescent smell like rotten food and garbage on the street, a sweet smell of perfume gone slightly bad from perspiration.

She took a deep breath and he left.

It doesn't matter now, Mrs. Fishbine thought. He's dead. She would work that out, rationalize it; but she would have plenty of time to mourn for him. After all, she thought, he'll still be walking about. But his father was another matter. He would take some time growing ugly and developing enough sores to cancel himself.

"Come on, now," she said. "What silly thoughts! Damon won't die. Skin cancer. . . . So let David stay with his father."

It was a commercial break. Mrs. Fishbine thought of food and decided to take a snack. It was snowing hard and the window was painted with frost. She turned off the television. Everything was quiet. The house didn't creak, the faucet didn't drip. She couldn't hear the wind. So she made noise, but it didn't work, for every word, squeak, cough, and snizzle seemed to come from another place, somewhere far away. She stood up and stamped her foot on the floor, but the sharp crack didn't have anything to do with her. It was a noise, but the connection of events wasn't causal. It was parallel, synchronistic. The worlds of sight and sound were only apparently connected.

But one of the worlds was dying, and Mrs. Fishbine had the feeling, the intuition, that simple, straightforward logic would have to break down, just a little. It was as if everything was now beginning to die and fall apart. What difference was David? she asked herself. He was only a second for his father, a bad image; so, of course, he would have to decay first.

Mrs. Fishbine fought the solid silence of the stone house and walked downstairs to the kitchen. Her feet padded on the carpet, but they were not her feet, they were a thousand ghosts occupying the same space. She felt heavy, but she was too brittle to melt away and become a dead sound.

She turned all the lights on—her house, squat and crumbling, would become a night beacon, a flare against death. She prepared a tray of cheese and crackers and tea to take upstairs. Tomorrow would be another day, she thought.

Tomorrow she would count the dead.

NIGHT VISIONS

Martin steps on the accelerator of his Naples-yellow coupe and prepares to die. It will be a manly death, he thinks, although he is somewhat saddened by the thought of his beautiful car lying wrecked in a ditch. He glances at the rectilinear information band that stretches across the instrument panel: the speedometer needle is resting neatly between the nine and the zero.

He feels a delicious anticipation as he cruises through the darkness and low-lying mountain fog. The high beams turn the trees preternaturally green; the moon changes shape to accommodate the clouds boiling above.

As the speedometer needle reaches one hundred, Martin closes his eyes and turns the steering wheel to the left. He envisions his car moving diagonally across the highway, then over the embankment, taking with it several guardrails, and plunging into the ghostly arms of fog below. He does not brace himself for the coming crash. Relaxed, he waits for the car to leave the highway and the events of his life to rush before him as if in a newsreel. Surely time will distend like a bladder, filled with the insights and profound despair that must attend the last instants of consciousness.

Martin resolves to keep his eyes closed; he *will* meet his destiny. But the car remains on the highway, as if connected to an overhead line like a trolley. The radial tires make a plashing sound as they meet each measured seam in the pavement. Curious as to why he has not yet crashed and died, Martin dreams of the splintering of bone, the blinding explosion of flesh, the truly cosmic orgasm.

Then, just as the left front and rear tires finally slip off the road, a siren sounds. Surprised, Martin opens his eyes to find that the car, as if under the influence of a bewitched gyroscope, has regained the highway.

A police car overtakes him; and Martin pulls over beside an illuminated glen of evergreen to accept his speeding ticket as if it were a penitent's wafer.

It is unfair that I should have to kill myself, Martin thinks, as his car dips in and out of the fog like a great warship on a desolate sea. Ahead, he can see the gray lights of a medium-sized city that is nestled between black hills. He muses in the darkness; soon the highway will become elevated and illuminated.

Martin regrets his life. What has he to show for it but one hundred and thirty-eight hack novels, two children, and a wife he does not love? He considers himself still a virgin, for he has never had sex with anyone but his wife. At thirty-nine years of age, he is still obsessed with sex. He has written thirty-five pornographic novels, yet never gone down on a woman. He thinks of himself as a writing machine, and machines don't have experiences. They have no free will, they don't love or get laid. They just operate until they are turned off or break down.

He slows down behind a small, foreign car. The highway is suddenly crowded, and Martin experiences a familiar claustrophobia: he remembers the Long Island Expressway during rush hour, the hypnotic seventy-mile-per-hour ritual of tailgating, the mile-long bumper-to-bumper traffic jams.

There can be no car-crashing here, for Martin does not wish the death of others on his conscience.

He passes a late-model convertible. A young man is driving, his arm around a pretty girl. Now, that would be a perfect car for an ending, Martin thinks—the wind whistling in your ears, drying your eyes, and no hard roof to protect skull from pavement.

Saddened by the thought that convertibles are no longer being made, he drives carefully onward. Safety poles whiz by him like teeth in some infernal machine; one wrong turn, a slight pull on the steering wheel, and the car would be smashed to scrap. But, always considerate of others, he keeps to the road. He passes a series of midtown exits, sees the blinking lights of a plane coming in from the east, and then the city and its dull glow of civilization is behind him. Ahead is a sliver of gray highway cutting through mountains, a low wall of nightfog, and heavy clouds hanging below an angry red moon.

Now Martin thinks he will slip into the darkness, which will absorb the impact of flesh and metal; and he will simply drift away like a ghost on the morning mist.

The highway becomes a two-lane road for the next few miles and fol-

lows the contours of the land. Martin's throat tightens in joyful anticipation as he closes his eyes and presses the accelerator to the floor.

He dreams of flight and concussion; he dreams that time is made of
rubber and he is pulling it apart. As he waits for his past to unfold, he
repeats a mantra that his elder daughter taught him.

He tries to visualize his wife, Jennifer. Although Martin knows her
intimately and can describe her in minute detail, he can no longer *see*
her. He remembers her now as an equation, as numbers complemented
by an occasional Greek letter to signify a secret part of her psyche.

She is probably phoning the police, calling the neighbors, making a
fuss and waking the children.

He pulls another band of time taut and dreams about his funeral.
His closest friends will all stand about the grave, then toss a few
clumps of earth into the hole; his children will be crying loudly while
Jennifer looks on quietly. All in all, a fine despair; a fitting end.

Martin wonders how long he has been daydreaming. Probably only
an instant, he thinks. He remembers his childhood.

And he turns the steering wheel hard to ensure his death. He
screams, anticipating the shattering pain and subsequent numbness.

But nothing happens.

He waits several more beats, then opens his eyes, only to find himself
negotiating a cloverleaf turnoff. He has unwittingly turned onto an exit
ramp and is now shooting back to the highway, heading in the opposite
direction.

He strikes the wood-inlaid steering wheel.

"Dammit, Jennifer, I'm not coming home. . . ."

There is very little time left; the sky is already becoming smudgy.
Dawn is not far away, and the thought of driving into a bleeding sunrise does not escape him.

It must be done while it is still dark, he thinks; the sunlight would
expose him to the world.

Shale palisades rise on either side of the highway like ruined steps.
But this time Martin does not shut his eyes. There is no time to dream.

He turns the wheel sharply, once again preparing for the bright explosion of death.

But the car runs smoothly forward, as if Martin had never turned
the wheel. The car follows the gentle curve of the highway. Martin is
only a passenger.

"No," he screams as he turns the steering wheel again. The car does not respond. He steps on the brake, but the car maintains its speed. Although he is screaming—long, sharp streamers of sound—he hears only engine noise. Perfect rows of numbers pass through his mind: all the coupe's specifications he had once memorized.

Half a mile to the next exit, the car decelerates, turns into the right-hand lane, and then into the thirty-mile-per-hour exitway. It rushes toward the sunrise, which is first a bleeding then a yellow-butter melting beyond the grey hills.

Home is only about twenty miles away.

Martin feels himself running down. He can barely move, for he is as heavy as the car. His hands rest upon the steering wheel as if he were in control. The air-conditioner blows a steady stream of cold air at his face. Numbers pass through his mind.

It is becoming a gritty day. Long, gray clouds drift across the sky, and Martin dreams that the sky is made of metal. He dreams that the world is made of metal, that he is made of metal.

In one last burst of strength, hope, and will, Martin commands his foot to press the accelerator to the floor. Once more, he dreams of the lovely shock of body and brain being pulped.

But the coupe maintains its speed.

Martin is almost home.

FRAGMENTARY BLUE

Eighty-three books, half that on psychology, were reflected in the antique silvered mirror. All out of date. Fleitman had stopped trying to keep up on anything long ago—these books were only a part of his ritual. I never liked to read, anyway, Fleitman told himself. And television had never been enough, even with cerebral hook-ins. He had stopped paying rent on the tiny machines when he had started to enjoy feeling the commercials. He could not rationalize having an orgasm over a cigarette advertisement.

Fleitman rested his forehead on the mirror: two clouds formed under his nose. If only you could forget where you are. If only you were young. But you should be content, Fleitman told himself. It is safe and calm here; there are no young people to intrude. Fleitman leaned back in his chair and smiled at himself in the mirror. He remembered when his professional degree had become obsolete. He remembered forty more years of soft jobs, jobs he could handle, jobs where his education and experience would be useful. He remembered working as a module superintendent.

Fleitman lit a cigarette and watched the smoke curl before his face. He experienced a vague sexual sensation. But he would not permit himself any more synthetic pleasures. He glanced around his room, all the familiar objects in their proper places, everything clean, ready for tomorrow. But the whole place will change, he thought—after this generation dies out. And you'll be dead.

Mercifully, the phone rang. A very white, wrinkled face appeared in the wall hollow; it smiled and without waiting for a customary greeting said, "You have a meeting, Professor Fleitman. Have you forgotten?"

Bitch, Fleitman said to himself.

"The Entertainment Committee is waiting for you. Shall I tell them you'll be right there?"

Fleitman watched his expression in the mirror. "All right. Tell Taylor I'll be there as soon as I get dressed."

"But you're already dressed, sir."

Forty years ago she might have had breasts, he thought, instead of dried-up gunnysacks. Where had he heard of gunnysacks? No image came into his mind. "Tell them I'll be there when I dress, Mrs. Watson."

Fleitman was happy that a meeting had been called. He needed the company, and a good argument would clear his head. And, as usual, everyone would end up hung in the feelies, Fleitman thought. He felt an urge to join them. No, he thought, and tried to forget about it. He felt squeamish about leaving his room.

He took a shuttle to the park. It would be a short, leisurely walk to the conference building. And he could forget all that mass above him, pushing down on his thoughts by its mere existence. As was prescribed, there was a thin drizzle. Fleitman had forgotten his raincoat, but the cold little bites of rain felt good on his arms and chest. His shirt clung to his skin.

The park stretched out before him. Haze hung in the trees and connected them into a pale ceiling supported by an undergrowth of frozen arms and legs, gnarls for chests and branches for limbs. A yellow chalk road sliced through the wall of trees. Fleitman did not look at the skyscrapers behind him, steel stalagmites reaching toward the bright surface of the dome above. The sunlights—the thousand eyes of the sphere that surrounded and supported the underground city built for the elderly—were turned on full. The sun-shower had been scheduled to last for an hour.

Fleitman walked along a causeway near the edge of the park and listened to the shuttle trains passing below him. The sidewalk enclosure shielded him from the rain. He watched a crowd waiting to step onto a slidewalk ramp. They were all wearing raincoats. Fleitman was repelled by their age, by their once-soft skin that had turned to parchment. Fleitman touched his own face. He left the park—it was a five-minute walk to the Entertainment Building. Like a somnambulist, Fleitman edged his way through the crowds, ignoring them. He took an escalator into the building and then an elevator to his floor.

He paused for a few seconds in front of the conference-room door, inches from the sensing line. He kicked at the air and the door slid open, revealing five old men seated around a polished metal table.

"'Bout time," Taylor said. He was seated at the far end of the table. "Christ, waiting for you for—"

Jake, who was sitting to the left of Taylor and opposite Sartorsky, said, "Sit down, Fleitman. We've got a great idea." He nodded at Sartorsky, who was studying his distorted reflection in the metal tabletop. Sartorsky's breath clouded the reflection. "Remember the old screen movies?" Jake continued. "I mean, you've heard of them."

Fleitman straightened his back to gain a few more inches of height. Relax, he thought. They're sitting down. He rested his palms against the back of the chair. No need to stand up, you old bastards. "The rules of order prescribe. . . ."

Good, Fleitman thought. Jake is going to be trouble. That will give me some time to think.

"What are the rules of order?" asked Sartorsky.

Sartorsky's blind, Fleitman thought. He fought down a gleeful urge to pull the black visor band from his eyes. "First of all, I received no notice at all of this meeting. Why was that?"

Tostler, who was sitting beside Fleitman's chair, winked at him. Fleitman had never seen him before. He was younger than the rest of the men. Fleitman ignored him.

"It was posted," said Toomis, who was sitting opposite Tostler and to the left of Fleitman.

"And you also got a call from me yesterday," Taylor said. "What the hell else do you want?"

"Out of order," Fleitman replied. An idea was forming. "Out of order, you sonovabitch." Everyone was playing the game, but they would not give Fleitman more than five minutes.

"Sit down, Fleitman," Jake said. "Listen for a minute. Sartorsky, over here, came up with a great idea." Jake looked at Sartorsky, but he was still looking down at his reflection. "It's good for the whole goddam sector, good enough for a couple of months at least."

"It stinks," Taylor said. "People want a feelie or, at least, a hook-in." Toomis nodded in agreement. Tostler smiled at Jake, waiting for him to reply.

Sartorsky looked up from the table. "Let me tell it myself. It's my idea."

"Shut up," Jake said. "I'm doing this for you." Tostler nodded in approval; Fleitman was not listening.

Popcorn, Fleitman thought. What the hell was popcorn? Popcorn—movies—dried gunnysacks. The words were there before the images.

"Let me tell this," Sartorsky said, propping his knee against the table and pushing his chair back. "It is a good idea. We could show a few screens a week for recreation."

"Movies," Toomis said, "not screens." Taylor grinned.

"Right, movies. There weren't that many that were available to us. We couldn't get anything popular." He held up a notebook. "These are the titles we can get right away: *Blood of the Artist,* by Cocteau; another one—it's only fifteen minutes—by Dali, but I can't read the title; another one by. . . ." He passed the notebook to Jake.

"Disney. Says it's a cartoon. What the hell is a cartoon?"

Cartoon. I'm getting near it, Fleitman thought. Little children running around, balloons. What's a balloon? Talking, laughing, gasping, whispering. Sideshow. Sonovabitch.

"Well, anyway," Jake continued, "there's a lot of them here." He passed the notebook to Fleitman.

"This is interesting," Tostler said. *"Freaks."*

"What's that?" Fleitman asked. Freaks. That felt right. Fleitman tied it into popcorn and gunnysacks. It still did not work. Soon, he thought.

"It's no good," Taylor said. "People won't give a damn about these movies, not without, at least, a hook-in. It has to be a feelie, or something like it."

"People want something different," Sartorsky said, tracing a line over his reflection with his index finger. "They don't have to experience everything through a feelie. People want something else."

"Do you?" Toomis asked.

Sartorsky flushed. "You know why I use the feelies. Let me put out your eyes and we'll see how well you can see with a visor band."

Taylor smiled at Toomis and relaxed in his chair. Fleitman was still standing, his palms red from his weight. He stood up straight.

"So what do you think, Fleitman?" Jake asked. "The girls should like it; hell, they suggested it, didn't they?"

Sartorsky grimaced.

It's not that easy, Fleitman thought. He could go one better; if not, he would side with Sartorsky. Fleitman could outyell Taylor. His ideas were still fuzzy, but a word came to mind and he blurted it out: "Circus. We can have a circus. That's better than a movie, that's almost real."

"What the hell is a circus?" Jake asked.

"Shut up, Jake." Animals, Fleitman thought. Pictures began to form in his mind. "We can pull thirty floors out of the rec building. Christ, it's a module, isn't it? The big top will be burlap." He had once filed this information, but he could not remember when or for what reason.

"What's burlap?" Sartorsky asked.

Tightrope walkers, lion tamers, trapeze artists, clowns. From a book? Horses jumping through hoops.

"What's wrong with the movie idea?" Jake asked.

Fleitman ignored him and sat down. Everyone was watching Fleitman.

"I know what a circus is," Tostler said. "It's like the movies, only closer to a feelie. The movies, I think, are flat. A circus is live people performing tricks. You can't get inside the performers, but you can watch them right in front of you. Not like on a board." Jake was silent.

"Is this thing a feelie?" Taylor asked.

Fleitman did not look at him; he looked at the wall over Taylor's head. "No, Stephen. It's not a feelie. You just watch it; the excitement is watching the other people, fearing for them."

"What people are you going to ask to perform? Is it dangerous? It must be, if it's as exciting as you say."

"No one performs. It's a projection." That would work, he thought. He would give in a little.

Taylor laughed and Toomis tittered. "Then," Taylor said, "it can be worked as a feelie."

"No," Fleitman said. "Then you lose the fun of being a spectator. And you lose the enjoyment of being with other people."

"We'd better do the movie," Jake said. "It's the middle of the road."

"It is not," Taylor said.

Fleitman allowed the badinage between Taylor and Jake to take its course. "O.K.," he said, "we can hook in the seats. Those who want cerebral hook-ins can have them, and those who just want to watch can do so."

"But why not a feelie?" Toomis asked.

"Because I want people to be in one place together. I don't want them isolated from each other in a feelie. I want them to smell each other, to touch each other."

"Why?" Taylor asked.

"Why are you in this meeting?"

"But that's almost the same thing we wanted to do."

· Sonovabitch, Fleitman thought. "No it wasn't, Jake. You would have used private screens or borrowed television time."

"Without hook-ins," Toomis added.

Sartorsky nodded his head. It was over, another meeting would be called to find out what had been settled, and Fleitman would begin on the circus. Alone. Everyone began talking at once. Jake started an argument. Fleitman doodled with his forefinger on the polished steel.

"Speaking of feelies," Tostler said, "why don't we all go down and hang?"

Fleitman nodded to Tostler and smiled. Get them the hell out, he thought.

"The hell with it," Jake said. "Let's go. Everyone agreed?" It was always the same: the feelies and to bed. "Are you coming, Fleitman?"

Taylor played along. "Of course he's not coming. That's not the real thing, is it, Fleitman?"

"Neither is his circus," Jake said.

But that's closer, Fleitman thought. He made a fist and extended his index finger. The room had become too dense. He counted the men as they left; Tostler was last. No courtesies—they had not even been introduced. That was Taylor's fault. But why didn't Fleitman ask? The door slid closed; Fleitman felt elated in the empty room. He looked forward to the work ahead; he could delegate permission formalities to the secretaries. They had probably changed the system again. He smiled. But not that much.

What the hell. The building will probably be razed within the decade. Why not an amphitheater for a day? The big top. The classic show of shows. And actors of actors?

He would busy himself with his secretary. That should build up anticipation and keep the walls at their proper distance. He tapped out her number on one of the table phones. Her face appeared in the wall hollow before him. He leaned his elbows on the table. Thanks for the idea, gunnysacks. A tic in her temple snapped in and out as she worked her mouth.

A generalized tape on the feelies. Bring back Mary. Bring back a body that felt right, not too loose on the bones. Skin pulled tight on your face—supple, won't crack when you smile. Fleitman suppressed these thoughts; submerged, they became anxiety. Projection isn't real; it's an excuse for a feelie.

"No, Mrs. Watson. It shouldn't take more than a day." Her tic snapped in and out a few times.

"Then quit, goddam it." Very good, Fleitman. Suck in your skin. Feel good. Stop the pressure, push out the walls, take in a feelie. Don't think about it. A tape can make you anybody. A-n-y—B-o-d-y.

Go. The whole morality had not been working very well. He walked down the hall to the elevator. The doors slid open before him. No good, he thought. You should get help. Fleitman, you're confusing morality with hard-on and you're too old for either. Fleitman had pushed the wrong floor button. He tried not to move his lips when he talked to himself. He sucked in the tic pounding in his cheek.

The elevator door opened and Fleitman walked past the feelie room. The door was open. Exhibitionists, Fleitman thought. He could turn around now. Say hello.

"I thought you didn't approve, Mr. Fleitman," Tostler said. "My name is Lorne Tostler; I'm sorry we weren't introduced." He shivered. "Cold."

"Then, use a robe."

"Uh, uh. Why use a cotton prophylactic?"

What's a prophylactic? Fleitman asked himself. You know, idiot. It's cotton that you don't know.

"I like your circus idea. Taylor refuses to recognize it, but the feelies don't permit enough freedom. You always know that you're twice removed from the action. Even when your emotions are juiced, you always know. But all that coming from you. After what I heard about you. . . . The circus idea reminds me of a place called the *Circus House,* in Santa Balzar."

"I think I've heard of it," Fleitman replied. "In Ecuador, I believe."

"It was the only house in the city where you could get away with losing two kidneys at roulette. Illegal everywhere else. Had quite an operating room set up. They also had a bordello called the *Slave Market.* Made for a good house. It was so damned realistic you talked Latin." He pushed his hands through the padded loops and watched the hollow in the wall opposite him.

He didn't wait for Fleitman to leave. He had stepped into the stirrups, rested his back against the long supporting pad that stimulated his spinal nerves, and activated the tape. His arms were already moving, reenacting a prefabricated motion, caressing a smooth face. His knees were buckling, and he looked as if he would collapse. He stared at the hollow, catching the electric impulses through his retinal wall, transmitting them through his optic nerve to his brain. The spinal pad quickened his heartbeat and at the moment was providing vague feelings of pleasure accompanied by a prescience of danger.

Fleitman found it difficult to breathe. But Tostler was smiling, then laughing. His torso cracked in a spasm of laughter. Then tears: rich, oily baubles. Made of plastic, Fleitman told himself. He backed out of the room, swallowing his guilt.

He walked to the nearest elevator. Fleitman had just desecrated Mary. But she was pulp, anyway. Thoughts of Mary spiderwebbed into bizarre images. But, he thought, everyone always went to the feelies after a meeting. At least they all said they did. No. They did. He had passed this room before. Don't think about that. Then, why was Tostler the only one there? And why was there only one feelie? There should have been ten racks.

He pushed the elevator button. *There were ten racks.*

Fleitman researched the circus from its birth in Rome to its end in Russia. He was fascinated with Astley, the former sergeant major who traced the first circus ring while standing on his horse's back. Fleitman would make the horses and their famous riders the major event of the circus. There would be a North, a Robinson, a Ducrow, a Salmonsky from the Baltics, a Carre, and a Schumann. And there would be a Philip Astley, surveying the acts around him, genuflecting to the great Koch Sisters performing on a giant semaphore arm. But the program could not be too outré. No one would care if the details were authentic or not, but for the sake of aesthetics he would do it correctly: First the overture played on a thousand horns, then the voltige, strong man, trained pigeons, juggling act, liberty horses, clown entree—how many clowns?—and a springboard act. And then he could have an intermission while popcorn and pretzels, beer and coke, ice cream and cotton candy were being passed out by red-nosed old men. (They would have to stay the same, he thought. Might be tricky.) The intermission ends with an aerial act—all the greats on the trapeze: the Scheffers, the Craigs, the Hanlon Voltas. He would leave no one out—Sandow, Lauck and Fox, Cinquevalli, Caicedo, and the Potters would all be there. Then the wild-animal act (Van Amburg could put his head in a lion's mouth), the wire walker, one hundred performing elephants, trick riding, and a finale of clowns. There were other choices: springboard acts, hand-to-hand balancers, artists on the rolling globe. But he had to stop somewhere.

Fleitman felt confident that he could reproduce a circus. And set it askew and ruin it. But it would be a perfect conception: the greatest show on earth. This is going to be real, he thought. It will breathe with realism: I'll forget I made it. But he knew that it was all wrong, too much to rationalize. Fleitman held the wand; he could direct his own purgation.

Fleitman spent most of his time four stories below street level in the computer complex of the Entertainment Building. The small, stark room where he worked seemed to grow warmer each day. Fleitman knew that this was impossible: the temperature was equalized on all levels. He worked in his underwear, constantly wiping his perspiring forehead with his wet forearm. The computers reproduced and projected all the circuses Fleitman had scanned earlier, superimposing one set upon another, suggesting proper costumes, proper colors, proper periods.

But Fleitman loved contrasts: He matched Roman gladiators and Victorian ladies, made the orchestra impossibly large, had the computers compose special music for the overture and finale. He exaggerated the clowns until they looked quite inhuman—short hair, long paste noses, cauliflower ears, exaggerated fingers and toes. Some were dwarfs, others were giants, and all were painted with bright colors—orange lips covering an entire jaw, accentuated age lines drawn in ocher, burntsienna moles, a beard of raw umber, baked blue buck teeth. He rejected the colosseum schematics and insisted on five stages surrounded by a hippodrome track, canvas walls, and wooden posts. The more changes randomly made, he thought, the more authentic it would become. He twisted the computers' suggestions into travesties as he giggled and wiped his forehead. His best idea had been to set a small fire in the tent during one of the high-wire acts. That would give the aerialists a chance to show their mettle.

Fleitman carefully created the performers, all manifestations of himself. He molded their emotions, exaggerated their possibilities. All pictures in an exhibition, all self-portraits. But he was careful to vary their physical appearance.

The computer room grew smaller each day as it filled with wraiths, painted clowns, and old acquaintances. Mary remained silently at his elbow, complimenting him on a good idea, shaking her head at a bad one. A midget gleefully mimicked him. He stood directly behind Fleitman, always out of sight; but Fleitman sensed his presence.

The room became more crowded. All the young men from his first job lined the walls. An old student roommate crouched on the floor. The juggler had left all of his pins and plates in the middle of the room where Fleitman needed to work. The juggler's assistant was making love with the strong man: it did not arouse Fleitman. Fleitman did not look up when the door slid back with a hiss. It was probably the blacksmith working his bellows.

"We haven't seen you lately, Mr. Fleitman," Tostler said, taking off his sennet straw hat.

Fleitman glanced up at him and scowled.

"I've begun to dress for the circus." Tostler always smiled when he spoke.

The room had emptied. The midget had disappeared; Fleitman could sense it. Suddenly, he felt exhausted and uneasy. Fleitman felt a chill; the temperature seemed to be falling.

"I hope you're ready for tomorrow," Tostler said. "Sartorsky's all excited. He thinks the setup is wonderful."

Fleitman did not remember showing Sartorsky anything.

"—And your friend Jake died."

Tostler's gums are blue, Fleitman thought.

"—You can still have a good-bye, if you like. Sartorsky, Taylor, and Toomis are having a party for him. They hooked a feelie into him."

Fleitman felt sick; he swallowed a lump of vomit. He remembered dead Ronson begging him to stop. Artificial men are better company, Fleitman thought. The room had become too important to him. "After Ronson, I thought we decided—"

"Always exceptions. It doesn't seem to bother younger people; it never bothered me to hook in with anybody."

It will, Fleitman thought as he vomited all over the juggler's equipment. He did not hear the door slide shut, but Mary was laughing at him. He told her to be quiet; he told her he was sick; but she continued laughing. And then the low bass of the weight lifter joined her laughter, and others joined in as they reappeared: the cowboys, the clowns, the aerialists, the midget, the redhead with her marionettes, the fat lady, the man with two heads, the snake woman, the popcorn man, and Tostler.

Fleitman returned to his apartment early and fell asleep. He would have to be alert for the first performance. He would eat tomorrow.

Fleitman arrived early. He sat on the uppermost tier and waited for the spectators. He had planned it all perfectly, even to the smell of horse dung in the stalls. In the center ring a tightrope walker was doing knee bends while five men in coveralls slung a net under the high wire above. Three acrobats were jumping on a trampoline in the center ring, their mascot hound crooning each time they shouted *hey*.

Everything seemed so real, Fleitman thought. He could not completely believe that it was only an illusion. The popcorn man yelled at him and threw him a box of popcorn. The box was made of transparent plastic and was warm to the touch. This did not feel right, although the computers had proved to him that it was indeed correct. Fleitman could smell the stink of the man. It was perfect.

A fight broke out in the side ring between the juggler and the unicycle clown. They were both immediately fired by the manager. This was one of Fleitman's touches—the computers would not fill in such a detail on their own.

The seal trainer ignored the fighting and firing, he shouted at his seals, promising them no food unless they came out of the water. They were a main attraction. He threw them a fish; it disappeared with a snap. Fleitman knew that if he were close enough, he would be able to smell the fish, a tart, stinging odor. He had made sure of everything.

Illusion, he thought. It can be rationalized. It's healthy. Forced feelie. Enjoy it. Don't hook in.

A few people came into the tent and looked for the best seats. Two old ladies sat down in front of him, giggling and hoisting their imitation leather skirts above their thighs. Fleitman looked up at the trapeze.

An hour later the tent was almost filled. A half hour after that, the tent was filled to capacity. Folding chairs were quickly provided for latecomers. Another one of Fleitman's touches: it would be authentic.

Fleitman watched an old man squirming on his bench, fiddling with his hook-in apparatus. Soon they would all be searching for their hook-ins.

Then the horns blared, and fifty red-uniformed Cossacks rode into the center ring, screaming and vaulting on and off their horses. One fell: it was not an accident. The next act was the strong man, and then the trained pigeons. Fleitman had substituted flying reptiles for effect. An acrobat, who had replaced the juggler, kept dropping balls; and the crowd hissed and booed and screamed and laughed. He could even blush.

When the clowns came out to announce the intermission, Fleitman had finished three boxes of popcorn. The clowns were well disguised, but too many of the performers resembled a younger Fleitman. An oversight, Fleitman thought. It would soon be over. It didn't matter. He threw popcorn at the clowns.

The second part of the program began with a wild-animal act in the center ring, flanked by hand-to-hand balancers and perch performers. An aerial act was performing above the right ring; below, a chain of elephants were bowing to a screaming audience. Fleitman watched the trapeze artists. The young man was Fleitman. And the woman somersaulting toward him was young Mary.

The crowd screamed. There was no slap of powdered palms. The click was missing. She fell toward the sawdust mounds, toward the clowns staging a mock fire. Her scream was absorbed by the roar of the crowd. Of course, some people were laughing: "It's not real."

Fleitman was standing up, perched precariously on a wooden runner board. He did not see the man shaking beside him, trying to pull out the jacks of the hook-in console. Another fell off the bench, dangled for a split second, and then with a silent pop, fell twenty feet. The old ladies sitting in front of Fleitman were vomiting, splashing an old man below, who thought it was funny.

This incident had not been planned. The safety net had been spread ten minutes before; Fleitman had watched. It had disappeared.

Two men dressed in white ran across the ring. As they swung her on the stretcher, the barker directed the audience's attention to the elephants. The men in white looked like Fleitman.

And then the springboard act, and more acrobats, and liberty horses. Out of order, Fleitman thought. The liberty horses should have been before the intermission. But the crowds were cheering again, hooking into their consoles, yelling at the handsome rider on a gray mare jumping through a flaming hoop. His saddle slipped, and he fell into the fire, straddling the hoop as his horse ran around the ring. Two men rushed toward him carrying blankets, but he ran away from them, his hair on fire.

Fleitman did not remember this. He counted the minutes to the finale. The small fire he had planned never occurred.

It was overdue.

The barker was waving his baton, telling the spectators of the next show, as the clowns led the parade of performers around the hippodrome. The horses stepped high, the young girls atop them curtsying; the acrobats glistened with sweat; the strong man bunched his muscles (but he should not have been there); and the strippers stripped. The old ladies shouted and screamed, the old men disconnected their hookins and got up to leave.

"Not yet," Fleitman screamed.

The tent darkened, the performers disappeared, the walls became translucent, revealing offices and meetings in session. People began to sit down. Fleitman fumbled with his hook-in. He was nauseated. It didn't matter; it would soon be over. The last time.

Fleitman leaned back, resting his head on the tier above him. The illusion was precise: the walls narrowed, almost seemed to be moving. Above, a dot of light growing smaller. Fleitman screamed with the spectators. Vertigo. He was in an elevator shaft. He lost his balance. One of the old ladies in front of him died. The other gurgled, pulled down her skirt, and skipped from tier to tier. The shaft was telescoping, pulling the crowd into its maw. Fleitman held his hands against his ears and screamed.

He does not remember this: he dreams that he is being swept toward the light. His heavy breathing echoes in the shaft, growing louder as it bounces from one wall to another. He awakens as he reaches the rim, as he opens his eyes to the glaring sunlight like an ant whose stone has been kicked away.

Fleitman was alone. The tent had disappeared, along with the sawdust floor and wooden beams. Floors, walls, and ceilings had been hurriedly joined to accommodate all the meetings scheduled after the show. Fleitman had been taking up too much room; as he moved, two panels slid together behind him to form a larger office. A snatch of conversation, and then a click as walls met to fill the space, as other walls opened up.

He followed a glowing blue line through corridor after corridor. He listened to the echo of his footsteps along the metallic floor. Another echo. Tostler was walking beside him, his sennet straw hat in his hand.

"Sixty-seven heart attacks. Not bad, Mr. Fleitman. Old Toomis died too. No one really bothered with him; they just wanted to get out. And you fell asleep."

Fleitman could see the elevator at the end of the blue line. He walked faster, but Tostler took him by the arm and led him down another corridor.

"Where are you going?" Fleitman asked, trying to break away from him. "You're off the line."

Tostler giggled. An old lady ran past them and collapsed, her arms flapping like a bird. "She was running around the center ring just like that," Tostler said. "Around and around. It's a wonder she got this far."

Fleitman stopped walking, but Tostler put his arm around Fleitman's waist and dragged him along. "Where are you taking me?" Fleitman asked.

Tostler smiled and his dimples turned into furrows dividing his face. "Why, you're going to the surface. That's what your whole gig was for, right? And that elevator sequence was beautiful. Pure wish fulfillment. And this is it. The idea had come up to pin a paper note to your apartment door and turn off the sensor. You know, a written note on parchment. But this way is better, don't you agree?"

Fleitman did not want to go. They turned a corner. He could see an elevator at the end of the hall.

"They moved an old lady into your room," Tostler said. "She likes it quite a bit." His grip grew tighter on Fleitman's arm. "Why didn't you just ask to get out?" The elevator doors opened as they passed the sensing line. "Silly question." He pushed Fleitman into the elevator.

Fleitman didn't resist. He positioned himself in the middle of the elevator. The doors closed. Fleitman thought he heard "Good show. Come back and see us sometime," but he knew that sound could not pass through the closed doors. The books suddenly seemed very important to him. But they have probably already been transformed, he thought.

The elevator walls seemed to disappear, and Fleitman could hear his heavy breathing echo along the length of the shaft, growing louder as it bounced from one wall to another. He closed his eyes and waited for the surface light to redden the insides of his eyelids. He dreamed of grotesque clowns waiting at the surface to jump into the elevator as the doors opened and stab him with their rubber knives. Fleitman was shaking.

The doors slid open. Children were pushing against him, trying to get into the elevator. They were breathing heavily from running, and perspiration glistened on their dirty faces. Fleitman stepped out, pushing children out of the way. The bright light hurt his eyes. The street elevator stood behind him, a huge gray monolith.

"What's that, what's that?" a twelve-year-old asked his playmate. She shrugged.

"We can't fit in there anyway," the little girl said. She turned to Fleitman and wrinkled her crinoline. "I'm Bozena Boobs. Do you want to do it?"

Fleitman did not understand her. He paid no attention to the children pulling at his hands and clothes. He kept shaking them off.

The buildings had risen much higher since he had been underground. And the sidewalk enclosures were shattered in places. The buildings, distorted by flaws in the enclosure plastic, blotted out the sun, formed their own gray horizon. Fleitman was dizzy. He thought of the levels of city beneath him, spider webs of corridors growing out of the dark like fluorescent spurs in a child's crystal garden. He felt suspended in the center of the city, and the heavy steel seemed to crush him from both directions.

The artificial light was too bright; it whitewashed the street and leveled the prominent features. The children's faces looked flat. Fleitman noticed that the slidewalks were not operating.

"Hey, old man," screamed a boy dressed in a blue zip suit. "Catch this." He threw a plastic scrap at Fleitman but missed.

"We've got to go," another boy said. "We can't wait. They'll catch us." He paused for breath and looked around at the other children. "Come on, let's go." He grabbed Bozena.

"Leave her alone," her playmate shouted, looking for a rock.

"I want to watch the old man," Bozena said.

"They can only take one of us anyway."

Fleitman thought he heard something in the distance: it sounded like the faraway rantings of a mob. The children were growing in number, clustering around Fleitman. Fleitman guessed there were about forty children. A little girl was screaming and crying. "We've got to go. We've got to go. He can't help us."

The children took it up. "He can't help us, he can't help us."

"He's a rag."

"He's a hag."

"He can't be a hag," a little girl said as she looked for something to throw.

There was a line of sediment around the buildings. Slowly, Fleitman thought, they were wearing.

"Bag."

"Scag."

"Fag."

Fleitman covered his face. They were throwing pieces of metal and garbage. A piece of yellow metal cut his face. They were chanting, "He can't help us, he can't help us, he can't help us."

"Rag."

"Scag."

"Hag."

"Glag," a crippled boy shouted.

"No good, cripple." More children joined in. "No good cripple, no good cripple," but it died quickly. They were all around Fleitman, wiping their dirty little hands on him, crying for help, spitting at him, caressing him, picking their noses, throwing stones, smoking cigarettes, coughing, giggling, belching. And a little girl kept screaming, "I'm afraid."

A piece of decayed food smacked against Fleitman's cheek. He felt it run down his neck into his high collar.

"Go back where you came from."

Fleitman ran around a corner. A rock hit him in the small of the back. The children easily stayed behind him, screaming and laughing, barely running. He crossed a street and turned into a main avenue. It was deserted, like the other streets, and the slidewalks were either broken or shut off. Fleitman noticed a large piece of plastic from the slidewalk enclosure propped against the side of one of the buildings. Three stories of window glass were broken.

There were about sixty children behind him now. His back had become numb. He felt a sharp pain in his chest as he inhaled. He sagged forward, his head lolling as he ran, his torso bent over.

Fall down. That's easy. They'll grind you, they'll crush your face.

He turned another corner. No garbage, he thought. No people. He couldn't see any windows in the buildings.

He stopped. A large crowd was pushing down the avenue. The children were behind him, the screaming adults before him. But the children turned and ran, and the crowd broke over Fleitman as so many waves in a hypothetical ocean.

Someone grabbed Fleitman's arm, but Fleitman broke loose, tripping over a young woman who had fallen down. Blood was welling from the collar of her zip suit.

The crowd was pushing Fleitman along. He was a dancer trying to keep his balance on an undulating floor. A young man waved to Fleitman and screamed, "This is a good one. Isn't this a good one?" He looked like Tostler. Fleitman noticed a number of men were wearing black robes, their hoods thrown back to reveal cropped hair.

The crowd stopped running, and Fleitman began to feel the ache of his new bruises. One of the children had been caught by the crowd. A little freckled boy kicked and shouted as he was handed from one person to another atop the crowd. Fleitman could not see any more of the children.

"This one, this one," screamed a young man next to him. Fleitman ducked as they passed the boy over his head. He thought he heard a voice whispering in his ear, more vibration than speech.

"What are you doing?" Fleitman asked the man next to him. The man wore a black cloth robe and his face was flushed with pimples and sores. He looked puzzled. "Well, you're in it," the man said, "aren't you?"

"In what?"

"You mean you don't know? Then. . . ."

The man was waving his arms. Fleitman allowed a few people to scramble beside him. The man was soon too far away to be a nuisance.

Fleitman listened. The murmuring in his head was barely audible; he could make it out. He could see the man in the robe grinning at him: it was Tostler.

The voice: *Do not unite yourselves with unbelievers; they are no fit mates for you. What has righteousness to do with wickedness? Can light consort with darkness? Can Christ agree with Belial, or a believer join hands with an unbeliever? Can there be a compact between the temple of God and the idols of the heathen? And the temple of the living God is what we are. God's own words are: "I will live and move about among them; I will be their God, and they shall be my people."*

This is brought to you by. . . .

Someone took a shot at the little boy. He was sitting on the priests' hands, his legs crossed in a lotus position.

"Well, he's imposing enough."

"He should make it into his thirties."

"Not that way."

A few more shots. An explosion. The little boy was crying and trying to break loose. The priests held him tightly, pressing his legs in place, crossing his arms. The crowd was howling, about to stampede. Fleitman saw a few of the children. They seemed to be enjoying the show.

Fleitman pushed his way to the edge of the crowd. He had only a few minutes before the crowd would break, pushing itself in all directions, crushing everything in its way.

"He's nothing without thorns."

Fleitman pressed himself against the building, merged with its grayness.

A few more shots. A priest's face exploded. Laughing children, dimly perceived. Fleitman closed his eyes: if he couldn't see them, they couldn't see him.

The crowd chased itself, unable to decide the fate of the new king. The screaming softened, and the crowd disappeared into the perspective lines of the street.

The shadows were all wrong—De Chirico's *Mystery and Melancholy of a Street*. Of course the shadows were wrong. Fleitman waited for the little girl to appear from a shadow pushing a hoop before her. And shouting, "I'm Bozena Boobs. Do you want to do it?"

Fleitman began to walk. He would look for other people. The eyeless buildings stood above him, watching him, not yet ready to topple over and crush him.

Kicking a plastic package of refuse out of the way, he turned a corner. The slidewalks were working. He stepped on the ramp and watched the buildings turn into a blurred gray wall. An old woman carrying packages stepped on in front of him. And another. Then a young boy and a few teenagers. A couple were holding hands beside him. A prostitute nudged his arm. He skipped to a faster ramp. But the slidewalk had become crowded. It was difficult to breathe. Pushing people out of his way, Fleitman worked his way to an exit ramp. He stepped off, ignoring the beggars and pimps.

The buildings were drab and undistinguished, but the smells were overpowering: defecation, spoiling meat, incense—orange, tabac—perspiration, exhaust fumes from makeshift engines. The foodstuffs piled behind the vendors' barricades were acrid and sweet—candies and oils, synthetic fruits and fetid sweetmeats. Fleitman watched three girls dancing on a podium in the street, their bodies oiled, electric tattoos decorating their paste-white skin. To his right, a respectable little shop with an imitation-wood portico. A pleasure ring was drawn around the large shop window to entice shoppers. Over the door an antique sign blinked on and off. Fleitman couldn't understand the lettering.

A balding huckster sat in front of the store and passed out loaves of burnt bread. A little girl walked toward Fleitman. She was furiously tearing a small loaf apart and stuffing it into her mouth. Fleitman remembered the food machine in his apartment. He wanted a piece of bread: its ugliness made it appetizing. The little girl walked past him, her hair crawling with tiny silver bugs.

Fleitman looked for a slidewalk, but most of the secondary walks were not operating. He passed street after street of markets, carnivals, and whorehouses—all interspersed with module office buildings and expensive shops. There should be more modules, Fleitman thought, not fewer. There probably were: this might be an isolated fad.

"Over there." The little girl had been following Fleitman. Crumbs of bread clung to the front of her dress. "There's something good over there. Come on, I'll take you. I'm old enough." She caught up with Fleitman, but he walked faster and she fell behind. "I can't keep up. I'm a cripple."

Fleitman slowed down. She limped as she walked; her right leg was shorter than her left. Why didn't I notice that before? Fleitman asked himself. Maybe it's not the same little girl. Fleitman was unconvinced.

"Turn left here. Come on, I know where it is."

"Where what is?"

"Right here," she said. "I'll show you."

Fleitman breathed through his mouth: she smelled. She led him into a crowd of people. Fleitman was nauseous.

"See, look up at the building."

A young woman was standing on the seventh-story window ledge of an old building that had been partly torn down. There was a space between the buildings. The sky was a gray mouth that had lost a tooth.

"All these buildings are old," the little girl said. "They started tearing them down. I watch them do it all the time. I like it; it's always the same."

The woman on the ledge was laughing and screaming at the spectators. She looks like Mary, Fleitman thought. He knew that it really was Mary. Her face was thinner than he had remembered. She was young, about twenty-seven. And she was suntanned, as always. Probably under a light, but he remembered the citizens' beach at Cannes; he remembered digging old beer cans out of the sand. Her hair and earlobes had been removed. She pointed at Fleitman and laughed.

The crowd was egging her on. Someone took a potshot at her. She laughed and waved her arms. There was only one refreshment man running in and out of the crowd; he was hurriedly doing as much business as he could before news leaked out and other vendors arrived. He was selling red-hots. The little girl bought two.

"Come on and eat one," she said. "This is a good one, isn't this a good one?"

Fleitman watched Mary. He pushed his way to the edge of the crowd. The little girl followed him.

"We better move, you know. She's going to jump soon."

"We've got to help her," Fleitman said.

"Why? She's having a helluva time. Look at her."

She was making obscene motions at the crowd. The crowd began to scream, "Do it now," in unison. Fleitman heard himself whispering with them. The little girl was jumping up and down.

Mary closed her eyes and held her arms out in front of her.

"Open your eyes," Fleitman screamed. He knew when she would jump: he had seen this already.

She leaned over the edge, her back arched. That's right, Fleitman thought. Very good. Fleitman noticed that he was screaming. Someone had drawn a pleasure circle around the crowd. Fleitman relaxed.

She jumped and fell in front of Fleitman, splashing herself on his slippers. He took a deep breath of her and counted the entrails before him. A good omen: the refreshment man had stopped selling red-hots.

"You want to take a walk?" the little girl asked. She smiled at Fleitman. He looked back, impatient for something to happen, and took the little girl's hand: it was cold and dry.

He listened to an advertisement softly buzzing in his brain.

THE DYBBUK DOLLS

Chaim Lewis had opened the store early. He did not especially mind Undercity, even though Levi Lewis, his half brother, told him he would become sterile from radiation (which was nonsense) and lose his eyesight. So after two children, why did he need to be potent, and what eyesight? If he went blind—which couldn't happen; Dr. Synder-Langer, his eye doctor, was a state affiliate and went to seminars—what did he care? He could get a cheap unit in Friedman City (Slung City they called it)—or if he had saved enough, he could plug a room into the self-contained grid built into Manhattan City. A bright façade of metal would be much better than the Castigon Complex. Shtetlfive, situated in the qualified section of the complex, was a very nice upside ghetto, very rich, semi-psycho-segregated, and sensor-protected. But Chaim would only move into a shtetlsection; he needed the protection of familiar thoughts and culture. That wouldn't be so bad. He could still visit Shtetlfive—it would not move for a while, maybe never. Business, unfortunately, was too good.

Above Shtetlfive was the tiny Chardin Ghetto. They gave all their money (which was considerable) to their colony on Omega-Ariadne. Koper Chardin ran one of the best pleasure houses in Undercity with impunity. He even advertised organ gambling, "for those who want to experience the ultimate gamblers' thrill." In fact, it was located on Chelm Street—which was rented by the Shtetl-Castigon Corporation at an exorbitant exchange—and had been built on mutual contract to better serve all business interests. Its overflow (and the poor that could not afford it) provided a moderate part of Chaim Lewis' business. But most of his money was made on collectors.

"Collectors they call themselves," Chaim said to no one in particular as he studied the afternoon trade sheet on the fax hidden behind his waist-high counter. The small room was dusty and badly lit, but it was expensively soundproofed so that only a low level of thoughtnoise could penetrate and influence his customers.

A young woman, dressed in a balloon suit, turned from a display of magazines on the wall and said, "Those *Stud* magazines. The price?"

She's got to be upside, very much upside, he thought as he closed his eyes in mock contemplation. And she's older than she looks. That's a falseface, he told himself.

"Well?" Her balloon suit changed color to fit the surroundings. This front room, the showroom, was dingy for effect. A dingy shop was a lure for the passing bargain hunter. Magazines protected by shock fields lined the soiled white walls, and plasti-glass cabinets displayed small telefac units, pornographic tapes, and assorted self-stimulation devices: secondhand handy-randies—robots designed and programmed to caress—and vibrators complete with controlled frequency and amplitude of vibration, variable size and surface texture, and temperature control. And a small sign above Chaim's counter read nontelepathically: DOLLS IN STOCK.

"Those magazines are very rare." Give her time, Chaim told himself.

"Price now; no bartering," she said, walking over to Chaim's counter. Her face was red and smooth—taut synthetic skin over a wire frame.

"Well," Chaim said, "twentieth-century porno, why the paper is itself worth—" He paused the proper amount of time. She did not respond properly. Instead of demanding price-by-law, producing a recorder, and then haggling within the well-known parameters determined by her own collectors' guild council, she pursed her lips and scanned the wall above Chaim's head.

Perhaps this is a new touch, Chaim thought, but his concentration was broken by the shouts and jeers of new customers. A boy of about nineteen, naked to the waist and obviously proud of the male and female sex organs implanted on his chest and arms, led a dozen people into the store. He wore his long blond hair in braids and his face was rouged and lined. He sported one large breast to prove he was a male. That was the latest fashion. The other six boys also flaunted sex organs on their arms and chests, but the women were modestly clothed, so Chaim could only guess at what was concealed.

"Where're your hook-ins?" asked the blond boy in undercity gutter tongue.

"In the next room," Chaim said. "But mind yourselves. There are plenty of sensors in there." Another thrill family, Chaim thought. Kinkies. He guessed from their accents that they were from one of the nearby manufacturing undercities, although one of them—a spindly girl with a large mouth and flushed face—spoke with an affected upside accent. All the undercities were identical spheres, one mile in diameter, buried one thousand feet below topground. But Undercity was the first; the others were named after such families and personages as Ryan, Gulf, Rand, Lifegarten, and other lesser luminaries. Lifegarten was the most powerful. It connected twelve spheres and had to be governed as a state with its own undergovernor.

The girl with the upside accent nervously shook her head—another upside affectation, Chaim thought—and flirted with the blond boy. She wore her long blond hair in greased ringlets that left tiny stains on her dress. "Dolls," she said. "This is the place that sells dolls. Herbesh was talking about—"

"Shut up," said another girl, her accent thick with factory twang. "When you're slumming with us, shut up."

"That's all right," said the blond boy, laughing. "She's not even a collector, much less a creep."

The woman in the balloon suit stiffened, but ignored the kinkies. They left to try the feelies, and the room was quiet once again.

So she is a collector, Chaim thought. But she doesn't want porn, she wants a doll. For the grace of God and fewer comments by that unsympathetic holy man, the Baal Shem, he would have to try to dissuade her. Chaim would have to hurry, though, for Levi would be here soon, and he did not believe in divine religion—he was trained by atheists in the Army. Now he's a spy, Chaim thought. And my own bloodspirit.

"You do, I believe, sell dolls," said the woman in the balloon suit. "I wish to purchase one, and I'm willing to stand here and dicker for as long as you like. I know price by law doesn't apply to alien goods."

"You seem to know what you want. But why want this—"

"Make it fast, but I've made up my mind."

"Then, you know about dolls?" Chaim asked, his thoughts drifting. Something about the kinkies bothered him, but he couldn't decide what it was. Perhaps it was something they said. "It's a perversion," Chaim said. "You cannot satisfy yourself with dolls."

"That's the idea, isn't it?" she asked.

"But sex is not supposed—"

"Sex doesn't concern me." She rested her hands on Chaim's counter. Her suit was changing color, affected by the shifting colors that streamed in through the small high windows shaped like pentagrams. "I'm a neuter—by choice, of course. You should be familiar with that. Doesn't your church advocate neutering your young until they are ready for marriage, to keep them pure?"

Chaim finished the sentence in his mind. *In the eyes of God*. He studied her face. It was too perfect a job, he thought. There were no character lines, no deviations, no pocks or scars, and her pug nose (that was the style) did not cover enough of her face and her mouth was too thin. But that's the way it's supposed to be, he thought. He could find no sensuality there, only bland purpose.

"So then, why do you want a doll?" he asked. "It is for sex where the thrill lies. What more?"

"That's the point; I want to experience it without my groin. I want it in my head."

"But dolls are for frustration, to build up pleasure and then trap it inside you until it becomes pain. Unbearable pain. Nothing can get out."

"Must we continue this? I have enough credit. You've done your duty. What more do you want? You Jews want to make money."

"We just want to live," Chaim said, thinking about the kinkies again. Something they said. He had been through this conversation too many times.

"Doing this?"

"This is all we're permitted. It's a long story, and like everything else, all politics."

"But your sect has money; in fact it's very rich."

Chaim sighed and ran his thumb around the reinforced edge of his pocket. *Live in Gehenna or be separated. The Diaspora of the rich.* But almost everyone is rich, Chaim thought. *To overthrow Satan you must know him. Know him, yet not be corrupted.*

"Money is only good for certain things," Chaim said. "That is part of Paskudnyak's plan. You have heard of that?" It was working. She might not buy a doll yet.

She laughed, her mouth twitching at the corners for effect. "That's a myth, a fairy tale. There's no test. No one is trying to corrupt you. No game. That's made up to scare your children."

She's intent on having that dybbuk, Chaim thought.

"Well," she said. "The doll. Price."

"If you even look at a new doll, it will take something away. Something good that lives inside you."

"Yes, I know." She grinned. "Price."

A fool, he thought. "It will actually take the shape of your frustra-tions."

"Price."

"It is not even known if the doll is some sort of mechanical toy, or if it is alive. No one knows."

"Price. Pricepriceprice."

So you win, he said to no one in the room. *Herbesh*. That was the word that upside girl used. Where had he heard it before? Herbesh. Something about—

"Your time is up," said Levi Lewis, stepping in from the street. For an instant the small showroom was bathed in a lurid yellow light. Old magazines turned yellow, silver handy-randies glittered, and Levi's face —framed between a red-and-silver beard, curled earlocks, and a black hat with a fur brim—looked withered and pocked. Then the door closed and the room became dim again. Levi was dressed exactly like Chaim. He wore a black caftan that reached to his knees. His pants were red, pleated and cuffed. A glitter belt separated mind and heart from his most corrupted parts.

"You've worked your requirement," Levi said. "That's the law." He winked at the woman in the balloon suit. Another yellow glare as a couple entered the store and browsed in the corner. Both wore sequined cloth dresses, lightbeads, and metal dangles in the form of stars and grotesque faces. "See," he said. "More customers to be titillated. My turn, Chaim. Go away.

"It's another *nechtiger tog* outside again," Levi said. "Day is night, morning is noon. Feh. They're using beadlights and that lousy hoof-foof thoughtnoise to make more business. And everything is yellow. I hate yellow. It hurts my eyes. May I help you?" he asked the couple in the corner, who were examining the poor selection of pornographic telefac tapes. They ignored him.

"So the street will earn its name," Chaim said after a pause. "Chelm, Chelm, a foolish place."

"Go get her doll," Levi said, suddenly serious. "You will not talk her out of it."

He's right, Chaim told himself. What matter; she's only a balloon. Although the room had returned to its former dusky state—the small pentagram windows could not offer much light and the lamps were turned low—her balloon suit was radiant. It seemed to bulge. Chaim could not look at her face. More *tsores* for me, he thought. Every day brought its share of troubles. Sticks to make a holy fire.

Chaim tried to shut out the thoughtnoise that was blaring in his head. The thoughtnoise had to be coming from somewhere inside the store, he thought, because it was too strong to be just echoes from out-side. It was giving him a headache.

"Well," the woman said. "I'm waiting."

So wait, Chaim thought. The fax screen was blinking. No one could see it but Chaim. It was set into a dead spot in the glasstex counter.

:Attention. Intruder FaChrm #4. Police notified/Sil. Pro.:

The kinkies set up a mindblock, Chaim thought. That's why I couldn't hear the alarm. Chaim was mindlinked with the store's alarm system. They must be rich, Chaim thought. Rich enough to disrupt with their own equipment the most expensive alarm and control system he could afford. He daydreamed for a few seconds. *Herbesh*. That same word swam in his mind. He remembered: Herbesh was a powerful member of a Chartist Clan. The shtetl had many political enemies, and the Chartists were the most rabid. Many money feuds had been lost be-cause of anti-Semitism. But the Chartists were more than just political enemies; they derived their strength and community from hatred and thus gained Machiavellian access into high-level politics.

Herbesh, Chaim thought. A Paskudnyak. They're one and the same. Paskudnyak was a Jewish myth, an ongoing legend born and main-tained out of paranoia. He was considered to be the focus of evil, "the mount of darkness." Some said he was deformed and called him Shi-men Hunchback; others said he was ugly as sin, but seduced all the beautiful women that came his way. Fruma, Chaim's wife, thought he must be beautiful, a misled innocent. A *nefish*. He was the imagined superman-conspirator who took on different faces at different times to frustrate the Jewish alliance. Chaim half believed in Paskudnyak. After all, he would tell himself, there obviously is a conspiracy against the shtetl.

One of the kinkies said something about Herbesh, Chaim thought. So they must be related to him. They have the money to steal, and buy mindblock equipment. They must want the dolls. *Gotenyu.* The kinkies would stuff themselves with the dolls and begin another scandal, another feud. But why steal the dolls? If they could afford mindblock equipment, they could simply buy the dolls outright.

Then, it must be a setup. What else? Chaim thought. And a setup could only mean scandal. Herbesh's kinkie clansmen would be psycho-logically deformed for life—that's what the fax would read. He could al-ready see tomorrow's scandalfax. Herbesh's *Reyakh*, who knows only one tune, will make up a new song. And Paskudnyak, who forces our lives, will win. That would be too much for the shtetl's weakened morale. They certainly had *chutzpa,* Chaim thought.

"Red light," Chaim said to his brother. Levi shrugged. There could be no blame on him: he wasn't officially working. Attempted robberies were common, and Chaim had made it a rule not to upset the customers. It was all routine. The sensors would mindscan every customer, deactivate any heat weapon, throw up a shock field if necessary, and notify the police. Since concealed projectile weapons were by law denoted "Civilian Punishable," it was the proprietor's choice. Chaim could not remember whether he had programmed paralysis (temporary) or mindshut. It didn't matter now, he thought.

"I'm going to see what's going on," Chaim said to Levi. The police were probably around the corner. It was probably too late to get out with the dolls.

"For what? It will be finished in a few minutes."

That's what I'm afraid of, he thought, as he walked across the room.

"But you place yourself in danger. . . ."

He should care, Chaim thought. He would lie with Fruma. He should be glad I'm not telling him. What could he do, anyway, but ruin everything? Mumbling a prayer, Chaim stepped into the feelie room. Both telefac units were being used, as were the less exotic cerebral hook-ins. A boy and girl, both naked, were strapped into the telefac stirrups, their backs resting against the supporting pads that stimulated their spinal nerves and activated the pornotapes. A network of microminiaturized air-jet transducers provided them with tactile information, and they also received audio, visual, and motion feedback. The girl's knees were buckling. The spinal pad quickened her heartbeat with a rerun of "Bestial Love." Her friend in the other telefac was in the throes of orgasm. The ultimate vicarious thrill.

Chaim looked away from them. The others, plugged into the small hook-in consoles, were dazed. But the blond boy and the upside girl were standing beside the back door. The door was open, revealing part of the sensor-protected storeroom. The dolls were hidden in a lockup at the far end of the storeroom wall. He hoped they had not been able to open the lockup and find the dolls.

"The police will be here soon," Chaim said. He tried to stop his shaking.

"We'll wait," said the blond boy. He reached for the upside girl's hand.

"So, it is a setup," Chaim said.

"No," said the girl. "It's for fun. We're just doing this to pull on your parts and have a good time. As children, we're entitled to a little fun."

"Are you part of Herbesh's clan?"

"He's my uncle," the boy said. "Aren't you afraid of Paskudnyak's wrath?" The girl giggled. "If he found out you were selling dolls to children, swamping their innocent souls with alien filth, it would make scandal. And then where would you work?"

"Hungry Jews," said the girl.

"You may be from Herbesh's clan," said Chaim, "but you're not children." Chaim knew they had him. Herbesh would call for a literal interpretation of the black-letter law, fold the courts, and denounce the shtetl on every fax channel for peddling filth to innocents. But if there were no dolls, there could be no proof.

"Police will be here soon," the boy said. "It's all set. You just might" —he slipped into guttertongue—"have enough time. Just a game."

"You know the commercial," the girl said. "Today's newsfax is tomorrow's scandalfax."

"Are the dolls opened?" Chaim asked. The boy and girl laughed at him.

"That's for us to know and you to find out."

"*Azes ponim,*" Chaim mumbled in a last effort at pride. They laughed as he walked past them into the storeroom. The storeroom had been ransacked: ancient magazines had been torn apart and left on the floor with streamers of telefac tape and broken plug-ins. A kinkie girl (Chaim wasn't sure, since he or she was undressed) huddled against the wall, hiding whatever organ was between spindly legs. Chaim hoped she was not cradling a doll against the wall.

The lockup was closed. But Chaim had no time. His ears burned. Like an animal, he thought, I'm running from these children—they should be running from me: they've broken the law. What's the difference? he asked himself. Eat dirt now, turn to dust later.

He had to get the dolls out of the store. A chill went through him—could they have done something with the dolls? What if they've tampered with the lockup? he asked himself. What could he do but close his eyes and pray. The police should be here by now, he thought. No time. So, let it be finished. Could they have fixed that, too? Sure, with the Shtot Balebos. What does he care?

Chaim slipped his fingers into a coded depression in the lockup cabinet. A soft burst of light, and the door opened revealing glasstex trays of neatly placed dolls. And each doll had taken the shape of a distorted human face. Chaim's face.

They've unpacked the dolls, Chaim thought. Plasticine packages were neatly piled on the top shelf.

Little tongues wrapped around little teeth, squinting porcelain eyes, wrinkles, and bald heads.

Petrified screamers.

All looking at Chaim from their glasstex trays.

Chaim screamed, pressing his palms against his eyes so the dolls couldn't reach into his head. But it was already done. Even with his eyes closed, he had "imprinted" each and every one of them. Within a fraction of a second he was transferring his every impulse and emotion to the dolls, namely fear. They drank it up, transmogrified themselves into a pattern best fitted to frustrate and titillate him.

"Dybbuks have entered me," he shouted, trying to exorcise the spirits. He could feel each one burrowing into his mind, confusing his thoughts, tasting his most sinful desires. Chaim could hear the kinkies laughing. Like tinkling bells, he thought. Let them laugh; it should be on me if it's God's choice.

"Scandalfax," the girl said. "You'd better gather up your dolls and take them with you. No time"—a slip into guttertongue, an upside affectation. "The police will be here soon, and the kids are hanging from the telefacs with red faces and erections and sitting on the floor with hook-ins plugged into their pink heads. Looks very bad."

"Very good," the blond boy said, pinching her cheek.

It was probably a ruse, Chaim thought. There would be no police. But he couldn't take the chance. Herbesh would not stand for opened dolls anywhere near his kin. The hook-ins and telefacs would only incur small punishment. Let Levi worry—that *loksh* spy.

"And we say you imprinted us with those dolls," said the boy, "while we scream and make obscene gestures and laugh and hold our heads. Alien thoughtscum, you know."

They must have used a mindblock to unpack the dolls, Chaim thought. He fantasized that the blond boy and upside girl were naked. They stood in the dark, heavy cloth stretched tightly over their puckish faces, and meticulously opened each package. *Gotenyu,* he thought. The dybbuks are changing me already, soiling my thoughts. He gathered up the dolls—they were the size of his large hands—and dropped them into a carrybox. They'll melt together, he thought. So let them. They'll suck out my soul. What black soul could you have? The girl is pretty, not fat and earthy like Fruma, but delicate and shriveled like Raizel the wet nurse.

"Take them home with you, sleep with them," the girl said, twisting a greased curl around her forefinger.

What small breasts she must have, Chaim thought. He felt strong unnatural urges welling up inside him, filling him up, beating against the inside of his skin to be free. His body was no longer a holy vessel, and he felt dispassionately removed from it. He drove it like a car toward the back door. His glands secreted the wrong juices, anesthetized him, fooled him with oceans of sexual sensation—all directed toward the kinkie girl, always ebbing instead of reaching new heights. Frustrating him. But there was sickly-sweet beauty in that frustration.

He could not, would not, have her. So the dybbuks pushed against him, sandpapered his delicate conscience against his flesh to produce guilt. That heightened the sensations, strengthened the brew. Chaim turned for a last look at the girl as he pressed against the door, and then stopped himself. No, he thought. God shouldn't see me brimming with filthlife. The dolls were not mechanical; they were alive.

The door opened, and Chaim was in the street, squinting his eyes in the strong yellow light. "Not even a look behind," he said to the dolls in his hand and the dybbuks in his head. Chelm Street was to his right, bustling with people, a river of rollers and slidewalks rushing in-town and back on the other side. Like boats on the water, platforms and movetels drifted slowly down the middle of the street. Beyond Chelm Street, and to his left, drawing an arc around him, the skyscrapers rose out of the yellow thoughtfog, sparkling like glass stalagmites in a crystal cave. Tiers upon tiers of fenestrated glasstex, studded with sunlights, reaching like inverted roots toward the bright surface of the dome above. Set into this glass landscape was a circular park, barely visible in the settling fog. Its boundaries were only a few yards from where Chaim was standing. A few feet from him was a transpod rut that extended as far as he could see to his left and descended into the ground a few yards to his right.

Chaim felt giddy. The fog was a lure. Its fumes and the hoof-foof thoughtnoise excited him, made him feel glamorous, a part of the party-crowd. A small transpod stopped in front of him. The silver egg was computer-controlled and driven by a propulsion system built into the narrow rut. Chaim climbed into the transpod with some trouble, intoning the eternal *oy-oy-oy*. He punched out the coordinates to go

home, called the shtetl to tell them of his dilemma, and by the time he
settled into a comfortable position he was almost topside.

He tried to compose himself. Just as I thought, there were no police,
he told himself. Looking at the carrybox on his lap, he thought: I
should throw this filth into the disposer. But who knew what would destroy it? By throwing it away, he might be putting the dybbuks out of
his reach forever, and their spirits would remain inside him, corrupting
him, until he was only a hollow shell filled with dybbukfilth. He
needed the dybbuks' flesh to exorcise them.

Chaim's heart was pounding. The car seemed to be getting smaller.
(You're making this up, Chaim told himself. Stopit.) He was afraid of
closed spaces again, like when he was a child locked in Makher's closet
with Dvora Shiddukah.

"So this is the way it is to be," he said, trying to ignore his fantasies.
He braced himself, arms outstretched, fingers touching the silver side
panels, and murmured the *Shema Yisroel*. The air was suddenly filled
with noxious smells. (Stopitstopit, Chaim told himself. This is a dream.
Don't set the stage.) He tried to pray. It was difficult to breathe. Too
hot. Chaim was sweating. (You are dry as a mat.) His *talis koton*, a
fringed cloth undergarment, was soaked through, defiled, he thought,
by his dreams. He found himself with an erection.

He dreamed about Dvora, sweet skinny Dvora with her bumps for
breasts and squeaky voice. The closet was dark and Dvora was naked
and making mouse noises. Air, Chaim said to himself, gagging. Too
small. Can't breathe. (Liar. Dybbukdreamer. You're smiling and
breathing clean recycled air.) Chaim reached forward to dissolve the
gray walls but couldn't touch the switch. (Stop acting and press the
button.)

And then he was pushing the switch and screaming. He was an actor
without an audience. But there was no release. His throat hurt and his
head ached. Now there was too much air and space. The city was all
around him, and he was being swept through a glass tunnel, one of the
billions of transparent cables that linked up the city, toward a canyon
formed out of glass and steel and light. Above him was a rush of perspective lines drawing together in the distance. A roof covered this part
of the city, melded all the buildings into a ceiling. Below him were
slidewalks and runshops and millions of people dashing about, spoiling
the clean, geometrical lines of the city ways. But Chaim was too high to
see them.

He hoped for a rush of relief. He was close to home now. But the exhilaration was too much for him. It became bone-crushing pain. And then just fear. He had only been afraid of heights once in his life, when he climbed onto a parapet on a dare. He slipped and almost fell. That's how he felt now. He was falling again, grasping for a transparent edge.

Before him was a glass wall. Then he was inside it. The transpod followed its course to a lift-rut, where it rose like an elevator toward the upper levels of the largest living units in New York. Castigon Complex consisted of two risers, each a thousand stories high and linked together by hookwalls and emergency passtubes. The uppermost stories looked down upon the smooth, snow-covered surface of the city's roof and swayed very slightly. But, from Chaim's position, the building was too large to be seen as anything other than interlocking linelevels and arbitrary shapes. It was as if these were risers that had been set into a glass template that was itself another building.

As the pod slowed to a halt, Chaim's head cleared and he sighed and closed his eyes. "Thank you, *Kvater* of both demons and angels." The door opened onto a platform strewn with plastipaper, but Chaim made no move to get out of the pod. A few people rushed by. He prayed. Thank you, Chaim said to himself. Let me rest a moment. A familiar face leaped out of his mind and dissolved before his mind's eye. It was Dvora. Her deep-set eyes were tiny blue stones set into the caverns of her bony face. He dreamed that she was lying on the glass parapet. She was waiting for him, breathing in short gasps, exposing her worm-white body to the chill wind. There would be no respite.

"But it's all illusion," Chaim shouted at the air. This is false as a telefac or hook-in, he thought. I'm drawing on my filthpile of carnal thoughts and experiences. But they're not real. (Yes they are.) I'm suffering for forgiveness. (God will punish. Liar.)

A group of children, dressed in knee-length caftans, heads shaved but earlocks untouched, all wearing *yarmelkehs* or black hats with imitation fur tails, were on their way home from *Kheyder*, where they had spent the morning studying Torah. They hooted and sang. High-pitched voices echoed. Translucent walls became mirrors of sound.

"Stop that," Chaim said. "It's a sin." Their echoes would dissipate their fragile souls.

"Bim, bim, bam," they sang. "Sleep soundly at night—
"And learn Torah by day. And you'll be a rabbi—
"When I have grown gray."

They walked backward past Chaim. For each step they took, so the legends told, their guardians or watchers would burn a year in Hell. Technically, at that moment, Chaim was a watcher. So he closed his eyes, but the children had taken at least five steps. They should play with shadows. *Sheyneh* loafers. (Stopit. Dybbukfilth.)

A buzzer sounded, reminding Chaim that he was taking up space. He tried to ignore it. Soon the pod would direct enough thoughtnoise at Chaim to make him leave. Think. Something about those children on the platform, he told himself. They were dressed like *sheyneh,* the rich, but they had the red faces of the *prosteh,* the poor. He felt a coldness in his groin. Think-think. Something familiar. (Another lie.) Something beautiful. (Dybbuktalk. Close your ears.)

Chaim squeezed the carrybox on his lap, felt a thrill radiate down his legs. A flame was coloring everything he thought and saw, dulling the ever-present frustration that glowed like coals on his lap. There was no rush, he told himself. He had to remember something. That's it, he thought. Those children all look like me. (Dreamer. Liar. Makeup-man.) Like my children. (Dybbukspawn.) Again, the coldness. His lap was wet. He shook off the dark things crawling in his mind and found himself kneading soft flesh, holding it between his large palms. His hands were inside the carrybox.

"*Gotenyu,*" he cried, pulling his hands out of the box and closing the lid. "Now they have my flesh, too." He watched the people rushing past the pod. Although there were a few women hurrying about in old dresses and work aprons, the men—dressed in knee-length caftans and sporting full, untrimmed beards and carefully curled earlocks—were clearly in the majority. There were several other pods backed up behind Chaim. It was still early, workers hadn't returned home yet, and housewives were in their rooms, frantically preparing for *Erev Shabbes,* the Sabbath eve. It was called "Short Friday," because after sundown no work could be performed. Any woman found in the building's ways on Short Friday became known as a *yideneh* and was shunned by the other women of her shtetl level, unless she had a good excuse. *Shabbes* was a time for the family, a time for prayer and study.

Chaim found that he could block out most of the thoughtnoise easily. He was having fantasies that Raizel the wet nurse looked just like him. Fearing for his life with every movement, he was making love to her on a parapet. He was a glutton, pulling the life juices out of her frail, skinny body.

"So what are you waiting for?" asked Feigle Kaporeh, an old woman wearing a rumpled ankle-length dress, a kerchief around her thick neck, and a wig over her cropped hair—she was known to be senile and still considered herself beautiful enough to attract sinful glances. "How much noise does the pod have to make before you get out?"

Still thinking about Raizel, Chaim swung one of his legs out of the pod. Feigle Kaporeh can't look like me, he told himself, as he pulled the carrybox along behind him. (Onanist.)

"*Oy,*" she said. "It's you. Get away from me. *Tatenyu.*"

"*Yideneh,*" Chaim mumbled and rushed across the platform, pushing through the few people that were in his way. He could smell the sweet fragrance of *challah,* the Sabbath bread, mingling with the stale air of the transpod tunnel. Chaim felt himself being pulled into a knot that would explode, flinging the trapped juices out of his corrupted body. I have to be alone with the dolls, he thought. Just for a few minutes. (Fight them.)

An arch decorated with golden lions and tablets of the Ten Commandments led into Shtetlfive's ways, a maze of hallways running parallel and perpendicular to a defunct rollway. The low-ceilinged rollway was the size of a small street or alley, and had become the neighborhood meeting place. It was poorly lit and poorly ventilated, but in an area where space was at a premium, this free tunnel was a luxury. It was hoped that the authorities would not be quick to turn the rollway into transients' space. Located nearby were the auditoriums and meeting rooms that functioned as synagogue, *besmedresh*—a study and prayer center, wailing room, Bundcongress, and local schools such as the *Talmud Toyreh* and *Gemoreh Kheyder.*

But there were few people about, only visitors, early workers, tardy gossipers, and children returning from trades and rich *kheyders.* The "Queen-Bride" of the Sabbath had to be escorted in; there was no time for dallying. The *shammes,* a synagogue functionary, was going about his duties early. He walked along the rollway calling, "Jews to the bathhouse," for the ceremonial *mikva* of purification.

"Hey, Chaim," he shouted. "We have news of what happened. Go quickly. Rabbe Ansky has found more than enough men to make a quorum. And, he-should-be-blessed, the Baal Shem from Menachem Ghetto will preside."

Chaim ignored him and stepped into a small corridor that would lead to his rooms. I must be alone, he thought. Just for a minute, just to see. . . . He would have to look into the box; there would lie his catharsis. But the quorum will save me. Why do I need Raizel, anyway?

he asked himself. I only need myself. (Dybbuktalk.) But Raizel is a lustbowl. No matter. I have it all inside me.

He could hear the buzz of garbled conversation before he reached his rooms. I have to get past their quorum, he thought. The doorslide was open. He walked into his front room and found it filled with people, more than enough for a holy quorum to exorcise the dybbuks. Chaim paused before his wife, Fruma, who took a step backward. She was wearing a black dress, a lace scarf over her matron's wig, and all her jewelry, which consisted of three gold pins, two necklaces with Mogen David dangles, and several silver bandbracelets. "I'm sorry," she said. "The year in Hell should be sent to me. It's the dybbuks—"

She, too, looks like me, he thought. The same strong face. (Stopit. Here is safety.)

"We heard from Levi," Fruma said. "This must be one of Paskudnyak's tricks. But we are strong. Look, the Baal Shem, he-should-be-blessed, and Rabbe Ansky will preside over the quorum. And, just in case, Mordcha Lublin has brought us the *shofar* from Newtemple."

Everyone but Rabbe Ansky stood behind the Baal Shem, a holy man of about eighty with a full white beard and greased earlocks. He wore a black caftan of the finest satin and a skullcap with a tassel. Fruma was about to speak again when the Baal Shem spread his arms for proper effect and said, "It is time. Let us begin. Chaim Lewis, give me that box of filth."

"You may prepare the other room now," the Baal Shem said to Fruma. "Then leave us. Your *zogerkeh*, or whichever woman you choose, will lead your prayers for Chaim in this room. But remember, do not listen to our holy words."

A few of the other men—prayer shawls draped over their shoulders, holy phylacteries strapped to their foreheads and bare arms—were already rocking back and forth, mumbling prayers. Chaim looked around the room. He knew most of the men: Yitzchak Meyvn, Solomon the cantor, Avrum Shmuel, Yudel, who cheats on his wife with his neighbor, and Moishe Makher, Yussel, Itzik, Yankel, and others whose names he couldn't remember.

"The box now, Chaim," the Baal Shem said. "We must hurry. *Shabbes* will not wait for us."

"No," Chaim said. "I must have myself alone." (Give them the box.) It's almost done, he thought. (The dybbuks are sucking you in.) Just for a moment. (You can't have yourself that way. *Treyftreyf*. Impure.)

"What kind of talk is that?" asked Rabbe Ansky, a dark man with a shaved head, frizzy earlocks, and a coarse black beard. He took a step toward Chaim. "Now, come on, give me that box."

Chaim tasted worms in his mouth. He ran toward the bedroom, knocking down Rabbe Ansky's wife, a small wrinkled woman who was screaming for help. Fat Yitzchak tried to cut him off, but Chaim had already passed Fruma. He pushed her out of the doorway and locked the slideshut. I'm safe from them for a few minutes, he thought. It would take some time to have the power shut off. Until then, they couldn't get in.

He pulled a chair into the middle of the room, sat down, placed the carrybox on the floor, and then greedily opened it. All the men in the other room look alike, Chaim thought. But they're only poor impressions of me. (Open the door.)

Chaim peered into the box. Hurry, dybbuks, he thought. Get it over with. His parts were clawing at each other. Spirit-pus. I'm filled up with it. I'll burst. Release me. (Open the door.)

The dolls had melted together into a gray lump of clay. Its shape changed as Chaim stared at it. It became a human head. (Stop it now.) It's only a mask, Chaim thought. Wait. The mouth was open, lips pulled over blue gums. (Stopit.)

Chaim saw what he wanted: his face without blood, without life. Give it back, he thought. But there could be no release. His soul was passing into the open mouth of dybbukflesh. He could not get back into himself. He would be stuck in the dybbuks' mouth.

Shaking and crying, he tried to fight the dark things that were sucking at his thoughts and memories. But he had lost too much of himself. I can't stay outside. (Then open the door.)

I can't.

The lights went out. Chaim paid no attention: he was drowning in his own thoughts. (Listen. The door.)

"Quickly, before he soils himself," said the Baal Shem, "remove him from that *thing*." The doorslide was stuck at an odd angle, and the men had to pull in their stomachs to squeeze through. Fruma and the other woman watched from the other room. The men lifted Chaim out of his chair and braced him in a standing position.

"Can you hear me, Chaim?" asked the Baal Shem.

"Yes," Chaim said. His heart was beating faster. A spot of goodness grew larger, then was swallowed by alien thoughts. He dreamed of Fruma, how she smelled and the noises she made. FrumaDvora. Panting together. Like me. They smell like me. Taste like me. He reached for Fruma, but could only find himself.

The Baal Shem began to pray. He rocked back and forth on his heels, sang, and raised his eyes toward the ceiling. "We must draw the dybbuks out of him," he said to the other men, who were praying with their hands over their faces. "You must not be afraid. Look at it. Destroy it. We will take it into ourselves, but with God's help we are strong."

As the men looked into the carrybox, the Baal Shem read the Ninety-first Psalm aloud. At first his words were strong and clear, but as he went on he began to falter. He gripped his prayer shawl until his knuckles turned red. "Look at it," he whispered to the others as he bent over to stare into the box. "Draw it out. God will protect."

Chaim could feel everyone's presence. He tried to pray, but his jaw was locked and the words were jumbled in his mind. The lump of dybbukflesh was changing. Sometimes it looked like the face of the Baal Shem, only wicked and full of lust, and at other times it looked like Rabbe Ansky, afraid and trying to become a woman. Chaim could see the faces of all the others in the clay lump. He knew their fears and thoughts. Yudel was spitting up blood, and Yussel was trying to run away from a man that he hated. The others choked quietly on everyone's memories.

> *"'He will cover you with his pinions,*
> *and you shall find safety beneath his wings.'"*

"Help me, Mayer Ansky," said the Baal Shem, as he dropped the holy book. But the Rabbe, like the rest of the men, could only stare catatonically into the carrybox.

"*'I will satisfy him with long life,'*" said Chaim. He had to fight for every word.

"*'. . . To enjoy the fullness of my salvation,'*" intoned the Baal Shem.

"Dybbuks," the Baal Shem shouted, "vacate the body of Chaim Lewis and the other members of this holy quorum. In the name of the most holy, go off to eternal rest."

The lump of clay was changing color. It would soon turn into dust. Chaim felt the darkness leave his mind, but the sour memories remained strong. The others had destroyed the dybbuks by making Chaim's sins their own. Now they were all stained. They would share each other's sins. They would always be bound together. The Baal

Shem would never become a martyr. Chaim could almost hear everyone's thoughts.

"*Mazltov*," said the Baal Shem. "*Shabbes* has come."

But Chaim and the others had fallen asleep. The Baal Shem, finally giving in to weakness, fainted. The "Queen-Bride" of the Sabbath would be escorted into Shtetlfive by sleepers to the trumpets of snorers.

CAMPS

As Stephen lies in bed, he can think only of pain.

He imagines it as sharp and blue. After receiving an injection of Demerol, he enters pain's cold regions as an explorer, an objective visitor. It is a country of ice and glass, monochromatic plains and valleys filled with wash-blue shards of ice, crystal pyramids and pinnacles, squares, oblongs, and all manner of polyhedrons—block upon block of painted blue pain.

Although it is midafternoon, Stephen pretends it is dark. His eyes are tightly closed, but the daylight pouring into the room from two large windows intrudes as a dull red field extending infinitely behind his eyelids.

"Josie," he asks through cottonmouth, "aren't I due for another shot?" Josie is crisp and fresh and large in her starched white uniform. Her peaked nurse's cap is pinned to her mouse-brown hair.

"I've just given you an injection; it will take effect soon." Josie strokes his hand, and he dreams of ice.

"Bring me some ice," he whispers.

"If I bring you a bowl of ice, you'll only spill it again."

"Bring me some ice. . . ." By touching the ice cubes, by turning them in his hand like a gambler favoring his dice, he can transport himself into the beautiful blue country. Later, the ice will melt; and he will spill the bowl. The shock of cold and pain will awaken him.

Stephen believes that he is dying, and he has resolved to die properly. Each visit to the cold country brings him closer to death; and death, he has learned, is only a slow walk through ice fields. He has come to appreciate the complete lack of warmth and the beautifully etched face of his magical country.

But he is connected to the bright, flat world of the hospital by plastic tubes—one breathes cold oxygen into his left nostril, another passes into his right nostril and down his throat to his stomach; one feeds him intravenously, another draws his urine.

"Here's your ice," Josie says. "But mind you, don't spill it." She places the small bowl on his traytable and wheels the table close to him. She has a musky odor of perspiration and perfume; Stephen is reminded of old women and college girls.

"Sleep now, sweet boy."

Without opening his eyes, Stephen reaches out and places his hand on the ice.

"Come, now, Stephen, wake up. Dr. Volk is here to see you."

Stephen feels the cool touch of Josie's hand, and he opens his eyes to see the doctor standing beside him. The doctor has a gaunt, long face and thinning brown hair; he is dressed in a wrinkled green suit.

"Now we'll check the dressing, Stephen," he says as he tears away a gauze bandage on Stephen's abdomen.

Stephen feels the pain, but he is removed from it. His only wish is to return to the blue dreamlands. He watches the doctor peel off the neat crosshatching of gauze. A terrible stink fills the room.

Josie stands well away from the bed.

"Now we'll check your drains." The doctor pulls a long drainage tube out of Stephen's abdomen, irrigates and disinfects the wound, inserts a new drain, and repeats the process by pulling out another tube just below the rib cage.

Stephen imagines that he is swimming out of the room. He tries to cross the hazy border into cooler regions, but it is difficult to concentrate. He has only a half hour at most before the Demerol will wear off. Already, the pain is coming closer, and he will not be due for another injection until the night nurse comes on duty. But the night nurse will not give him an injection without an argument. She will tell him to fight the pain.

But he cannot fight without a shot.

"Tomorrow we'll take that oxygen tube out of your nose," the doctor says, but his voice seems far away and Stephen wonders what he is talking about.

He reaches for the bowl of ice, but cannot find it.

"Josie, you've taken my ice."

"I took the ice away when the doctor came. Why don't you try to watch a bit of television with me; Soupy Sales is on."

"Just bring me some ice," Stephen says. "I want to rest a bit." He can feel the sharp edges of pain breaking through the gauzy wraps of Demerol.

"I love you, Josie," he says sleepily as she places a fresh bowl of ice on his tray.

As Stephen wanders through his ice-blue dreamworld, he sees a rectangle of blinding white light. It looks like a doorway into an adjoining world of brightness. He has glimpsed it before, on previous Demerol highs. A coal-dark doorway stands beside the bright one.

He walks toward the portals, passes through white-blue conefields.

Time is growing short. The drug cannot stretch it much longer. Stephen knows that he has to choose either the bright doorway or the dark, one or the other. He does not even consider turning around, for he has dreamed that the ice and glass and cold blue gemstones have melted behind him.

It makes no difference to Stephen which doorway he chooses. On impulse he steps into blazing, searing whiteness.

Suddenly he is in a cramped world of people and sound.

The boxcar's doors were flung open. Stephen was being pushed out of the cramped boxcar, which stank of sweat, feces, and urine. Several people had died in the car and added their stink of death to the already fetid air.

"Carla, stay close to me," shouted a man beside Stephen. He had been separated from his wife by a young woman who pushed between them as she tried to return to the dark safety of the boxcar.

SS men in black, dirty uniforms were everywhere. They kicked and pommeled everyone within reach. Alsatian guard dogs snapped and barked. Stephen was bitten by one of the snarling dogs. A woman beside him was being kicked by soldiers. And they were all being methodically herded past a high barbed-wire fence. Beside the fence was a wall.

Stephen looked around for an escape route, but he was surrounded by other prisoners, who were pressing against him. Soldiers were shooting indiscriminately into the crowd, shooting women and children alike.

The man who had shouted to his wife was shot.

"Sholom, help me, help me," screamed a scrawny young woman whose skin was as yellow and pimpled as chicken flesh.

And Stephen understood that *he* was Sholom. He was a Jew in this burning, stinking world, and this woman, somehow, meant something to him. He felt the yellow star sewn on the breast of his filthy jacket. He grimaced uncontrollably. The strangest thoughts were passing through his mind, remembrances of another childhood: morning prayers with his father and rich uncle, large breakfasts on Saturdays, the sounds of his mother and father quietly making love in the next room, *yortseit* candles burning in the living room, his brother reciting the "four questions" at the Passover table.

He touched the star again and remembered the Nazis' facetious euphemism for it: *Pour le Sémite*.

He wanted to strike out, to kill the Nazis, to fight and die. But he found himself marching with the others, as if he had no will of his own. He felt that he was cut in half. He had two selves now; one watched the other. One self wanted to fight. The other was numbed; it cared only for itself. It was determined to survive.

Stephen looked around for the woman who had called out to him. She was nowhere to be seen.

Behind him were railroad tracks, electrified wire, and the conical tower and main gate of the camp. Ahead was a pitted road littered with corpses and their belongings. Rifles were being fired, and a heavy, sickly-sweet odor was everywhere. Stephen gagged, others vomited. It was the overwhelming stench of death, of rotting and burning flesh. Black clouds hung above the camp, and flames spurted from the tall chimneys of ugly buildings, as if from infernal machines.

Stephen walked onward; he was numb, unable to fight or even talk. Everything that happened around him was impossible, the stuff of dreams.

The prisoners were ordered to halt, and the soldiers began to separate those who would be burned from those who would be worked to death. Old men and women and young children were pulled out of the crowd. Some were beaten and killed immediately, while the others looked on in disbelief. Stephen looked on, as if it was of no concern to him. Everything was unreal, dreamlike. He did not belong here.

The new prisoners looked like Musselmänner, the walking dead. Those who became ill, or were beaten or starved before they could "wake up" to the reality of the camps, became Musselmänner. Musselmänner could not think or feel. They shuffled around, already dead in spirit, until a guard or disease or cold or starvation killed them.

"Keep marching," shouted a guard as Stephen stopped before an emaciated old man crawling on the ground. "You'll look like him soon enough."

Suddenly, as if waking from one dream and finding himself in another, Stephen remembered that the chicken-skinned girl was his wife.

He remembered their life together, their children and crowded flat. He remembered the birthmark on her leg, her scent, her hungry lovemaking. He had once fought another boy over her.

His glands opened up with fear and shame; he had ignored her screams for help.

He stopped and turned, faced the other group. "Fruma," he shouted, then started to run.

A guard struck him in the chest with the butt of his rifle, and Stephen fell into darkness.

He spills the ice water again and awakens with a scream.

"It's my fault," Josie says as she peels back the sheets. "I should have taken the bowl away from you. But you fight me."

Stephen lives with the pain again. He imagines that a tiny fire is burning in his abdomen, slowly consuming him. He stares at the television high on the wall and watches Soupy Sales.

As Josie changes the plastic sac containing his intravenous saline solution, an orderly pushes a cart into the room and asks Stephen if he wants a print for his wall.

"Would you like me to choose something for you?" Josie asks.

Stephen shakes his head and asks the orderly to show him all the prints. Most of them are familiar still lifes and pastorals, but one catches his attention. It is a painting of a wheat field. Although the sky looks ominously dark, the wheat is brightly rendered in great, broad strokes. A path cuts through the field and crows fly overhead.

"That one," Stephen says. "Put that one up."

After the orderly hangs the print and leaves, Josie asks Stephen why he chose that particular painting.

"I like Van Gogh," he says dreamily as he tries to detect a rhythm in the surges of abdominal pain. But he is not nauseated, just gaseous.

"Any particular reason why you like Van Gogh?" asks Josie. "He's my favorite artist too."

"I didn't say he was my favorite," Stephen says, and Josie pouts, an expression that does not fit her prematurely lined face. Stephen closes his eyes, glimpses the cold country, and says, "I like the painting because it's so bright that it's almost frightening. And the road going through the field"—he opens his eyes—"doesn't go anywhere. It just ends in the field. And the crows are flying around like vultures."

"Most people see it as just a pretty picture," Josie says.

"What's it called?"

"Wheatfield with Blackbirds."

"Sensible. My stomach hurts, Josie. Help me turn over on my side." Josie helps him onto his left side, plumps up his pillows, and inserts a short tube into his rectum to relieve the gas. "I also like the painting with the large stars that all look out of focus," Stephen says. "What's it called?"

"Starry Night."

"That's scary too," Stephen says. Josie takes his blood pressure, makes a notation on his chart, then sits down beside him and holds his hand. "I remember something," he says. "Something just—" He jumps as he remembers, and pain shoots through his distended stomach. Josie shushes him, checks the intravenous needle, and asks him what he remembers.

But the memory of the dream recedes as the pain grows sharper. "I hurt all the fucking time, Josie," he says, changing position. Josie removes the rectal tube before he is on his back.

"Don't use such language, I don't like to hear it. I know you have a lot of pain," she says, her voice softening.

"Time for a shot."

"No, honey, not for some time. You'll just have to bear with it."

Stephen remembers his dream again. He is afraid of it. His breath is short and his heart feels as if it is beating in his throat, but he recounts the entire dream to Josie.

He does not notice that her face has lost its color.

"It's only a dream, Stephen. Probably something you studied in history."

"But it was so real, not like a dream at all."

"That's enough!" Josie says.

"I'm sorry I upset you. Don't be angry."

"I'm *not* angry."

"I'm sorry," he says, fighting the pain, squeezing Josie's hand tightly. "Didn't you tell me that you were in the Second World War?"

Josie is composed once again. "Yes, I did, but I'm surprised you remembered. You were very sick. I was a nurse overseas, spent most of the war in England. But I was one of the first women to go into any of the concentration camps."

Stephen drifts with the pain; he appears to be asleep.

"You must have studied very hard," Josie whispers to him. Her hand is shaking just a bit.

It is twelve o'clock and his room is death-quiet. The sharp shadows seem to be the hardest objects in the room. The fluorescents burn steadily in the hall outside.

Stephen looks out into the hallway, but he can see only the far white wall. He waits for his night nurse to appear: it is time for his injection. A young nurse passes by his doorway. Stephen imagines that she is a cardboard ship sailing through the corridors.

He presses his buzzer, which is attached by a clip to his pillow. The night nurse will take her time, he tells himself. He remembers arguing with her. Angrily, he presses the buzzer again.

Across the hall, a man begins to scream, and there is a shuffle of nurses into his room. The screaming turns into begging and whining. Although Stephen has never seen the man in the opposite room, he has come to hate him. Like Stephen, he has something wrong with his stomach; but he cannot suffer well. He can only beg and cry, try to make deals with the nurses, doctors, God, and angels. Stephen cannot muster any pity for this man.

The night nurse finally comes into the room, says, "You have to try to get along without this," and gives him an injection of Demerol.

"Why does the man across the hall scream so?" Stephen asks, but the nurse is already edging out of the room.

"Because he's in pain."

"So am I," Stephen says in a loud voice. "But I can keep it to myself."

"Then, stop buzzing me constantly for an injection. That man across the hall has had half of his stomach removed. He's got something to scream about."

So have I, Stephen thinks; but the nurse disappears before he can tell her. He tries to imagine what the man across the hall looks like. He thinks of him as being bald and small, an ancient baby. Stephen tries to feel sorry for the man, but his incessant whining disgusts him.

The drug takes effect; the screams recede as he hurtles through the dark corridors of a dream. The cold country is dark, for Stephen cannot persuade his night nurse to bring him some ice. Once again, he sees two entrances. As the world melts behind him, he steps into the coal-black doorway.

In the darkness he hears an alarm, a bone-jarring clangor.

He could smell the combined stink of men pressed closely together. They were all lying upon two badly constructed wooden shelves. The floor was dirt; the smell of urine never left the barrack.

"Wake up," said a man Stephen knew as Viktor. "If the guard finds you in bed, you'll be beaten again."

Stephen moaned, still wrapped in dreams. "Wake up, wake up," he mumbled to himself. He would have a few more minutes before the guard arrived with the dogs. At the very thought of dogs, Stephen felt revulsion. He had once been bitten in the face by a large dog.

He opened his eyes, yet he was still half asleep, exhausted. You are in a death camp, he said to himself. You must wake up. You must fight by waking up. Or you will die in your sleep. Shaking uncontrollably, he said, "Do you want to end up in the oven, perhaps you will be lucky today and live."

As he lowered his legs to the floor, he felt the sores open on the soles of his feet. He wondered who would die today and shrugged. It was his third week in the camp. Impossibly, against all odds, he had survived. Most of those he had known in the train had either died or become Musselmänner. If it were not for Viktor, he, too, would have become a Musselmänn. He had a breakdown and wanted to die. He babbled in English. But Viktor talked him out of death, shared his portion of food with him, and taught him the new rules of life.

"Like everyone else who survives, I count myself first, second, and third—then I try to do what I can for someone else," Viktor had said.

"I will survive," Stephen repeated to himself as the guards opened the door, stepped into the room, and began to shout. Their dogs growled and snapped, but heeled beside them. The guards looked sleepy; one did not wear a cap, and his red hair was tousled.

Perhaps he spent the night with one of the whores, Stephen thought. Perhaps today would not be so bad. . . .

And so begins the morning ritual: Josie enters Stephen's room at a quarter to eight, fusses with the chart attached to the footboard of his bed, pads about aimlessly, and finally goes to the bathroom. She returns, her stiff uniform making swishing sounds. Stephen can feel her standing over the bed and staring at him. But he does not open his eyes. He waits a beat.

She turns away, then drops the bedpan. Yesterday it was the metal ashtray; day before that, she bumped into the bedstand.

"Good morning, darling, it's a beautiful day," she says, then walks across the room to the windows. She parts the faded orange drapes and opens the blinds. "How do you feel today?"

"Okay, I guess."

Josie takes his pulse and asks, "Did Mr. Gregory stop in to say hello last night?"

"Yes," Stephen says. "He's teaching me how to play gin rummy. What's wrong with him?"

"He's very sick."

"I can see that; has he got cancer?"

"I don't know," says Josie as she tidies up his night table.

"You're lying again," Stephen says, but she ignores him. After a time, he says, "His girlfriend was in to see me last night, I bet his wife will be in today."

"Shut your mouth about that," Josie says. "Let's get you out of that bed, so I can change the sheets."

Stephen sits in the chair all morning. He is getting well but is still very weak. Just before lunchtime, the orderly wheels his cart into the room and asks Stephen if he would like to replace the print hanging on the wall.

"I've seen them all," Stephen says. "I'll keep the one I have." Stephen does not grow tired of the Van Gogh painting; sometimes, the crows seem to have changed position.

"Maybe you'll like this one," the orderly says as he pulls out a cardboard print of Van Gogh's *Starry Night*. It is a study of a village nestled in the hills, dressed in shadows. But everything seems to be boiling and writhing as in a fever dream. A cypress tree in the foreground looks like a black flame, and the vertiginous sky is filled with great, blurry stars. It is a drunkard's dream. The orderly smiles.

"So you did have it," Stephen says.

"No, I traded some other pictures for it. They had a copy in the West Wing."

Stephen watches him hang it, thanks him, and waits for him to leave. Then he gets up and examines the painting carefully. He touches the raised facsimile brushstrokes, and turns toward Josie, feeling an odd sensation in his groin. He looks at her, as if seeing her for the first time. She has an overly full mouth, which curves downward at the corners when she smiles. She is not a pretty woman—too fat, he thinks.

"Dance with me," he says, as he waves his arms and takes a step forward, conscious of the pain in his stomach.

"You're too sick to be dancing just yet," but she laughs at him and bends her knees in a mock plié.

She has small breasts for such a large woman, Stephen thinks. Feeling suddenly dizzy, he takes a step toward the bed. He feels himself slip to the floor, feels Josie's hair brushing against his face, dreams that he's all wet from her tongue, feels her arms around him, squeezing, then feels the weight of her body pressing down on him, crushing him. . . .

He wakes up in bed, catheterized. He has an intravenous needle in his left wrist, and it is difficult to swallow, for he has a tube down his throat.

He groans, tries to move.

"Quiet, Stephen," Josie says, stroking his hand.

"What happened?" he mumbles. He can only remember being dizzy.

"You've had a slight setback, so just rest. The doctor had to collapse your lung; you must lie very still."

"Josie, I love you," he whispers, but he is too far away to be heard. He wonders how many hours or days have passed. He looks toward the window. It is dark, and there is no one in the room.

He presses the buzzer attached to his pillow and remembers a dream. . . .

"You must fight," Viktor said.

It was dark, all the other men were asleep, and the barrack was filled with snoring and snorting. Stephen wished they could all die, choke on their own breath. It would be an act of mercy.

"Why fight?" Stephen asked, and he pointed toward the greasy window, beyond which were the ovens that smoked day and night. He made a fluttering gesture with his hand—smoke rising.

"You must fight, you must live; living is everything. It is the only thing that makes sense here."

"We're all going to die, anyway," Stephen whispered. "Just like your sister . . . and my wife."

"No, Sholom, we're going to live. The others may die, but we're going to live. You must believe that."

Stephen understood that Viktor was desperately trying to convince himself to live. He felt sorry for Viktor; there could be no sensible rationale for living in a place like this. Everything must die here.

Stephen grinned, tasted blood from the corner of his mouth, and said, "So we'll live through the night, maybe."

And maybe tomorrow, he thought. He would play the game of survival a little longer.

He wondered if Viktor would be alive tomorrow. He smiled and thought, If Viktor dies, then I will have to take his place and convince others to live. For an instant, he hoped Viktor would die so that he could take his place.

The alarm sounded. It was three o'clock in the morning, time to begin the day.

This morning, Stephen was on his feet before the guards could unlock the door.

"Wake up," Josie says, gently tapping his arm. "Come on now, wake up."

Stephen hears her voice as an echo. He imagines that he has been flung into a long tunnel; he hears air whistling in his ears but cannot see anything.

"Whassimatter?" he asks. His mouth feels as if it is stuffed with cotton; his lips are dry and cracked. He is suddenly angry at Josie and the plastic tubes that hold him in his bed as if he were a latter-day Gulliver. He wants to pull out the tubes, smash the bags filled with saline, tear away his bandages.

"You were speaking German," Josie says. "Did you know that?"

"Can I have some ice?"

"No," Josie says impatiently. "You spilled again, you're all wet."

". . . for my mouth, dry. . . ."

"Do you remember speaking German, honey, I have to know."

"Don't remember, bring ice, I'll try to think about it."

As Josie leaves to get him some ice, he tries to remember his dream.

"Here now, just suck on the ice." She gives him a little hill of crushed ice on the end of a spoon.

"Why did you wake me up, Josie?" The layers of dream are beginning to slough off. As the Demerol works out of his system, he has to concentrate on fighting the burning ache in his stomach.

"You were speaking German. Where did you learn to speak like that?"

Stephen tries to remember what he said. He cannot speak any German, only a bit of classroom French. He looks down at his legs (he has thrown off the sheet) and notices, for the first time, that his legs are as thin as his arms. "My God, Josie, how could I have lost so much weight?"

"You lost about forty pounds, but don't worry, you'll gain it all back.

You're on the road to recovery now. Please, try to remember your dream."

"I can't, Josie! I just can't seem to get ahold of it."

"Try."

"Why is it so important to you?"

"You weren't speaking college German, darling, you were speaking slang. You spoke in a patois that I haven't heard since the forties."

Stephen feels a chill slowly creep up his spine. "What did I say?"

Josie waits a beat, then says, "You talked about dying."

"Josie?"

"Yes," she says, pulling at her fingernail.

"When is the pain going to stop?"

"It will be over soon." She gives him another spoonful of ice. "You kept repeating the name Viktor in your sleep. Can you remember anything about him?"

Viktor, Viktor, deep-set blue eyes, balding head and broken nose, called himself a Galitzianer. Saved my life. "I remember," Stephen says. "His name is Viktor Shmone. He is in all my dreams now."

Josie exhales sharply.

"Does that mean anything to you?" Stephen asks anxiously.

"I once knew a man from one of the camps." She speaks very slowly and precisely. "His name was Viktor Shmone. I took care of him. He was one of the few people left alive in the camp after the Germans fled." She reaches for her purse, which she keeps on Stephen's night table, and fumbles an old, torn photograph out of a plastic slipcase.

As Stephen examines the photograph, he begins to sob. A thinner and much younger Josie is standing beside Viktor and two other emaciated-looking men. "Then, I'm not dreaming," he says, "and I'm going to die. That's what it means." He begins to shake, just as he did in his dream, and, without thinking, he makes the gesture of rising smoke to Josie. He begins to laugh.

"Stop that," Josie says, raising her hand to slap him. Then she embraces him and says, "Don't cry, darling, it's only a dream. Somehow, you're dreaming the past."

"Why?" Stephen asks, still shaking.

"Maybe you're dreaming because of me, because we're so close. In some ways, I think you know me better than anyone else, better than any man, no doubt. You might be dreaming for a reason; maybe I can help you."

"I'm afraid, Josie."

She comforts him and says, "Now tell me everything you can remember about the dreams."

He is exhausted. As he recounts his dreams to her, he sees the bright doorway again. He feels himself being sucked into it. "Josie," he says, "I must stay awake, don't want to sleep, dream. . . ."

Josie's face is pulled tight as a mask; she is crying.

Stephen reaches out to her, slips into the bright doorway, into another dream.

It was a cold, cloudless morning. Hundreds of prisoners were working in the quarries; each work gang came from a different barrack. Most of the gangs were made up of Musselmänner, the faceless majority of the camp. They moved like automatons, lifting and carrying the great stones to the numbered carts, which would have to be pushed down the tracks.

Stephen was drenched with sweat. He had a fever and was afraid that he had contracted typhus. An epidemic had broken out in the camp last week. Every morning, several doctors arrived with the guards. Those who were too sick to stand up were taken away to be gassed or experimented upon in the hospital.

Although Stephen could barely stand, he forced himself to keep moving. He tried to focus all his attention on what he was doing. He made a ritual of bending over, choosing a stone of a certain size, lifting it, carrying it to the nearest cart, and then taking the same number of steps back to his dig.

A Musselmänn fell to the ground, but Stephen made no effort to help him. When he could help someone in a little way, he would, but he would not stick his neck out for a Musselmänn. Yet something niggled at Stephen. He remembered a photograph in which Viktor and this Musselmänn were standing with a man and a woman he did not recognize. But Stephen could not remember where he had ever seen such a photograph.

"Hey, you," shouted a guard. "Take the one on the ground to the cart."

Stephen nodded to the guard and began to drag the Musselmänn away.

"Who's the new patient down the hall?" Stephen asks as he eats a bit of cereal from the breakfast tray Josie has placed before him. He is feeling much better now; his fever is down and the tubes, catheter, and intravenous needle have been removed. He can even walk around a bit.

"How did you find out about that?" Josie asks.

"You were talking to Mr. Gregory's nurse. Do you think I'm dead already? I can still hear."

Josie laughs and takes a sip of Stephen's tea. "You're far from dead! In fact, today is a red-letter day, you're going to take your first shower. What do you think about that?"

"I'm not well enough yet," he says, worried that he will have to leave the hospital before he is ready.

"Well, Dr. Volk thinks differently, and his word is law."

"Tell me about the new patient."

"They brought in a man last night who drank two quarts of motor oil; he's on the dialysis machine."

"Will he make it?"

"No, I don't think so; there's too much poison in his system."

We should all die, Stephen thinks. It would be an act of mercy. He glimpses the camp.

"Stephen!"

He jumps, then awakens.

"You've had a good night's sleep, you don't need to nap. Let's get you into that shower and have it done with." Josie pushes the traytable away from the bed. "Come on, I have your bathrobe right here."

Stephen puts on his bathrobe, and they walk down the hall to the showers. There are three empty shower stalls, a bench, and a whirlpool bath. As Stephen takes off his bathrobe, Josie adjusts the water pressure and temperature in the corner stall.

"What's the matter?" Stephen asks after stepping into the shower. Josie stands in front of the shower stall and holds his towel, but she will not look at him. "Come on," he says, "you've seen me naked before."

"That was different."

"How?" He touches a hard, ugly scab that has formed over one of the wounds on his abdomen.

"When you were very sick, I washed you in bed as if you were a baby. Now it's different." She looks down at the wet tile floor as if she is lost in thought.

"Well, I think it's silly," he says. "Come on, it's hard to talk to someone who's looking the other way. I could break my neck in here and you'd be staring down at the fucking floor."

"I've asked you not to use that word," she says in a very low voice.

"Do my eyes still look yellowish?"

She looks directly at his face and says, "No, they look fine."

Stephen suddenly feels faint, then nauseated; he has been standing too long. As he leans against the cold shower wall, he remembers his last dream. He is back in the quarry. He can smell the perspiration of the men around him, feel the sun baking him, draining his strength. It is so bright. . . .

He finds himself sitting on the bench and staring at the light on the opposite wall. I've got typhus, he thinks, then realizes that he is in the hospital. Josie is beside him.

"I'm sorry," he says.

"I shouldn't have let you stand so long; it was my fault."

"I remembered another dream." He begins to shake, and Josie puts her arms around him.

"It's all right now; tell Josie about your dream."

She's an old, fat woman, Stephen thinks. As he describes the dream, his shaking subsides.

"Do you know the man's name?" Josie asks. "The one the guard ordered you to drag away."

"No," Stephen says. "He was a Musselmänn, yet I thought there was something familiar about him. In my dream I remembered the photograph you showed me. He was in it."

"What will happen to him?"

"The guards will give him to the doctors for experimentation. If they don't want him, he'll be gassed."

"You must not let that happen," Josie says, holding him tightly.

"Why?" asks Stephen, afraid that he will fall into the dreams again.

"If he was one of the men you saw in the photograph, you must not let him die. Your dreams must fit the past."

"I'm afraid."

"It will be all right, baby," Josie says, clinging to him. She is shaking and breathing heavily.

Stephen feels himself getting an erection. He calms her, presses his face against hers, and touches her breasts. She tells him to stop but does not push him away.

"I love you," he says as he slips his hand under her starched skirt. He feels awkward and foolish and warm.

"This is wrong," she whispers.

As Stephen kisses her and feels her thick tongue in his mouth, he begins to dream. . . .

Stephen stopped to rest for a few seconds. The Musselmänn was dead weight. I cannot go on, Stephen thought, but he bent down, grabbed the Musselmänn by his coat, and dragged him toward the cart. He glimpsed the cart, which was filled with the sick and dead and exhausted; it looked no different than a carload of corpses marked for a mass grave.

A long, gray cloud covered the sun, then passed, drawing shadows across gutted hills.

On impulse, Stephen dragged the Musselmänn into a gully behind several chalky rocks. Why am I doing this? he asked himself. If I'm caught, I'll be ash in the ovens too. He remembered what Viktor had told him: "You must think of yourself all the time or you'll be no help to anyone else."

The Musselmänn groaned, then raised his arm. His face was gray with dust and his eyes were glazed.

"You must lie still," Stephen whispered. "Do not make a sound. I've hidden you from the guards, but if they hear you, we'll all be punished. One sound from you and you're dead. You must fight to live; you're in a death camp; you must fight so you can tell of this later."

"I have no family, they're all—"

Stephen clapped his hand over the man's mouth and whispered, "Fight, don't talk. Wake up; you cannot survive the death camp by sleeping."

The man nodded, and Stephen climbed out of the gully. He helped two men carry a large stone to a nearby cart.

"What are you doing?" shouted a guard.

"I left my place to help these men with this stone; now I'll go back where I was."

"What the hell are you trying to do?" Viktor asked.

Stephen felt as if he was burning up with fever. He wiped the sweat from his eyes, but everything was still blurry.

"You're sick, too. You'll be lucky if you last the day."

"I'll last," Stephen said, "but I want you to help me get him back to the camp."

"I won't risk it, not for a Musselmänn. He's already dead; leave him."

"Like you left me?"

Before the guards could take notice, they began to work. Although Viktor was older than Stephen, he was stronger. He worked hard every day and never caught the diseases that daily reduced the barrack's numbers. Stephen had a touch of death, as Viktor called it, and was often sick.

They worked until dusk, when the sun's oblique rays caught the dust from the quarries and turned it into veils and scrims. Even the guards sensed that this was a quiet time, for they would congregate together and talk in hushed voices.

"Come, now, help me," Stephen whispered to Viktor.

"I've been doing that all day," Viktor said. "I'll have enough trouble getting you back to the camp, much less carry this Musselmänn."

"We can't leave him."

"Why are you so preoccupied with this Musselmänn? Even if we can get him back to the camp, his chances are nothing. I know—I've seen enough—I know who has a chance to survive."

"You're wrong this time," Stephen said. He was dizzy and it was difficult to stand. The odds are I won't last the night, and Viktor knows it, he told himself. "I had a dream that if this man dies, I'll die too. I just feel it."

"Here we learn to trust our dreams," Viktor said. "They make as much sense as this. . . ." He made the gesture of rising smoke and gazed toward the ovens, which were spewing fire and black ash.

The western portion of the sky was yellow, but over the ovens it was red and purple and dark blue. Although it horrified Stephen to consider it, there was a macabre beauty here. If he survived, he would never forget these sense impressions, which were stronger than anything he had ever experienced before. Being so close to death, he was, perhaps for the first time, really living. In the camp, one did not even consider suicide. One grasped for every moment, sucked at life like an infant, lived as if there were no future.

The guards shouted at the prisoners to form a column; it was time to march back to the barracks.

While the others milled about, Stephen and Viktor lifted the Musselmänn out of the gully. Everyone nearby tried to distract the guards. When the march began, Stephen and Viktor held the Musselmänn between them, for he could barely stand.

"Come on, dead one, carry your weight," Viktor said. "Are you so dead that you cannot hear me? Are you as dead as the rest of your family?" The Musselmänn groaned and dragged his legs. Viktor kicked him. "You'll walk or we'll leave you here for the guards to find."

"Let him be," Stephen said.

"Are you dead or do you have a name?" Viktor continued.

"Berek," croaked the Musselmänn. "I am not dead."

"Then, we have a fine bunk for you," Viktor said. "You can smell the stink of the sick for another night before the guards make a selection." Viktor made the gesture of smoke rising.

Stephen stared at the barracks ahead. They seemed to waver as the heat rose from the ground. He counted every step. He would drop soon; he could not go on, could not carry the Musselmänn.

He began to mumble in English.

"So you're speaking American again," Viktor said.

Stephen shook himself awake, placed one foot before the other.

"Dreaming of an American lover?"

"I don't know English and I have no American lover."

"Then, who is this Josie you keep talking about in your sleep . . . ?"

"Why were you screaming?" Josie asks as she washes his face with a cold washcloth.

"I don't remember screaming," Stephen says. He discovers a fever blister on his lip. Expecting to find an intravenous needle in his wrist, he raises his arm.

"You don't need an I.V.," Josie says. "You just have a bit of a fever. Dr. Volk has prescribed some new medication for it."

"What time is it?" Stephen stares at the whorls in the ceiling.

"Almost 3 P.M. I'll be going off soon."

"Then I've slept most of the day away," Stephen says, feeling something crawling inside him. He worries that his dreams still have a hold on him. "Am I having another relapse?"

"You'll do fine," Josie says.

"I should be fine now; I don't want to dream anymore."

"Did you dream again, do you remember anything?"

"I dreamed that I saved the Musselmänn," Stephen says.

"What was his name?" asks Josie.

"Berek, I think. Is that the man you knew?"

Josie nods and Stephen smiles at her. "Maybe that's the end of the dreams," he says; but she does not respond. He asks to see the photograph again.

"Not just now," Josie says.

"But I have to see it. I want to see if I can recognize myself. . . ."

Stephen dreamed he was dead, but it was only the fever. Viktor sat beside him on the floor and watched the others. The sick were moaning and crying; they slept on the cramped platform, as if proximity to one another could ensure a few more hours of life. Wan moonlight seemed to fill the barrack.

Stephen awakened, feverish. "I'm burning up," he whispered to Viktor.

"Well," Viktor said, "you've got your Musselmänn. If he lives, you live. That's what you said, isn't it?"

"I don't remember; I just knew that I couldn't let him die."

"You'd better go back to sleep; you'll need your strength. Or we may have to carry *you*, tomorrow."

Stephen tried to sleep, but the fever was making lights and spots before his eyes. When he finally fell asleep, he dreamed of a dark country filled with gemstones and great quarries of ice and glass.

"What?" Stephen asked, as he sat up suddenly, awakened from dampblack dreams. He looked around and saw that everyone was watching Berek, who was sitting under the window at the far end of the room.

Berek was singing the Kol Nidre very softly. It was the Yom Kippur prayer, sung on the most holy of days. He repeated the prayer three times, and then once again in a louder voice. The others responded, intoned the prayer as a recitative. Viktor was crying quietly, and Stephen imagined that the holy spirit animated Berek. Surely, he told himself, that face and those pale, unseeing eyes were those of a dead man. He remembered the story of the golem, shuddered, found himself singing and pulsing with fever.

When the prayer was over, Berek fell back into his fever trance. The others became silent, then slept. But there was something new in the barrack with them tonight, a palpable exultation. Stephen looked around at the sleepers and thought, We're surviving, more dead than alive, but surviving. . . .

"You were right about that Musselmänn," Viktor whispered. "It's good that we saved him."

"Perhaps we should sit with him," Stephen said. "He's alone." But Viktor was already asleep; and Stephen was suddenly afraid that if he sat beside Berek, he would be consumed by his holy fire.

As Stephen fell through sleep and dreams, his face burned with fever.

Again he wakes up screaming.

"Josie," he says, "I can remember the dream, but there's something else, something I can't see, something terrible. . . ."

"Not to worry," Josie says, "it's the fever." But she looks worried, and Stephen is sure that she knows something he does not.

"Tell me what happened to Viktor and Berek," Stephen says. He presses his hands together to stop them from shaking.

"They lived, just as you are going to live and have a good life."

Stephen calms down and tells her his dream.

"So you see," she says, "you're even dreaming about surviving."

"I'm burning up."

"Dr. Volk says you're doing very well." Josie sits beside him, and he watches the fever patterns shift behind his closed eyelids.

"Tell me what happens next, Josie."

"You're going to get well."

"There's something else. . . ."

"Shush, now, there's nothing else." She pauses, then says, "Mr. Gregory is supposed to visit you tonight. He's getting around a bit, he's been back and forth all day in his wheelchair. He tells me that you two have made some sort of a deal about dividing up all the nurses."

Stephen smiles, opens his eyes, and says, "It was Gregory's idea. Tell me what's wrong with him."

"All right, he has cancer, but he doesn't know it and you must keep it a secret. They cut the nerve in his leg because the pain was so bad. He's quite comfortable now, but remember, you can't repeat what I've told you."

"Is he going to live?" Stephen asks. "He's told me about all the new projects he's planning, so I guess he's expecting to get out of here."

"He's not going to live very long, and the doctor didn't want to break his spirit."

"I think he should be told."

"That's not your decision to make, nor mine."

"Am I going to die, Josie?"

"No!" she says, touching his arm to reassure him.

"How do I know that's the truth?"

"Because I say so, and I couldn't look you straight in the eye and tell you if it wasn't true. I should have known it would be a mistake to tell you about Mr. Gregory."

"You did right," Stephen says. "I won't mention it again. Now that I know, I feel better." He feels drowsy again.

"Do you think you're up to seeing him tonight?"

Stephen nods, although he is bone tired. As he falls asleep, the fever patterns begin to dissolve, leaving a bright field. With a start, he opens his eyes: he has touched the edge of another dream.

"What happened to the man across the hall, the one who was always screaming?"

"He's left the ward," Josie says. "Mr. Gregory had better hurry if he wants to play cards with you before dinner. They're going to bring the trays up soon."

"You mean he died, don't you."

"Yes, if you must know, he died. But *you're* going to live."

There is a crashing noise in the hallway. Someone shouts, and Josie runs to the door.

Stephen tries to stay awake, but he is being pulled back into the cold country.

"Mr. Gregory fell trying to get into his wheelchair by himself," Josie says. "He should have waited for his nurse, but she was out of the room and he wanted to visit you."

But Stephen does not hear a word she says.

There were rumors that the camp was going to be liberated. It was late, but no one was asleep. The shadows in the barrack seemed larger tonight.

"It's better for us if the Allies don't come," Viktor said to Stephen.

"Why do you say that?"

"Haven't you noticed that the ovens are going day and night? The Nazis are in a hurry."

"I'm going to try to sleep," Stephen said.

"Look around you; even the Musselmänner are agitated," Viktor said. "Animals become nervous before the slaughter. I've worked with animals. People are not so different."

"Shut up and let me sleep," Stephen said, and he dreamed that he could hear the crackling of distant gunfire.

"Attention," shouted the guards as they stepped into the barrack. There were more guards than usual, and each one had two Alsatian dogs. "Come on, form a line. Hurry."

"They're going to kill us," Viktor said; "then they'll evacuate the camp and save themselves."

The guards marched the prisoners toward the northern section of the camp. Although it was still dark, it was hot and humid, without a trace of the usual morning chill. The ovens belched fire and turned the sky aglow. Everyone was quiet, for there was nothing to be done. The guards were nervous and would cut down anyone who uttered a sound, as an example for the rest.

The booming of big guns could be heard in the distance.

If I'm going to die, Stephen thought, I might as well go now, and take a Nazi with me. Suddenly, all of his buried fear, aggression, and revulsion surfaced; his face became hot and his heart felt as if it were pumping in his throat. But Stephen argued with himself. There was always a chance. He had once heard of some women who were waiting in line for the ovens; for no apparent reason, the guards sent them back to their barracks. Anything could happen. There was always a chance. But to attack a guard would mean certain death.

The guns became louder. Stephen could not be sure, but he thought the noise was coming from the west. The thought passed through his mind that everyone would be better off dead. That would stop all the guns and screaming voices, the clenched fists and wildly beating hearts. The Nazis should kill everyone, and then themselves, as a favor to humanity.

The guards stopped the prisoners in an open field surrounded on three sides by forestland. Sunrise was moments away; purple-black clouds drifted across the sky touched by gray in the east. It promised to be a hot, gritty day.

Half-step Walter, a Judenrat sympathizer who worked for the guards, handed out shovel heads to everyone.

"He's worse than the Nazis," Viktor said to Stephen.

"The Judenrat thinks he will live," said Berek, "but he will die like a Jew with the rest of us."

"Now, when it's too late, the Musselmänn regains consciousness," Viktor said.

"Hurry," shouted the guards, "or you'll die now. As long as you dig, you'll live."

Stephen hunkered down on his knees and began to dig with the shovel head.

"Do you think we might escape?" Berek whined.

"Shut up and dig," Stephen said. "There is no escape, just stay alive as long as you can. Stop whining, are you becoming a Musselmänn again?" Stephen noticed that other prisoners were gathering up twigs and branches. So the Nazis plan to cover us up, he thought.

"That's enough," shouted a guard. "Put your shovels down in front of you and stand in a line."

The prisoners stood shoulder to shoulder along the edge of the mass grave. Stephen stood between Viktor and Berek. Someone screamed and ran and was shot immediately.

I don't want to see trees or guards or my friends, Stephen thought as he stared into the sun. I only want to see the sun, let it burn out my eyes, fill up my head with light. He was shaking uncontrollably, quaking with fear.

Guns were booming in the background.

Maybe the guards won't kill us, Stephen thought, even as he heard the crackcrack of their rifles. Men were screaming and begging for life. Stephen turned his head, only to see someone's face blown away.

Screaming, tasting vomit in his mouth, Stephen fell backward, pulling Viktor and Berek into the grave with him.

Darkness, Stephen thought. His eyes were open, yet it was dark. I must be dead, this must be death. . . .

He could barely move. Corpses can't move, he thought. Something brushed against his face, he stuck out his tongue, felt something spongy. It tasted bitter. Lifting first one arm and then the other, Stephen moved some branches away. Above, he could see a few dim stars; the clouds were lit like lanterns by a quarter moon.

He touched the body beside him; it moved. That must be Viktor, he thought. "Viktor, are you alive, say something if you're alive." Stephen whispered, as if in fear of disturbing the dead.

Viktor groaned and said, "Yes, I'm alive, and so is Berek."

"And the others?"

"All dead. Can't you smell the stink? You, at least, were unconscious all day."

"They can't *all* be dead," Stephen said; then he began to cry.

"Shut up," Viktor said, touching Stephen's face to comfort him. "We're alive, that's something. They could have fired a volley into the pit."

"I thought I was dead," Berek said. He was a shadow among shadows.

"Why are we still here?" Stephen asked.

"We stayed in here because it is safe," Viktor said.

"But they're all dead," Stephen whispered, amazed that there could be speech and reason inside a grave.

"Do you think it's safe to leave now?" Berek asked Viktor.

"Perhaps. I think the killing has stopped. By now the Americans or English or whoever they are have taken over the camp. I heard gunfire and screaming; I think it's best to wait a while longer."

"Here?" asked Stephen. "Among the dead?"

"It's best to be safe."

It was late afternoon when they climbed out of the grave. The air was thick with flies. Stephen could see bodies sprawled in awkward positions beneath the covering of twigs and branches. "How can I live when all the others are dead?" he asked himself aloud.

"You live, that's all," answered Viktor.

They kept close to the forest and worked their way back toward the camp.

"Look there," Viktor said, motioning Stephen and Berek to take cover. Stephen could see trucks moving toward the camp compound.

"Americans," whispered Berek.

"No need to whisper now," Stephen said. "We're safe."

"Guards could be hiding anywhere," Viktor said. "I haven't slept in the grave to be shot now."

They walked into the camp through a large break in the barbed-wire fence, which had been hit by an artillery shell. When they reached the compound, they found nurses, doctors, and army personnel bustling about.

"You speak English," Viktor said to Stephen as they walked past several quonsets. "Maybe you can speak for us."

"I told you, I can't speak English."

"But I've heard you!"

"Wait," shouted an American army nurse. "You fellows are going the wrong way." She was stocky and spoke perfect German. "You must check in at the hospital; it's back that way."

"No," said Berek, shaking his head. "I won't go in there."

"There's no need to be afraid now," she said. "You're free. Come along, I'll take you to the hospital."

Something familiar about her, Stephen thought. He felt dizzy and everything turned gray.

"Josie," he murmured as he fell to the ground.

"What is it?" Josie asks. "Everything is all right, Josie is here."

"Josie," Stephen mumbles.

"You're all right."

"How can I live when they're all dead?" he asks.

"It was a dream," she says as she wipes the sweat from his forehead. "You see, your fever has broken, you're getting well."

"Did you know about the grave?"

"It's all over now, forget the dream."

"Did you know?"

"Yes," Josie says. "Viktor told me how he survived the grave, but that was so long ago, before you were even born. Dr. Volk tells me you'll be going home soon."

"I don't want to leave, I want to stay with you."

"Stop that talk, you've got a whole life ahead of you. Soon you'll forget all about this, and you'll forget me, too."

"Josie," Stephen asks, "let me see that old photograph again. Just one last time."

"Remember, this is the last time," she says as she hands him the faded photograph.

He recognizes Viktor and Berek, but the young man standing between them is not Stephen. "That's not me," he says, certain that he will never return to the camp.

Yet the shots still echo in his mind.

THE MARKS OF PAINTED TEETH

Faro led the way down the fire escape. The alley below was quiet. It was too early for much movement. Later, it would be too warm. There were a few derelicts sleeping in doorways and on the street. The garbage that covered the street served them as a soft, moist mattress. Faro picked out a sleeper with a dirty felt hat pulled over his ears and a cigarette stub hanging from the corner of his mouth. Faro jumped over him, kicked him, and grabbed his hat. The man snorted and turned over, catching his cigarette stub in the folds of his chin.

Doug, who was a little crippled, dropped behind Faro. Faro didn't mind; he quickened his stride and tossed the hat through a broken window. Doug fell further behind and asked Faro to slow down. Faro stayed out of the way of the few people that hurried past him. A fallen road lamp barricaded the street, already littered with the rusting remains of automobiles. Faro walked slowly, watching for glass. A splinter could easily cut through his worn soles.

"When we going to be back?" Doug asked. "I couldn't eat last night. No food. I got to try to get food. Can we get food?"

Faro answered his own questions. "Going to stay together now. Maybe even leave the city. Get food together. But we're going to be what we want, anything we want, everything. It's never going to be like this anymore."

"Like what?" Doug asked.

"Like what we are now. If you want to be an airplane, you can be an airplane. Or a piece of wood. You can't do that now, not without help from Dorcas. Going to be different, you'll see."

They found Bennie sleeping on the steps of the Primitive Church of Christ, a squat modern building that seemed to cower between two ten-story apartment houses. Both of the buildings beside the church had been bombed, and the debris rested on the church roof: piles of burnt gargoyles.

Bennie's smart to stay in the open, Faro thought, remembering a time when he was trapped in a basement. He counted four escape routes.

"I'm not coming," Bennie said.

"Why not?" Faro asked, but Bennie only stuck out his tongue and gave him the finger.

"Come on," Doug said in a whine.

There would be no sense arguing with him, Faro thought as he turned around and started to walk away. Doug would follow. Bennie's strong, Faro thought, fighting down an urge to turn around. But that would spoil it. Bennie was shouting good-natured obscenities at them and making squealing noises.

Faro blocked out everything behind him, including Doug, and concentrated on his heels clicking on the pavement. Doug drew up next to him, his limp more exaggerated than usual. He chattered away, smiling, then frowning.

Faro imagined that he was pulling Bennie down the church steps by his testicles. He squeezed harder and chanted, "By the balls, by the balls," under his breath, as he tried to spark something inside himself. He felt a rush of power; his face flushed. Bennie screamed and bounced down one step.

"Then, get off your ass and come on," Faro thought. Doug was screaming, but Faro was not listening. He gave a twist, and then another, but Bennie had worked up his own power and held his ground. Bennie was mouthing obscenities, his eyes closed in concentration. Faro tried again, but Bennie was too strong. But that's wrong, Faro thought. I'm supposed to be stronger. Now Dorcas would have to get him later. Faro tripped Doug and, ashamed of himself, helped support his weight for a few blocks.

They found George playing in the mud.

They found Alan dead, his head severed.

I'll have to make up for Alan, Faro thought as he left Alan's building and crossed the street, passing a grocery and an elevator garage. But Dorcas had told him that he would find new people.

"Alan told me that some kids live in there," George said, pointing at the garage.

"When did he tell you that?" Faro asked.

"The last time we were all together with Dorcas. He told me to tell you, but I forgot. I don't know why he wanted me to tell you, usually he makes me tell Dorcas things."

Faro grinned and walked into the garage. He heard a noise above. There was a slight echo. Faro looked for stairs, but it was difficult to see in the dim light. Faro noticed that part of the first tier had collapsed and cars were piled on top of each other. Faro heard a loud giggle and called out. His voice echoed and he shouted again. A pause, and then another giggle, a laugh. Faro found a metal ladder bolted to the wall. He yelled a few more times and followed the giggles to the third tier, where he found a boy and a girl, twins, sitting in a car. They had found a car with a workable battery and were listening to the static on the radio.

The twins, Sal and Sandra, followed Faro quietly down the ladder. Faro introduced them to Doug and George and quickly forgot their names. He didn't like them; they made him nervous, especially the girl. She was still undeveloped, he thought. He pushed both of them out of the way as he walked out of the garage. He decided to ignore the girl, even though she had a pleasant scent. He would use it to cover up bad odors.

After they left the garage, Doug and George became very quiet and tried to keep up with Faro. The twins walked behind Doug, grinning at him when he turned around, and chanting, "Step and a half, Step and a half, we're marching behind Step and a half." Doug's limp became more pronounced. Faro did not try to stop them.

Three stops for the girls: Sue could not be found. Faro would have to make do with someone who looked like Sue. He would have to remain in Sue's neighborhood until he found a substitute. Faro tried a few apartment buildings and an old cellar café operated by some gang girls from his own neighborhood. Doug and George remained behind for support; the twins kept drifting away. Faro found a few girls in a small bowling alley. They had found a bottle of whiskey in the backroom bar. Faro plucked the drunkest from the group and named her Sue. She insisted that her name was Nan, but Faro would not believe her. Her features were already changing; soon she would look exactly like Sue, then she would be Sue. It's a shame that her hair is falling, Faro thought. He liked long hair. But Sue wore her hair bobbed.

Doug went ahead to find Fenny, since he had a crush on her. Fenny's hair was the same color as Doug's; they could weave their hair into a red basket when they made love, Faro thought. But Doug wasn't old enough for such things: Faro would soon have to show him.

Faro ducked into a hallway and waited for Fenny and Doug. George followed him. The twins played in the street, oblivious to the people staring at them, some of them wearing gang jackets. Faro did not recognize the emblems on the street boys. By the time Fenny and Doug returned, holding hands and smiling, a few boys were teasing the twins. The twins looked around, but did not turn. A boy with short black hair threw a rock at Sandra and hit her squarely in the face. Sal just stared at the boy and tried to smile.

Faro ran into the street shouting and grabbed the twins. He ran down the street, paying no attention to the shouts behind him. He blocked out everyone but the twins. A piece of metal flew past his head. He tried to make everything behind him heavy. He slowed everyone down, and then remembering, opened a path for Fenny, Doug, and George.

They did not stop running until Doug collapsed.

"That was stupid," George said, wiping his face with his hands and then running them through his gray hair. "You ran right out in the middle of them. You should have gotten killed."

Faro's face flushed. He had to bring the twins back for Dorcas; he had already lost Alan and Bennie. It would be better to be used up by the gang than go back without them. "You were just as stupid. You followed me out there."

George whispered, "I didn't want to be alone," but Faro heard it and chuckled.

"Chickenshit." Faro felt better. He slowed down and walked with Doug and Fenny. The twins stayed behind. Sandra's face was cracked and bleeding, but nothing was broken. A stream of blood oozed from her nose. Sal would periodically wipe it with his hand.

"You know what I want to do?" Faro asked Doug, ignoring Fenny, who was trying to be noticed. Doug shook his head. "I want to suck on Dorcas' toes."

"How come?"

"I don't know." Faro could feel everyone around him. They were all quiet. He blocked them out, anyway. "She's got six toes on her right foot. One kind of comes out the side."

Faro wondered how everyone would act together. He was not used to strangers. But Dorcas had said that everything had changed, that anybody would be all right, that she'd know just the same. Faro pretended to understand, but he could only intuit a few things. But Dorcas had told him he was learning fast. She joked that soon he would know too much and she would have to botch him up. Faro wished that Dorcas wasn't so strong.

Sue ran ahead of Faro—Nan's identity was rapidly disappearing—and then slowed down to a walk, wiggling and swinging her arms. Faro could almost see her long hair, although he knew that it was short now. She even has bumps, Faro thought. For an instant she reminded him of Dorcas, but that shouldn't be, Faro thought.

Dorcas had said that she thought up Faro first. Faro insisted that he had thought up Dorcas. Then Faro thought up Bennie, which at the time made him feel better about himself. He was worried about Bennie's strength. Bennie then probably thought up Doug, although there was something wrong about that. Maybe Dorcas thought up Nan to be Sue, just for the fun of it. Where was the real Sue? It didn't matter now, Faro thought as he looked at the girl walking in front of him. The last vestiges of Nan had disappeared; this Sue was the same as the other. He wondered if she had six toes, also. He glanced at her feet, but she was wearing leather shoes instead of the sandals that Dorcas liked to wear.

It would be a long walk to Dorcas' basement, especially now that more people were on the streets. Soon the road would become too crowded and Faro would have to find new paths to skirt the strangers. As they walked uptown, the air rapidly became stale. It became hazy and more difficult to see. George began to cough and Doug had a severe fit of vomiting. Although Faro found it difficult to breathe, he liked the bad air; it kept people from the streets. Everything had become soft and fuzzy; the only reminder of sharpness was the stinging in his nose and throat. Faro coughed up some phlegm dotted with blood. He could see some lights ahead, yellow blobs hanging in the afternoon dusk. "Probably protected neighborhoods," he thought.

Faro found a dead water rat when he stopped to catch his breath. It had been freshly killed and was only partly mutilated. Faro circled the area and found an underpass. Crouching in the darkness, cooling themselves in the dampness, they ate the animal. There was no time to cook the dark, bloated rat, but no one seemed to mind, except Doug, who could not keep it down. Faro saved a few pieces for him—Doug could cook them later.

Sue sat down beside Faro and said, "I don't need makeup to be beautiful." She pressed her face against his. Faro recoiled at the sound of her loud voice. He imagined it cutting through the dull fog and reaching unfriendly ears. Faro told her to shut up, but she only laughed louder.

"And I can wear a bra if I want, see? And I have six toes."

Her image wavered. She was turning into Dorcas, her mouth a sneer. Faro stood up quickly and everyone laughed. Dorcas was erasing Sue's face, as Sue had erased Nan's, only faster. Her skin became brittle, then fell away to reveal new flesh underneath, full of pocks and scars.

It was Dorcas: red hair framing her face, two missing teeth, a mole at the corner of her mouth, long oval eyes that didn't seem to blink. Yet there was still something missing. Did Dorcas really look like this? Faro asked himself. He remembered short-cropped hair and a smooth, dark face. And she had larger breasts than that. She was at least fifteen. This Dorcas was younger, although she was starting to bloom and knew how to exaggerate her sexuality.

Faro turned and looked at Doug, who was standing near the opening of the underpass. He looked different than he had a few moments ago. A small boy holding a paper bag was standing beside him. His head was half shaven and he was missing a front tooth. He was wearing pants that were much too large for him.

"That's Stephen," Dorcas said. "We haven't made him into anybody special yet, but we will." Dorcas told the boy to sit down. He sat down on his haunches and played with some pebbles. "Don't worry," Dorcas said, taking off her shoes and exposing her toes. "It was easier for me to meet you here. It would have been a long walk to my basement and this is a safe place and we're all together. Anyway, you can't breathe uptown and there were a lot of fights near my basement, big ones, too."

"But you don't look the same," Faro said.

"Neither do you," Dorcas said as she drew an imaginary line across his face with her index finger.

Faro felt his face. It was fleshier than he remembered, and his ear-lobes were smaller.

"And you're the same person. Right? Anyway, we're going to paint ourselves up." She took a small package out of her pocket and laid it on the ground. "There won't be many people along this way; the slum clans are pushing everybody east."

"But what about us?" Faro asked.

"They started farther over; they missed us. Anyway, we've got Bennie."

"Where?"

"Stephen can be Bennie," Dorcas said. "He'll make a good Bennie. And Bennie knows everybody, you know that."

"But that's not Bennie. He doesn't even look like Bennie. And anyway, Bennie only knows a few of those people. If there's trouble, it won't make any difference."

"Of course it will. And that's Bennie." His features had begun to change. Dorcas took five colored bottles and a small paintbrush out of her package. She unscrewed the caps and placed them beside each bottle. "First the red—that's my favorite color." She painted her upper front teeth red, carefully wiped the brush on her dungarees, and dipped it into the green, then the blue, yellow, and black. The lacquer dried quickly on her teeth, but the colors bled into each other and created strange shapes in her mouth. She passed the brush to Doug, who kneeled over the bottles, decided on green, and painted the outside and inside of his teeth. But he used too much black for effect and as a result became toothless.

"Now you'll really have trouble eating," Dorcas said. Everyone laughed except Fenny and Faro. "You'd better paint them again." She dipped the brush in yellow and handed it back to Doug.

Faro was brooding, waiting for Dorcas to notice him. She would have passed him the brush first, but she was angry. Why should he paint his teeth, anyway? he asked himself. Should he paint them blue as the sky and then have to eat cotton to satiate himself? Or black like Doug's and lose them? Or green like a salamander crawling through the grass? But Faro could not remember what a salamander looked like; he could only remember the animal book where he had seen a picture. Why should he do it?

"Because we have to be everything. If we want, we should be able to be anything." Dorcas sat down, legs crossed, in front of Faro. Faro wanted to squeeze her breasts, but she was too strong to touch. "You're different now than you were before," she said. "Look at your ears. Where are your cauliflower ears? You didn't like them so you changed them. Right? And remember that old movie we rigged up at the Strand? You wanted scars, just like that guy, remember? Now you have them all over your face. But that's not much of anything. Just a few little changes. But with the paint you can be anything; you don't have to be people. That's the next step. I could be that piece of stone over there, or dirt, or that broken pencil. I could be that rock and never get older or that beetle Fenny's stepping on."

"But you don't need paint to do that. You said you could do it."

Dorcas smiled. "But you do. Try it." She gave him a bottle of blue lacquer. "Use your finger. Make your teeth blue, so when you open your mouth in the day, you'll have a tunnel right through your head into the sky."

Faro rubbed the paint on his teeth. It was sticky and wouldn't rub off his fingers. He allowed his fingers to stick together and pretended that he was wearing mittens. His hands began to sweat.

Doug and Fenny were jumping around, glaring at each other with new teeth, and making faces at Bennie and George. Bennie was afraid of the paint, but Dorcas assured everyone that he would be all right in a little while. Faro tried to quiet everyone down, but Dorcas announced that no one could hear them because they were surrounded by an invisible shield. She had heard about that on a TV tape. Doug thought they were trapped inside the shield, but Faro didn't think it mattered.

It was late afternoon. The underpass was cool. Faro still had difficulty breathing, but he had stopped coughing blood.

"Do you have more paint?" Fenny asked, holding an empty bottle of lacquer. She had left Doug to vomit by himself and paid no attention to his whimpering.

Dorcas shook her head and said, "If we need paint now, we'll make it ourselves. We'll make it out of air—we all know what we want to look like."

Dorcas moved closer to Faro. She rubbed his leg and picked at his scab. "I had a funny dream," she said. "I dreamed about an evil little animal that looked like a snake and had horns and ate all the other animals. But then God came from four corners—or maybe he was four gods—and gave rebirth to all the dead animals."

"I want to to be one of the gods," Bennie said, swinging his brown bag back and forth.

"Then, paint your teeth," Dorcas said. "Then I dreamed I went to Heaven, where everyone was dancing with their clothes off; and I went to Hell, where angels were doing good deeds. And then—I don't know how I got to this part of the dream—a lot of small animals scared me, and then they grew tremendous and one of them ate me. And then the animal became a small mouse and was penetrated by worms, fishes, and human beings. That represents the four stages of the origin of mankind."

"Where are we now?" Bennie asked. He had painted his teeth like a barber pole.

"I guess we're up to the fishes," Dorcas said.

"I want to be one of the gods and give rebirth to all the dead animals," Bennie said.

"Me too," Fenny said.

Everyone wanted to be a god; but Dorcas would have to choose, because it was her dream. She pointed at herself and then at Faro, who was smiling. She asked Bennie for his brown bag, which had become soggy, and told him that he could not be a god yet; he would have to wait until his features changed. She pulled out Alan's head from the bag and, holding it by the ears, showed it to everyone. "Bennie collected it on his way over here, kind of as a penance. But it will still take a while, Bennie." She placed the head against the wall and folded the bag neatly beside it. "And one more god to go, but we'll have to wait. We've got a lot of things to do before then, anyway."

"I want to be a god too," Fenny said.

"You've got to be other things first, maybe a spirit," Dorcas said.

Faro touched Dorcas' toe and imagined that the underpass was a cave, silent and cool, with a narrow waterfall splashing down one side.

"No," Dorcas said, "you're doing it wrong. You've got to be things, not just think them around you. Like this. . . ."

And Faro disappeared into the craggy walls, splashed into the water, cooled inside the clay below the cave, and spread under the children, enjoying their body heat. He shook in the spray from the waterfall and examined the smooth rock behind it. He counted out the length of his cave, memorized the play of light on the walls, then on his body. He learned the surface, then dropped below to examine the bones and dirt. He cut his finger on an Indian flint, sunk lower, found some larger bones. The bones support the mud, he thought. He spread out his hands and pretended he had no flesh.

"That's right," Dorcas said. "From now on this is a cave. And you can only get out from there." She pointed at Faro. "Everybody's got to think this is a cave for it to work. No one can hurt us in here." As she described the cave to the other children, it changed. She pointed out how the light should play on the waterfall. The waterfall turned bright green and the walls became luminescent. Faro felt a chill: the cave had become very damp.

"But I'm still hungry," Doug said, "and we're trapped in here, unless we get out through Faro. And we can't see the sky unless Faro's mouth is open. And it's closed."

"Then, we'll make an animal," Fenny said, "and make you all better." She stood up and nodded to Dorcas, obviously pleased with herself. Dorcas was silent.

"If I eat something good, I'll stop vomiting," Doug said. "What kind of animal do you want to make? Something that lives in caves? Like a bear? Or an eel?"

"I've never seen a bear," Fenny said.

"How about a dog?" Faro asked. "Dogs are good." Everyone laughed. Faro scowled at them, but they only laughed louder, their lips drawn back from painted teeth.

"What's so funny?" Faro asked.

"Your mouth," Fenny said. "When you open it, we can see right outside the cave. Your mouth's a hole in the ceiling."

"Does anyone want to be the dog?" George asked. "That would make things a lot easier."

"Shut up," Dorcas said. "We'll make a dog, like Faro says. What kind of dog do you want, Faro? Big, gray one with lots of meat?"

Faro nodded, careful not to open his mouth.

When Faro yawned, Dorcas climbed out of the cave and stood on top of it. Faro could see yellow flecks in her hair when she shook her head. He could also see that her dungarees were torn at the crotch. He used Sandra's odor to mask her sweet smell. Everyone crowded around Faro. Sandra touched him as Sal whispered something to himself. Each time Faro would close his mouth, Dorcas would scream and everyone would laugh, especially Fenny. Faro could not keep his mouth open much longer.

"O.K., here it is. Get ready to catch it," Dorcas shouted. She dropped the dead mongrel through the hole and Faro jumped aside, shutting his mouth. The dog looked like a German shepherd, but for an instant Faro thought it was something else. He put the image out of his mind. The dog's fur was ash gray, and gray whorls mottled the pink flesh of its tail. A geyser of blood spurted from its chest, staining its fur and forming tiny puddles and streams on the rough stone. The dog was large enough to feed everyone twice, Faro thought. George examined its ear with his finger.

"Well, open your mouth," Dorcas shouted. "I don't want to stand out here all day."

Faro opened his mouth and yawned; Dorcas jumped on top of the dog, a felt hat in her hand.

"Where'd you get that?" Faro asked.

Dorcas smiled and said, "I found it on top of the cave. There are lots of things there: stones, bullets, birds, monsters, cans, chewing gum, cigarettes. See?" She put a cigarette butt in her mouth and let it dangle on her lower lip. "You know who I am now, don't you?"

Faro did not want to look at Dorcas. She was too strong. She was influencing the rest of the children, distorting the shape of the cave, canceling and creating new forms and noises. Faro knew that she would look like the bum he had jumped over and kicked in the alley. Faro remembered the cigarette dangling from the bum's mouth, catching under his chin when he turned over.

When everyone had finished eating, Dorcas pulled the derelict's swollen head out of the heap of animal remains and displayed it to the children. Then she laid it down against the wall beside Alan's head. Doug screamed, "I didn't eat that, I didn't eat that." The twins, paying no attention to Doug's shouting, asked Dorcas where it came from. Dorcas ignored them. She put the felt hat on the head and pushed the cigarette butt between the lips.

Faro noticed that the bones strewn around the cave were growing larger. He watched the dog's scapula, gnawed clean and thrown into the refuse heap, mutate into a human pelvis. Dorcas told Faro not to worry about it: they were now past snakes.

Dorcas tried to make the heads talk to each other, but the twins shrieked when Alan's mouth began to move. The froth clung to his teeth as they chattered, forming intricate white spider webs. Faro stopped further conversation by dropping the brown bag over Alan's head.

Faro was tired; he moved to the far end of the cave and fell asleep. He could hear whispers, George's high-pitched laugh, water trickling down the wall. Dorcas lay down beside him and was soon asleep; she had said that she needed to dream. Faro opened his mouth and dreamed he was looking through the opening in the top of the cave. He watched the gray sky turn dark blue, then black. He had forgotten clouds, but it was too late, stars were flickering above him. He tried to count them, but they dimmed and turned into fog. The fog passed through the opening, filling the cave. Faro quickly closed his mouth, but some of the mist settled on his face. He awoke coughing.

Dorcas moaned and threw her arm over Faro's chest. Her skin was pale and droplets of perspiration clung to her jaw. Saliva formed at the corners of her mouth as she shook her head back and forth. Faro watched her dream. Gray birds grew out of her skin, flapping their wings wildly, cawing and pecking at each other. They covered Dorcas completely, although occasionally she would shake them off her arm.

We'll probably leave in the morning, Faro thought, relieved. He fell asleep quickly and dreamed that swarms of gnats obscured all the stars above him except one: a bright, twinkling light. He could not shut the stars out; he was snoring, his mouth open for air. Faro could feel Dorcas watching him. And the flaming yellow star grew larger as it fell toward him. It crashed through the opening and embedded itself in his mouth. Dorcas giggled but told him that it was a good dream. But the dream continued: All the other children burned up except Dorcas, who was sitting before the fire in a new dress.

Dorcas woke everyone up the next morning. Faro took it as a compliment that she was wearing the dress he had dreamed about.

Dropping the derelict's head into a bag, she said, "We're moving today. We can take the cave with us. All we have to do is think about it when we need it. We're going to practice being spirits and becoming other things and being a part of everything."

"Am I going to be a god, too?" Bennie asked. He was trying to chip the enamel paint off his front tooth, but it would not come off.

"No," Dorcas said, "but you'll be a spirit. There can only be four gods, and that's me, Faro, and Alan—'cause he was dead, and the bum —because you ate him." Doug started screaming that he didn't eat the bum, but Dorcas ignored him. "Everybody else can be a spirit."

"Which way are we going?" Faro asked Dorcas.

"That way," she said, pointing her finger toward an overhead highway ramp. "Downtown."

"But that's dead people down there."

Dorcas did not reply, but Faro started to walk. She's too strong, Faro thought. Dorcas dropped behind Faro and gave the bag of heads to Sandra. Each time one of the heads said anything, Sandra would howl and drop the bag. They soon became silent. Sandra tried to give the bag to Sal, but he refused to carry it.

Faro led the way, and Dorcas walked with Fenny, followed by Doug, George, and Bennie. The twins were last; they mocked and chided everyone but Faro and Dorcas. Doug was the butt of most of their jokes, because he was crippled.

By habit, Faro kept to the back streets, but they were more crowded than usual. The main avenues, with their traders and police gangs, would be faster and more fun, but they were also more dangerous. Faro walked near the edge of the curb, looking for cigarette butts; there were none to be found. He had to cross the street a few times to avoid fights, but they were small ones. The other children stayed close behind him.

As they walked downtown, they encountered more fights. They detoured around a large park that stank of garbage to avoid a mob charging down the street. They were probably Screamers, Faro thought, but he would take no chances: even Screamers could be dangerous.

"Go down that street," Dorcas said, pointing to a street piled with wrecked cars and unused rolls of barbed wire.

"Too dangerous," Faro said. He saw something move in the narrow street. "See?"

"All right," Dorcas said. "Fenny goes to check it out. She's the first one to practice being a spirit. Fenny?"

Fenny nodded and smiled.

"Nothing can hurt you now," Dorcas said. "You just change into something. But you've got to be fast or it won't work."

"I'll go," Faro said, humiliated.

"No. Fenny goes. And we watch. Watch Fenny, everybody."

"But we don't need to go there," Faro said. "We don't need to check it out."

"She needs practice," Dorcas said. "We're gods; we tell spirits what to do. I want to go that way. That's the way we go. You're a god, so watch." Dorcas put her arms around Faro's waist and pressed herself against him. Faro giggled.

Everyone huddled together behind Faro and Dorcas and watched. The few people walking down the street paid no attention to them. Fenny crossed the road, paused, then walked into the smaller street, and after a pause, screamed. A short sallow man had grabbed her arm and was dragging her toward a doorway.

"I can't see," Bennie said.

She screamed again and Doug, finding his courage, ran toward the street.

"That's not right," Dorcas said. "It's not time. But it will have to do. He will make a poor spirit."

Doug reached Fenny, and the man hit him in the face, crushing his nose. Doug fell to his knees, and the man hit him again.

"Don't worry," Dorcas said. "It's just practice. Watch." Faro was having trouble catching his breath.

"We don't have time to wait for him to change," Dorcas said, looking at Faro. "He'll find something and do it himself. That way he'll learn not to be hungry all the time. He's probably thinking something up right now. See, he's turning into the man's hand. He's the fingers. He's touching Fenny. Now he can help her. She's almost all changed."

Faro tried to distort the image that Dorcas was creating, only to test his own power, but she was too strong and he could feel his fingers being crushed in her hand. When everyone was satisfied that Doug and Fenny were all right—and maybe they were, Faro thought—Dorcas nudged Faro to continue the journey.

"Why are we going downtown?" Faro asked.

"We need practice," Dorcas said. "If it's too long a walk, we'll just be gods and spirits and fly . . . if you still want to go on. I'm going to scrunch up this whole city, bring everything together so I can see it. You can get other people from somewhere, but not from here, and fight me. Then we can make wars and intercede for each other."

"What about me?" Bennie asked.

"You'll be a spirit," Faro said, mimicking Dorcas. As he walked, he thought above the cave, how he would like to sleep against its cool, hard walls.

They walked all afternoon. It was very warm. The sun was barely floating on the buildings behind them. Faro saw fewer people on the street, and those he saw were sick with plague. The twins screamed when they saw the first corpse. Soon the streets were littered with decaying bodies. The few people that passed held handkerchiefs against their faces. They passed a mound of bodies in front of a barbershop. The stench was unbearable; Faro tried to conceal it with Sandra's odor, but it didn't work. He watched a man, jumping over bodies, disappear around the corner. Faro turned around, his hands pressed against his nose and mouth, but could not see the twins. Everyone else was coughing and getting sick except Dorcas, who seemed pleased.

"We'll stay here," Dorcas said, pointing to an alley leading off the secondary street they were on. "Plague is working well. It's making me an army. Remember," she said to Faro, "you've got to get yours somewhere else, if you can get one. You'd better learn to fly. This is just like my dream."

"Where're the twins?" Faro asked.

Dorcas ignored his question. "I'm hungry," she said.

Everyone thought up the cave and crept in while Dorcas imagined an animal for them to eat. Once in the cave, they were safe. The smells of the dead streets disappeared. Dorcas told Faro to open his mouth. She jumped through the opening of the cave and looked around. It was gray outside. She dropped two rabbits through the opening and followed them. They were already skinned and ready to eat. They were very large, too much for everyone to eat now, and had orange eyes like a cat. Their fur was gray and their rattails were pink and covered with spikes.

"I think that's what they're supposed to look like," Dorcas said. "If you touch the tails, you can get poisoned."

Faro watched the twins' shadows wavering around the large pieces of meat. He could see Sandra's shadow drifting above the smaller piece; he could almost detect her odor. This time Faro decided he would not eat, although he was suddenly hungry.

"Don't worry," Dorcas said. "The twins are all right. They're hiding inside Bennie's face. See? The bald side is Sal, and the side with hair is Sandra. They're staying with Bennie for a while."

Faro could see the twins in Bennie's face. They were both trying to talk at once, contorting Bennie's mouth, changing his facial expressions as quickly as his muscles would allow. But Faro could recognize Bennie's tiny, trapped eyes staring at him. The odor of fresh meat reached Faro and he sucked in his cheek.

This wasn't even the real Bennie, Faro thought. He might even change again. Faro looked at Bennie's face, but the twins had disappeared. Bennie stuck his tongue out at him and giggled. It didn't matter, Faro thought. He sliced off a piece of meat and sat down beside Dorcas. George sat down against the far wall and talked with Bennie and the twins.

Dorcas, her eyes closed, talked about giving birth to all the dead animals and making her army. As she talked, she dissolved the cave. Faro choked on the bad air. While Faro was coughing, she stood up and said, "I'm going to look for the heads. Since the twins disappeared, I can't find them."

It was dusk. Faro watched her stepping carefully over the bloated bodies, her head down, looking for a familiar face. In the dusk light, the bodies looked like ivory figures, not yet yellowed by age. Only Dorcas looked like an ancient piece of tusk, her brown skin contrasting nicely with the corpses. Faro watched her bend down, almost becoming one of the corpses, then move on again.

Bennie sent George out to help her. "She said I could before," Bennie said. "Anyway, he's got the plague, or will have it soon. Dorcas won't find those two heads. She's not even looking for them."

"Then, what's she doing?" Faro watched George fall in the street.

Bennie smiled and took off his saddle shoes, revealing six toes on his right foot. The sixth toe, swollen and without a toenail, overshadowed the little toe, which was perfectly formed. Faro looked at the toe, his face against the cooling cement. "But Dorcas is out there looking for missing heads."

Bennie laughed. His image wavered. He was turning into Dorcas. Dorcas deftly erased his face and substituted her own. "No I'm not," she said. "But Bennie's out there. And he's really dying, just for the fun of it. Not like George, who just falls down. Bennie's not trying to change into anything else, because he knows I'll resurrect him soon, anyway." With a shrug, Dorcas assumed her own shape.

Faro pressed his face against the cement, but he could not stop himself from moving toward Dorcas' foot. He tried to assume a fetal position, but she straightened him out. Dorcas was giggling and, for effect, changing into Bennie.

"But we have to decide who's going to be good and who's going to be bad," Faro said. "You have to wait for me to get an army too. And all those dead bodies are still lying there; you've got to resurrect them first."

As Faro crept closer, his face bleeding from rubbing against the cement, the toe grew larger. Just one look, Faro thought, as he tried to turn around. Bennie was laughing hysterically.

"Go ahead, turn around. I didn't cheat. Take a look."

Faro looked at the corpses, just as dusk was turning into evening. Their mouths were open to reveal painted teeth. He thought he saw one of them move, but it was already too dark to be sure.

AMONG THE MOUNTAINS

1

The men sit on their woven mats in front of the village *dinh* and pray loudly as they wait for ghostly visitations and true signs from their holy ancestors. The silvery *dinh* is the oldest structure in the village and is now used as a longhouse and meeting place for the various clans. Just as their ancestors have done, the men shiver in the night air, gabble, pray, inhale the dark effluvia, and watch the sky.

Like a rainbow, the ring arches across a sky afire with stars and meteors.

"And I will tell you the story again," Vo Kim Lan says to the children who are playing on the mossy lawn that extends from the *dinh* to the pebble garden. The children giggle, smirk, laugh, make terrible faces, and wave their arms at him.

Because of his wrinkled face, the children call him Giay—the paperman who can read and make up stories. He knows all the stories, and every year he makes up more. Every year he invents the world. He renames the gods and mountains and ghosts and demons and has a name for every star. He has renamed the evening star and claims that he can change the heavens with only words. He says that the mirrorlike glitterwings are holy, because they are made of the same silvery stuff as the village *dinh*.

"It was on a night just like this that Tan Ming Hoang, the ruler of the world, called in his sorcerer and ordered him to construct a bridge to the stars," Giay says. He pauses, shifts his gaze from child to child. "And do you know why he wanted such a bridge?"

"I do," says a skinny twelve-year-old named Du. "Tan Ming Hoang was not happy with his world. It was not enough. He wanted Heaven, too."

"That's right," says Giay. "So the sorcerer destroyed the ruler's finest palace and threw the broken pieces into the sky to make the ring you see in the sky tonight. Then he made a beautiful rainbow and told the ruler that it was the road to Heaven. The ruler left for Heaven immediately, but when he reached the sky, he found that he still couldn't touch the stars. He had been tricked."

"What then?" asks a young woman kneeling behind Du. She knows all the right questions. The ceremony is the same every year.

"When Tan Ming Hoang recognized his ruined palace, he let out a shriek and swore that he would kill the sorcerer." Giay pauses, waiting for a proper question.

"But why didn't Tan Ming Hoang kill his sorcerer?" asks Du.

"Because he could not return to the world, for the sorcerer had removed the rainbow which was the bridge to the sky. That is the reason you never see rainbows at night, only the ring. Without a rainbow, Tan Ming Hoang was stranded."

"But he could have just waited for another rainbow," Du says.

"Then he would have had to wait for daylight," says Giay. "But have you ever seen the ring in the day? It is in the sky only at night. You see, the ruler could not return."

"So what did he do?" asks Du.

"He waited, just as he waits now," Giay says. "He's still up there, looking down at us. He hates the world, because he cannot have it. And he hates us. That is why he throws his stones of fire." Giay points to a meteor shower. "Yet the world doesn't burn."

All the children sigh and make *tssing* noises, as they have been instructed to do, and Giay leaves them to the women, who have prepared a special feast for the solstice festival. The children will snack on *banh tet* and *dua hau,* delicious small cakes wrapped in mirror-bush leaves and cooked over an open fire.

Giay has joined the men in prayer. They pray for the wandering souls of the dead. They pray to their ancestors and the beings that make the winds and rain. They ask for dispensation and then they recount the lives of the cross, all this to exorcise the *ma quy*—the evil souls responsible for bad crops, death, and sorrow.

It is altogether a supernatural night, for both adults and children. It is a holiday of the fantastic, where all thoughts and prayers and conversations are directed toward the holy ancestors and the invisible beings that crowd the air.

Bao Lam, a boy of fourteen who is now approaching his manhood, sits beside Giay and prays. He has left the place of his family to study and learn. For almost two months he has not touched the soil with his hands, has not done an errand for anyone but Giay, and—until tonight —has not even talked with his family. If he is to become a sorcerer, this will be the most important year of his life.

So he watches and listens and prays. He tries to remember the names of all the ghosts, spirits, and demons that inhabit the days and nights. Although he has learned Giay's stories and followed some of his magicks, Bao still feels like a baby and a know-nothing. But he understands that he must one day replace Giay as sorcerer, or the village will be taken by *ma quy*, all the crops will die, and his townspeople will be turned into the smoky dreams of demons and forest ghosts.

Bao thinks it is only natural that he should become a sorcerer and follow Giay, for he was born during the equinox, on a clear night when the sky took a bite out of the ring and Charmian and Iras turned coppery red. Ever since he was old enough to understand, he has been told that his birth date was astrologically significant, for just as the ring had been broken, so would he be forced to undergo an uncertain trial.

As the men pray and wave their arms to the invisible spirits, Bao dreams of the outside world. He imagines that "everywhere" is just like the village, only inhabited by different peoples and spirits. But perhaps different magicks work in different places, he tells himself. Although he would like to venture outside the environs of his village, he is afraid, especially now that he knows Giay's prayers and stories.

He knows that if he should have the misfortune to die outside of his village, his spirit would become *ma quy*. By leaving the sacred grounds of his ancestors, he would sever all ties to the world of men. He would deny his ancestors a future—and that, he thinks, would be a terrible responsibility to bear.

But he is curious about the great war—a concept he does not completely understand. He also wants to know more about *moi*, those boys and girls who sometimes came into the village to preach about freedom and unity, the greater family, and the holy trinity of men and soil and state. Although *moi* always spoke in Bao's language, their words were only words. He could understand the meanings of the words but could not make sense of the general concepts.

"Wake up," says Giay, who is already standing. "Iras has lifted into the sky. Our prayers are finished for now. Stand up. Were you sleeping with the spirits?"

His vision still blurred with sleep, Bao stands up and smiles at Giay. They embrace and then walk around, nodding and shouting with the people, as they wait for the women to stoke the fires and prepare the food. Bao tries to hide his excitement under a mask of indifference, for tonight men, women, and children will remain together. The feasting and talking and praying will continue until dawn banishes Tan Ming Hoang's ring from the heavens. Tonight is a night for magicks and spirits. Bao can almost hear ghosts whispering in the wind and chattering in the fires.

"Dunk, dunk, dunk," sing the children as they wave fish-shaped lanterns to ward off noxious spirits. They dance around a *khanh*, a small gong mounted on a thirty-foot pole. Clay bells and colored glass tinkle, and the village becomes the center of the world. The ring and stars and meteors are merely the gaudy lights of the village reflected in the sky.

Bao follows Giay to the edge of the pebble garden, where woven mats have been laid out for them. A pregnant girl with short-cropped hair brings their food: rice covered with golden flowers, sour meats, porkplant, shed yolk, mooncakes, sugarseeds, chao gruel, bo-bread still hot and soggy, and candies that seem to bite the tongue. As tired as Bao is, he laughs and chokes down all his food. The ghosts and spirits and demons are thick in the air tonight, he thinks, and they will be watching how he performs.

After the feast, the men talk, then pray; then they retire to the pebble garden to commune with their ancestors. Bao follows like a dog on a leash. He feels awkward and unsure of himself, especially now that the men look to him to help lead the prayers.

"Don't be afraid," Giay whispers to him. "You are praying to the spirits and your ancestors. Don't pay attention to the stares of old men."

After glimpsing a ghost out of the corner of his eye, Bao leads the prayers with conviction. He shouts, waves his hands just like Giay, smiles, nods to the spirits, and recites all the prayers and proper singsongs. The night goes quickly. By the time Charmian is in the sky, the children are asleep with aunts, sisters, mothers, and grandmothers. They are all safely inside the *dinh*, where washing-bowls and morning wine have been set out on mats for the men.

The men are still praying and talking, although some of the oldest are nodding. But tonight the men must remain conscious to ward off the spirits and *ma quy* that would enter their mouths to take their souls. Bao fights sleep by staring at a *bat quai*, an intricate design painted on a piece of turned wood. His studies with Giay have been rigorous; there has been little time for sleep. As he plays with the wood, turning it over and over in his hand, he wonders when Giay ever finds time to sleep. Giay is an old man, Bao tells himself. Yet, buried inside that old husk is a playful little boy. Bao looks into the concentric lines of the *bat quai*. Draws himself into the design. Imagines that his old age is buried inside him. And with his eyes wide open, he dreams of dragons and numbers. . . .

The blaring of horns wakes the village.

Although the rest of the men entered the *dinh* at dawn, Bao and Giay are still outside, singing the last prayers for ancestors and village spirits. It is early morning and Caesar is driving the purple shadows from the mountains. A few clouds scud overhead, as if trying to escape from the sun.

"*Moi* have returned," Bao says to Giay, but the old man's face retains its fixed expression. Bao watches as the noisy parade makes its way through the village. First come the boys and girls dressed in costumes of black and red. They wave flags and swing incense tapers back and forth. They are followed by other *moi* dressed in festival costume: a black dragon with green paper teeth and orange claws, a great fish with faces peeping out of its gill-slits, silvery sectos hung on the branches of walking trees, a king gator that cannot quite co-ordinate its movements, a hoplite wearing slippers, a hipposaur, and a big polypus with red paper tentacles. Then come young men and women who shout and smile and drop papers that bear the *bat quai* symbol. And then come the trumpeters, who are followed by fabers. The fabers dance and mimic the *moi*. With their short arms and strangely jointed legs, their iridescent scales reflecting the morning sun, and their great golden eyes, they look like human grotesques.

Bao imagines that the fabers are inhabited by demons, and he remembers what Giay had once told him: "Every man—and animal, too —might be driven by ghosts and demons. A demon can enter your mouth as you breathe. Once inside you, it will take your thoughts and force you to live in its dreams. So you must be careful, lest you yawn and find that *ma quy* has stolen your thoughts."

"Why do *moi* parade for us?" Bao asks Giay, who is tweaking his thin, gauzy whiskers.

"The outsiders come to teach us their ways," Giay says, picking up a piece of the *moi*'s yellow paper, which a breeze has carried along the ground. "They think they can show us a new world by dancing about and dropping *bat quai* and singing the variations of the alphabet. But they think that *their* world is the real one. They think only *their* world produces correct dreams. Have you talked with *moi?*"

Bao nods his head.

"Then, you know that they have different dreams. We have no such need for dreams to guide our every action—the demons could do that well enough, if we let them. Their words and dreams are without meaning, just as they are empty. They are phantoms, shadows that can speak and withstand light."

"Then, what do they want with us?" Bao asks.

"They think they can change us and pull us into their dreams," Giay says. "But we will not take new things—new magicks—or we tear away our roots. And our roots are in this ground, not in the neverlands or shadows of the caves. Those other worlds cannot have meaning for us and, if you are to become a sorcerer, you must learn to make *moi* disappear. You must see through them, as if they were demons or *ma quy.*"

"But I can see them," Bao says, watching a young woman dance about. She looks at Bao and smiles, then skips away.

"What do you see?" Giay asks.

"Just what you see. *Moi.*"

"And you know that *moi* are only shadows. What do you hear?"

"I hear songs and shouts and horns and the clanging of bells," Bao says.

"Tell me again what you really see," Giay says as he closes his eyes, and Bao remembers what he has been told about the snakes of time and all the difficult paths to sight. So Bao counts and dreams of dragons and tries to find his own snake of time. He travels in circles, as if following the lines of a *bat quai.* Then he is outside of his seconds and minutes— he has found his snake and is peering into its dreams. The snake dreams of Bao. And time crawls along very slowly.

"Now open your eyes," Giay says. "What do you see?"

Bao laughs and says, "I see shadows."

"And what do you hear?"

"I hear the tinkling of bellflowers and the buzzing of sectos," Bao says as he watches his neighbors leave the safety of the *dinh* and join the parade. Old men and women dance about, as if to the beating rhythms of their strong hearts. Children rush into the melee. They laugh and wave their arms. Although Bao can no longer see *moi,* he senses them as a directing force, a force that will quickly pass through the village and into some impossible world of dreams. Meanwhile, Bao sits and watches and smiles and yawns noisily for his ancestors who might seek passage into his soul.

"Now you can see clearly," Giay says. "What you see with your eyes is not always real. Your mind can see much more clearly." Then Giay stands and walks briskly toward the crowd of dancers. Villagers move out of his way, for he walks like Duc, the blind beggar who brings luck to any farmer who feeds him. Giay turns, both arms outstretched, and shouts for Bao to follow.

Reluctantly, Bao joins his teacher and prays that his eyes will not fail him by admitting false visions and shadows. "Why do we do this?" Bao asks Giay as they weave through the crowd. Bao tries to ignore the phantoms that dance beside him and disappear when he turns to look directly at them. He prays to exorcise the unseen monsters that jabjabb and chitter and sound like stormwinds soughing through windertrees.

"We do this to show our kinsmen that shadows are not people, that they must be ignored, that they do not exist except as false visions inside our heads."

"But no one will pay attention," Bao says. "They will see what they see."

"No," says Giay. "They will see what they want to see, what they must see. Our burden is to lead them in the proper direction."

"And how do you know that direction?"

Giay looks upward, as if to share a joke with heaven, and laughs. "Why, all the ghosts and spirits are shouting the correct answers. Every ancestor of every ancestor points out the same direction. Just listen to them. Look at them."

Bao looks around, and sees that some of the children are already miming Giay. They walk around as if they are blind. Their arms are extended before them. Nut-brown faces smile, as if the very young could reflect the very old. Bao can almost believe that Giay has taken them over, that he is hiding behind their dark eyes and baby faces. Then the adults, taking their cues from the children, become blind to *moi*. Soon Giay and Bao are the center of the group. Once again, the village is its own world, governed by its own laws and spirits.

"So you see," Giay says, "the *moi* are easily defeated by the ghosts of our land. The village is as it was."

Giay and Bao lead the villagers away from the shadows of *moi*. The sun has climbed higher into the sky. Bao looks upward and gives thanks to the spirits that cluster about him, even though they are invisi-

ble. But he looks away from the sun, for Caesar is the blinding eye of
God.

The holiday is over. Magic must give way to work. It is time to return to hutches and fields and paddies. Bao looks past a row of hutches
and imagines that even now women, wearing loose trousers, conical
hats made of silverleaf, and wooden clogs, are working in the rice paddies beside the dinobryon forest which climbs up the steep face of a
mountainside. But somewhere in the mountains is the door-through-
the-world. Giay claims it is a huge cave built by giants. He says that
anyone who steps into the darkness of the cave will find himself back
on earth, the hell that burns forever in cold flames.

Suddenly the sky darkens. Storm clouds appear like phantoms skat-
ing on blue ice. Thunder rolls in the distance. And the villagers run for
cover. Bao looks around, sees only the familiar faces of village folk and
the *moi*-shadows. Time seems to slow down as the world awaits a deluge. It is *mua mura*, the rainy season, a special time to reaffirm the
sacred ties of family, neighbor, and clan.

Then, an instant later, the world collapses. The village is attacked.
Villagers fall to the ground as if playacting. Drops of rain fall like tiny
bombs. Mist seems to be pouring out of the ground. Every sound is
magnified, as if in a dream, but there are only sharp screams and the
crackcrack of rifles.

Another instant and the village is afire. Hutches are burning, their
woven bamboo walls and sarissa roofs swelling into flame, burning with
a popping and cackling, as if ghosts and demons are laughing and
mashing their teeth. Soldiers and fabers dressed in filthy green and
brown uniforms run across the mud, then disappear in the mist. But
the fires they set glow redly in the storm-created twilight.

Bao shakes his head, as if a dream could be broken or thrown aside
by a simple gesture. Demons are running around, burning, shooting,
raping girls and women in the open, in the mud and rain. But *moi* are
also falling. *Moi* are killing *moi*, Bao thinks. They are only men, Bao
tells himself, surprised that he is lying on the ground under cover of
rotbush and crying-vines. He tastes the bitter soil and wonders if he is
hurt or dying.

He watches the pregnant girl, who had brought him his dinner,
being raped. Help her, he tells himself, but he is frozen. He cannot
move a finger, and he has wet his pants. He cries, then breaks out of
his fright, stands up, and rushes toward the *moi* and the shrieking girl.

The girl stops screaming. Perhaps she's dead, Bao thinks. He feels he is trapped in a dream of slow motion.

He wrests the rifle from the *moi* and shoots the demon in the head. But it isn't a demon, he tells himself. It isn't even a man, just a boy with a shaved head. The girl beneath the dead *moi* does not move, does not even seem to notice Bao. Her hair is full of mud, and her face is bleeding. Bao sees that her nose is broken.

Get out of here, he thinks as a fusillade of shots breaks the momentary calm. The air smells sour. The downpour is over. A light drizzle falls from an angry gray sky. Soon the mist will lift. Bao shivers and sees that his rain-soaked overshirt is spattered with *moi* blood.

He stands up, looking for Giay, forgetting for an instant about the attack. But Giay is nowhere to be seen. Perhaps he's dead and demons have carried his body into the sky, Bao thinks. He dreams, then remembers where he is, and runs. He runs across the pebble garden and past burning hutches and trees, past the well-kept shrubs and Venus Mirrors, which smell sweet and heavy. Dead bodies litter the ground. Bao hears commands barked in a familiar tongue. *Don day. Durng lai. Tuan lenh khong toi ban.* But the tones and accents are wrong. The words are slurred, as if spoken by drunken men.

But Bao does not think about orders or bodies or burning hutches. He has forgotten Giay, the pregnant girl, the dead *moi*, the smells of death and feces and urine, the fusillades of shots, the rain, the mist, the screams. He thinks only of his family. Perhaps they are alive. His family had left the solstice celebration early. They did not even eat with their neighbors, for Giay had told them that Bao would lead the last prayers. From now on, Giay had said, Bao could have no family but the village.

The sky begins to clear. The mist lifts, disappears as if it had never been.

Bao runs blindly, and the universe lets him pass. He feels he has already lost his soul to some *ma quy* that is too powerful to be exorcised. He imagines that he is a shadow, no better than *moi*. Perhaps that is why *moi* can't see me, he thinks. But he tells himself that he is being prepared for something else. Just as the ring was eaten by the sky when he was born, so must the path of his life be dark and difficult. But why must my path to the cross lead me home? he asks the imagined spirits of the air.

He skirts the rice fields and smells the swamp-stink of stagnant water. He imagines that he has become two beings. One being watches the other. It talks, tells the other being that time is still passing. The other being listens and screams.

Bao sees his house, a medium-sized hutch built of sarissa, wood, and mud. It overlooks a canal that irrigates the adjacent rice paddy.

He runs across open land dotted with sarissa and Christmas memory. It has become a beautiful morning. The sun has burned away the clouds, the sky is a cool blue, and the sectos are buzzing as if to prevent the world from going dumb. Bao is trapped in a pastel dream where spirits rule kindly and the sun always shines.

But when he enters his hutch, he finds his mother and father and sister hanging upside down from a ceiling truss. His mother and sister are naked. They are all bound with brown rope. And they are all, clearly, dead. Light beams cut into the darkness like yellow swords.

He sits down on a woven mat before the hearth. Cooking utensils have been strewn over the hard-packed dirt floor. Bowls are broken, bark baskets torn apart. The cramped family room is heavy with body stink and the sweet smells of gravy oil, mooncakes, sugarseed breads, bamba peels, glazed meat, shed yolk, roasted carryseeds, wine, and milk-liquor. Four places have been set before the hearth, each with wiping cloth, eating sticks, and a painted bowl. One of the settings is for the wandering spirit who brings good luck, long life, and happiness. Bao tries not to look at the wood-plank bed on the other side of the hearth. The reed pad is soiled with blood. But the altar is in its proper place against the wall. It seems that *moi* did not wish to antagonize the spirits of the hut.

Taking the food sticks in his hand, Bao makes a blessing over the food and begins to eat. With every mouthful of festival food, he feels more removed from the apparent world of cause and effect. And he descends, as if through the scrim layers of a gentle dream, to a synchronistic universe. He drifts backward, only to be swallowed by the snake of time. Now he finds everything is just as it should be. He is in perfect harmony with *yin* and *yang*, the two opposing forces of the universe. He is easily transformed. He dreams that the universe is a wheel. Every event must repeat itself in slightly different form. Flesh and spirit are themselves movements of the great wheel.

He watches as all the cycles reveal themselves. He feels possessed by Heaven's will. I must remain here in this house, he tells himself. Then he prays to the spirits of the dead and the not-yet-here, to the monsters and ghosts of the past, and the growing spirit-creatures of the future. Bao sees only with his mind. He falls into his past, dreams that he is eating and talking with his family. He has captured all the familiar smells and words, all the textures of time past. If I can feel the past as the present, then I have turned the wheel, he tells himself. I have truly left this cycle and journeyed to a gentler time.

But his eyes betray him. He finds himself staring at the dead bodies of his mother and father and sister. They have become empty husks; their spirits have escaped from their open mouths. Bao has not been watchful. He has lost their souls. They have drifted away to become *ma quy*.

With a scream, he stands up and pummels his father's corpse with his fists. He screams for death, for its bone-crushing touch, and hopes that *moi* will hear him and end his life right now. A timely death would be the perfect resolution. Perhaps he can still join the spirits of his family.

Bao sits down in front of his father, then retreats into gentle dreams. He looks at his father's upside-down face and imagines that the hutch is filled with sympathetic spirits. They make the air heavy. They smell of grass and sweat and night effluvia. They have the faces of his family.

"*Remain here,*" says his dead father without moving his lips. Bao ignores the spirit voice inside his head. It might be a demon or false spirit trying to trick him.

"*You must listen to your father,*" says his dead mother. "*Your path must end here. You must remain with us, for only through you can we have any spirit life. You close the circle of our existence. Together, we are like the great wheel. We belong to you now. And you belong to this house, to the soil and the wood and sarissa, and to every ghost in the air.*"

Bao understands that death must not be an end, but a transition. He remembers Giay's words: "Man is a breeze, stilled only by death. Then he becomes like the earth. But the earth is sacred and must be maintained by prayer. Each generation must sing the same prayers, or our ancestors will be cut off from the world."

"*You cannot leave,*" says Bao's father. "*Your past and future lie here.*"

"*You must provide for your ancestors,*" says his dead sister. "*When we are buried in sacred soil, we will not be able to follow you. You must not leave.*"

"*You must provide,*" sing the spirits.

"No," Bao says to the dead. He steps out of the hutch and shouts, "Where are you, *moi*? I am here. Kill me." The world whispers, but will not listen. Wind soughs through sarissa and highvine. Sectos chirp and buzz. A hipposaur lows in the distance.

Bao walks away from the hutch and the paddies and the village. He does not look for cover. If *moi* cannot kill him, then he will find the door-through-the-world. He will enter the cave built by giants and descend into Hell.

He skirts the edge of Ban Dem Forest, where spruce, pine, willow, and oak create a twilight world for sleeping demons and shadowy ghosts. It is as if the tall trees are waging a slow battle for space and light with the indigenous yellow-crawlers, flatfronds, and the weblike silverfrost. Bao's feet pad upon a soft turf which is a spongy mulch of dead leaves, crawlers, and rot. He cries, hacking out his pain and loss as if they were pieces of raw meat. The forest absorbs his noises. He retreats into the dark world of bough and leaf. The spirits of family and village cannot follow him here. They are lost to him forever. By simple intention, Bao has become *moi*. He has decided to die outside of the village. He has broken the circle and smashed the wheel. And like the circle, Bao is broken. One half of him is rage, the other half is quiet: *yin* and *yang*. The circle is true, even when broken.

Dark forest gives way to scrub and mossy uplands. Bao detours around silvernets that have trapped small winebirds and silver fliers. Forest green has been replaced by the umbers and ochers of high ground. Swarms of smidgins darken the air like storm clouds. They fly toward Bac Mountain, to the door-through-the-world, where all manner of beasts and Hell's monsters are spawned.

It is early afternoon when Bao reaches the crags and sheer rock faces of Bac Mountain. He begins his climb to the roof of the world. He has defected from the world of men. Here, among the mountains, he is less than a demon, more fragile than a ghost. He has lost past and future. All that is left to him is the constant present. But his soul cannot be confined in such a narrow place. As Giay had said, "The soul is a flower made of the very stuff of time. Its soil is the past, its air is the present, its water is the future. If we forget our past, or are blind to our future, then the soul wilts and dies. We become husks without hearts."

Bao climbs until he is exhausted. He has worked his way from ledge to ledge, foothold to foothold. The sun hangs in the clear sky like an angry eye. It watches Bao and saps his strength. There is no shade, no cover for a *moi* climbing into Hell. The world has turned to stone. Below him, the blue-black shadows are as tangible as the blades of butcher knives. Above him is the door-through-the-world.

It takes him an hour to reach the stone lip of the cave. He crawls through a narrow passageway into darkness. Now he can die. The shadow-spirits can take him. He shivers, feels cold stone against his cheek. Gradually, his eyes adjust to the darkness and he sees stalagmite towers in the distance. The cave is aglow with a cold, phosphorescent light. Bao imagines that he has come upon a subterranean city. The rainbow-hued stalagmites and stalactites might be the grotesque dwellings of the dead. He might be bathing in the cold light of Hell.

"I am here," he shouts, and his voice, carried by ghosts and demons, echoes through subterranean halls. But the dead will not answer him. They mock him with his own words. He walks on, through the many chambers of the dead. He is soon lost in the caverns, some of which are completely dark.

He loses his sense of time. He sleeps and walks and dreams. His hunger is a constant, a dull ache he imagines to be his companion. He dreams of his father. He dreams of *moi*, the weapons of God. The caverns are full of scrabbling, chittering life. It is a dark universe of worms and clickers and scuttlers. Reptiles splash in unseen pools and bats shriek for lost spirits. White-winged moths fly overhead like ghosts floating in darkness.

Bao dreams of bright light. He crawls out of the darkness, as if he is stepping out of time. He has smashed the wheel of his life. He falls and vomits. Demons rush out of his mouth.

In his dream, the creatures stand above him and talk. He cannot understand their words. He wonders how long he has been in the caverns. He dreams of his village and begins to shake.

But it is too late, Bao thinks. He is dead, just another *moi*. He dreams that his spirit has already become *ma quy*, a demon wanderer. He touches the edges of his dream and pushes toward the darkness that is either death or empty sleep. . . .

2

Lying in a prone position, Bao Lam peered through a field glass at the valley below. It was as he remembered it, only more verdant and beautiful. The forests were in bloom, their colors so bright that they confused all sense of distance and space. Foreground and background seemed to bleed into each other. As he used to do in his childhood, he counted all the colors of choehoa—the pastel-tinted pseudoblooms. In his old language, the equivalent word for color was light-of-God.

Below him, past the straw-colored rock, below the small brown fists of scrub, the land became a green mat of moss sloping gently downward to meet a forest of saucerleaves. Shiny green and yellow fronds swayed in the wind. Vines of silverglitter reflected the twelve o'clock sun, and Bao could make out a copse of redknob. He turned up the magnification to see if the sweet-smelling plants had attracted any fliers. Seeing that the sticky knobs were covered with rotting carcasses, he quickly looked away. He remembered the stink, the furrowed surface, the sticky ooze of redknob. He remembered the burning sores it had once left on his fingers.

He searched the entire valley with his field glass, carefully scanning an area from right to left, raising the glass and scanning again. When he caught sight of a rice field, he stepped up the magnification and watched several women transplanting rice seedlings. The water reflected the bright colors of the world. Bao imagined that these women were dipping their hands into rainbows.

Although Mun Village was well hidden, Bao knew its exact location. He felt as if he could see through the barriers of flora, past saucerleaves and silverglitter, past oak and yellow-crawlers and scatterbush and high sarissa, right into the sleepy little village which was its own world. This was the heart of Casca Mountain country. Bao knew that this hidden village would look like every other village he had passed through. It was as if he had spent his childhood and the long years of the war in the same village. It was a *ching*-game. He followed his programmed dreams, led dimsimple fabers, watched them die, won villages, lost villages, hid, slept, and fought. He had lost the past and future. He was a blind spirit submerged in a dead present. He had dreams and food and fabers. He was a child of the people.

"Take your group around the rice field and enter the village from the north," Bao said to Le, one of his two command fabers. Le's face had a different structure from the simple soldier's: a high forehead and small crest, a flexible mouth that could form words and express basic emotion. "Call in, and I'll follow with Chi."

Chi, who was a double for Le, remained beside Bao as Le rose and screeched at the company of fabers. The soldiers had grouped behind Bao. They kneeled, as if praying, their large yellow eyes looking blankly upon a world they were not engineered to comprehend.

"So now we wait," Bao said, ostensibly to Chi, but he was only talking to himself. He watched the women in the field through his field glass and tried to ignore Chi and the remaining fabers. As he stared at the women, looking for something unusual, any change in their rooster-walk movement, he felt all the walls of the world separating him from his own kind. These villagers seemed more alien to him than his green stick-figure soldiers. Perhaps, he thought, if I look into a mirror, I would find that I have become a faber. He turned to Chi, who sat beside him and stared ahead, as if into nothingness. The faber's scaly armor was iridescent in the sunlight.

Bao turned his field glass toward the women again and tried to imagine the people of this village. There was time for a *ching*-game. He dreamed of Pi, the image of grace, and he shaped his dream as if he were making love to one of the slender girls working in the paddy. But Pi is composed of Ken, the mountain, and Le, the fire. *Fire at the foot of the mountain: the image of grace.* The dream grew dark as Bao manipulated Po, the inferior forces, and the dreamworld of the girls in the paddy shattered like glass.

"Village clear," said Le's voice amid radio static.

"Take your group and clean out every hutch," Bao said to Chi. Bao did not expect trouble. The mountain people had become passive to the comings and goings of their war of liberation. They had taught themselves not to "see" the enemy. And the few who could be trained to fight changed sides as often as they ate. The war was like a *ching*-game, Bao thought, but it was a game directed by unseen forces, forces Bao could only imagine.

Bao waited and watched the girls working in the field. He wondered what it would be like to have a woman, then shuddered, remembering his mother and sister hanging like carcasses on redknob. But his memory of mother and sister was quickly pushed out of his mind. Almost as quickly as the thought had surfaced, it was forgotten. Bao had no need of such memories; he had *ching*-games to replace the pains of the past. He had the present.

He heard shots, short bursts echoing, as if carried from the village by gleeful demons.

"Ambush." Chi's voice was raspy over the radio.

"Where are they?" Bao asked, speaking into a tiny ovoid communicator. He held the communicator close to his lips, as if *moi* could hear him, as if they were standing right behind him, listening, but afraid to kill him. That would ruin the game.

The static was a barrage of tiny explosions, the quickened sounds of guns and shouting and death. "They have moved back to the silverglitter. I have ten soldiers left. Moving them out."

Bao heard more shots, but he was already moving, directing his remaining fabers. He remained several paces behind the group for safety, but four fabers guarded him, protected him with their scaly bodies, mimed his every action like green shadows born of a dream. But Bao paid them no attention. They were merely a part of his surroundings. They might as well have been walking plants or stones. They lived and died without awareness like simple beasts. They had no past or future, only a present.

The shots had become sporadic. Bao imagined that *moi* had once again left the silverglitter and were carefully cleaning out one hutch after another. Perhaps the *moi* attack was a fluke, he thought. Or, more likely, they had known his whereabouts. *Moi* might be behind him right now, tracking him like silent animals patient for their kill. And Bao knew that nearby a Pindarian missionary was directing the attack. If only I could get *him*, Bao thought.

Bao would not reply to Chi. Perhaps he could still gain some surprise. Walking through the saucerleaf forest that flanked the western edge of the village, he felt that only an instant had passed since he was a child running from his village, from *moi* and demons and family spirits. An instant ago, his life was before him—to learn, conjure, marry, pray for his ancestors and the world. But he had broken the cycle and was now condemned to an eternal, empty present. He thought about the war and this place, and concluded that he understood nothing. He was under the control of demons who wore pink faces and had given him tools and *ching*-dreams. He had all the correct memories and information. He knew every mile of this country, even the places he had never seen.

As if waking from a recurrent dream, he forgot, once again, what it was all about. He could only remember *ching*-games. Everything around him seemed to be in constant motion. The fronds made shushing sounds as he slid past them. The supple saucerleaves were slippery to the touch and veined as if they were great pieces of green flesh. The faber-soldiers moved smoothly through their natural habitat, as if they had never been biologically engineered to be fodder for a war of liberation. The ground was spongy. It was a floral cemetery of dead leaves, humus, twigs, crawlers. Colorful pseudoblooms flourished everywhere, giving a colorful palette to what would otherwise be a monotonous green and yellow world. Bao had a sudden desire to take off his boots and run through the forest in his bare feet.

Bao had thought to surprise the *moi* in the brush, but he could find no sign of *moi*. Everything was quiet. Too quiet, Bao thought. He directed his fabers to enter the village just north of the *dinh*. They "leapfrogged" from hutch to hutch, keeping away from the pebble garden and mossy open ground. Dead fabers and villagers littered the village common area, the place of *thinh hoang*, the village guardian spirit. They looked like wooden figures, spirit-dolls dropped by hungry children called to dinner.

Bao remained behind, using a ramshackle deserted hutch for cover. There were several hutches on the edge of the village which were maintained for lesser spirits. Bao felt the forest's presence, as if it were an enemy staring at the back of his neck. He did not move. He sensed something was about to happen. It was a soldier's sense, a smell, a tickle that became a pressure between his eyes, centered in his pineal.

He recognized Le, who was lying dead in the pebble garden, his arms and part of his chest blown away by a *moi* projectile. Bao began to scan the village with his field glass. And the enemy opened fire on him. He hit the ground. The hutch was in flames. It began to fall, spreading out on the ground, sending out feelers of fire. Bao's fabers returned the fire, and a few *moi* fell. But they were moving toward Bao. He was worth a thousand fabers.

You were sloppy, he told himself as the ground exploded. Yet he felt he had enough time to think and dream. Everything was moving in slow motion. Soon the world would freeze. But right now demons were walking about, tearing the guts out of his town.

His town. That was how he had thought of it. He felt as if he were back in his village. Why not die here? he thought.

"Because we won't have you." A ghost whispered inside his head. It was the memory of his childhood. It was Giay. It was his parents. His ancestors. All dead. All living in the air, wandering because of him. Die, he thought; but, just the same, he crawled back into the forest like a scuttler seeking darkness. His shoulder felt cold and numb; it was oozing blood. Bao wondered just where the bullet had lodged—if it was a bullet. It might have passed right through him. Don't look, he told himself. It doesn't matter. It doesn't hurt yet. You'll go into shock. In shock now. He thought of Giay, imagined that the ghost was crawling before him, motioning him forward.

"You remember how to 'see,'" Giay said. *"You must will* moi *out of*

existence. Push them from your thoughts. Think of the village. That is where your ancestors and friends and family live. The rest is emptiness. Ignore moi-demons."

Bao crawled into the forest, his hands digging into damp, black dirt, his eyes staring ahead at a ghost. He felt the earth's coolness and the weight of a green and yellow world above him. It was as if he were at the bottom of an ocean. He was a water spirit about to fall asleep as he looked up at the seafronds and weeds swaying gently to the silent music of cool, blue water.

You are sloppy, he told himself. And this isn't even your village. The past can't kill me, he thought. My ancestors are *ma quy*. Dead spirits. They'd have no use for a *moi*-soldier.

He remembered his slogans and *ching*-games, which had usurped his past. *Ching*-variations ran in his mind like wheels of words and memories. The wheels turned, sparking familiar slogans.

"You are a child of the people," shrieked the voices inside his head. They drawled out old lessons, reminded him of obligations. And Bao realized that he had never seen a city, although he had dreamed that he was once inside one. He had never taken a fly-by, dressed up, hooked in, read a book, watched a holo, or loved a woman. Memories roiled like smoke from burning hutches. He began to dream, creating a *ching*-game, but he forced himself awake. He reached for memories. He had memories, he told himself. They must count for something. But were his memories real? Perhaps only *ching*-games and dreams were real.

I have seen things, he said to himself. But he could not quite remember what he had seen. He felt as if he had always been in these forests. His life was this land. He had always skulked through villages, fought *moi*, eaten rations, directed fabers, talked to villagers who would not believe his slogans because he was a soldier. He belonged to the land, yet he had lost his village and his ancestors.

When had he last talked to a human being? He could not remember. Yes, he thought. I have talked to. . . . He remembered that he had talked to his fabers.

"You have become a faber," Giay said. He sat in lotus position under a huge dinobryon.

"I'll return to our village," Bao said to the ghost. "I'll pray for my ancestors and become a sorcerer."

"You have no village," Giay said. *"Everyone you know is dead."*

And as Bao fell toward dreamless sleep, he heard Giay say: *"You are already dead."*

"You must not remain here," Chi said, pulling Bao to his feet. Bao's shoulder was bandaged and felt sticky. His chest ached. He felt numbed and tired. He imagined that he was caught in hookervine. He could not move or think. But he was a soldier. And the slogans were still wheeling.

"Report," Bao said. Once again, he felt as if he had two selves. He was two beings, each one fighting for control. His darker, more subterranean self howled gleefully.

"You are approximately fifteen miles west of the village. You have thirty-two soldiers. Le is dead. Wounded were left behind. The soldiers are in spread retreat. I carried you under cover."

Bao looked around but could not see any soldiers, although he was sure they were nearby. They would be well hidden and without uniform. If *moi* happened upon them, the soldiers would be mistaken for natural fabers.

As Chi carried him through dense forest, Bao slept fitfully. He dreamed he was crawling through a dark cave. He dreamed that he could crawl backward into his previous life. "Am I dead?" he mumbled, dreaming of Giay's ghost. He could not remember. Do I have family? he asked himself. Or am I a soldier? Always fighting. Never praying. A child of the state. No, he thought, as if he were caught midway between darkness and light. He dreamed of imaginary places. I do other things, he told himself. I know other things.

"What do I know?" Bao asked Chi. He grabbed the faber's scaly arm, which held him gently. It was cool to the touch.

When Bao awakened, it was dark and humid. The air was still, Charmian was in the sky, and stars shone through the dimly glowing dust of the ring. Bao could make out Orion and the constellations of the Buckle, the Two Fishermen, the Smidgens, the Khanh, the Serpent, and the Ship. He knew the sky; it contained all the shapes of his dreams. It was a silent friend, this resting-place of spirits and ancestors.

Shifting his gaze from the bright night sky, he looked past the cliffs and canyons of Casca country to the Northern Mountains, in the distance. As a child, Bao had been told that friendly spirits had pulled the mountains out of the ground to keep out *moi* and demons. But demons passed through the mountains and took their revenge.

Bao traced his fingers along his shoulder wound. There was still some pain, but he could move about. Nothing had broken. Chi had worried out the bullet and applied fastflesh to quicken the healing process. Bao counted himself lucky that the bullet had not been treated with a sacworm poison or scored so it would explode on impact.

As Bao stared at Chi, he was reminded of a machine that had been shut off until it would be needed again. Chi stood perfectly still, as if he were a great, scaly plant that grew among saucerleaf and yellow-crawlers. Bao understood that the altered fabers were sauroids, and were related to hipposaurs, gators, hoplites, and the huge-winged flying deltasaurs.

"Try control post again, and we'll get moving," Bao said to Chi. Bao was worried. He had not been able to contact control post or base *hai*, which was his assigned recovery area. As he had very few soldiers, he could at least make a reconnaissance of base *hai* and try to discover what was wrong.

Bao looked away as the faber raised the ovoid radio transceiver and began to speak. If Bao did not look at Chi, he could pretend that the faber was human. He needed the illusion that he was not alone. But the faber could not carry on an extended conversation. It could respond to questions and follow orders, and—under certain circumstances—could even initiate action. But the faber had no soul, Bao thought. It was a biological machine with a life only for the state.

If only I had a laser transceiver, Bao thought. But it was enough that he had rations and fabers and weapons. Movement was the key to a guerrilla war. It was the engine of revolution. Each man commanded his own army. He was given an order and an objective. Then he was on his own.

Bao stood up and motioned to Chi to start moving. Chi, in turn, motioned to the soldiers. Although Bao could not see the other fabers, he knew their approximate positions. They were spread out in a wide fan formation. If they were discovered by *moi*, the soldiers would draw the enemy fire while Bao took cover.

As Bao walked through rough country, he listened intently to the night sounds—the scratchings and clickings of sectos, the shushings of breezes through flatvine and saucerleaves, the faraway crashings of white water. A bluebat shrieked and, as if in reply, a mountain-hog howled. Bao imagined that he was working his way through another *ching*-dream, one that he had not experienced before. The world was trying to speak to him. It was full of dream figures. He had only to recognize them. He looked to the north and imagined that the chalky cliffs that formed a long, uneven palisade were a demon's teeth. Beyond the cliffs were mountains shrouded in mist.

Bao kept to rocky terrain which afforded sufficient cover from *moi* and avoided the fieldmoss of open ground. When he reached Nho Forest, he took a last look at the cliffs. He remembered that the meaning of any *ching*-dream depended on the interaction of *yin* and *yang*. And he comprehended his fears. The world had become an enemy that concealed all manner of ghosts and demons. He was afraid of the very ground that protected him from *moi*.

He did not stop to rest until he was out of the forest. Before him was hill country, where he would find mossland, fields, paddies, villages, and, farther west, base *hai*. The cold, gray light of dawn had turned the world into a misty ghostland. Bao waited, and shivered in the dampness. His chest and shoulder still hurt, the pain pulsing as if to keep time with his heartbeat. He could not just take a pill and move on. He would have to sleep. He needed to dream, experience a familiar *ching*-dream, or play the *ching*-game. But he could not find a dream. He was wide awake.

The soldiers sounded the alarm. It was the high whine of the wild faber.

Bao stayed behind as Chi reconnoitered, then followed when the faber waved that it was safe. Chi led him to a mossy rill flanked on all sides by earth elm and Christmas memory, which were fighting an impossibly slow war for space and light. About twenty Dardanian fabers lay dead, as if sleeping on the cool moss under the shade of the trees. They were all wearing the same colors as Bao, except some of the uniforms had been torn open.

Bao was met by their stink, which was almost human—it was the universal smell of death, of rotting flesh and trapped feces. But as Bao examined them, he began to panic, as if this were the first time he had encountered death. Once again, he felt as if he were dreaming. He remembered entering a hutch and finding his mother and father and sister hanging upside down from a ceiling truss. He remembered running across open land dotted with sarissa and Christmas memory. He dreamed that he was going home again.

The soldiers had died of the plague, the great weapon that would end the war and turn all the people into children of the land. Bao had listened to the propaganda. As he understood it, the faber-specific plague would destroy only *moi* fabers. All Dardanian fabers were to be immunized.

Then, why weren't these fabers immunized? Bao asked himself as he stared at them. Their scale-plates had begun to fall away from their flesh, which had turned color. The fabers were bloated. He found ooz-ing sores under their loose scales.

The plague was not supposed to do this, Bao thought. It was just supposed to kill like smoke poison or a bullet to the heart. He felt him-self begin to dream. He could dream, yet remain awake. He had been taught to dream by the state. Just as dreams were supposed to replace dead memories, so would the revolution erase the past.

In the dew-dampness of morning, the world was a new and colorful place. The sun, which had burned its way into a clear sky, was now blurred by clouds skiffing past. Great cumulus clouds soon closed up the sky as they moved like great silent engines made of air. Then lightning shot like chords of gold from cloud to cloud, followed by the crack and crash of thunder. The earth boomed, as if the sky were a tight skin that demons were pounding and trying to tear. And there was a deluge. A mist rose in response.

Bao walked stoically through the rain. He ignored the ache in his chest and shoulder. The wound was healing. When he reached base *hai,* he could rest and sleep while Chi reconnoitered. But now he would use the rain for cover. *Moi* would have difficulty finding him in this downpour.

The storm raged for another hour, then suddenly ended, leaving a mist on the land. Beyond the next rise was base *hai,* the small farming village that had been taken so easily from *moi* last year. When the Dar-danians had directed their forces to the north, the *moi* retreated into the south. So base *hai,* formerly Son La, was now inside the triangle of Dardanian-held country. But the lines constantly shifted. And another *moi* offensive was due.

When Bao stopped to rest, the mist had lifted. The clouds had scud-ded away like frightened white animals. The world was bright and clean. Bao felt the warmth of sun on his face as he gazed at the valley below. A mossy lawn of varying shades of green gave way to furrowed fields and paddies. An irrigation canal reflected the morning sun into a stream of molten gold. Even without a field glass, Bao could make out the village hutches and part of the *dinh.* But something was wrong. There were no women in the fields, which was unusual, as this was prime working time. The rootstalks had to be tended daily. They re-sembled high sarissa but were extremely light-sensitive. By nightfall they would be submerged in the muddy water of the paddy. Like wa-terweed, rootstalks glowed under water.

Bao sent Chi and a few soldiers to scout around the village. In the meantime, he scanned the village and its environs with his field glass. He could not see anyone about. No smoke rose from any of the hutches he could see. He scanned the paddies and fields, even the forest and scrubland. He had time for a *ching*-game. It would renew him, give him peace of mind and proper thoughts. But he had become uncomfortable with his dreams lately. Just as *yin* was not wholly *yin*, so the medicine could become a poison. When Bao dreamed, forgotten memories rose out of his unconscious like prehistoric creatures crawling out of the darkness.

Once again, Bao tried to dream, play a *ching*-game. He dreamed of Tun. But Tun is composed of Ch'ien, the heavens, and Ken, the mountain. *Mountain under heaven: the image of retreat.* The dream grew dark, and Bao saw himself as a child beating his dead father. The *ching*-game was spoiled.

He felt nauseated and feverish when he came out of the dream. The fastflesh should have taken care of any infection, he told himself as he bent over, touching his knees with his chin. No more dreams, he thought. Such memories could not serve the state.

It was early afternoon before Chi called in. So far, the fabers had found nothing. Bao told Chi to search the village and report what he found. Although his shoulder still hurt, Bao felt rested after a heavy, dream-ridden sleep. He felt warm but not feverish. The nausea had not returned.

"The village has been checked," Chi said. His voice sounded raspy over the transceiver. "All the hutches are clear of villagers. Many villagers are dead."

"What have they died from?" Bao asked, looking at the familiar cliffs and gutted hills which spread to the north. Perhaps *moi* had swept through on a raid, he thought.

"They look like the soldier-fabers found in the woods," Chi replied.

So the plague had spread, Bao thought. It was killing villagers and soldier-fabers alike. Bao remembered the faces of the soldiers he had found. Their faber faces looked almost human. In death we all look the same, he thought, suddenly feeling dizzy. And this is a new death.

"What did you find in the headquarters hutch?"

"Only fabers," Chi said. "Dead. No men."

"Is the cache-cellar locked?" Bao asked.

"Yes."

Bao would have to go into the village, for the heavy steel doorslide of the cache-cellar was keyed only to soldier-missionaries. Neither fabers nor *moi*-missionaries could gain entrance. But Bao would find supplies and safety in the comfortable bunker. And he could use the laser transceiver to call command post for new orders.

Before he could stand up, the nausea returned. He coughed, and vomited a thin, yellowish bile. He would rest a moment. His strength would return. But he was caught in a dream. He fought it. Old memories woke and left their dark places. Bao shouted. He was in a cold sweat.

And then he remembered that base *hai* had once been his home. He could not go back there, he told himself. Everyone he had known—the children he had grown up with, his teachers, Giay, the old men, the women—would be ghosts or spirits or strangers who thought the same thoughts, believed in the same divine cycle, and lived in the same dream.

He tried to shut out his memories, for he belonged to the state. He should not have memories, for the state had replaced them with *ching*-games and dreams and noble thoughts. Nevertheless, he remembered. Now he had a past. But he was lost. His memories were tearing him from the sacred web of state, the one true authority that presided over the earth and maintained the precarious balance of *yin* and *yang*.

Bao tried to forget his past, which had formed like frost on cold metal. But it was too late. Memories crawled out of the filthy caverns and stinking closets of his mind. He stood up and directed his fabers to fan out around him. Then he began walking toward his village. He imagined that he was already dead.

He was finally going home.

Bao entered the village from the east. He followed a muddy path around hutches that were in various states of disrepair. In this climate, the crude huts had to be mended daily. Village life was a constant battle against wind, rain, *moi*, and the ever-encroaching jungle of flatfronds, saucerleaf, silverglitter, and crawlervine. Beyond the hutches was the silvery *dinh*—the village longhouse—and beyond that was the pebble garden, which contained the eternal spirits of the village.

As Bao approached the *dinh*, he was overwhelmed by the stench of putrefaction. Villagers were sitting and praying inside a circle of dead bodies. Women, children, old men, and fabers had been laid out to form a mandala of flesh. The human corpses were black and blue; they looked as if they had been beaten. Their bellies were distended, and their bloated bodies were covered with large sores. The few fabers that were laid out on the outside edge of the mandala were also swollen and discolored. Their scaleplates had fallen away to reveal sores and mottled gray flesh. Effigy-dolls hung from high poles that were positioned north, south, west, and east of the mandala. They represented the four keepers of death.

"What are you doing there?" Bao asked the villagers, who stared past him as if looking into private worlds or watching invisible spirits swimming in the clear air.

No one answered him. Even the children seemed to be lost in the magic of the mandala. But Bao remembered something Giay had said to him long ago: "What you see with your eyes is not always real. Your mind can see much more clearly." Then Bao understood that the mandala of the dead was made to keep out *ma quy*. The villagers could see only their village spirits. They were blind to anything outside the mandala.

Keeping a good distance away from the villagers, he walked over to headquarters hutch, which had been scorched and structurally damaged. The villagers probably did it, he told himself. They would blame the plague on *outsiders*. He could almost visualize the brown-mud-and-sarissa hutch as a great wounded animal hunched over on its forepaws. He stepped over the bits and pieces that had once been a porch. Chi was waiting for him in the doorway.

"Three faber-soldiers were found inside," Chi said as he helped Bao into the hutch. Bao felt weak and sweaty again. He sat down in a worn wooden chair.

"Where are they now?" Bao asked, looking around the room. Then he looked outside at the faber-soldiers regrouping in front of the hutch. They huddled close together, as if to keep warm.

"They were taken behind the third hutch."

"Bury them," Bao said as he activated the doorslide to the cellar-cache. As the door slid open and the bunker lights blinked on, he heard a woman's voice speaking in a soft monotone.

". . . remain calm . . . an antidote has been found . . . remain at your posts . . . help will arrive . . . shortly . . . in the meantime . . . keep your distance from anyone . . . faber or human being . . . who . . . the symptoms of the virus are . . . corpses must be burned immediately . . . attention. . . ."

Bao climbed into the bunker and switched off the laser transceiver. The room stank. A missionary was slumped over the small workbench beside the transceiver. Bao did not touch him, as he could see the sores on the man's hand. He called Chi, told the faber to have the dead man taken outside, where he would be burned. Then Bao checked the storeroom, which was little more than a closet. Although most of the food and medical supplies had been removed, Bao was grateful for the few ration packs and food canisters that he found.

The men must have used the tunnel, he thought, resting his hand on the metal latch of the tunnel hatch. The tunnel was a narrow passage-way, barely wide enough for a man to crawl through, which opened behind a copse of redknob outside the village.

Just as he was about to leave the bunker, Bao experienced a slight delirium. And he felt something growing inside him, something alive and slippery, something with tiny claws at the end of thinsmooth feelers. He fell, and the room seemed to be whirling around him. His fingers scrabbled about on the floor like live things searching for dark-ness and cool safety.

When he awakened, he found that he was drenched in his own sweat. He shivered, made a resolve to fight his weakness, and crawled out of the bunker.

"All the corpses must be burned," he said to Chi, who had been waiting in the hutch for further orders. Then Bao stepped out of the hutch into the bright sunshine. He took a deep breath of fresh air and imagined he was breathing the effluvia of death.

Before him, just beyond the pebble garden, the villagers sat inside their mandala, their backs outward. They chanted the prayers of exor-cism. Bao walked to the edge of the garden and shouted to them. But they ignored him. He was only *moi*.

Bao signaled to Chi, and the fabers moved in to carry away the corpses. A pyre of sarissa and softwood had been prepared behind the hutches, well away from the village center. The corpses would have to be burned immediately.

But the villagers would not permit their mandala to be disturbed. They snarled and shouted and prayed. They pummeled and kicked the faber-soldiers, called them death-*moi*, shouted at Bao, told him to take away his demons, for he was *ma quy*, and he would never find his way into their souls. They would hold their breaths if he came near; they would not breathe his death fumes.

Bao understood their threats. He felt like a ghost or a demon, a maleficent spirit that had somehow escaped from the darkness of the caves of Hell. He fired a warning shot over the villagers. They became silent and turned away from him. The soldiers quickly removed the corpses to the pyre, which had just been set afire.

As Bao watched the corpses blacken in the flames, he remembered events and emotions of his childhood. He imagined that his past was just another corpse burning in the fire. His memories were streamers of black smoke drifting skyward.

But they would return, he thought, as the black rain of his dreams.

The *moi* attack came with dusk. The new offensive had begun. It was as if the gray-turning-into-darkness had brought all the noise and shadow-figures and pinchbombs. Hutches exploded. Villagers were shot as they ran toward the *dinh* or into the fields, which had been set aflame. *Moi*-fabers rushed into the village. They tripped mines, died in trapwire and automatic crossfire. But still they came. It was as if they had been spawned from dragons' teeth. For every *moi*-faber that fell, there would be another to replace him. Everything was soon covered in smokeover mist. The crackcrack of rifles and the yellow flares of small bombs became the thunder and lightning of a deadly storm.

Bao knew that he could not hold against this attack. Although his fabers still held their positions and slaughtered *moi* in a carefully planned crossfire, they would soon be overwhelmed by sheer numbers of *moi*-soldiers. Somewhere in the hills, Bao told himself, there was a missionary directing this attack and watching the smoke and fire from a safe distance, as if he were playing a *ching*-game that would come out right in the end.

But Bao was sick. He vomited every few minutes. The yellowish bile stank, and he imagined that he was rotting from the insides. Still, he tried to make his way to headquarters hutch. His only chance was the tunnel, he told himself as he took cover and rested for a moment behind a hutch. The hutch burst into flames. The heat was a wave pushing outward, overtaking him, wafting over him. He rolled away and screamed. His past had overtaken him.

Chi pulled him behind another hutch. Bao could hardly see in the smokeover. He hoped *moi* would shoot him. He imagined that ghosts were drifting through the smoke.

"*Stay here,*" Giay said. He had become just another smoke-ghost. "*If you leave, your soul will remain behind with the bones of your ancestors. You'll destroy your past and future. You'll have nothing left but an eternal present.*"

"*This is your home,*" his mother said as she drifted in the flames.

Bao cried as an explosion changed the pressure in his ears. He could hear only a constant roaring. Something knocked him over, and he was lost in darkness. He dreamed that the world was slowing down, unwinding, dying.

He dreamed that he was dead.

When he awoke, he felt Chi's dead weight on top of him. He pushed himself away from the faber and crawled through the roiling smoke to die alone. He laughed and imagined that he was a smoke-ghost. *Moi* could not find him, he thought. He dreamed that he was crawling with Chi. He had only the present, the dead comfort of *now*. Each *now* was a dream, an empty space. *Yin. Yang.* Only *now*.

Bao had made it out of the smoke and fire. He rested near a copse of sleeping willows and Christmas memory. Below him, past sarissa and paddies aglow with rootstalk, the village was buried in smokeover.

It didn't matter if he was caught now, he told himself. His diseased spirit would escape through his mouth to deliver death to the enemy. He would be a tool of the state. But Bao did not care: it could be *yin* or *yang*, love or hate, the wheel would still turn. Perhaps not, he thought. Then the divine cycle would be broken. He felt the gentle touch of childhood memories.

Above him, above the ticktick rattling of rifles, the sparkling fragments of the ring were moving imperceptibly across the clear night sky. It was as if the hidden fires of the village were reflected in the heavens, Bao thought. He remembered the legend of Tan Ming Hoang, the ruler of the world who was trapped in the sky.

A flare burst beyond the mountains. It was a white flower of pure daylight. Shadows lengthened, then faded back into the soft depths of night. Bao listened for the barking of rifles but heard only familiar night sounds.

He awoke, as if from a dream of grace, when he saw the ocean of red light behind his closed eyelids. He sat up and watched the red flowers blooming on the western horizon beyond purple mountains. The sky was like dark water, and a red dye was leaking, taking over the night with bleeding arms. As Bao watched the distant fires, he understood that the cycle had been broken. The ring could barely be seen in the sky. Surely Tan Ming Hoang could make his way back to earth now.

This was the time to leave, he thought, trying to die. But he could not push himself into death so easily. He stared into the bright night and waited, knowing that beyond his land a greater war had begun. . . .

JUNCTION

I.

Junction: white picket fences, one small perfectly rectangular park, rows of little houses with no glass windows, yards meticulously tended, distances marvelously the same, as if plotted for the blind.

Children heel beside mothers who never wear hats and sport ugly dresses dyed in pretty colors, prayer meetings are held in the reconverted and blessed Desert Midland Bank (where the boys and men and especially Ned Wheeler can sit on the third level and look down through the broken glass and watch the whores getting laid in the Congress Bar).

As Ned had been told: "Glass to let in the many eyes of God. A transparent mountain of perfection," with its broken windows and pilasters and naves for the bankers' ghosts. But who needs money now? Everything's the same, only different.

And five barns in "Center City" of the village, a racial memory of a medieval status symbol. And lands held in fief and in fee and in common and in escrow as the fathers saw best to govern the town-island that promised the last hope in the civilized world for God and man.

And it was the last hope.

Ned Wheeler stood in the high grass and watched the mountain form in the distance. It pushed itself out of the ground silently. Snow-capped peaks reached into a slate sky colored with blue streamers of cirrus. He waited for the mountain to dissolve, merge with the robin's-egg clouds, or explode into a shower of hypercubes to provide fourth-dimensional moisture. Anything could happen.

Before him, gray tundra extended from the grassy plain to provide a dividing line between two realities. And beyond the tundra, a mountain grew, belching amorphous rock, forming new mountain chains, silently proclaiming a new geologic era.

Behind him, Junction, unchanging, still the same, prim, pretty, only today a bit noisier than other days. Junction was a democracy. So elections were being held and ale being drunk and the whores were working overtime. President's Day was a time for hymns and anthems and good pot, a time to jump and scream and not be jailed or whipped or clamped in stocks or thrown into the urine pit.

But today Junction was too noisy for Ned, and everyone would be using his favorite whores. If he stopped at the Congress Bar, which smelled of perspiration and soil, they would probably put him to work. So here he was, hand in his pocket, awed by nature freaking out before him, thinking about Hilda's heavy hips and Sandra's heavy breasts.

He was frightened of the growing black mountains; they were great bears lumbering toward him, mouths slavering, needle teeth glinting under a black sun. (Ned had never seen a bear, had only read about them in a golden book in the library.)

Before him was Hell. As Ned had been told: "And to punish sinners, God sundered cause from effect." And Ned believed it; he was watching it. Out there, nothing was predictable. Water could crack, the sun was black or green or sometimes (after he had smoked some very good pot) it was a golden insect sucking up the world, peeing green lettuce, saturating the world in vegetable rain.

But Ned still liked to stand on the edge of reason, on the perimeter of God's hope, and try to outguess Hell. At least it wasn't boring—the only things in Junction that weren't boring to Ned were the accouterments of Hell: whores, ale, and pot.

The mountain couldn't keep growing, Ned thought. So it did. It grew and grew and the sun turned green and it was Halloween and the grass swayed in the wind and the birds crowed above him.

And something moved, just beyond the tundra. Ned felt a chill. A rabbit running, he thought, and dreamed of stew and the golden book. He could barely make out the creature running toward the tundra. Running faster, just reaching the tundra, but never crossing over.

Ned was relieved. A creature from Hell could not reach Heaven. That was a reassuring thought. But it was still running, never quite reaching the grayness of sand and rock and plain. It would shriek and crawl and beg, but the distance was too great.

Bolstered by higher knowledge and faith, Ned was no longer frightened. He studied the monster and tried to make out its features. Was it a woman? Did it have pointed teeth? How many arms and legs?

Enjoying his vision and thoughts, he pulled a milky-white weed from its sheath and slid it into his mouth, between his upper gum and cheek. The raw brown juice burned his throat. Perhaps the creature was a bird of Heaven trapped in Hell. He thought about that, trying to recall a phrase from the book. Ezekiel the Wishwasher saw in a vision beasts with wings that were called angels. That was in the book. "And they were full of eyes round about them." He didn't quite know what that meant. If the monster trying to escape into Heaven were only a bit larger; he still could not make it out.

He thought of St. John the Diviner and remembered his father, who could memorize anything, recite: "And before the throne *there was* . . ." —he would raise his hands above his head at this point—". . . a sea of glass like unto crystal: and in the midst of the throne, and round the throne, *were* . . ."—he threw up his hands again—". . . four beasts full of eyes before and behind.

"And the four beasts had each of them six wings about *Him:*" Father breathing with difficulty, looking to the ceiling. "And they were full of eyes within, and they rest not day or night, saying, Holy, holy, holy, Lord God Almighty, which was, and is, and is to come."

Full of reverence, if not for the vision at least for being able to remember it, he strained his eyes to see the creature. It could be a lion, but a lion couldn't run upright. But neither could the rest.

Eyes straining. Ned could see it now. The creature was crawling, its wings were flapping. It jumped into the air and rolled into the tundra.

The mountain turned to glass, reflected the black rays of the sun.

Ned screamed.

The angel from Heaven was after him, the sinner. It had escaped from Hell. Or worse yet, perhaps it was a creature from Hell coming to claim him. Could this only be a vision, a vision of conversion?

The monster lumbered across the tundra.

But which monster did he see? Was it only a figure of his imagination? He could see it better now; it became larger as it bridged the distance. It investigated the new ground. Ned could see that it was neither an animal nor a human being. And it was too big to be just his imagination, he thought.

But it had come from Hell and Ned wasn't going to wait. He ran through the high grass to Junction Road, looking back only once.

And found nothing but grass and a sunny day behind him. The creature had disappeared or, perhaps, had never been there in the first place. Ned, gaining courage, walked back several paces to investigate, then several more. Before him, the mountain of glass had turned to gelatin and was shaking and melting.

Although Ned Wheeler was awed by the religious moment, he still wanted some good pot, a touch of spider brandy, and a good fat whore. It would be a long walk through the grass, woods and wastes, commons, meadows, and lammas lands.

II.

Junction consisted of two great streets running parallel with each other between the hillside and the river—which some said was fed from Hell. It was around and about Main Street that the church and the whorehouse bars could be found. Riverside Drive, a hated but still used name, was a market and residential street. In the middle of Main Street there survived, against town law, a large farmhouse with all its agricultural and pastoral appurtenances: horses and oxen in the stalls, and a dung heap of gigantic size in the front yard.

That house, known conveniently as "The Stone House," was the president's residence. The oxen and horses were displayed as a symbol of feudal power. And since a president could serve—or be served—for only one year, Thomas McCall, the incumbent, was moving out. He would return to his old trade as a mason.

"The Stone House" was a curiosity; most of the houses in Junction were made of timber, and a fire became a village holiday for the children.

Ned Wheeler found Main Street crowded with election-day celebrants. Dressed in Sunday best, courteous to one another, singing, laughing, giggling, they all walked to church or a bar or a lover or favorite whore. Men lifted their caps to the ladies, who had not bathed in weeks. All wore the neatly powdered look of celebration and humility. These Victorian faces possessed certitude and thin-lipped righteousness.

"Hello, Ned Wheeler," said Miss Jenkens, a squat old woman wearing a faded black dress and a veil. She was an old schoolteacher of Ned's. "Are you off to church?"

"Yes, ma'am," he said, walking a bit faster.

A man without a shirt, chest covered with ashes, winked at him as he passed. Ned bowed his head at a group of ladies prancing by. They giggled and pointed at him, their pungent smells preceding them. The youngest one, a saucy blonde, scratched at her crotch and Ned looked away, wishing for a swim and a smoke. But he would go to church and pray for true conversion—at least for a little while.

The church was two blocks away. There were not very many vendor stalls in this area. He passed The Hanging Tree, a small whorehouse that was doing a good trade today. But the girls were not up to par, Ned thought. They were jealous of the Congress girls and were always starting fights. Ned remembered a skinny redhead who painted her toothless gums and had given Sandra the long pink scar that ran across her face. But that had been years ago, when he frequented every house in town.

Ned sighted a piece of glass in the gutter and stooped to pick it up. That would bring good luck—glass had taken on religious significance. Most of the church glass that had once littered the immediate vicinity of the bank had been picked up. Although some had been donated to the tabernacle, most was kept for luck and private prayer.

Much of Ned's whoring money had been made by selling these sharp trinkets. But no more, he thought. He slipped the sliver into his handkerchief and put it into his pocket, sure that it belonged to the bank and was holy.

Miss Jenkens caught up with Ned and, puffing, said, "Your father's worried about you. Do you know that? Do you know that he's in church right now?"

"Yes, ma'am."

"He's a good, religious man. And he's worried about you, worried you're going to walk right into Hell. 'The sinner will be bibbed into Hell.' "

Ned looked around the street; there was no escape. He did not see a familiar face. Already, he regretted his vision and possible new conversion.

"I saw you pick up a piece of holy glass. Don't you know that's a sin? You're not allowed to touch it. Your fingers will burn in Hell. And it's against the law; only a clergyman is pure enough to touch it. What if I told on you? What then? Are you going to give it to one of your whores?"

"No, ma'am."

"Aren't you worried just a little bit about being poisoned in Hell with your whoring and smoking and drinking?"

"Yes, ma'am, I am," Ned said. And he meant it, although he dreamed about Sandra and some good pot. But that would just be another sin.

"Ned Wheeler, if you're really going to church, I won't tell."

"Thank you, ma'am," he said, listening to the laughter from the Congress Bar. He thought he could hear Hilda's husky voice; she loved to laugh and bite when she tumbled.

"Then, I'll walk along with you." She handed him her Bible and took his arm.

"Your sin will be on me," she said, "but I think I can better stand it than you. Now that you have it, perhaps God will see to look into your soul."

There were a few horses and wagons in the street. Ned kept to the carriage side of the road, so as not to be splashed by garbage. A bag fell from a third-story window-hole and exploded beside Miss Jenkens; its putrescent smells were immediately picked up by a warm breeze and wafted down the street.

Ned climbed the stone church steps slowly, the schoolteacher hanging upon his arm. He tried not to look at the Congress Bar, on his left. The side door had become the official entrance to the church; only the children used the front entrance.

Some of his friends stood outside the Congress Bar and called to him.

"Hey, Ned; you're missing a hellofa party."

"Hilda's been asking about you. She misses you."

"Going to church with Miss Jenkens. Ned's got religion. And he's using the side door, too."

Ned felt his face flush.

A catcall from the second story, a strident voice screeing, "Ned, honey. Going to church? We're having an election party."

Once inside the building, his heels clicking on the faded red-and-blue parquetry, he could hear the congregation singing, his father's voice the loudest of all. He followed Miss Jenkens to her seat in the first pew on the main floor. He could smell the mold of the pulpit carpet in front of him. A heavy man with thinning hair combed up into a pompadour was leading the services. The notes of "My Country, 'Tis of Thee" echoed in the open vaults where Ned used to play hide and seek and had once banged the carpenter's daughter. (At the time, the carpenter had been president, and his daughter was, indeed, a prestigious prize.)

Miss Jenkens sat down and patted the seat beside her, motioning Ned to stay with her. But the smells and her devotion were too much for him, and he excused himself by telling her that he had to look for his father.

"You're probably going to sneak out the front and run across the street. Your friends are probably still calling you."

"No, ma'am," he said as he watched her breasts rise and fall as she breathed. At one time, it was rumored, she had been a beautiful woman, with a full face and long black hair. She had had a few lovers, one of them his grandfather, or so he had overheard his father say. Looking at her veined, wrinkled hands, he imagined her old, shriveled breasts and wondered what she had been like.

"Well, all right. Go look for him if you must," she said, rubbing her eye. "At least you're respectful. Could I borrow your handkerchief for a minute? I've left mine at home, and I think I've got something in my eye." She took off her hat and veil. Her hair was dyed red and she was slightly bald in the back. A bug crawled to the surface and then disappeared again into her red forest, which had been patiently stiffened and combed. "Well?" she asked.

Ned laughed a bit too loudly, and he felt everyone watching him as he walked toward the stairwell. Then up three flights of stairs, past the sitting room—which was the drinking room—and down the hallway onto the balcony. The balcony was accidental: the third floor had given way years ago, and the masons had simply smoothed the ragged edges into an oval and the carpenters had strengthened what was left.

Ned's father was standing up and praying, left hand holding the book, right index finger pointing out the lines to whoever might be interested. He was very proud of his reading proficiency. Behind him was a large window that overlooked the street and the Congress Bar.

Squeezing between his father and Mr. Brownlaw, a city official and fervent churchgoer, Ned sat down. His father, without even looking at him, handed him a book, and Ned held it open and waited for his father to sit down.

A half hour later, after all the young men were happily seated, he sat down. "Why did you bother to even come? It's almost over."

Ned knew that there would be at least four hours left, five, probably, for his father. "I had a vision of Hell. That's why I came."

His father was suddenly interested. He brushed back his gray hair and picked at a mole on his forehead. Where the father was ruggedly handsome—features sharply defined and body well kept—the son was overweight and his face was soft and familiarly average. Of course, he resented his father for that, but the whores liked Ned. And he was three inches taller than his father.

"I told you to stay away from the tundraland. You shouldn't even go near there. Tell me about your vision."

Ned told him what had happened, and his father nodded and smiled, as if he had experienced that vision many times before.

"Haniel, Kafziel, Azriel, and Aniel. You saw one of the monsters from Heaven. A wonderful sight. And you found nothing when you went back. Well, visions are only to see once. I knew this would happen one day. Sit and pray. I'm very proud and very happy." He turned the pages of Ned's Bible to the correct prayer and began intoning the words.

Ned stared at the true book and remembered Miss Jenkens, who had taught him to read it. She had a habit of raising her eyes to Heaven whenever she said an important word. Once, on a dare, he had looked up her dress as she embraced the sky and said, "Amen." She used to scold him when he went to the Old Library, now a stowbin, to read the other old books. She had told him about "trash" and why the old books didn't count or work anymore. "That was before God punished us and raised Hell to Earth," she had said.

Ned's Bible had seen too much wear, but, then, it had not been made to stand up to normal use. The binding was torn, and the script was smudging. Upon closer inspection, Ned could see that it had been transcribed in haste. Sam Sence, the town scribe, was paid only a few pennies for each book he produced. So quality was compromised by quantity. The new Bibles were not as thick as the old versions. Through the years, each succeeding Bible became slightly thinner as proclaimed authoritative councils decided what would be the true and correct portions of the New English Bible.

Mouthing the words, Ned tried to find meaning in the many ciphers. He sang and smiled at the congregation. He glanced at his father, who had turned his head to sneak a peek out the window behind him. The second-story window-hole of the Congress Bar was just visible. On the pulpit, below them, the mockministers had donned white garments and pointed, conical caps. With arms outstretched and fingers parted to form the sacred sign, they blessed the congregation and prayed to hold back the advance of Hell.

The congregants closed their eyes so as not to witness the holy sign, and beat their chests. Ned's father clapped his chest the loudest and cried as he sang. Ned tried to imitate him.

It became warm and stuffy; Ned could smell the pungent odors of old men. And the services went on. Ned's father was so happy that he wouldn't sit down. Whenever Ned would sit, his father would knit up his eyebrows. And Ned would sigh and stand. As the hours passed, the glass behind him seemed to draw his face. And every turn of his head that brought him closer to God's glass, ironically, brought him closer to Hell.

Sandra was hanging out the window-hole of the Congress Bar. Ned turned around and saw her, but could not hear her shouts. At his father's glance, he turned toward the pulpit and said a prayer, already feeling the old discontent of being forced into God's lap. The chair, although more comfortable than the pews downstairs, was beginning to hurt his buttocks.

Word had passed that Forester, the featherwaker, was coming upstairs to see if anyone had fallen asleep. With his approach, everyone nudged his neighbor and sang louder. Forester's bald head was polished with perspiration; that's why he had acquired the nickname "Chromedome."

But what was chrome? A strange way to say shiny, Ned thought. "Another mystery of life," his father had said.

The glass pulled Ned around just in time to see Sandra unbutton her blouse and dangle her tits at someone below. She glanced at Ned and winked. Although she wasn't his best lay, she was his favorite girl. She sucked her fingers and Ned sat down again, covering his lap with the book. His father raised an eyebrow, but it did no good: Ned would not stand. His face flushed as his father prayed.

Another hour passed. It was getting dark. Ned wondered if the mountain was still growing out of Hell. There, it would probably be sunny as noon. Remembrance of his vision brought prayers to his mouth.

Another hour. Behind him it seemed that the entire town was trying to squeeze into the Congress Bar. That's where a closed meeting was being held in the wine-cellar—the traditional room for caucuses and political brawls—to decide who would be the next president. Of course, the president had no power—that was reserved for the king. But no one knew who the king was. It was rumored that the king was a myth and the president really did hold power; but every president denied that.

Ned had to go to the bathroom, but it was considered unholy to leave the church on a prayerday. He could see Sandra still hanging out the window, looking for customers. She had put a sweater on to counter the night-chill, but expediency forced her to expose her breasts. Looking at her only strengthened the feeling of fullness Ned was trying to hold back.

Without asking permission, he stood up and left his father. He would return, he thought. After all, did his father expect him to become a complete convert in a day?

Ned relieved himself in the street outside. There was a cool breeze, and the street smelled of good sweat and food and urine. Behind him, the great windows of the church were yellow with flickering light from the candles. A candle for each sin, the flame of penance. His father had probably already lit one for him, he thought.

He forced himself to walk back up the stone church steps. His father had not, would not, ever learn. As long as he could stand and pray, he would badger Ned with religion. Ned could never be religious enough to satisfy his father.

Make him happy, Ned thought, inhaling deeply, pretending he was smoking some good pot and lying with Sandra and Hilda. Stay with him tonight, he told himself. The vision was true—you're converted.

"Hey, Ned," shouted John Sewall, one of the town smiths. He was standing on the porch of the Congress Bar. "Come on. Party, party, party. They're thinking up the next president in the cellar. Aren't you interested in eavesdropping?"

"No, thanks," Ned said, but he stopped on the stairs and waited to be persuaded.

"Everybody else is using up Hilda. Must be thirty guys jumped on her belly today. Give her a dose for you. And you're up there praying with your highfalutin father."

"Shut it."

"Come on," shouted Baldanger, the shoemaker, from a second-story window-hole above the porch. "We see you. Everything's just about started, and who are we going to tumble the whores with? Old Herman trying to bounce long enough to come?" Baldanger whistled past a chipped tooth as he spoke.

"Come on, Ned."

Behind Ned, a glass cathedral reaching for Heaven, shimmering yellow to relieve him of sin, its money vaults now collecting alms and prayers for the poor.

And before him, the devices of Hell.

Ned leaned out the second-story window-hole and watched the revenants promenading along the green in front of the church. A central bonfire provided light and warmth for the cool night. The figures looked grotesque in the flickering firelight. Ned tried not to look at the church, for he would see his father praying for him, the "almost convert."

Would it take a bash on the head, Ned asked himself, to make me believe?

"Is this for me?" asked Hilda.

Ned turned around. Hilda had searched his pockets and found the shard of holy glass in his handkerchief. She held it before a candle and examined it.

"I always know when you have glass by the way you fold your handkerchief. This is a pretty piece. It looks green at the edges. How come you always find the glass? It seems to grow out of the dirt wherever you walk. Baldanger never finds any."

"Give me that," Ned said.

She ducked out of reach, layers of fat jiggling as she moved, thick auburn hair hiding her freckled face. "Come on, honey. For all the free tumbles and drinks and pot when you said you didn't have a dollar." She lay down on the floor, legs spread and raised in the air. "Come on, a new position for the glass. You owe me a present."

"Hell I do," he shouted, and jumped on her, straddling her wide stomach. She laughed and kept her arm out of his reach.

Laughter from the door. Sandra and Baldanger, arm in arm, were hooting and shouting at the wrestlers.

"And look," said Sandra, "Ned with a hard-on. Very impolite."

Baldanger looked around the room. He had not been able to find his clothes and was wearing one of the girls' robes. He was a lanky man with a deep tan and thinning blond hair, which he combed over his forehead. Sandra, by contrast, had black hair cropped short at the ears, and pale, almost translucent skin. The delicate network of veins was clearly visible on her throat and breasts. She was wearing an open-front robe that exposed her breasts.

"Stop it," Sandra said. "We've got some news. Give Ned whatever he wants and listen."

Hilda gave him the piece of glass and curled up in the bed to sulk.

"Have you seen my clothes?" asked Baldanger.

"Shut up," Sandra said. "Do you know who's in the cellar? Well, from what I hear, there's almost no South Side representation. It's all Central." Sandra peeled back a broken fingernail, pausing for effect. "Old Herman is down there, and Stan and Freeglass and practically everybody but you and Baldy. You've got most of us to yourselves."

Baldanger stuffed some green pot into his pipe and passed it around.

"What about East Side?" asked Ned. "*They* must have people down there."

"Yes, they do," said Baldanger, curling his lip over his chipped tooth to stop the whistle—it didn't work. "But not as much as last year. When the mayor picked out the electors, he probably figured it was only fair that we get more representation after what happened last year."

"East Side, West Side, they don't even exist," Hilda said, twisting her hair into knots. "What do you need political parties for? They're as imaginary as the cow pasture they represent. What are they but an excuse to get drunk and slide between our legs?"

Everyone ignored her. It was bad taste to discuss the parties seriously.

"It's a fraud," she continued. "What do we need a president for, anyway? He has no power, doesn't do anything, lives off the public tit like a God damn lord for a year, and he's elected by a bunch of drunks. Everyone respectable is over there in church." She pointed toward the window.

"That's not true," said Baldanger. "Hell, the Reverend's down there. The altarmen are covering for him at the church."

Ned ran his thumb over the surface of the glass. "Nobody knows if the president's got any power, because they never tell," Ned said. "Even Sam, after he finished his term, would only smile when anyone asked him about it." He made a fist around the holy glass. "And look at all the old presidents; they've all been smart, even if none of them had any education. As drunk as the electors get, they always elect someone smart. And how come there's always some clergy down there? Did you ever think of that?"

Hilda giggled. "Ned's going over to the other side."

"He was in church most of the day," Sandra said, "turning around—just like his father—to look at my tits."

"Shut up," Ned said. "The presidents have all had something to do with religion. Even old Sam was going to church three times a week when he was in office."

"That's because he had to," Baldanger said.

"That's right," said Ned. "The president represents tradition and religion. Remember, the presidents used to rule over everything. So what does that mean since God changed everything and put Hell all around us? It means that the president, at least symbolically, rules Hell and Earth. And Junction, whether we like it or not, is Earth."

"What's symbolically mean?" asked Sandra.

Baldanger filled the pipe again and gave it to Hilda, who was still pouty. The candles in the room were low, and everything looked soft and yellow. Ned could hear the chatter of the congregants as they left the church for home and clean living. The girls would soon be working overtime.

Ned passed the pipe to Sandra and watched the smoke curl in the yellow light. A breeze wafted into the room through the window-hole, circulating the bad air and banishing the smoke. Baldanger lay down on the bed with Hilda and Sandra. Sandra protested that she'd have to go downstairs soon, but she leaned against the wall, her leg draped over Baldanger's crotch, and seemed to enjoy the company.

Sitting alone in front of the window-hole, Ned watched the congregants below. Were they waiting around for the electors to decide? he asked himself. But that would take all night. And what did he care? He did not want to face his father tonight. He would stay here until morning.

"You know," Baldanger said, "Ferris Angleton was downstairs, higher than a sonofabitch, and telling stories. He said he saw a monster that looked like a bird running across the northwest pasture. Christ, he even brought in his daughter Flora—the one with the game leg—to say she saw it too."

"I heard something like that," Sandra said, "only from Alex Eitrides."

Ned was developing a sense of fate. He looked at the church and thought about the monster that was stalking him—somehow, he was sure that it was looking for him. He dreamed of the church and the smells of the pulpit and traced his father's face in the street outlines. Shadow and line, a sparkle of glass, the holy building before him. To remind him.

He listened to the springs squeaking under the weight of Baldanger and Sandra, concentrated on the candles in the church. One by one they were slowly going out, substituting grayness for each yellow halo.

III.

Ned awakened with a start. He was in Hilda's bed, arm propped up against the wall, leg resting on the coarse hide rug. The thin, worn blanket lay in a pile on the floor. In her hand, unbeknown to Ned, she clutched the shard of holy glass.

The room was filled with people who were shouting and laughing. The electors had not slept and were still drunk. They had been followed by the girls, townsfolk, and clergy. The strong morning sunlight streaming through the window holo revealed the starkness and shabbiness of the room and the blanched faces that only rest could restore to life.

A tattooed whore pinched Ned's buttocks and shouted, "Out the door, out the door."

"And don't forget his whore," a red-faced farmer shouted.

"Ned Wheeler, king of the whores."

"The sleeper's a president."

"Life to the president."

"Here, here."

Hilda was picked up and passed out the door by strong hands that playfully squeezed her soft parts. After a few seconds, her screams turned to yelps and giggles.

Most of the people in the crowd were Ned's friends. He could see Baldanger, Herman and Stan, Sam Sence, Ferris Angleton, Alex Eitrides' little girl, Reverend Surface, and, of course, all the girls. But there were unfriendly faces in the crowd.

Fairchild Sewell, a slightly built man wearing a discarded guildsman cap, knuckled Ned in the neck and called him a sonofabitch. Sewell had been a Central City party prompter before he defected to the North Side to become a professional elector. His brother Cravett, who outweighed Fairchild by seventy-five pounds, tried to knuckle Ned, but was kneed in the crotch by Sam Sence. Most of the members from the other parties were waiting outside on the green.

The crowd carried Ned and Hilda downstairs, past the bar, out the front door, and onto the small village green. Everyone on the green was shouting and waving at Ned. The crowds spilled onto Main Street, which formed a circle around the perfectly rectangular park. The church looked on blankly with its broken glass eyes. Farther down the street—which was roughly paved with cobblestones, but fouled with mire and the accumulation of garbage thrown from the adjacent houses —the shops were closed, although a few vendors were talking business, oblivious to the festivities occurring up the street.

A high-pitched voice shouted, "Speech, speech, give us an inauguration speech."

"Yes, a speech from the newly elected president."

They all began to chant, "Speech, speech, speech." Mugs and ale had been taken from the tavern, for the Central City Party people were drinking and waving their flagons.

The electors, backed up by the crowd, pushed Ned and Hilda up a crude stairway onto the stocks platform in the middle of the park, where a hangman's tree and an assortment of wooden stocks and whipping posts served as warnings to any would-be offender. From the platform, Ned could look over the heads of the crowd and see Main Street winding its way downtown. Houses and shops were scattered along the route, clumped together to form subsections of the central village, their tidy roofs sloping toward the road and crowned with chimney pots in which birds built their nests. Before Ned, the glass cathedral, the tallest building in Junction. He looked up at the tall oak tree beside him, wishing he could climb it into Heaven and be done with all this embarrassment.

"Say something," Hilda said. "They're waiting for you to say something."

Ned began to speak, cleared his throat, faltered, and began again. He could not think of anything to say, so he just said whatever came to mind and hoped that his unconscious would carry him through. He looked over the heads of the townspeople at the church, stared into the small, unpaved alley beside it.

"Well, come on," said a guildsman. The guildsmen stood together and smiled condescendingly at everyone else.

"I thank all of the electors and all of you who elected the electors who elected me to this office. I don't really understand why I was picked for this. . . ."

Something moved in the alley beside the church. Ned could not tell what it was. He averted his eyes, his attention wandered.

". . . but for whatever I do, I shall do my best. I may be mistaken, but I believe that this office confers sacramental powers and responsibilities upon the holder, even if that be the upholding of a tradition most of us have forgotten the meaning of. I imagine this office to represent all the world through God. . . ."

The crowd was laughing, guffawing, trying to drown him out with a song. Fat Cravett led with the first verse:

> "Back and side, go bare, go bare
> Both hand and foot go cold,
> But belly, God send you good ale enough
> Whether it be new or old!"

The tattooed girl, her eyes closed and mouth open, tried to unbutton her blouse, but the older women quickly covered her and slapped her face with the backs of their hands.

Ned tried to leave the platform, but the crowd blocked his way. When they had finished their song, they began to chant, "Speech, speech, finish your speech."

"Some think that the presidents used to rule the world, even the outside, even Hell." Ned listened to his words flow, amazed that it was really his voice speaking. "Even the most thoughtless of us—me, for instance—live under the shadow of eternity. All around us lies Hell. We know its geography, its climate, its monsters, as well as we know our own land. . . ."

"You may know its monsters," someone from the crowd shouted, "but we don't."

Another voice: "We don't look upon Hell."

"It's bad luck," said an old man holding a mug, his face scrunched up and wrinkled as if he were forever peering at the sun. "And you've certainly got it." Everyone laughed, and the younger men patted him on the shoulder.

"You are right," Reverend Surface shouted to Ned. "That office does confer responsibilities upon you. That's why we taunt you and laugh at you. That's why we will love and respect you for a year, even though we may blacken your face now and bloody your skin. Perhaps you will rule over Junction and Hell for us. But they are words from other books, books to which we cannot give complete credence. But we'll take no chances. We'll laugh at the books and obey them, mock them for being apocryphal, love them because they might be God's."

The crowd cheered, now given excuse to throw mud and dung at the foolpresident.

"April fools," they shouted.

A guildsman, wearing a red cap befitting his rank, beat his chest in mock solemnity. Ned was reminded of his father. Would he be proud or ashamed? Ned asked himself. Beside him, Hilda was teasing a potential customer, another guildsman.

When will they let me down? he asked himself, ducking a clump of dung and grass that passed over his head. Ned could not see his father in the crowd. As he looked, a clump of mud caught him squarely in the face, followed by a dungball.

"Good shot," Miss Jenkens shouted.

"Look at the kingpriest, the foolpresident, the ruler of Hell."

"He's full of shit."

Even Reverend Surface was laughing. He accepted a drink from the burly peasant beside him.

Ned wiped his face and thought about tomorrow. Tomorrow Junction would return to its normal state. It would be quiet and respectable and dull. And the whores would not shout or dangle their breasts from the window-holes. And the Reverend would not laugh. And Ned would be in The Stone House. And everyone would ignore him and pay attention to lifting their hats for the ladies that stank. And the farmers and peasants would be working in the fields, careful not to glance into Hell. The shopkeepers could make money, and the guildsmen could protect their own.

Let them throw their garbage, he thought. He looked at the church and then into the alleyway beside it.

A figure with a plastic face and a yellow beak stood in the alley, ankle deep in muck, and leaned against the church. Its mottled yellow body was covered with eyes, some closed, some blinking, each a different color of Heaven: henna, Milori blue, topaz, fluorite, viridian, stammel, umber. One iris looked as if it were made of black glass, pure and untainted by the grays of Junction reality. The angel from Hell wore a halo around its head that killed any insect that chanced to be near it.

Ned pointed at the creature when he saw it, but it stepped back into the darkness before anyone could turn around. Ned thought he heard it speak inside his head. It said, *I am not ready yet.*

The crowd turned to look, found nothing, became angry, and pelted him with more dung and garbage. The outer fringes of the crowd were falling away. People were going home, to an illegal job, a sewing circle, or a whorehouse. As the crowd began to disperse, other people appeared on the street, those who had not wanted to see the foolpresident's inauguration, but were religious enough to make an appearance. Those who had stayed home would spend an extra eternity in Purgatory.

Ned tried to push his way down the platform stairs. The crowd gave way a bit and he descended a few steps.

"Wait for me," Hilda said, her arms folded over her breasts to protect them from pinching fingers. "I'm part of this too."

Baldanger shouted and waved his hands to attract Ned's attention. "Wait," he said. "They'll carry you to The Stone House."

Ned pushed at the crowd, trying to bury himself in the mass of sweating flesh and become just another peasant. But what did it matter? he thought. The angel from Hell would find him. But why? And for what?

Hands grabbed his arms and legs, passed him atop the crowd, which was shouting, "Take him home, take him home."

About three hundred people made up the homecoming procession. Others were hanging out window-holes of adjacent buildings to see Ned. The crowd held Ned face up to the sky, his legs splayed as far as they would stretch. They carried Hilda behind him, passed her back and forth, squeezed her extra portions of breasts and thighs. Although she screamed and prayed, her nipples stood erect.

Ned watched the sky, examined the strange angles and lines of the buildings that pointed to the sun. He tried not to look at the people hanging out the window-holes. They smiled and leered and shouted at him. An old woman spat at him, spraying his face. He closed his eyes. But he felt his face being pulled to the right.

"*Look at the building,*" said a voice inside his head.

The angel from Hell sat atop one of the old metal buildings on a girder, all eyes open, halo attracting and killing insects.

Or perhaps anything that came near it, Ned thought.

He screamed and closed his eyes, unable to pray.

IV.

Almost none of the old buildings were left in Junction. Scripture has it that when God raised Hell all around Junction, he also leveled the buildings to cleanse the land from sin. The only buildings that were completely untouched were The Stone House and the Desert Midland

Bank. The bank was converted into a church, and The Stone House had become the president's palace.

It was considered a miracle that the churchglass had been left intact after God slapped the land causing the earth to quake and the buildings to fall. It was later on, Ned had been told, and because of Junction's accumulated sins, that the glass cracked and shattered in places. It was sin that caused the third floor to fall. The other old buildings that remained were only skeletons, reminders of God's wrath for future generations.

The Stone House was situated in the middle of Main Street, below the shops. Its neatly tended lawn and garden served as a boundary line between "Center City" and the South Side, although both districts claimed the landmark as their own. Behind the house stood three small barns and stalls for the oxen and horses. Two of the three barns were in disrepair. The dung heap in the corner of the barnyard was near "Trespassers' Path," and the wealthy guildsmen's wives would delicately place tiny rags to their noses as they passed the contaminated area on their way home.

The large front doors of The Stone House opened into an empty anteroom that led into a hallway. To the left and right were once-luxurious sitting rooms and a library without books. A recently constructed staircase led upstairs to the bedrooms. To the rear of the house, a small kitchen was connected to a pantry and sunken dining room. A kitchen stairway led into the cellar, where food and wine were kept.

Ned Wheeler was sitting in the library waiting for his father and Reverend Surface. The room was bare except for a couch and a few simple wooden chairs. The parquetry on the floor had faded from use, and the stairs leading up to the hallway were due for repairs. A vase of daffodils rested on one of the empty bookshelves that ran the length of the room. A Bible, the only book permitted in the house, lay open on the desk. All the other books had been removed decades ago. Above the desk hung a framed photograph; the original subject had long ago bleached into the background.

Looking out the window-hole before him, Ned watched a few people running across the front yard. Probably on their way to church, he thought. He heard a scream, then another. By now the church would be full of supplicants praying for the birdfaced beast's return to Hell. Each would pray that he was not the object of its errand.

But Ned would wait for the messenger from Hell. Now that he was president, he could not outwit his fate.

The library doors opened and Reverend Surface and Ned's father walked into the room. Reverend Surface pulled a chair beside Ned and patted his shoulder. Ned's father nodded, but preferred to stand an uncomfortable distance away from his son.

Ned's first thought was that the Reverend smelled, but that was not the minister's fault, for the clergy were supposed to smell like the people—and Reverend Surface was known to hang around the dung pits and talk with the workers. He wore a black-and-gray coat of coarse material that was called cary, and his overhood was so full of holes that his hair stuck out of it. His toes peered out of his worn shoes with their thick soles, and his hose hung about his ankles on all sides. Although the church and its vassals held large amounts of wealth and power, they wore the vestments of the poor.

And the poor accepted it when they were not drunk and in their senses, and pretended to believe that only God held the riches death would bring. In the meantime the Desert Midland Bank held the money.

"You, no doubt, know that the creature from Hell is still about in Junction," Reverend Surface said. "Everyone's afraid that the Last Days have come, and the birdbeast is the messenger. And he just might be. . . ."

"It's up to you to meet him," Ned's father said. "He's looking for you. You saw him first. You must see him again." Ned's father was dressed in a simple, loose overshirt with faded brown pants and leather sandals.

"You did tell your father that you saw a beast cross from Hell into Junction," said the Reverend. "And since you saw him first, it is felt that you should see him again. The people believe that he is looking for you. You are our Jonas."

"But others saw it too," Ned said.

"That doesn't matter," said the Reverend. "You are the president. Since you hold the power of office and represent us, it is feasible that you would be the one it's looking for. Anyway, everyone is waiting for you to meet it and find out what is to happen."

"It is significant that you saw it first," Ned's father said. "And then you were elected president. Can't you see God's plan? You must follow His orders. You have been chosen."

"Just like that," Ned said.

His father leaned against the bookshelf, resting his arm on the old dark board and running his fingers along the surface of the vase, and solemnly nodded.

Ned looked at Reverend Surface. "And if I don't go? If I stay here? Then what?"

"Well, most of the people are afraid to be out now. The hours are short until dark. But in the morning, when it's safer, they'll gather together and force you out of Junction, push you into Hell. You'll be their sacrifice. You will be the holy lamb tormented in sulphurous flames before the holy angels. Now you have their faith. Tomorrow, if you have failed, they will try to destroy you in desperation and fear of the coming days."

"You must go now," Ned's father said. "Find out what it wants with us. You have been chosen. We will light the church, and those who are unafraid to leave home will pray there for you and ourselves. So go now. We will wait."

"There is one thing," said the Reverend. "The beast has been seen in several different places at the same time. Your father suggested that they saw the four holy beasts, Haniel, Kafziel, Azriel, and Aniel, that Ezekiel saw in his holy vision. But I don't think that's so, because five beasts had been seen at the same time—as you know, there can be only four holy beasts—and they all looked alike."

"That doesn't matter," Ned's father said. "One of the beasts could have been an untrue vision."

"But it is possible that there are more than one, so be forewarned. Anyway, it has been officially decreed that there is but one beast."

Ned curled his lip into a practiced sneer and asked, "Why hasn't the Bishop come? I was looking forward to seeing him. And where are the Reverend Priests MacDonald, Briar, Shorter, and Blues? And where's Small Henry?"

"The Bishop doesn't exist, my son," said the Reverend. "And the others are calming the people. For our purposes, you are the Bishop."

He laughed, thinking he would leave the room without saying good-bye and make a good exit. He laughed to conceal his fear and anxiety. But he stopped at the door, thereby spoiling his exit, and asked, "Why can't I just wait here?" As soon as he asked the question, he felt ashamed. He had spoiled his moment, and he already knew the answer.

"Because," Reverend Surface said, "you cannot be sure that the angel from Hell will come for you. It has stayed outside, never once entering a house. And if it were coming here, wouldn't it have already arrived?"

"You must find it," Ned's father said. "That's what it wants. You must seek out the Lord."

Ned felt his face flush. He slipped on the smooth parquetry and did not close the doors behind him.

Outside, the streets were empty. Brushing invisible spider webs from his face, he walked down Main Street toward Junction Road. The wind was slight; it tickled him. Children peered down at him from window-holes and greeted him with jeers and shouts. They threw flowers and garbage. Peasants in adjacent buildings praised him and blessed him and sang his songs. But none would step on the street, and some had closed their window-holes with boards in preparation for the miasma of evening.

Playing the hero, Ned marched down Main Street and ignored the occasional bombardments of garbage. In a few minutes it would be dusk. Behind him, the candles in the church were being lit in his honor. Ned thought about Hilda; she was probably hiding in a closet or wasting a tradesman's semen.

As he turned left onto Junction Road, the human sounds became muffled, to be replaced by crickets and birds and the scratching of wind in bush. Ned had never been out of Junction-proper this late—he shivered and walked faster.

And each step brought him closer to Hell. Junction Road ended before the high grass that gave way to the tundra, the gray boundary between order and disorder. Ned wondered if the mountain was still growing, or had it been transformed into something else?

Dusk came quickly and turned into evening, revealing a new moon surrounded by a pale white halo. Ned concentrated on his heels clicking on the old cobblestones overgrown with weeds and grass. As the evening deepened, the moon turned from gray to silver, creating shadow-specters that seemed to jump out at Ned.

Fighting an urge to run, Ned stopped to get his bearings. He was almost at the end of Junction Road; before him was tundra, and then Hell.

And the angel from Hell said, "Hello."

Surprised, Ned screamed and took a step backward. By squinting his eyes, he could make out the outline of the birdbeast standing against the background of high grass. Its beak glinted yellow, and all of its eyes were closed except those that made up its face.

"I've been waiting for you," it said. "Don't worry about my halo; it won't hurt you."

"What do you want?"

"I want you to come with me into Hell."

Ned could almost see the mountains growing behind the birdbeast in the moonlight.

"Yes," the birdbeast said. "They are still growing. Those mountains proved to be quite an obstacle."

Ned noticed that the creature's beak did not move when it spoke, and he wasn't even sure if he was hearing a true voice.

"Are you a creature of God or of Hell? And why do you want me?"

"Because of those mountains. You created them, you know. They've been growing since you imagined them that day."

"I don't believe that."

"And," the birdbeast said, "I'm neither from Heaven nor Hell."

"Then, what are you?" Ned asked.

"A lure, I think. The dream stops here. Now we're on our own."

Ned could see the mountains changing behind the birdbeast. The mountains are alive, he thought. They're bears with stone claws and icicle teeth.

And in tempo with the black mountains, the birdbeast began to change into a man. All but two watery eyes disappeared, and his beak turned into a chin that could be construed to be weak. The beast became a short, stocky man with an overlarge mouth and short-cropped black hair.

Ned watched the transformation, then screamed.

"This is what I really look like," the man said. "I'm just like you. You don't have to be afraid."

"You're Satan," Ned said. "You change at will. Why do you want me? You're bringing the Last Days, I know that."

"No, I'm not Satan. My name of Kaar Deaken, and I'm just a messenger from another town. A town like Junction, only a thousandfold larger. And that's where I want to take you."

"What if I don't want to come?"

"You have no choice," Deaken said. "If you don't come with me, I'll remain in Junction and the townspeople will push you out to exorcise me."

"But you're a man now," Ned said.

"Shall I change for you again? I can change into God's monster, if you like. But we don't have much time, because this is a dream that will begin and end again. You don't have to understand that now. Just come with me. But if I must, I will change into God's beast."

"Then, you aren't really from Hell?" Ned wished he hadn't said that —it was the whine of a child needing comfort.

Ned followed Deaken into the tundra. In the moonlight, scattered bushes gave form to the desolation, acted as God's scarecrows to frighten impetuous trespassers. Before them, the mountains appeared to be still growing, reaching for the moon. Deaken hurried toward them, urging Ned to keep up with him.

Deaken stopped a few hundred paces from the mountain wall and said, "I don't know how we will get past them. I came through over there." He pointed at a new mountain growing to fill the empty space, reaching toward the rock faces of its neighbors. "We can't get through there now. By the time we reach it, it will be a mile high." Deaken's eyes darted back and forth, looking for a break in the mountain wall.

Ned watched the mountains moving toward him, bursting out of new ground. Soon everything would be rock and hard-packed dirt. The sky would be blotted out by the sheer bulk of stone.

"The mountains will swallow us," Ned screamed as he turned to run. But new mountains had grown up behind him. Stone arms were reaching out to surround the trespassers. A stone stalagmite pushed out of the ground and touched Ned's hand. It was the seed of a new mountain. "It's growing beneath us," he said.

"We'll never outrun them," Deaken said calmly. The mountains had gained another hundred paces. They would soon merge together, fuse into a single block. "They're real. But you've let them get out of hand. You're afraid of them. Look for a way through; I can't find it."

Ned faced Junction and watched the tiny stalagmites bursting out of the ground in even rows, swelling and merging together to form another mountain wall.

"You won't find it back there," Deaken said. "We haven't been having that dream over and over for you to just return to Junction. The way out must be through those mountains." He pointed at the mountain before him. It had gained another hundred paces.

And Ned found an opening in a rock face. No stalagmites grew in front of it.

Stepping over growing stalagmites that blocked their way, they reached the opening and crawled into the damp tunnel. The opening closed behind them as the mountains fused together. If Deaken was right, Ned thought, and the mountains were real, then he could never go back to Junction.

It was completely dark and slightly damp in the tunnel. Ned didn't

mind the dampness—he was used to sleeping in a cellar. But the darkness frightened him.

Although Ned was tired and his arms and legs ached, he followed
Deaken's droning voice. He could not understand very much of what
Deaken was talking about, but he would remember and think about it
later. Ned could not tell how long they had been walking. The loss of
sight expanded time. Deaken kept up a continuous stream of conversation. Ned remembered Hilda and Sandra and, tired as he was, could
feel himself stiffen a bit.

And then Deaken suddenly stopped talking. And Ned was alone.

Ned had finished shouting. He pressed his back against the cold rock
wall and listened to his voice tumble away, echoing before him.

"Deaken, come back." It was almost a whisper. Ned waited for the
words to die. He knew that Deaken was not in the tunnel.

Perhaps I had stopped and fallen asleep, Ned thought.

No, he said to himself as he rubbed his eyes and relished the purple
splotches darting across his retinal field. Deaken would not have let
him lag behind. Ned had been awake, walking and listening to Deaken
speak about Hell and New York City and the future and minds
dreaming.

"*What you call Hell,*" he had said, "*is a place where physical laws
have become indeterminate. Hell is a substance, a quality that can be
affected by mind. It is unformed potential, the substratum of reality.
Your town Junction exists because people will it, and it remains as
small as they believe it must be.*

"*But there are other things contained in that substance, past realities
that remain outside of your vision and mind. Just as, until now, I had
remained outside of your vision and mind. . . .*"

Ned could not understand that. For him, Hell was simply the ab-
sence of God. But he thought about it again and fought another spasm
of fear. He sat on the cold tunnel floor and talked to himself. His back
ached.

I'm alone, he thought. He mouthed the words over and over. But it
had been his own unbridled fear that had formed the mountains. He
was safe in the tunnel. It was a place to be alone. And if he was alone,
he rationalized to himself, then he could not be harmed. The thoughts
comforted him, reminded him that he was tired and hungry.

"*Since the world is indeterminate,*" Deaken had said, "*the arbitrary
distinctions of time are of no use. Clock time has become dream time, a*

state in which past, present, and future exist at the same time, as possibilities. Time can no longer be thought of as a straight line or a continuous and connected series of events. It is a loop. All experience consists of loops. There is a loop for every memory pattern. A recurring dream is a loop, as is remembering the future; but you might not remember the same future as others. Overlaps are haphazard. They could only be consistent if one mind is providing continuity.

"Perhaps one mind is providing continuity. . . ."

Even after Deaken had explained Jung and determinism, Ned could not understand why Deaken did not see the obvious: tomorrow comes after today, and dreams are made of sleep.

And sleep is made of darkness, Ned thought, but the darkness of the tunnel still frightened him. Pressing his palms against his eyes, he waited for the familiar purple splotches to appear on his retinal walls. This time, the fluorite spots were richer and more intense. He waited until they filled his entire field of vision, and then opened his eyes. Before him, the tunnel was aglow with phosphorescent light, which provided security and humid warmth. Ned noticed that the walls were smooth, without seams or cracks. And he had forgotten about his hunger.

He walked into the fluorite light, stretching his arms before him. Ned was comfortable and secure. But as he walked, he began to feel a chill wind on his back, pushing him on with icicle feelers. Behind him it was dark.

"Telepathy and psi phenomena," Deaken had said, "did not seem to be ruled by any known physical laws. But now that physical laws in the past are gradually becoming more indeterminate, psi has become more consistent.

"Every night eleven million, five hundred and seventeen thousand people in New York City are dreaming about Junction. And you. Every night they remember the future. Everyone, every child and adult. That's why I've come for you. Perhaps that will stop the dreams. All the dreams are centered on you. What will we dream when you are in our present? . . ."

Ned could not understand how so many people could live in one place. He imagined that New York City was a huge monster of flesh and steel and glass waiting for him at the end of the tunnel. Its metal jaws were ready to swallow him and make him join the screaming crowds that lived in its pores.

I could turn the tunnel into Junction, Ned thought. Ned had made the mountains and the tunnel, Deaken had said. This tunnel led into the past, into New York. And New York City was real. But he could return to Junction right now and be squeezing Hilda and sucking Sandra. But that would not be real, Ned thought. That would only be a place in my mind.

He felt a chill draw across his spine. He told himself not to think about the mountains or Junction. The fears he had been repressing would produce monsters in the darkness behind him. And once created, they would eat him.

Before him, at the end of the tunnel, was New York City. That place was real—it was not in his mind. And behind him was Junction. That place, too, was real—it had spawned him.

But Ned wasn't quite sure. If Junction wasn't real. . . . He didn't want to think about it. If nothing was real but himself, he would be left with monsters.

He quickened his step.

Ned could see the end of the tunnel. It was a black dot that grew larger with every step. He forced himself to keep walking and let it draw him into its mouth. The chill breeze behind him ruffled his clothes. Ned could not turn back now: darkness and mountains blocked his way to Junction. The mountains were real. They had become independent of their creator. They were permanent. Turning around would be more frightening than going forward.

Ned hoped he would not meet his dreams. His only chance to return to Junction lay somewhere in the growing darkness ahead.

A tiny light flickered at the end of the tunnel. It turned red, then green, and blinked out. And the phosphorescent light was becoming dim, losing its power and warmth. It was being sucked into the darkness ahead. As Ned soon would be.

Ned fought a self-destructive urge to turn around and face the blackness. Its presence was so near that he thought he could touch it and grasp it if he outstretched his arm. He imagined it would be cold and wet. It was a tail looped behind him, pushing him forward into its wet mouth.

He screamed and ran to the end of the tunnel, hoping for death and purgation and the blond face of God. Instead, he found himself beside a subway train screaming to a halt.

People were milling around him, clawing each other, pushing for a better position, trying to reach the glass and metal doors that would soon slide shut. Men in suits, holding briefcases close to their chests,

burst out of the cars first, pushing eager entrants out of the way. The
men were followed by women in business suits and girls wearing
sweaters and dungarees, ladies in shorts and torn stockings, some holding babies with gray faces and screaming obscenities, others quiet and
shy. But they all had to fight the onrushing mob pushing and squeezing through the rubber-trimmed doors.

Ned was wet with perspiration; his coarse overshirt clung to his skin.
It was in the high nineties in the subway station. He looked around for
an exit. He had to get away from these people, from their pushing arms
and fetid breath and sweat-clogged clothes. And they looked outlandish
and frightening in their business costumes.

He spied an escalator ahead, its metal steps climbing forever. Perhaps
the moving stairs were a stairway to Heaven, Ned thought, and then
screamed as the train noisily left the station. The chalk and blackboard
sound of steel grinding steel. And another train screamed to a halt in its
place, a shining metal warrior hungering to fill up the empty space.

Ned pushed toward the moving stairs, his hands clasped to his chest
and elbows raised like fins to swim through a new rush of people. It
was truly a monster, Ned thought. All of these people, breathing
through a thousand mouths, sweating in a million places, might as well
be one.

"Hey, it's Ned," an overweight schoolgirl said to her companion.
They were both dressed in identical blue sailor outfits.

"Hey, look, it's Ned," they shouted at the crowd as they ran after
him.

Ned ran for a door made of iron bars. Beyond the door was a stairway in a metal cage filled with people hurrying up and down. Some
turned to look at Ned.

"It's the one in the dreams," shouted a man in a faded blue suit, acne
sores and collar rash visible on his neck.

"Well, get him," shouted a young woman carrying an armload of
books.

Ned ran past the turnstiles, pushed his way through the door, and
was pulled into the waiting crowd. Poking and pushing, it reached out
for him.

A boy in a torn black leather jacket crawled through the crowd that
had formed around Ned. He stood up and grabbed Ned's arm. The boy
had a smooth, unshaven face, and his greasy black hair was combed
back in a ponytail. Other boys wearing black leather jackets appeared,
and they pushed him through the crowd.

Arms reached out toward his face. Ned tried to disengage himself from the youths, but they held him too tightly. Someone hit him in the face. Numbness. He spat out a tooth and swallowed salty blood. Closing his eyes in fear and resignation, he let the crowd pummel him.

"Come on, man," said an olive-skinned boy with high cheekbones and sunken cheeks. "We can't drag you up the stairs."

"Up the stairs, we got Ned. Shit, we got Ned."

"Get out of the way," shouted the smooth-faced boy at anyone who might try to stop them. He waved his gravity knife and the crowd opened to let him pass. "Chicken bastards, we got Ned. And we're all going to Junction."

Ned opened his eyes and concentrated on the golden bear embossed on the black leather jacket before him. The boys were all around him. Ned smelled their pomade and wondered if it was a strange blend of black honey. Ned found it difficult to breathe. He coughed and swallowed blood.

The crowd followed the gang that held Ned. They seemed to be waiting for the right moment. They shouted and, gaining confidence, began punching the youths. One of the boys fired a pistol into the crowd. That drove the crowd into a frenzy. Ned turned to watch a group of young girls pull the smooth-faced boy down the stairs. They scratched his face and kicked him with small, deft strokes.

As the gang toughs were swallowed by the crowd, Ned tried to propel himself forward to the top of the stairs. But ready arms were waiting to seize him and pass him through the crowd. Together all the selfish entities made up a synergetic, unselfish whole. They were content to handle Ned for a few seconds, perhaps scratch and gouge him, and then pass him on.

Behind him, Ned could hear the crowd chanting, "Get the Dreamer, Ned. Ned. Ned's ahead. Ned's ahead. Get the Dreamer before he's dead."

And someone started singing a familiar song:

> "Back and side, go bare, go bare
> Both hand and foot go cold,
> But belly, God send you good ale enough
> Whether it be new or old!"

"Let him alone," cried a nun dressed in white with a black cowl that framed her pink face.

Others took up the song, and it spread through the crowd. "Don't hurt him, don't hurt him. He's the president, bim, bim, bim."

"He's the president?" shrieked the nun, and then she fainted.

Fifty feet from the stairway, they dropped him to the floor. A fat woman wearing bright orange lipstick sat on his chest and pushed her breasts together. Ned gagged from the sudden weight and closed his eyes. But this huge room on the main floor was etched under his eyelids; for a few seconds it would remain intact, a fading image soon to be relegated to memory.

The ceiling was high and crusted with carbon. Cement slabs and temporary, makeshift rooms broke up the parallel attraction of perspective lines. A hamburger stand with tiny stools and smeared plexiglass containers on the counter faced metal doors and compartments and turnstiles. Numbered luggage lockers lined the walls, jutted out to provide corners and alleys. Overhead signs and arrows pointed to the IRT and BMT and D and N and RR. Sharp contrasts of black and white, shadow and light. A cave lit by bare light bulbs.

Ned moved his arms close to his body to protect his hands from clumsy feet. But they would kill him anyway, he thought. The scum on the floor bunched up under his fingers. Ned knew if he opened his eyes, he would see the sticky city dust falling through the air. He thought about metal. It fascinated him. It reflected faces and lights and sparkled, yet would not break like glass.

He visualized a large window fronting an underground record store on the far side of the room. Latin music blared out of nowhere. Could this be Heaven? he thought, with glass and music played by invisible musicians?

Thoughts jammed into his mind.

"*It's a phonograph. That's what makes the music.*"

"*Can't you hear him? He's shouting.*"

"*His mouth isn't moving.*"

"*Neither is yours.*"

"*Let him alone.*"

Silence. General agreement. Group telepathy. Ned sighed and the grays behind his eyelids turned black. For an instant, he thought he was back in the tunnel. Alone. But he could feel the weight of the people above him, pushing down on him with their pulpy hands and scouring minds. Entering him. Now trying to revive him. Mass penance.

They became a huge toeless foot about to step on him. And he was an insect waiting for two-dimensional death.

V.

Washed and bandaged, hair neatly combed and smelling of soap, Ned stared out the window at the street below. He pressed his nose against the cold glass, felt the cool rush of air from the air-conditioner vent beneath the window. He looked at the blank theater billboards and the crowds in the street. The street had been cordoned off by police and no cars were permitted in the area.

As Ned watched the crowd below, he remembered the faces he had seen in the subway. They passed before him, portraits locked in the cellar of his memory. He examined their scars and birthmarks and wrinkles and expressions. And his mind wandered into new rooms of recent memory. He remembered being carried from the subway station by uniformed men who wheezed and snorted in the heat. Ned could still hear the screeching of subway machines and taste the rubber of the gas mask that was pushed into his face as tear-gas bombs bloomed over the scum floor.

Ned could feel the crowd below tugging at him. They would not let him alone. They wanted him, needed him. He dreamed of crashing through God's windowglass and falling into their outstretched arms.

But I'll be safe here, he told himself, trying to believe it. I'll control it the next time. The crowds tried to pull his face against the window-pane. They waved to him. Ned tried to feel secure within this large room with its smooth white walls, twin leather couches that faced each other across an expanse of rich brown carpet, dining table surrounded by high-backed chairs, ceiling-high bookcases filled with musty-smelling books and bric-a-brac of Hummel china, end tables covered with glass, and well-stocked bar and early-model television. This room was a haven from the harsh realities below. But it was a precarious, transparent nest.

Ned's warm breath fogged the windowpane.

"Everything's gradually changing," said Renny Weissman, the plainclothes policeman assigned to stay with Ned. He wore a blue serge suit and a brown striped tie, was well over six feet tall, and combed his thick brown curly hair into a pompadour that reminded Ned of a flight of stairs.

Ned didn't turn around, although he could feel the pressure of Weissman's gaze on the back of his neck. He felt the pressure increase as Weissman stepped closer to the window.

"It's stable for a while, and then there's another change. Take this hotel. It used to be the Astor Plaza, a fairly new office building. I was in there a few times, but I didn't like it—it was too big and sterile, reminded me of a hospital.

"Before the Astor Plaza, there was the Astor Hotel. This hotel. It had been here for years, a tourist hotel—this is the center of the theater district. It was a landmark. And then they tore it down to build the Plaza building.

"Well, after a change—we get them every few days now—the old Astor Hotel had replaced the office building. It was almost the same as the old one, except for those gargoyles on the ledges."

Ned looked at the ledge that passed under the window. It was discolored by pigeon droppings. By pressing his face against the window, Ned could see a gargoyle's outstretched arm. But Ned remembered what the gargoyle looked like: a mottled marble body covered with eyes, some closed, some open. He had seen similar gargoyles in the hospital lobby. They stood under a stained-glass window that depicted the baptism of Christ by St. John.

"I don't mind the change at all," Weissman continued. "I always liked the Astor. Used to stop at the coffee shop on Sunday mornings in the old days.

"Strange thing, though, is that when the office building blinked out and the hotel took its place, all the hotel people were at their old jobs. And the office workers—anyone who had been in the building when it blinked out—were all missing. But it happened around one o'clock, and all the executives and company presidents were out to lunch. We lost about four hundred office boys and secretaries.

"Anyway, the city government proclaimed the hotel to be government property—the mayor and mayor's mansion had disappeared too, that day—and fired all the workers. Some scientist came to the conclusion that the hotel workers couldn't be real. Well, they are. I tracked them down on the welfare books."

Ned didn't reply. He watched the people below. They were carrying placards and silently shouting at him. Ned listened to the hum of the air-conditioner. And heard their thoughts.

"We believe in God and Ned."

A young girl, dressed in dungarees and a paint-stained pullover sweater, held up a pane of glass and tried to reflect the sun into Ned's eyes. *"Glass is holy. God protect us from encroaching Hell."*

"We are penitent. We await Purgatory, knowing that God's in sight."

"Give us another dream. Tell us what to do."

"Another dream. Another dream. Tell us. Tell us."

Ned drew his finger across the steamed window and dreamed about Junction. He imagined how everything was changing, growing more indeterminate for a few moments or hours, and then settling back into known reality, waiting for the glue of newly created reality to harden.

He listened to Weissman's thoughts, theories, and fears, and then reached out into the city. Beyond New York were other cities and towns and farmlands and mountains; but Ned sensed that they were changing faster, that they would soon be swallowed up by Hell. Only New York would remain. And Junction, somewhere in the future.

He let his mind wander into Greenwich Village. He smelled the marigolds, peonies, petunias, geraniums, tulips, and laughed. The streets had been transformed into gardens and flowers bloomed everywhere. Flowers of every description grew on lawns that had once been cement. Bluebonnets, red clover, goldenrod, black-eyed Susan, pink and white lady-slippers, iris, dogwood, red roses, Indian paintbrush, bitterroot scented the air, choked the allergic with pollen. Cars and shops became hothouses for tropical plants.

Ned investigated Wall Street, the small roads and high buildings of the business section. The old mixed with the new. Ned grew impatient and left. His mind lingered in the Brooklyn-Battery Tunnel, then floated uptown, past himself and midtown, through Harlem and the Bronx, up the Henry Hudson Parkway, to settle on the cold steel of the George Washington Bridge. Soon, he knew, that, too, would be destroyed, the last door into Hell closed.

Ignoring Weissman and the crowd below, Ned investigated Westchester through the minds of those who lived there. But the crowd below was stabbing him, tearing off his defenses, thrusting unsure fingers into him.

"Help us. We believe in God. We believe in you.

"We believe in you. We believe inyou. Webelieveinyou.

"WebelieveinyouWebelieveinyouWebelieveinyouwebelieveinyou.

"Ned. Ned. Ned. Ned. NedNed. NedNedNednednednedned."

People in Westchester heard the chorus, reached out to Ned and augmented the drone of thoughts. Ned tried to talk, but could only broadcast fear. He pressed his face against the window and screamed.

Weissman's large hands locked over Ned's arms, pulling him away from the window. He tried to break loose and said, "I want to stay. Leave me alone." But he thought, *Please help me, get me away from them, everyone leave me alone, give me the tunnel. I can't stand flesh.*

And then it was over. Weissman crossed the room to the bar and mixed himself a drink. Ned returned to the window. He pressed his face against the cool glass. They were still in the street below, shouting, raising their placards, praying and beating their chests.

But Ned couldn't hear them. He was shut inside his hotel room.

VI.

Ned and Weissman were alone in the hotel. The maids and other necessary personnel were permitted inside at certain hours, but other than that the hotel was empty. But it was well guarded. Policemen manned the roof and ledges and formed a human wall around the hotel. A double pane of bulletproof glass had been substituted for the old, imperfect window glass. Ned would not allow the windows to be covered. Although he yearned for the solitude of the tunnel, he had to be able to see into the city, its glass and steel and people. Ned could not understand this ambivalence.

Although Ned was comfortable for the time being, he did not like policemen walking on the roof. He could tolerate them during the stable periods; but during the indeterminate times they would bear down on him with their thoughts. And he would feel the weight of every cell in their bodies.

It was curious, Ned thought, that the position of a body could so affect his mind. Perhaps its cause could be traced to the Mount Sinai Hospital, where white-capped nurses with small breasts had constantly watched him and doctors in white smocks came in and out without warning. They had tested him for everything, given him GI's and spinals, pricked his fingers, tied hoses around his arms, measured his brain waves, drugged him with this and that, waited for him to dream, X-rayed him, probed, asked questions, would not permit him a whore and told him that he had recently contracted a venereal disease. Penicillin had been in order, and then more smears and psychological tests. And visits by scientists and historians and a philosopher and a few members of the trade press.

Ned had screamed to be let alone, so he was drugged and re-examined. They had found spots on his lung. They measured him and bathed him and collected his urine. And all the tests had proved to be negative (except, of course, the Wassermann).

Ned had taken to sleeping for long periods in the hospital. When awakened, he had refused to talk with anyone. And during the indeterminate times he would squirm in his electric hospital bed and scream and shout that he couldn't stay there. He had said that he couldn't stand everyone dying around him, and that the ghosts of the previously dead were piling up on the soon-to-die.

And they waited. They were interested in his dreams and had wanted to know why everyone else had stopped dreaming about him. Ned had told them that he couldn't remember his dreams, but the psychiatrists and psychologists would not believe him. They told him that he was repressing his fears. And they had seemed to know that everyone would soon dream of him again.

So Ned had told them that he could not dream correctly in the hospital. He said that the ghosts of the soon-to-be-dead were crowding into his sleep and taking his dreams. The politicians finally persuaded the doctors and psychologists to move Ned to a dream-conducive atmosphere. Ned asked for a hotel, because he had read a book by that name one Sunday afternoon in Junction.

Although it was easier in the hotel, Ned still could not remember his dreams, nor affect the dreams of others. And the indeterminate times were becoming worse: too many minds clawed and raked him, gleefully sucked out his energy. When it became intolerable, Ned would fortify himself with Demerol and wish for dreams, Hilda, and some good pot.

Ned stared out the window at the crowds below. The crowds had thinned until there were more white-helmeted policemen than spectators. The spectators were losing faith and drifting away, leaving the policemen with no one to watch but themselves.

These city people were different from anyone else, Ned thought. They were so greedy for something more, that when they found it they tried to tear it apart. Although they wanted to merge—a primeval urge— tradition and morals and blocks of cement and steel and gray skies choked with dust and ennui assured separation. In desperation—or just for fun—they built and then destroyed, one a rationale for the other.

Weissman stepped out of the bedroom and, pulling his narrow brown necktie under his collar, said, "Come on, Ned. Get away from the goddam window and get dressed. Those people will be here in a few minutes."

Ned ignored him and thought about Hilda. In the indeterminate periods, he dreamed about her jelly-fat body and auburn hair and tried to make her real. But something was wrong—he could not give her substance. He tried Sandra. She remained a pleasant memory: a pale chiseled face, a pouting mouth, short cropped hair, and black fuzz around her large nipples.

"Come on, Ned, dammit." Weissman finished tying his necktie and smoothed it against his starched white shirt.

"Alright, alright." Ned turned away from the window. Although he was sweaty and needed a change of clothes, he didn't feel like washing and dressing for company. Since he left the hospital, Ned had taken to wearing flamboyant silk shirts—notably those with colorful Hawaiian patterns—and dungarees. The dungarees reminded him of the coarse trousers he used to wear in Junction. In the last few days everything—smells, sounds, the play of light on a skyscraper—reminded him of Junction. Memory was beginning to color the past and replace it with its own reality. Past pain and discomfort were, for the sake of pleasant memory, forgotten.

"I'm not going to change," Ned said. "I like this shirt, anyway."

"Well, you'll have to; there's some important people coming up. So take a bath."

"Screw them," Ned said. "What do they want?"

Weissman stretched out on the couch beside the bedroom door, patting his kinky hair in place before he rested his head on the worn leather armrest. "It's something important," he mumbled.

"What's so important?"

Weissman closed his eyes and his left leg slipped from the couch. He buried his toes in the rug. "Something that will happen, can't quite. . . ."

"What's the Hell's wrong with you?" Ned asked, shaking his shoulder. Weissman grunted and smiled. His face softened. By clenching his teeth and sucking in his cheeks, Weissman could tighten his face and give the illusion of alertness and strength. But sleep restored it to its true form. It was as if loose layers of skin were draped over his skull, ready to be pressed and pulled into a desired mask at will.

Weissman had always waited until Ned was asleep before he would catnap. And he would never sleep for more than two hours consecutively. Now Ned could daydream without feeling the pressure of Weissman's gaze on the back of his neck. He could freely walk around the well-provided suite without being followed or spoken to. Or he could try to dream up Sandra or Hilda or even one of the street girls. But everything around him was hard and cold, impervious to his thoughts.

Trying to rationalize a sin he was about to commit, Ned started for the bathroom, which was adjacent to the bedroom. And he remembered his father's words: "Onanists will forever fall through the mirrors of Hell."

Ned's father had once told him that Hell could not claim any glass. That's why Satan invented mirrors, which are made out of darkness and can only show up the evil nature of people. There were no mirrors in Junction. It was said that they had all been thrown into Hell, where they reflect and magnify sorrow and pain.

But there was a mirror over the sink in the bathroom. And all the monsters of Hell were on the other side, watching and laughing. The bedroom was even worse: it sported full-length door mirrors and a vanity. Ned could not lie on the bed without being seen by monsters on the other side. In the bathroom, at least, he could duck out of sight of the Hellglass.

Yet he had not asked Weissman to have them removed. If he was going to stay here, he would live with mirrors and Hell, as God had prescribed. He would watch himself sin and grow ugly; he would tolerate Weissman and the men on the roof. And he would give the monsters behind the mirror an eyeful before Weissman woke up.

Ned's wry grin turned to rictus when he saw his father's face in the bathroom mirror. Ned leaned against the sink for support.

"How do you like it here in the midst of Hell?" Ned's father asked.

"How did you get here?"

"Go to sleep and I'll tell you."

Ned noticed that his father's hairline had receded since he had last seen him. Perhaps this was not his father, but a creature from Hell. A misdirection.

"Are you my father?"

"Does it matter, son? Go to sleep and I'll explain."

Ned went into the bedroom and watched his father in the vanity mirror.

"Well," his father said, "lay down and go to sleep."

Ned hesitated, prayed it was his father—but if it wasn't, then it was God's fate—and lay down and held his breath for luck. As he exhaled, he heard his father speak.

"You dreamed that scene in the bathroom, you know. Time can be cut up anyway you like. Substitute the middle for the end, the end for the middle. It doesn't matter. The bathroom scene was hung in the middle of the dream. I reshuffled it so that it would make sense to you. And make you go to sleep."

"But I thought I *was* asleep."

"In a manner of speaking, you were. Different states of consciousness equate to different levels of sleep. At any rate, I simply turned things around. For example, you could easily conceive a child before you were born. And, in fact, you did. Remember Donatello Toth? No, you wouldn't; he died from Parkinson's disease when you were very young."

"Are you my father?" Ned asked.

"No," the voice said after a pause. "If you like, you can be with him. But eventually you've got to face this, me, if you like. It is a piece that cannot be ignored if all the reasonable alternatives are going to be—or are, or were—experienced."

Ned tried to open his eyes, but he couldn't. A light flickered before him and he dreamed that he was back in the tunnel.

"Would you like to see Donatello Toth?"

"That's crazy," Ned said, mumbling in his fitful sleep.

"No, it's not. Consecutive time is a mnemonic device, that's all. Cause and effect are only pieces that happen to fit together."

What's a mnemonic device? Ned thought. The voice had lost all its affectations and pomposity. It did not sound like his father and was developing a Brooklyn accent. It rose in register until it sounded like Weissman.

"You know what that is," the voice said. "Push yourself forward, or backward, to wherever the answer lies."

And Ned remembered what a mnemonic device was, although he had never heard of one before.

"You really know everything that has been accomplished through evolution. And, of course, everything that has been lost. So, in a way, you know everything."

"Then, what's the end?" Ned asked, gaining confidence in this game.

"What we're doing now. And what we'll do later. But this will lead into it. We don't have to worry, because we don't have to stay there."

"Here?"

"Open your eyes."

Spread out before Ned was a field scattered with boulders, moss clinging to the interface between rock and soil. But Ned wasn't sure. The field flickered, turned into a forest, and then into Junction.

Ned stood upright. "Am I walking in my sleep?"

"Don't worry," the voice said. "Everyone is watching you. You won't fall."

Ned searched the outskirts of the town, looked for a familiar face. He could not see the glass church, the highest building in Junction. The ground and stones and nearby brook seemed to be whispering, holding conversation, a dialectic he could not yet understand. But Ned did not let himself move randomly. He fought for control, for a graspable succession of events. By choosing cause and effect, he permitted one event to lead into another and ignored the psi handholds that would make him dizzy.

And he found that he was not looking into Junction.

Large split-level houses sported tiers of windows that overlooked rolling hills and pine forests. Swimming pools filled with blue water and bikinied girls with dark tans (and wealthy men with bald heads and pinky rings) became the private oases of this summer-green desert. Sleek cars, as yet not invented, moved slowly along the picturesque winding roads.

"Call it Goshen," the voice said. "We'll meet here."

"Why?" asked Ned. "Why do you want to meet with me?"

"Not only with you."

"With whom, then?"

"They're on their way. Wake up."

VII.

"Come on, Ned," Weissman said. "Get away from the goddam window and get dressed. Those people will be here in a few minutes."

Ned ignored him and thought about Sandra. In the indeterminate periods, he dreamed about her pouting mouth and the black fuzz around her large nipples and tried to make her real. But something was wrong—he could not give her substance. He tried Hilda. She remained a pleasant memory: a freckled face, jelly-fat body that smelled of potatoes, and thick auburn hair.

"Come on, Ned, dammit." Weissman finished tying his necktie and smoothed it against his starched white shirt.

"Alright, alright." Ned turned from the window. A bath was in order: he was sweaty and his hair smelled sour.

Ned was not in the violet-scented lukewarm tub water for five minutes before Weissman insisted that he get out and dress. While Ned glued his light brown hair to his scalp with orange pomade, Weissman laid out a conservative blue suit and white shirt on the bed for him. But Ned wore a red and blue flowered shirt with a long white collar and tartan trousers.

There was a knock on the door. Weissman, who had been in telephone and radio communication with the guards and police, placed the receiver on the cradle and walked to the door. Ned stared out the window into the darkness—that was a good posture for effect. But the darkness turned the window into a mirror and Ned watched Weissman pat down his cowlick before opening the door. "One should always look *through* a window, not *at* a window," Ned's father had said. As Ned watched the door open, he added another sin to his list.

But I'm important now, Ned thought. I'm in New York, a city made of glass. And mirrors, he added as an afterthought. Here his sins would pile up faster. "A great man has more sins to repent for, more crimes to be forgiven, and a longer stay in Purgatory—if he does not go to Hell," his father had said one Passover when Snapover, the tailor, sat for dinner. After that, Ned had been quite sure that Snapover would certainly go to Hell.

Ned turned around to greet the guests that entered the room.

"Good evening, Ned," Dr. Kheal said. "I hope you've had a pleasant day." Dr. Kheal, a tall, skinny man in his early forties, had light brown hair that was beginning to turn gray, and a smooth, relaxed face. His green jacket with brown elbow patches was frayed at the cuffs, and his black trousers had lost their crease. Ned noticed that he needed a shave.

"I'd like you to meet Miss Ingrid Oolan, who has been waiting quite some time to meet you. She's a parapsychologist from St. John's University." She had long black hair and pale, almost translucent skin. The delicate network of veins was clearly visible on her throat.

Is this just chance that she looks like Sandra? Ned asked himself. She wasn't wearing a bra, and Ned could see the outline of her nipples on her open-collared shirt. Her black hair and dark skirt contrasted with her pale face and white shirt. She was a pen-and-ink drawing on white paper, Ned thought. But her features were different from Sandra's. Her lips were thin and her eyes were set a bit too close together, giving her the appearance of always staring. Ned wondered if she, too, had black fuzz around her nipples.

"And this is Dr. Michael Taharahnugi," said Kheal. Taharahnugi, an albino black of medium build, stood beside Ingrid, his pale hand almost touching hers. His pink eyes were buried deep in his square face, and he wore his kinky white hair long—it framed his face in a bleached halo. Ned guessed he was a sociologist, then reminded himself to stop sidestepping, lest "cause should be sundered from effect," as his father would probably say.

"And you know Dr. Ladislas, of course." Nicholas Ladislas had a lined, sour face and a shock of white hair that was thinning in the back. He had what was known as "lazy eye," and his heavy-lidded eyes never seemed to move. Ned knew that he sometimes wore an eye patch, but that was an affectation. Ned didn't like him, sensed he had an inflated, fragile ego, and then told himself to stop sidestepping. There were too many people in the room. He hoped they would leave soon— he was beginning to feel the effects of claustrophobia.

"And here's someone you haven't seen in some time," Kheal said.

It was Deaken. Ned had not recognized him. He was much thinner than Ned remembered, and his face was drawn, giving him an older appearance. He looked like a cadaver, Ned thought. His large, dark eyes were sinking into his face. Although his movements were shaky, he handled his cigarette with aplomb and brushed off the ash with his pinky finger.

No doubt he's ill, Ned thought. Could be a tumor of the gastrointestinal tract. Or Hodgkin's disease. It was probably lymphosarcoma. Ned remembered a few of his father's homilies and forced himself to think along previously earmarked paths. He told himself that he had to stop wandering and sidestepping.

"I hope you have found New York interesting, Ned," Deaken said, using one cigarette to light another.

"You look different," Ned said.

"Do I? I don't feel any different. Well, it all worked out, didn't it? You're finally providing New York with its dreams."

"Yes, you certainly are," said Taharahnugi.

Ned was sure Taharahnugi was a sociologist.

"Everyone's been dreaming each other's dreams for a week," Kheal said. "The dreams ran in a sequence and we've just come to the end of it. I think we have enough information now. We've come to talk to you about your dreams."

"But it's not a week," Ned said. "I can't remember having any dreams until tonight."

"Well, that's news to me," Weissman said.

"Let's sit down," Ned said, motioning Ingrid Oolan to the couch near the bedroom door. He sat down between Ingrid and Kheal. Ladislas sat down on a soft chair beside Taharahnugi, who had claimed the antique rocker and was drumming his long fingers on the small end table, while Deaken pulled one of the high-backed chairs away from the dining table. They were mapping out a tight, defensible niche in the overlarge living room.

Ned let his hand slip from his lap until it touched Ingrid's leg. She tensed for a second, then moved toward Kheal and crossed her legs, showing off blue climbing veins that reached for her knees.

Weissman brought out drinks for everyone: a sherry for Ingrid and cognac for Kheal, bock beer in tall frosted glasses for Deaken and Ladislas, and soda water for Taharahnugi. Before retiring to the couch at the other end of the room, Weissman served Ned the last bottle of a particular Mexican beer that had a green tinge when held to the light. Ned loved it. Weissman had once tried it and suffered the next few hours with diarrhea.

"Tell us about your dream," Ladislas said, rubbing his eyes as if he would soon go to sleep.

Ingrid stretched her legs out and Kheal nodded to Ned. So Ned told them about the apparition in the mirrors and Donatello Toth (who could not be) and Junction and Goshen, where they all would meet.

They asked him questions and argued among themselves. But Ned felt himself losing the drift of their conversation. He tried to remain alert, but his head kept lolling forward, dipping into sleep. In his dreams the words would take on a life of their own. They became animated film characters running through their own pathos of life and death.

And Ned would awaken with a start, feeling fuzzy and warm, only to dream again of words and cartoon animals.

"Although our dreams were different than the boy's," Ladislas said as he scratched at the corner of his eye, "we all received the same directive to go to Goshen."

"But I can't believe that an alien presence is responsible for the breakdown of our known continuum and laws, as Ladislas suggests," Taharahnugi said. When he wasn't talking, he would drum his fingers impatiently on the end table.

"I think the answers might as easily lie within ourselves," Kheal said. "Everyone will agree, I think, that this is, at least in part, a psi phenomenon."

Ned fell asleep again and dreamed of Ingrid's blue-veined legs. Words and letters acquired form and personality and passed before him. It was strange, he thought, that the others did not recognize this as another indeterminate period. Yet the presence of other people did not bother him as it had in the past.

He allowed himself to drift freely through the unformed potential, dimly realizing that he was holding the stuff of the room together.

But walls and doors could just as easily become trees and snow.

And trees and snow could easily become sand and stone.

Ned dreamed that he was lying in reddish yellow desert sand. His crotch itched. A scorpion was making its way toward his extended arm, its feelers touching the ground, sensing and feeling movement that was miles away. It would crawl a few inches, curl up and wiggle its pincers, clean them with its lobster legs.

Ned could hear the creature whispering to him, but its comments were too simple to be understood. Ned found that his arm was pointed toward a church carved out of the soft, porous tuff of a stone cliff. He knew that he was seeing through the stone into its holy insides. He glimpsed the fresco-secco portrait of Emperor Constantine Porphyrogen-itus in the narthex entrance hall and the chapels to the east and the ceiling domes resting on vertical cylinders of stone. And the fading frescoes on the walls and ceiling depicting scenes from the life of Christ. He remembered that around the ninth century in Cappadocia, a province in central Turkey, monks had whittled God's stone into this church, cutting into the rock from above to reveal a church they would create inside.

From the outside, the spires, cones, and folds of rock were overpowering in their monochromatic contrast of white and black. They hid hundreds of God's monasteries and churches. Jutting into a pale, cloudless sky, they stood as a true synthesis of man's way and nature's display.

"Do you want another beer, Ned?" Weissman asked. "You'll have to take bock, we're out of the Mexican stuff."

Ned shook his head and tried to retrace the conversation. The change was over: Ned felt alert and restless. Ingrid was still sitting beside him, her legs crossed, right hand just touching Ned's leg.

"Yes, I agree," Ingrid said. "The fact that we all dreamed of that desert church is indicative of psi phenomena. And the religious symbolism corresponds with Ned's beliefs. In fact, the paintings on the walls looked very much like the sketches Ned had done for Dr. Court. Ned is quite talented; they could easily be dream paintings." She pressed her hand against Ned's leg.

"And all the figures Ned imagined in the Rorschachs had white haloes," Kheal said.

"I made them up," Ned said. "I didn't really see them in the ink splotch; I drew them in myself."

"Well, that's what you do with that kind of test," Ingrid said, patting his hand.

"No, it's different," Ned said, resting his knee against her leg. "All the other stuff, I saw."

"But how could Ned know anything about the place we've been dreaming about?" Ladislas asked, resting his head on the back of his chair and staring at the wall from under half-closed eyelids. "Goreme is in Turkey."

"I just dream it," Ned said.

They ignored him.

"Well, why couldn't he dream about Goreme?" asked Kheal.

"Because Junction is isolated," Ladislas said. "It's surrounded by chaos, their conception of Hell. And who knows—"

"Goreme would have been in a library book," Ingrid said. "And Ned read everything he could find."

"Yes," Ladislas said, sitting up, "and he remembers all the titles he read, which is a considerable amount. He has a photographic memory, yet he did not remember anything that could even remotely tie in with Goreme. It seems that Junction has destroyed everything relating to geography and world history, except for a few biblical accounts. Ned could not dream an exact duplicate of Goreme, detail by detail, by chance."

"Yes, he certainly could dream Goreme, just as I dreamed Junction," Deaken said. He sounded as if he was out of breath. "As the world becomes more indeterminate, our arbitrary distinctions of time must break down. They seem to work here only part of the time. We have also experienced the breakdown of certain spatial relationships. But what we simultaneously experience as space does not necessarily have to correspond with real space. We can overlay our experienced space onto its equivalent geometer's space and then merge any overlaps. Just as in aerial photography, the overlaps ensure reliable mapping. But in aerial photography, when we have blank spaces, we have to use our imagination to fill in the gaps. That is our only available means of connection. Mankind is and has always been split in time and space. It is through Ned that we have established contact with another community beyond our time. . . ."

"Aren't you forgetting about yourself?" Kheal asked. "You initiated the contact, remember that."

"And that contact was possible because time is not a straight line," Deaken continued. "It is made up of loops, or may be a loop itself. The only way I could reach Ned was by imagining the necessary overlap into the future, that's how I stepped into a possible future. The same holds true for the past, as witnessed by Ned's journey here."

"And what do you think will happen when all the overlaps merge, if they ever do?" asked Ladislas.

"I don't know," said Deaken, "but I think we will soon find out."

"Bullshit," Taharahnugi said. He stopped drumming on the table.

Ingrid's hand was actively pressing Ned's leg. Could I have dreamed this to happen before? Ned asked himself as he put his arm around Ingrid, resting his hand on her shoulder.

"No, I don't think it's bullshit," Kheal said. "Deaken did not exactly imagine his way to Junction. He dreamed it. And the way things are now, that's just as real."

"Oh," Ladislas said. "Then, you're dreaming me and everything else, and I'm dreaming you and everything else so cleverly that our dreams match."

"I didn't say that, but it's possible. An interesting solution."

"Then," Ladislas continued, "there might be an integrating force drawing us to Junction, dreaming us all."

"Your alien?" Kheal asked.

"Hooray," said Ned. He glanced at Taharahnugi and smiled. "Dreaming works as good as anything else. Hell, how do you think I manage to oogle Ingrid, if not by fooling around with the stuff of change?"

"That's all been set up," Ingrid said. "We've all been dreaming about it for a week. All those moves have already been plotted."

"And we've been dreaming of going on a trip to Goshen-Goreme," Deaken said. "Perhaps we'll find some answers there."

"Can we all be ready by tomorrow morning?" asked Kheal.

Ned knew the answers, saw the end of the dream; but they had dreamed different endings, so Ned played along. As they fussed over details, he nodded and pretended to pay attention and fondled Ingrid's leg. It didn't matter, he thought. Although Ned felt a compulsion not to drift away from the immediate present, he was becoming impatient. And Ladislas was talking too much.

"All right," Kheal said, "I guess that's about it."

Ned waited for the others to leave. Ingrid acted as hostess and escorted them to the door, laughing and promising to be ready in the morning.

"Well, are you coming?" she asked Ned as she stepped into the bedroom.

Ned followed, leaving Weissman in the living room to read his New York *Times* and smoke hand-rolled Cuban cigars, a commodity that had suddenly appeared on the market after the last change. Ned wondered if his noisy lovemaking would bother Weissman. Probably not, he thought. But Ned wheezed like a seal when he reached a climax.

Rationalizing his uncountable sins, Ned watched Ingrid in the full-length mirror. He dreamed of all the hollows in her body where he could rest his face, all the fleshy handholds he could squeeze as he came.

"All we have to do is do it," she said as she combed her long black hair. "It's all been set up, we just follow along."

"Well," Ned said, "you do have a choice. You don't have to mimic your dreams."

"No, I've made my choice. I agreed to it." She stared at herself in the mirror and unbuttoned her blouse.

"Well, I didn't," Ned said as he took a step toward the door.

As she took off her shirt, exposing her breasts fed by visible arteries, she smiled and said, "Wait a moment, Ned. As you will see, they do have hair around the nipples."

And a smile of even white teeth drew Ned back into the room.

VIII.

The crowds filled the street and backed up against the windows of the plush Park Avenue shops. Fleeing from their dreams, they chanted and sang songs. They co-opted policemen, gray ladies with tiny clubs, and pompadoured boys to help them break through the many weak points of the police line. Secretaries in colored scarfs and office boys sporting sideburns and dirty shirts threw handfuls of confetti from skyscraper windows. Sparkles and streamers spun and danced their way to the street below. They would soon be swallowed up by sweeping machines intent on restoring the world to a sober gray.

Ned waved to the crowds from the back seat of a Cadillac limousine. He sat between Weissman and Bunker, a young detective with a pock-marked face and a swollen lower lip. Bunker's aloof style and quiet manners reminded Ned of the "cool fifties." Lately, Ned had found it easier to remember details of a past he had never experienced.

"Sit back in the seat," Weissman said.

Ned settled back into the cushioned seat for a few seconds and then sat up to watch a girl climb onto the hood of the car. Facing the windshield, she straddled the silver hood ornament. Long blond hair covered her shoulders and part of her thin face. She wore a loose dress, and Ned could see her tiny breasts jiggle with each movement of her arms.

"How the Hell did she get up there?" Weissman asked. Bunker, of course, would not answer. He pleated the fabric of his trousers and sucked in his cheeks.

"Ned. Ned. Get out of bed," she screamed as she pounded on the windshield with red fists. Two policemen with red armbands pulled her off the hood and were swallowed by the crowd.

Ned thought he heard her scream, "Ned. Ned. I want to love you before you're dead." He looked around at the crowds he passed. Faces focused for an instant. Everyone was shouting with the girl's voice, singing her songs.

"Ned. Ned. Ned. We want to love you.

"Before you're dead.

"Dead Ned."

Boys with painted faces sang contralto. Someone thudded against the car and rolled under the tires, giving himself for his faith. Ned watched his proselytes disrobe as he passed. A wave of his hand and new faces appeared out of a pastel fog of confetti.

"Christ is here and Ned is His prophet," shouted a curly-haired boy in a white robe. He prostrated himself in the road. Ned felt the car lurch as it crushed the boy's chest. The crowd was singing. A policeman with his cap cocked over his left eye gave him the finger. A blond girl cupped her breasts for him. Onanists lined the street.

Ned prayed that this would not become a difficult indeterminate period. He could not suffer a change now, not with these thousands of people threatening to crush him inside the soft interior of the car.

A rock bounced off the unbreakable windshield. A pistol was fired twice. Screams, laughter, more confetti snow for the departing hero. Ned sat up straight in the car, braced himself, played his role, and waved with an open hand, fingers aflutter. A perfumed silk handkerchief would complete the tableau, he thought.

"Alright, Ned," Weissman said. "That's enough. Stop waving. I'm tired of your hand fluttering in front of my face."

"But that's what they want," Ned said.

"I don't care."

Ned stopped waving and the crowds pushed past the police lines to converge on the car. They beat their fists against the windows, slashed the tires, crawled over the hood, and some were crushed as the car slowed to a halt. Screaming for Ned and God and a new order, they rocked the car, picked it up and dropped it. And then picked it up again. Ned was thrown against Weissman, who was swearing with his best Brooklyn accent. Regaining his balance, Ned readied himself for the next shock.

The crowd paused, like a weightlifter slowly inhaling and curling stiff fingers around a steel bar, and flexed its muscles by throwing the car on its side.

"Sonovabitch," Weissman screamed, as Ned and Bunker squeezed him against the door. Ned banged his knee on the floorboard, trying to move out of Bunker's way.

The window shattered. Shards of green-tinged glass were followed by long fingers and fists. Bunker fired several shots, and a skinny girl fell through the window. She smelled of perfume and sweat. As Bunker pushed the girl out of his way, a man in a green suit crawled through the window and grabbed his arm.

"Get out of the way, Ned," Weissman said, pointing his pistol at the man in the suit.

Well, fire, Ned said to himself, feeling another change coming on. The girl beside him moaned. Her arm flopped behind her head, which was wedged against Ned's knee.

"Mother of God," Bunker screamed as he was pulled out of the car by his hair. Weissman fired into the window, but there were more people than bullets.

"God is the mother of Ned," the girl whispered. Her left eye fell open.

"Get Ned," screamed the crowd.

Weissman pulled Ned under him, straddled his head with his legs, protected him with his muscular body. Ned thought he could hear Bunker screaming as he was swallowed by the crowd. He sidestepped and watched an old lady pinch Bunker's cheeks, then stick her fingers in his eyes.

"We love you Ned. We love you," the crowd screamed with one voice.

Weissman screamed as his ear was torn off.

"Save the world for mankind."

"God is the mother of Ned."

And a dissenting voice. "Fuck you."

Ned was aware of the exploding CS and CN tear-gas grenades. But it took such a long time for a second to pass. A fog machine belched HC smoke. Canisters of Nausea gas and Blister gas exploded into the crowd. Finally a propellent canister of Mace was shot into the car by a giggling policeman.

The policeman was quickly replaced, but not before the canister exploded, filling the car with smoke. Ned choked, still remembering the pungent odor of Weissman's crotch.

Ned coughed, and arms reached into the car to pull him out. He was passed among the crowd, worshiped and beaten. Ned smelled the rubber of a gas mask being fitted over his face. He gagged and remembered the subway station, its noises and people with their pushing arms and fetid breath and sweat-clogged clothes.

"Don't kill Ned," they shouted. "Love him. God is his mother. Mother of God."

Ned vomited, but the reluctant police were a wall around him. They tried not to become part of the crowd. They screamed for his blood, but held on to their sanity.

Ned listened to the shots being fired. He sidestepped and slowed down the bullets so he could watch them. A few screams, a few deaths, and Ned was still protected. He pulled at his mask and tried not to think about Weissman as everything went white before him.

"Don't protect me," he screamed. "I want to do it." But it wasn't much of a feat, since he was so close to the Pan Am Building.

The elevator doors opened and Ned found himself on the roof of the building. Standing on this concrete shelf, he could look down on the smaller spires of the city, a pincushion carpet of steel and cement. But the heliport was smaller than he expected. The clarity and fullness of Ned's memory overshadowed the prosaic immediate reality. Ned had stopped worrying about sidestepping into a past he had not experienced. He wandered into the past and future for diversion or information.

His party was already in the Vertol helicopter. Ned knew that the helicopter was turbine-powered—whatever that was; he did not care to search his memory just now—a commercial version of the U. S. Army YHC-1. Although it was ungainly on the ground (how could such a pregnant fuselage be supported by those frail rotor arms?) Ned thought it was beautiful. Its six tiny portholes reminded him of sailing ships he had never seen. And it was painted white, the color of Heaven and virtue.

But would the air in Heaven hold them up? Ned asked himself, hoping that God would provide an answer. The sky was gray, filled with pollutants. But he didn't have to worry yet: he was still a safe distance from Heaven.

The pilot hurried him into the copter. Ingrid waved as he entered, and he sat down beside her. Ned remembered that she had left his bed at four o'clock that morning. Too tired to start an argument, he had feigned sleep.

"How are you, Ned?" she asked as he sat down. Taharahnugi, who was sitting across the aisle with Kheal, frowned and adjusted his seat to a reclining position. "Aren't you a bit frightened?" she asked in a condescending tone. "I certainly am."

Ned nodded his head and let his hand slide to her leg. She crossed her legs and huddled close to the window. Ned left his hand where it was, deciding what to do next.

"I wanted to have a chance to talk with you," she said, moving slightly closer to him but watching his hand. "I've been very interested in your dreams—the ones you didn't share with the rest of us."

"Why?" Ned asked.

"Because I feel that they might be a key to this puzzle."

Ned sidestepped, searched into the future, enjoyed a lapse into the past—Ingrid looked beautiful when she made love, especially when she came—and said, "They're not important. They're only distortions of my fears and have no relevance to this trip."

"Well, why don't you let me be the judge of that?"

Ned leaned toward her and whispered, "Why did you leave so early? You had more time to stay. We could have made love again."

"I beg your pardon. I don't know what you're insinuating, and I don't like the way you're talking to me. I'm not one of your Junction sluts. You've been dreaming too much."

"You seemed to enjoy it at the time. And I didn't dream this," Ned said, squeezing her breast. He could feel the padding of her brassiere.

She bit her lip and slapped him squarely on the mouth with her open hand. "You awkward, boorish sonovabitch," she said, adjusting her bra.

And with that the engines started. A FASTEN YOUR SEATBELT, NO SMOKING sign blinked on over the aisle, and the pilot checked everyone to make sure the seatbelts were fastened tightly. As the pilot walked to the forward compartment, Ned noticed that he had a slight limp.

Ned listened to the rotors cutting the air with a whooshing sound, like a scythe cutting grass. Ned liked the rhythm and followed it as it gained momentum. As the helicopter lifted, Ned leaned his head back against the headrest and closed his eyes. He let himself be sucked into the machinery of God, concentrated on the whirring of cogs and blades. But even with his eyes closed he could see Taharahnugi's smiling face. And Kheal's close beside it. Ned dreaded a long indeterminate change, but it passed quickly and he awoke with a start.

"Sorry," he said to Ingrid after jarring her elbow. She nodded, gave him a wan smile, and returned her stare to the porthole.

They were over an urban area. Gray buildings jutted into a gray sky, reaching for, but never skewering, the gray wafer clouds that drifted by. The clouds above were a worn insulation for the city, a sham protection from the unformed potential that was engulfing previous reality.

In another future, Ned thought, New York would be only a part of the Bos-Wash Corridor, one of the pincers of urban drift. But that was not for this future. Soon he would see Tarrytown in the distance and the first mimicries of open country. But Ned felt that something was wrong. He turned his gaze from the porthole and leaned toward the aisle, away from Ingrid's tightly laid-out psychological space.

"Well, then, what do you believe?" Kheal asked Taharahnugi. Ladislas, who was sitting with Deaken behind Ned and Ingrid, leaned forward in his seat and looked very interested.

"I believe in 'Dreamin,'" said Taharahnugi sarcastically. "That's the aborigines' word for the dream time of the primordial when the Earth Mother Goddess and the Rainbow Serpent were born out of dreamstuff. After the Rainbow Serpent created The Road, the Earth Mother dreamed the world around it. Does that satisfy your need to know?" He smiled and stared at the ceiling.

Ladislas shook his head and muttered to himself, but Deaken only smiled and said, "That's very interesting. Perhaps the Rainbow Serpent symbolizes time and the Earth Mother Goddess space. Then your aborigines' dream time might be something like a collective unconscious where past, present, and future exist at the same time, as possibilities. We are not so removed, after all."

Taharahnugi chuckled and folded his large hands on his lap.

"Perhaps we are on the road right now," Kheal said.

"Look out your porthole," Ingrid said. "Something looks wrong out there. How long have we been traveling, anyway? This trip should only take twenty minutes, more or less."

"Well, we haven't even been in the air five minutes," Deaken said.

"What?" said Ladislas. "We've been flying for at least a half hour."

"No we haven't," said Ned. "But we haven't been flying for any five minutes either."

"And so it starts," Taharahnugi said. "Remember, no one else has ever returned."

"Shut up," said Ladislas.

There was not a cloud in the robin's-egg sky. As Ned looked past Ingrid's hardened face and out the porthole, he could not find where the sky ended. It had swallowed up the ground below.

Now Ned realized what had been bothering him before: the skyscrapers and four-lane highways and rivers and hills and grasslands and towns had not been believable. Their reality had been so diluted that they became illusions. But it was a gradual process.

No one could have survived in the towns they had left behind—they were just palimpsests to be erased. Real flesh would have withered, and the countryside could only become a painter's wash on a blank, white canvas. And now, Ned thought, everything was erased. Natural law had fallen apart behind him. Chaos was, for the time being, blue. But blue was as good a color for the stuff of the universe as any.

As the engines sputtered and the rotors lost momentum, the plastic blue potential for a new cosmos congealed around the helicopter. It slowed the blades to a halt. The copter was stuck in the sky, like a fly in amber.

"What the Hell is this?" Ladislas shouted, his sleepy eyes wide open.

"That's it," said Taharahnugi. "It's Hell, the pit, the serpent's living room." He began to laugh hysterically and then screamed. "We're with the snake in the belly of the Mother. The snake will wrap itself around us until we can't see."

"Quiet him down," said Deaken, but Taharahnugi shook his head at Kheal and ran to the forward compartment.

"Open the door," he shouted, banging it with his fists.

"Well, something's wrong," said Ladislas. "Why doesn't the pilot answer? And why doesn't he come out of his cabin?"

"Because he probably doesn't want to be attacked by a lunatic," Deaken said.

"He can't just stay in there and do nothing. Why didn't he say anything to us?" And with that Ladislas got up and helped Taharahnugi wrench the cabin door open. The others just watched.

And finally the door gave way. But there was no pilot or forward compartment. Only blue sky pushing into the doorway. Taharahnugi screamed and tried to jump, but Ladislas grabbed him, pushed him out of the way, and kicked the door closed.

Ladislas ran down the aisle away from the door, screaming, "Help, I'm falling." Taharahnugi lay unconscious against the raised seat platform. Deaken made sure that Taharahnugi was all right while Kheal tried to quiet Ladislas. Ingrid stared calmly out the porthole.

"Well, what do you think?" asked Kheal.

"I don't know," said Ingrid.

As she spoke, the outside blue turned to gray. Ned could almost

make out the slight definitions that could mean hills and sand and arti-
facts.

"Look," Kheal said to Ladislas, who had begun to scream again.
"Something's happening out there."

"I don't want to see it," Ladislas said.

"Are we making that happen?" asked Deaken, leaving Taharahnugi
to sleep in the aisle.

"Yes, I think so," said Kheal. "That's real; soon it will set. But is this
Goshen?"

"How do you know what's real?" asked Ladislas. He laughed in a
high-pitched voice, an operatic mockery.

"No," Taharahnugi whispered, "this isn't Goshen. This is the road,
and that, that is the Earth Mother." He yawned and mumbled in his
sleep.

The helicopter shuddered, and a buzzing sound swept through the
fuselage. This illusion of shaking was only a manifestation and magnification of their fears. And without being told, they all seemed to
realize it. Ned knew that the copter was at rest forever.

"Just another illusion," Taharahnugi mumbled and then chuckled.
He was having a fitful sleep.

"Spatially, perhaps, we may be in the vicinity of Goshen, but that's
quite meaningless now," Kheal said.

Growing impatient, Ned closed his eyes and dreamed. The desert
spread out around him, silently sucking the life out of the soil and
warm creatures and replacing them with reddish yellow sand and soft
tuff. The spires, overhangs, and cut cones of rock were overpowering in
their monochromatic contrast of light and shadow. Rough-hewn cathe-
drals jutted into a pale, cloudless sky. A breeze pushed the sand into
waves and bit microscopic pieces out of the rocks, which would soon
become reddish yellow sand again.

And the others watched the plastic-coated walls of the helicopter
melt into the sand and rock around them. Taharahnugi was still asleep
and started to snore. Ned found himself lying in the desert sand. His
crotch itched. A scorpion was making its way toward his extended arm,
its feelers touching the ground, sensing and feeling movement that was
miles away. It would crawl a few inches, curl up and wiggle its pincers,
clean them with its lobster legs.

Ned could hear the scorpion whispering to him, but its comments
were too simple to be understood. But as it came closer, the creature's

thoughts became stronger and Ned compensated for its lack of intelligence.

"You would do better in the shade," it said. "There, in the temple where your arm points."

"Why can you talk?" asked Ned, sifting the coarse sand through his fingers, then scooping out another handful.

"Because I am conscious, as is everything hereabouts. You're supplying the words and conceptions; I'm just communicating a sensation, and a simple sensation at that."

Ned watched its slow, agonized movements toward his outstretched arm. Ned was wary of the euphoric feeling that was beginning to come over him. It dulled him, made him wish for Hilda and Sandra and, perhaps, Ingrid and great chunks of green-tinged glass.

"Of course," the creature said, "if you don't move, I will poison you."

The scorpion was only a few inches away from Ned's fingers. Ned curled them into a fist, hoping to gain time. He was sluggish and could feel the energy being sucked out of him. And he thought he could hear himself snore.

Ned sensed the infinity of sand around him. It seemed to whisper as it covered him. The sky was a blue ceramic bowl with a cloud pasted inside for effect. Slowly it was flattening out, soon to crush him into glass.

The sky hummed. Ned did not listen to what it was saying. There was no time: the vainglorious scorpion was hoping to deliver death, or at least a respectable sickness. With a supreme effort of will, Ned pulled his arm to his chest and stood up. He was dizzy, as if his head were filled with water sloshing from side to side.

His thoughts were jumbled into the desert sounds. Everything was whispering, whistling, and humming. He listened to the broken syllables and almost words. The scorpion inched past Ned's foot, but Ned was too far above to understand its simple cursing.

I don't see a temple, Ned thought, secretly addressing the scorpion, which was burrowing its way into the sand.

"Go straight ahead, in the direction of your face," said a voice inside Ned's head.

"What about the others?" Ned stood motionless, waiting for a reply.

"Forget them for now," the voice said. "You'll know what they're doing."

Was this a directive from an outside source? Ned asked himself. Or was it his own intuition? Unable to find the scorpion, Ned walked on.

The sand sucked on his feet, trying to bury them. Each step was an attack on the sand and a retreat from its grasp.

As he quickened his pace, the desert noises became louder. The sky hummed. The sand whispered, occasionally finding its voice and drawling out a few syllables. And the air gave him enough space to walk in. Soon the smooth waves of sand would give way to rougher ground enclosed in a crown of stone spires and cliffs.

"It's both," said the voice inside Ned's head.

"What?" asked Ned.

"This voice inside your head constitutes both your own intuition and an outside intelligence. One nudges the other. You know: feedback. A cozy synthesis."

"What are you?" asked Ned, once more feeling his energy being sucked away. He imagined that he was falling to his knees in the hot red sand.

"I'm more than the scorpion and the sand sucking on your feet. But I'm just a part of the whole thing."

"Shit," said Ned.

"Now you sound like Taharahnugi." The sand whispered, "Haha," each tiny grain adding its own measure of mirth as the wind ran its fingers toward the east.

"How do you know about Taharahnugi?"

"The same way you do," said the voice. "I know everything that you know, or could know if you looked. And I know what you're in the process of learning."

"And what's that?" asked Ned. He focused his eyes on the brown bumps in the horizon that would soon become hills and cliffs.

"That everything here is conscious: the sand, rock, scrub, and crawling creatures, even the air. In this place, every particle of dust and mote of sand is in perfect empathy with everything else. The sand under your feet feels joy when a spider is hatched; and the spider sees, senses, and suffers when a bird falls from the sky. They suffer for you and the wormwood you kick out of your way. We are the unformed potential you first talked about with Deaken, who, incidentally, is dead now. Died of lymphosarcoma.

"But we are all the bits of an ordering principle or mind, if you like, that has created itself out of its own potential. Everything around you is made up of the stuff of mind. We think around you, and with you. We are simply taking the natural direction of matter, for entropy is only an aberration, albeit a widespread one. But soon the entire cosmos will become conscious. . . ."

Ned found himself stepping over rocks. The voice had become a buzz and would not answer his questions. Making his way into the rough Turkish hinterland (that hadn't been there before), Ned could make out the cliffs ahead. They jutted into the pale, cloudless sky to form a roughly hewn crown. Natural shapes for God's church, Ned thought. An object lesson in perfection.

As Ned gained the top of a ridge, he saw a field of rock cones that seemed to continue forever. It overwhelmed the distant mountains, which might be only larger cones, fields upon fields to cover the world, a cosmos of gray stars in a stone heaven.

Ned stopped to dry-heave. He gagged on his tongue and pressed his palms against his wet forehead. As his eyes unfocused, the landscape became a smear of charcoal and umber. His body needed food, drink, and rest. Ned would appease it with sleep.

"These cones are called *peri bacalari,* or fairy chimneys," the voice said, leading him into deeper levels of sleep. "The peasants in the region of Urgap believed that a thousand harmful spirits dwelled in the cone fields. There are many myths, of course. One claims that the cones are the tents of a vast ghost army waiting to take its vengeance when the horns of God break the world into pieces."

The cones did look like tents, Ned thought. Each one cast an inky shadow on the parched ground.

"The grotesque shapes are the stuff of myths and dreams; many men imagined that they saw the dominions of the afterlife in those rocks."

"Where are the peasants now?" Ned asked.

"They're all dead, but their souls make up part of the world. The universe conserves its souls, just as it does mechanical energy. Look around you. Conscious souls are rising from the earth. They're growing lighter and stretching into the sky."

Ned watched the ghosts cavorting from cone to cone before they rose into the blue sky and disappeared into Heaven. Some were transparent specters, others were full-bodied, complete with hair and rouged cheeks.

"The transparent ones will rise first," the voice said. "See?"

"But the others are human," Ned said, his eyes moving back and forth to follow the dream.

"Yes, of course," said the voice. "The monsters are still inside the cones, soon to be spewed out and merged with the rest. They are the local gods, still hoping to be resurrected and worshiped by surviving natives. But they confuse ghosts with flesh. So they've been dying for quite a while."

The voice guided Ned across the cone field. It directed him over the ghost-laden rocks and around the well-worn cones. Guided by his sleep-walker's intuition, Ned investigated his dream images with fascination. He watched the ghosts rising into Heaven, each adding its bit of consciousness to the stuff of the universe, and waited for the gods resting inside the earth.

Ghosts with long noses and thin lips reached out to him. They spoke softly inside his head, invaded his private thoughts, rested in his memories. Transparent specters drifted around him, passed through his skin on their way to Heaven.

"They are pure life energy," the voice said. "Each one is etched into reality."

"But you're losing them," Ned said. "They're floating away."

And a chorus of voices shouted inside Ned's head. Each voice was that of a ghost. They laughed and giggled, held conversation, and filled Ned with new languages and thoughts, new songs and sensations. They proved their reality by inhabiting him.

Ned listened for the voice that had guided him here, but it was silent.

"You don't need that voice anymore," said a ghost who was losing his hair.

"We'll show you around now," said a specter that could barely be seen. He spoke in Kazan Tatar, a Turkish dialect, which Ned could now understand.

"We're not lost," said a ghost that had once been a peasant girl. Her face was smooth except for brown sacs of skin that hung under her deep-set black eyes. She had been dead for a long time, for she spoke Old Turkish.

"We're just passing away," said another ghost, who seemed to be growing out of the peasant girl's stomach. "Just as water turns into steam, so are we passing into another state. But as we pass into each new state, we become more complex and fewer in number."

"You see," said the specter that spoke Kazan Tatar, "by losing ourselves, we're becoming more conscious."

"And he's well on the way," said the ghost who was losing his hair. "I can hardly see him. But what about you?"

"We can certainly see you," said the peasant girl. The ghost growing out of her stomach was giggling.

"You're better off than the monsters below you," said the ghost, try-ing to extricate himself from the peasant girl. "But Ned, Ned, you're not dead."

The chorus took it up. "Ned, Ned, you're not dead."

Ned stopped snoring, began to climb out of the upper dungeons of sleep.

"Do you know where you're going, Ned?" they asked. "You're pass-ing away too. Running just ahead of the monsters trying to break out of the ground. But your skin's too tight. Loosen it. Die a little."

Ned broke into consciousness with a howl. The ghosts ignored him and went about their business of ascending into Heaven. Ned pressed his hands against his face and listened to his fingers break. He felt for his flesh, which would soon dissolve, layer by layer.

IX.

The cone field, with its thousands of fingers protruding from the ground, was behind Ned. Everything was quiet except for the wind, which screamed as it pushed itself into the crown of cliffs ahead. Work-ing his way up another hill, Ned listened for voices but could hear only the crack of his eardrums as the air pressure changed.

As he neared the minarets and jagged cliffs of stone, Ned could dis-tinguish the hermitages, monastic complexes, and churches from the natural lines of the rock. To his left, thirty feet up a smooth rock face, was a small opening. But the pulley ropes were rotted, and the monks-basket had long since been swallowed by the sand. That church must have had other sources of light, Ned thought, scanning the rock for other openings.

He felt himself being drawn toward a stone fist that stood sixty feet high. A foot-wide staircase hewn out of the rock led into a large opening.

Ned stepped up the stairs and paused in the narthex entrance. Des-ert light streamed through the opening and illuminated the entire church. Ned recognized the fresco-secco portrait of Porphyrogenitus to his left: it was just as he had dreamed it.

As he looked into the church, he saw a room measuring about one thousand square feet, which had been chiseled out of the raw stone by some unknown carver-architect. But the structure had always been there, even before the carver began, somehow implied in the soft tuff. The carver was only God's tool used to coax and torture the rock into a work of art.

The plan of the church was a cross inside a square; the principal dome was situated over the crossing and the four subsidiary domes over the corners. But the structural rendering was idiosyncratic, almost pagan in its rawness and disregard for neat geometry and detail. Since the carver-architect did not have to worry about structural safety, he could create as he pleased. The cracked, tilted ceilings seemed as if they would cave in; their cupolas were stone bubbles about to burst and bury Ned in God's ruins. Painted arches didn't quite match each other, and the walls, too, were uneven.

Intrigued by the paintings and designs that covered the walls and ceilings, Ned walked into the church. The Pantocrator, represented by Christ, was the largest and most detailed painting in the church. It dominated the central dome, which was surrounded by the celestial hierarchy. The architect-artist had envisioned Heaven as a very busy place: The four evangelists were crudely painted in the pendentives. The eastern apse contained the Virgin Mary. Arches and vaults were filled with saints and holy scenes. Lesser saints, martyrs, church dignitaries, events of the earth and the flesh were left to the lower portions of the walls. And for the faithful, now dead, the Last Judgment was painted in dramatic detail on the back wall. However, most of the paintings and designs were faded or marred by fissures in the stone.

"So it all comes back to this," said a voice inside Ned's head. "Look for me. I'm here."

Ned scanned the walls and ceiling.

"The arch. Right above you."

And Ned found a faded fresco of a middle-aged man dressed in a gray suit and blue tie, holding a crumpled fedora in his hand. His face was strong, only softened by a curly red beard. He talked, but his lips were not synchronized with the words inside Ned's head.

"I'll speak to you this time," he said, his lips forming a stylized smile. A piece of his face fell off as he talked.

"Were there other times?" Ned asked.

"Yes. Many other times. They're all passing by right now."

"Who are you?"

"Right now I'm a plaster metaphor for Ahasuerus the Jew, who shouldn't even be here. But I think it's a nice touch. What I really represent looks more like this. . . ."

Ned felt himself turning over in his sleep. He looked around the church, found that it was held together by the things growing inside. Deities and saints smiled at him.

And a soft, thin tentacle curled around his leg.

"Don't be afraid," said Ahasuerus. "That's only to secure you for the moment."

"Moment?"

"As long as you like. Now follow the other tentacles outside. You can see them probing, growing, closing synapses."

Ned felt a tentacle take his hand and another wrap itself around his neck.

"We now inhabit the whole continuum of psychological space. Each tentacle reaches into another reality, another dream state."

Ned started to gag, but his tongue was between his teeth.

"Don't worry," Ahasuerus said. "We're holding you tight. You've just sunk inside reality. It's much thicker than the diluted stuff you're used to."

"I'm drowning," Ned said, spitting up phlegm and clenching his fists.

"No, you're not," said Ahasuerus. "You're dreaming for everyone. We're linking up humanity's dreams, organizing them. Dreams add another layer of reality to the world, an ever-thickening atmosphere of consciousness. And every soul contributes an idea, a thought, or simply the density of its being. So idea encounters idea. Your ideas. You're a contributor."

"But why me and Ladislas and Taharahnugi and Kheal? And where are they now?"

Ahasuerus laughed and was joined by the four evangelists. The Virgin waved from the eastern apse to the Christ in the central dome. The martyrs, church dignitaries, and venerated saints were chattering among themselves.

"It doesn't matter," Ahasuerus said. "Anybody could replace you. And everyone does. That's where the rest of your friends are: standing here. Dreaming you as you dream them. New York and Junction are only extensions of you. And you're only extensions of them. We all participate together. We all dream together."

"Then everything is just a dream," Ned mumbled.

"Dreams are made of thoughts," Ahasuerus said, "and the world is more like a thought than you'd imagine. Our thoughts, emotions, and ideas are like dust motes in a clear light—reflecting, tumbling, constantly creating new patterns. Our thoughts are converging to create a new atmosphere. Imagine one thought filling the universe. Becoming the universe."

"Who *are* you?" Ned asked, imagining that the minions of humanity were choking him, crowding him into a space that didn't fit.

"Just an instigator. Pushing matter into its natural direction. The alchemy of evolution turns things into thoughts. So I trace out patterns and match your dreams with those of everyone else. (Ladislas was right about that.) You could have done it yourself. In fact, you had a good start. But now you face unity. The only thing of value you have to bequeath to the world is your consciousness; only consciousness will survive matter and time. It is not enough to create great works and have ideas. You must give up your very self to the collectivity."

"No," Ned mumbled, trying to wrest his arm away from a tentacle. Other tentacles curled around his arms and legs. Ned dreamed of Hilda and Sandra, their puckered faces and loose skin, their high-pitched voices and clawing nails. Each soul locked in flesh. Flesh to knead and squeeze and enter. Soft parts to push against. Single entities. Fitted tools.

"I'm thirsty," Ned said, his swollen tongue scratching against the roof of his mouth. He opened his mouth to breathe and a tentacle slid down his throat to suck his insides away.

"Don't worry," Ahasuerus said. "It will go away. Dream about water for the time being. Ascend to Heaven.

"As I was saying, your purpose, and the purpose of all life, is to become a unique mirror of the universe, or, if you prefer, a lens to focus its thought. And as every soul merges with every other soul, we evolve into our destiny of total consciousness.

"And it should not be surprising that some greater soul should evolve out of this new collective consciousness. Just as matter evolves into mind, so do souls converge into deity.

"Granted, the universe cheated a bit by going indeterminate here. But impatience is universal. Life needed a catalyst. It's only chance, of course. What difference is a few billion years?"

Ned began to sense everyone else's dreams. They were all here, packed into this place, squeezing Ned out, suffocating him.

"And you're the soul of souls," Ned said, trying to sneer. He tried to break free from the tentacles, but they shrank to choke him.

Ahasuerus smiled. "I'm just a fading paint job." And to prove his point, the stone crumbled, leaving only his face and fedora. His mouth and nose were rapidly disappearing. His eyes were cracks in the soft tuff.

The church was filled with dreamers, each one asserting his own presence. Ned recognized most of them: faces from all the crowds he had ever seen, ghosts with long noses and thin lips, memories from books and Junction, and doctors and nurses and Baldanger. And Snapover, the tailor.

Ned screamed as the scavengers carefully picked him apart to taste his experiences. He tried to conceal his dreams from them, tried not to remember the taste of Hilda, the gaunt face of his father. But they were now universal experience.

"I'm still here," Ahasuerus said. "We'll disappear together."

"I need more space," Ned said. "They're pushing inside me. Too much weight." A ghost passed out of his mouth and hovered above him, pinching its nose.

"Well, let them in," said Ahasuerus. "Give yourself up. The universe has taken your form. It has personified itself."

"They're taking off my arms," Ned screamed.

"Let them in," said Ahasuerus.

Another scream as they pulled Ned out of his flesh.

And Ned dreamed them all and watched all the possibilities simultaneously. He had a choice of eyes and minds and personalities. Hilda would be fun. Sandra danced out of view. His father was ill.

"Let's go," said Ahasuerus, and the arch crumbled.

X.

Ned squeezed out of the church. Light exuded through his pores, followed by sweat and desert grime. He could hear Ahasuerus chuckle inside his head.

"I hope that's just an affectation," Ahasuerus said.

"Are the rest here too?" Ned asked.

"Yes," said Ahasuerus. "Everyone is locked in your head and vice versa. They're all there. Instant communication. Just float along."

"What's vice versa?"

"No need to ask anymore," said Ahasuerus. "Sidestep. We'll hold you up. Fall down. We're all here."

Voices chanted inside his head. Ned could hear Hilda shouting above them all. And there was Baldanger's toothless whistle. Faces flashed before him, and he turned a corner.

And passed the old Desert Midland Bank. The glass had been repaired, and it was no longer a church. Customers in suits and matching hats were walking in and out clenching checkbooks and brown envelopes. Although things had changed, Ned knew where he was. Houses and shops would be scattered along the route downtown, clumped together to form subsections of the central village, their tidy roofs sloping toward the road and crowned with chimney pots in which birds built their nests.

Behind him was the park, with its hangman's tree and assortment of wooden stocks and whipping posts. But it was summer vacation and the children had taken it over with their games and carbonated sodas. Grass had been swept away for a baseball diamond. The swimming-pool pumps gurgled. Steel swings and curlicue slides glinted in the yellow sun. Basketballs bounced on cement.

Ned passed a skyscraper. Another effect, Ned thought. But whose? The Congress Bar was doing a Saturday-afternoon business. The girls hooted at him and the men smiled. But where were Hilda and Sandra and Baldanger? And Reverend Surface was usually sniffing around this area at noontime.

"I'm sleeping," said a voice inside Ned's head.

"That was Reverend Surface," said Ahasuerus.

Ned noticed that the road was now paved with tar instead of cobblestones. Garbage cans neatly lined the street. All the shops were open, selling wares from New York and Goshen. Selling swimming pools and cameras and radios and televisions and cultivated hash and grain whiskey.

"Where's Hilda?" Ned asked.

"Find out for yourself," said Ahasuerus. "You're too lazy."

"And where's Sandra?"

"Just keep walking."

"That's Sandra," said Ahasuerus. "Now leave me alone. I'm sleeping."

Ned found downtown Main Street crowded with celebrants. Dressed in Sunday best, courteous to one another, singing, laughing, giggling, they all walked to church or a bar or a lover or favorite whore. Men lifted their caps to the ladies. They all wore the neatly powdered look of celebration and humility.

"You're *my* favorite whore," said a woman's voice inside his head. It did not sound like Sandra, Ned thought. Ahasuerus was snoring.

"Who are you?" Ned asked.

"Ingrid."

Ned blocked the thought for the moment. He found Taharahnugi sitting naked on a stoop in front of a barbershop.

"I like the way the barber pole twirls around," Taharahnugi said. "I also like your halo. It fits your image. You know, young boy with strong cock who loves the world. Sandra will be right out. She went to get me some holy water."

"For what?" Ned asked. He noticed the fine scars that covered Taharahnugi's shoulders.

"So I can bring strength to the weak. Watch."

An old man with jowls and a silver rim of hair around his freckled head kneeled before Taharahnugi and begged forgiveness.

"See?" asked Taharahnugi. "Right off the street. Just like that. Where's the holy water?" he shouted.

"Right here," said Sandra, stepping out of the barbershop. She held a large glass pitcher against her chest and pulled her wet slip away from her crotch.

"You're spilling it," Taharahnugi said as he reached out and took the pitcher. He shook some water over the old man's head and said, "Yes, you are forgiven."

"Hello, Ned," Sandra said. She kissed him and slid her pinky finger inside his shirt. "Don't be possessive. He's a sociologist."

Ned didn't restrain himself from hugging her and sneaking a feel.

"You don't have to sneak," Sandra said.

The old man thanked Taharahnugi, stood up, and kissed Sandra on the forehead. She giggled when he tried to maneuver his hand up her slip.

"Don't even think about it," Sandra said to Ned. "I'm very busy for the afternoon. Bringing strength to the weak. Let's do it later at the Congress. For old times."

"Do you want forgiveness?" asked Taharahnugi. He rolled his eyes and winked.

"Where's Deaken?" asked Ned.

"He's dying," said Taharahnugi, splashing water in Ned's face.

"And Kheal?"

"I'm in the Congress." It was Kheal's voice.

"That's him," said Ahasuerus between snores. "He's in your head."

"You were in too much of a hurry," said Kheal. "You passed us right by. Ladislas and I are having a party with Hilda. Very nice. But what were you looking for?"

"He's baiting you," said Taharahnugi.

"You're still my whore," said another voice inside Ned's head.

"That's who you're looking for," said Sandra. "Very nice."

Ned watched Ingrid cross the street. She wore a brown business suit and matching yellow bracelets on both arms.

"This is, of course, only one possibility," she said, slipping her hand into Ned's. She smiled at Sandra and Taharahnugi. "What do you want to do with it?"

Baldanger, dressed in a suit and open-collared shirt, ran past them and shouted, "Hey, Ned. See you later at the Congress. Big party."

"I'm doing it," Ned said to Ingrid as they walked down the street. "I'm very comfortable right now. Right here."

"Comfortable?"

Ned noticed a few more skyscrapers and another Desert Midland Bank. He could hear factory bells. Business people nodded as they passed.

Ned held a short conversation with Deaken and began to feel tired again. "I'm tired," he said, looking up at the blue sky that always threatened to drop. He laughed and winked at it. Taharahnugi approved.

"But you've got responsibilities now," Ingrid said. "Hell is no longer an unformed plenum. It's a city. Look." And a thousand modern buildings burst out of the ground to form a new horizon. "There are freeways and subways and spaceports and people to be governed and laws to be made. And you're the president. It's your job."

"Not anymore," Ned said, looking down at the street.

"I'm over here," said the scorpion.

Ned squatted down in the middle of the street beside the scorpion.

"I'll stay here with you," Ingrid said.

"I'm not anybody's whore," Ned said as he lay down in the street and extended his arm toward the scorpion. It moved toward him, its feelers touching the ground, sensing and feeling movement that was miles away. It would crawl a few inches, curl up and wiggle its pincers, clean them with its lobster legs.

"While you're sleeping," Ingrid said, "I'll dress the city up for you.

Watch. There's another factory. Ball bearings. Very useful in industrial society. And a university complete with graduating students."

"Hurry up and bite my fingers," Ned said to the scorpion. It winked at him and composed a tune:

> "Back and side, go bare, go bare
> Both hand and foot go cold,
> But belly, God sent you good ale enough
> Whether it be new or old!"

And then it crawled into his shirt through the entrance between the first and second buttons.

"And later I want to do it again," Ingrid said. "In a double bed. And then on the beach. And on stones."

Ned looked around at Junction before he fell asleep: white picket fences, one small perfectly rectangular park, yards meticulously tended, distances marvelously the same, as if plotted for the blind, rows of little houses with glass windows framing flowerpots and Hummel bric-a-brac.

He yawned and looked up at the sky for a wink. The glass from the line of little houses (and skyscrapers) reflected the sun into his eyes.

And as he fell asleep, Ahasuerus was just waking up.